The Best American Mystery Stories™ 2002

Edited and with an Introduction
by James Ellroy

Otto Penzler, *Series Editor*

HOUGHTON MIFFLIN COMPANY

BOSTON • NEW YORK 2002

ISSN 1094-8384
ISBN 0-618-12494-2
ISBN 0-618-12493-4(pbk.)

Printed in the United States of America

DOC 10 9 8 7 6 5 4 3 2 1

The Best American Mystery Stories 2002

Contents

Foreword

ON A RECENT TRIP to one of the South's literary meccas, Oxford, Mississippi, I had the pleasure of spending a great deal of time with literary folks — authors, booksellers, editors, publishers, professors — who take books and writing very seriously. Included with visits to William Faulkner's home, the University of Mississippi's special collections library, Square Books (at which John Grisham happened to be doing a signing), were many hours spent with good wine, cold beer, and conversation.

This wasn't ordinary conversation, at least not to me. It was among people who love literature as much as I do and who care about it passionately. The talk swung freely: a writer is described as "a little full of himself" but is then quickly conceded to be one of the best writers in the state, a discussion immediately followed by a roundtable argument of which of his books is the best and which is the worst, with more than one drinker — oops, I mean *conversationalist* — cogently quoting beautiful lines from his work.

The reason this discussion is appropriate (at least I *think* it is) is that, without exception, those involved in the conversation love mystery fiction. While one argued that Thomas Wolfe is a better writer than either Faulkner or Hemingway (I excused him on the basis of his having consumed nearly a case of Budweiser) and others tussled over whether Cormac McCarthy is as good as or better than Faulkner (remember, this occurred in Faulkner's longtime home, so he was used as the measuring stick for all American writers, although most of us know that Hemingway was the greatest writer of the twentieth century, closely followed by Raymond Chandler), there was agreement on one point. Mystery and crime fiction ranks with the best literary production of these times, as it has for a long time.

Every person engaged in these nightly confabs was acutely familiar with this series of anthologies from Houghton Mifflin. A few of them had work appear in its pages, and several were disappointed (permit me to state it gently) that theirs hadn't yet been selected. Not one of them is what would be described as a "mystery writer." They were writing the best, most powerful, passionate, realistic fiction that they knew how to do. Yet all had written stories or novels in which murders or other criminal acts were committed.

As has been true for the first five volumes in this series, the twenty stories that make up this distinguished collection help broaden the boundaries of mystery fiction, which I define as any work in which a crime or the threat of a crime is central to the theme or the plot of the story. Detective stories are merely one subgenre of this very wide-reaching literary form.

This year's guest editor reflects that stretching of the borders. James Ellroy, described by Joyce Carol Oates as "our American Dostoevski," began his career as a writer of traditional mysteries, albeit with a hard edge and an original prose style. His first book, *Brown's Requiem,* is a private-eye novel. His second, *Clandestine,* is a police novel, as are his next several novels. Although the police, and even private eyes, continue to have a place in his work, many layers of politics, jurisprudence, and social history have been added. He has helped blur the lines between mystery fiction and serious fiction — as if they ever needed to be separated in the first place. The suggestion that Dashiell Hammett, James M. Cain, Horace McCoy, Raymond Chandler, Ross Macdonald, and Robert B. Parker weren't writing social commentary while also writing first-rate mystery fiction means only that the reader missed much of the point.

On a different subject, more or less, a word needs to be said about the possibility of perceived favoritism, or nepotism, or some -ism or another.

In addition to this series for Houghton Mifflin, I also edit other mystery and crime anthologies and have done so for many years. These other books are different in that I commission stories specifically for them. In 2001, those mystery anthologies had specific themes of baseball *(Murderers' Row)* and boxing *(Murder on the Ropes)*. It seems to me only natural that I would request stories from authors I admire, which is what I did.

As the end of the year approached, I was looking for the best original mysteries of the year; I could not ignore the books I edited nor the authors who wrote for them. Sure enough, they produced some of the best mystery stories of the year, and several of these stories will be found on these pages, as Ellroy agreed that they were outstanding and deserved to be here.

The danger of having too many stories on a single theme is that a collection can seem to be too heavily weighted with a single type of story. Find three boxing mysteries in one book and you're going to think there's an awful lot of boxing around here. The same would be true if there were great anthologies about perfume or blues or zebras (there are already too damned many about cats, if you ask me).

This is not an apology, mind you, but an explanation. The fact of the matter is that the boxing stories in this book are truly wonderful, and so are the baseball stories. If anything, I may have been a bit tougher on some of the authors who wrote for those anthologies because I was overly aware of their origins. In this year's anthology — there's no getting around it — you will get a disparate number of sports stories. However, I believe they are among the most original and memorable stories that have ever appeared in the six years of this series.

One more thing. The only criterion for selecting a story for this book is the excellence of the writing. Last year's book contained stories by only a handful of authors with whom I was familiar. It's different this year, as some of fiction's greatest names appear between these covers. When you read these triumphs of superb prose, you will instantly see that they are here because of how good they are, not because of who wrote them.

Enormous thanks and gratitude go to James Ellroy for taking the time to work so dedicatedly on this volume. His introduction conveys a great deal with the same alliterative and flamboyant flair that distinguishes his other work, most recently *The Cold Six Thousand,* which appeared on the *New York Times* bestseller list last year.

And of course, thanks to my colleague, Michele Slung, the world's best reader, without whom this annual volume would require three years to complete. She culls the mystery fiction from all the magazines and books with original fiction all year long so that I can read the likely suspects and bring the list down to the top fifty, from which the guest editor then selects the final twenty.

Despite reading every general consumer magazine and hundreds of smaller periodicals, as well as books and the electronic publishing sites that offer original fiction, we live in fear that, unlikely as it may be, we'll miss a worthy story. Therefore, if you are an author, editor, publisher, or someone who cares about one and would like to submit a story, you are encouraged to do so. A tearsheet or the entire publication is fine.

To be eligible, a story must have been written by an American or Canadian and first published in a U.S. or Canadian book or periodical during the calendar year 2002. If it was initially published in electronic format, you must submit a hard copy. The earlier in the year I receive a story, the more I'm inclined to welcome it with a happy heart, since reading more than a hundred stories when the rest of the world is celebrating Christmas and the entire holiday season (as occurred last year) makes me very Scrooge-like.

Please send submissions to Otto Penzler, The Mysterious Bookshop, 129 West 56th Street, New York, New York 10019. Thanks.

O.P.

Introduction

THE SHORT STORY is the novel writ small. It's reduced for revelation. Its features are epiphany and lives in sharp duress. Miniaturization is difficult. It's the watchmaker's trade revised for words.

I prefer the form of the novel. I dig the short story dictum of "every word counts" in concert with the sweep of lives in *deep* duress. I've written twelve novels and an equal number of short stories. The novels required years of work. The short stories required more time per page, more time per sentence, more time per word. An editor friend dragged me into the craft. I'm glad he did.

The short story balances narrative line and characterization and limits the scope of plot. The short story form teaches the novelist to conceive more simply and condense the payoff. The short story form taught me to think more surely and directly. The short story form taught me to assume the reader's perspective and curtail my reliance on plot. The short story form taught me to gauge thematically and employ brevity to make my characters pop.

My editor friend brought me to the medium kicking and screaming. I owed him favors. My commitment to the short story paid off the debt. The debt proved to be a gift disguised as hard work. The short story is the novelist's alternative universe. It's a respite from sustained concentration and a crash course in concentrating that much harder in the moment. It's a reprieve from the vast borders of scope and a primer on scope contained. It's the watchmaker's trade taught to architects and large-scale engineers.

Plot and character must merge and meld quickly. Revelation must grab and hold hard. A world must build from overt phrase and implication. Balance must fall perfectly.

The *mystery* short story is a craft within a craft. The necessity for plot makes that balance tough. Mystery fiction is crime fiction. Crime fiction is mainstream fiction possessed of superior story-line and equal character-development skill. Casting plot-nets *wiiiiiiiiiiiiiiide* is relatively easy. Constricting them to short story dimensions makes a novelist hurt. Yeah — but the hurt is so goooooooood.

Concision. Precision. Distill the essence or succumb to your reader's derision. Sting with story, rap with revelation, *plotz* with your plots.

You can't languor with language. You can't dither in discourse. You can't indulge idle idylls. You have to see, select, say.

The form liberates as it impinges. Crime and mystery fiction has always celebrated the extraordinary more than the prosaic. Personal honor and corruption. Societies divided. Murder as moral default. The Big Themes of crime and mystery fiction maul mainstream minimalism and minutiae. They enrapture, edify, entertain. They often orbit in orgiastic excess. They muddle as murky melodrama. They occasionally log in as literature — vibrant and vulgarized.

The crime and mystery novel is that extraordinary world captured large. The mystery short story is that world microscopically magnified.

A writer's skill skirts that orbit of excess. Righteous writers wrangle with murky melodrama and writhe their way out alive. Crime and mystery fiction dissects and extols larger-than-life events. It's a trap and an option to fly.

Bad crime and mystery novels meander in murk. Their depictions of large events play preposterous and make minimalism look good. Bad mystery short stories are contrivances undermined by their size. They waft wickedly worse as wastes of the watchmaker's trade.

Yeah — but when they're *good*, you get everything.

Bam — deft psychology meets a crystallized time and place. Bam — you're someplace all new. Pop — there's the surface of lives in stasis. Pop — they're not what they seem.

You get a mystery. It may or may not pertain to a crime. You get that time and place laid out in layers. You get suspense and surprise. You watch characters ascend and deep-six. Fear fillets you.

Heartbreak and hurt hammer home. The story is *short*. It may be densely packed for its size. It may hinge on a simple conceit or premise. You're wrapped up *rapidemente*.

The good short story is a reader's sprint and a knocked-back cocktail. It hits strong, it's over quick, it induces heat and lingers when it's done. The abbreviated form makes the reader's role more interactive. There's a crime to be solved or a mystery plumbed. There's a revelation within rapid reach. The scant page count itself creates tension. You can read short stories in one sitting. You *should* read them that way. Whap — you circumnavigate quicksville. You get the big jolt, the instantaneous assimilation. Then it's yours to savor and mentally mess with over time.

Reading sprints will sap you, drain you, jazz you, move you, scare you. The mystery short story will astound you with its diversity and range. Many fine writers work the watchmaker's craft in this book. Read, sprint, and fall prey.

JAMES ELLROY

The Best American
Mystery Stories 2002

JOHN BIGUENET

It Is Raining in Bejucal

FROM *Zoetrope*

I

IT IS RAINING when the letter arrives. But when is it not raining in Bejucal? When do the tin roofs of the settlement not clatter under the endlessly falling pebbles of water? When do the few windows not waver with the slithering trails of raindrops beading down glass? When is the brown face of the river not pocked like old Doña Ananá's, who contracted smallpox when she was twelve during the one visit to her cousin in the capital?

Yes, the letter arrives in the rain. A barefoot man, his sandals slung around his neck, slops across the road from the ballast-board cabin of the Southern Crescent Trading Company with the damp blue envelope already curling in his hand. He pauses on the veranda of the cantina to slip on his shoes and remove his straw hat. Even though he is the company foreman, he has no choice; the implacable Doña Ananá would chase him back into the rain just like any other man who dared enter her café with a hat on his head or without shoes on his feet. "It is a respectable establishment, no?" he has heard her bellow at prostrate peones cowering beneath her raised machete. So, still dripping from every fold of his poncho, the foreman slicks back his hair.

The men of the town are all there, hunched over tables, sipping maté, waiting for the rain to break. They are in no hurry: what doesn't get done today will get done tomorrow, or the next day maybe. At some tables, men sit saying nothing. They have grown up together, nearly all of them. They know everything about one another. And they have quit talking about the weather, years ago. So what is there to say?

The foreman, called Tavi by everyone who knows him, nods at Doña Ananá. She smirks. Even as a boy, he sensed the old woman didn't care for him. He strides up to José Antonio López, who straddles a stool at the bar, grasping an empty beer mug in both hands. The foreman sits down beside the man and, without speaking, slides the blue envelope blotched with raindrops in front of his old friend, to whom it is addressed. Tavi has passed the letter with the surreptitious gesture of a man paying for a crime another will commit for him. He has always had a taste for the dramatic. In another place, he might have been a notary or a salesman, but in Bejucal he is simply the guy who organizes the work crews for the company, the guy who gets his orders from the circuit manager every fifth week, the guy who delivers a letter that has floated three hundred miles up the river from the capital to this outpost in the jungle.

Doña Ananá is scowling at two Indians playing dominoes on the bench against the wall. Tavi catches the eye of the old woman. "Señora, a beer, and one for this man, too."

When the foreman lays down a ten-peso note for the two warm drinks, she makes change from the pocket of her apron. "Big shot," he hears her grumble. José Antonio's left thumb conceals the return address on the blue envelope while the old woman snaps the coins, one by one, onto the bar in front of Tavi.

"So you going to open it?" Tavi almost whispers after she disappears through the stained curtain into the little kitchen.

"In a minute." Now José Antonio is holding the letter in both hands, running his thumb back and forth across the embossed address of the Office of the National Lottery. Both men already know what it must say, the letter. The Office of the National Lottery does not waste a sheet of its official stationery, folded into one of its pale blue envelopes, to inform a citizen that after the annual drawing in the capital, his ticket still remained at the bottom of the great iron cage among the thousands of others unplucked by the archbishop.

They know this because for the past thirty-two years, ever since the two classmates were fifteen and each old enough to enter the lottery, they have failed to receive such a letter informing them with profound regret that they have lost yet again. They have come to understand, without saying so or even acknowledging it to themselves, that this is the lesson of the lottery: the inevitability of loss. Why waste paper on the confirmation of the obvious?

Nonetheless, the agent of the lottery arrives each autumn under the protection of the Southern Crescent circuit manager and his payroll guards. The little man sets up on a table in this very cantina the framed placard announcing the unimaginable prizes to be awarded the following spring. Then he unlocks the cash box and, like the last year and the year before and the year before that, once again enrolls each of the villagers in his ledger. Each name is inscribed beside an ornate number printed in the margin, a number matching the one stamped on the blue ticket the bespectacled gentleman offers as a receipt of the wager.

So José Antonio need not draw his knife from its sheath between his shoulder blades and splay open the seam of the envelope to know he has been invited to present his ticket at the Office of the National Lottery in Puerto Túrbido, where he may claim his prize.

"Come on, amigo, let's see it," pleads Tavi.

But slipping the envelope into a pocket, his friend is firm. "Later." José Antonio nods toward the tarnished mirror behind the bar, which flickers with the reflections of dark figures crowding the room as they wait out the downpour.

Tavi sighs. "I'll bring a bottle, yes?"

"Yeah, later . . ." The voice trails off into that trackless waste of memories and dreams where Tavi has often lost his friend.

The foreman finishes his drink and pats the other man on the shoulder. "God smiles on you," he whispers. But he knows José Antonio doesn't hear him.

2

The house, his since childhood, has fallen into disrepair these last few years. The roof leaks, of course. In the bedroom upstairs, scattered pots cluck with dripping water. It sounds as if something is beginning to boil, as if José Antonio is making tea for the whole village.

At least, that is what he is thinking as he takes his siesta, half asleep in the bed he has dragged to the center of the floor, the one dry spot left in the room. The Virgin watches him from her framed portrait on the wall, her hands cupping a heart in flames, tears weeping from her eyes.

He has only to glance at the picture of Our Lady, he knows, and he will be back in the doorway, once again the five-year-old answering his mother's screams in the middle of the night as his father, still cursing the woman, pushes past him and flees down the stairs. The Virgin was the last thing she saw, his mother, as the sheet dampened beneath her in this very bed. He remembers the blood oozing, just in front of his face, between the long fingers she pressed against the gash in her belly and how it pooled red, and then darker than red, in the hollow of her curled body.

Even after his great-aunt had scrubbed the blood from the coarse linen with lye on the bank of the river, working the sheet against the washing stone worn smooth by generations of Indian women, the stain's brown shadow lingered as though scorched there by a hot iron. But the old woman, too frugal to discard a possession with use still left in it, slept on that soiled sheet in her niece's deathbed for the next twelve years until the afternoon she herself died, delirious and cursing the priest.

In his memory, José Antonio cannot distinguish his mother's face from the face framed on the wall. There was no photograph of her, Elena. As a boy he convinced himself that maybe she did look like the Virgin, with pursed lips and blue eyes saddened for her son. When he told his great-aunt about it, though, she cackled. "Blue eyes?" the old woman scoffed. "One of us?" But then she softened. "The Mother of God is the only mother you have, niño, so yes, your mother has the face of the Virgin."

From then on, the old woman had the child say his prayers each night on his knees before the portrait. Every year at Eastertide, she replaced the small palm branch wedged above the frame with a new frond blessed by the priest. The spine of green needles protected the houses of faithful Christians and all those who dwelled there, she believed, just as she believed every other superstition countenanced by the Church. In fact, the fury she unleashed upon the itinerant priest who administered her last rites had sprung from the failure of his holy water to shrink the tumor in her gut. At first she had dipped two fingers in the carved font just inside the door of the crude chapel before Mass each month and slipped them under her skirt to rub the swelling. But then near the end, when the pain had clawed her into a whimpering madwoman, José Antonio found his great-aunt lapping the water from the font like a scrawny monkey drinking rainwater cupped in the crook of a tree.

He had the old woman wound in the stained sheet on which she had died with knees clutched to her shriveled bosom against the agony of her last hour. The young man had thought to bury his mother's ghost in his great-aunt's grave, but when he came home after the funeral, he found it still there, the shadow of Elena's death, blurred on the ticking of the mattress. He sees it still every time he strips the bed and stuffs the mattress with fresh husks, smoothing the clumps of sheaths with arms sunk all the way to the shoulders through the slits of the bedding. And there have been times when, kneeling beside the bed with his cheek on the brown stain of his mother's blood, his fingers deep inside the mattress to find the hard core of withered chaff that disturbs his sleep night after night, José Antonio could have let himself weep like a child.

Thinking of his mother, he lowers himself to his knees before the image of the Virgin and repeats the prayer he has offered for more than thirty years, professing a vow that now — thanks to the lottery — can finally be honored, a vow to find and kill his father.

Then, making the sign of the cross, he pulls himself up along the wall and slides his hand behind the frame of the holy picture. Just beneath the barbs of the palm frond he has continued to replace each year since his great-aunt's death, slipped into the groove of the frame that locks the mat against the picture, a delicate strip of paper rustles under his fingertips. Reassured, he smiles to himself as he riffles the slip of blue paper, stamped, he knows, with a string of maroon numerals and emblazoned with the ornate crest of the Office of the National Lottery.

3

The steamer that has delivered José Antonio's letter will leave at first light tomorrow morning on the return voyage to Puerto Túrbido; Southern Crescent trades at no villages farther upriver. Already Tavi has gathered a crew to load the crates of rare orchids and the baskets of iridescent butterfly wings gathered by Indians along the slopes of an unnamed valley six hard days' trek from Bejucal. Because it is the rainy season, the company warehouses are nearly empty. The lumber, black with water, is too heavy to cart back through the rutted mud of the logging roads, and the jungle crops can't begin to be harvested until the rain breaks in another month or two. So this time of the year, the company sends the little boat, and it does not bother to stop for long at the small settlements on its way back to the capital.

José Antonio finds his friend on the landing, checking a bill of lading, and the two men walk together to Tavi's office. Rain licks their faces with its hundred small tongues.

Inside the company cabin, Tavi bends before the safe that Southern Crescent has provided each of its outposts. The one at Bejucal is an antique; his father taught Tavi its sequence of numbers twenty-two years ago. Now without even repeating the code to himself as he spins the brass knob to first one number and then another, twirling it back and forth between his thumb and finger, the foreman opens the safe and counts out the wages owed since the last payday nearly three months ago. As José Antonio signs the ledger to document the transaction, Tavi realizes he will never see his old friend again. Why would a man return to this godforsaken place?

"Bring a case of whiskey when you come home," he says as he locks the red ledger back in the safe.

"For a fiesta," the voice behind him promises.

There is much to be done, and José Antonio is not used to being rushed. With his pay and if he sells his father's gold watch still locked in the strongbox that is squirreled between two joists of the floorboards of his bedroom, the man will have enough for his journey to the capital — even with the debts he has to settle before he leaves the village. He owes Doña Ananá for a month of drinks at her cantina. There is the money for the ax he borrowed from Xavier and lost in a hole of the river when his canoe capsized last spring. And then he has to do something about Maciza.

He needs a mat to sleep on and a new hat, one with a band on the inside that keeps the straw from scratching the forehead. He has to wash his clothes and pack them in the woven bag an Indian traded him for a pocket mirror on the mudflats below San Ignacio Falls. He has to sharpen his knife, he reminds himself.

The day drizzles away. José Antonio dislikes being pursued by obligations yammering after him like pups snapping at his ankles. It is already dark before, finally finished with everything else, he sends a boy for Maciza.

A bottle forgotten beside his rocker from last night or the night before glistens in the lamplight with a finger or two of rum. José Antonio pours the dregs into two glasses and carries them upstairs to the woman who, already undressed, waits for him in his bed.

Maciza sniffs the drink when he hands it to her.

"Go on, it's rum."

"Why do we drink tonight?" She senses his unease.

"Tomorrow, I'm taking a trip." He feels her eyes on him. "A long trip."

"How long?"

He shrugs and swallows the black liquid. Then he loosens his clothes.

She lays her cheek against the mattress, her knees beneath her. Maciza will let herself be rolled onto her back, but it embarrasses her to be taken like a white woman, and her shame stifles the whimpers of pleasure he likes to hear her make. So he kneels behind her on the sagging bed, rolling his hands along the curve of her back until he seizes her shoulders and holds her fast.

Afterward, he tells her to live in the house until he comes back.

"Come back?" she laughs. "Why would anyone come back?"

"You never know," he whispers in the dark. "Maybe I'll miss you."

"Oh, hombre," she purrs, pleased.

"And if I don't come back, you keep the house."

The woman, her back still to the man, is both touched and hurt by the promise of his gift to her.

4

After an hour or so, José Antonio no longer notices the pistons huffing below the deck. Sitting upon a bale of blouses embroidered at the cuffs and the bibs with tribal talismans, he observes the roiling water the stern leaves in its wake. But lifting his eyes, he sees the churning ease, then calm just twenty yards back, as if the boat had never passed.

He has never felt the need of a watch, not in his entire life. But now, gliding over the brown river that thickens behind him before he's even taken its next bend out of sight, the man asks a crewman what time it is.

"Ten minutes," the sailor assures him impatiently, "since the last time you asked."

"Ah, sorry. It goes slow on the water."

"Not if you have work to do," the man snaps as he lashes a tarp over the three bales of blouses and aprons and festival skirts carted from Xinutlan to Bejucal for shipment to the capital. They store textiles on deck; the dampness in the holds would mildew and stain the cloth long before they reached Puerto Túrbido.

José Antonio waits for the man to move on to other duties, then stretches out on top of the tarp and the three stacks of clothing it covers. Drowsing on the makeshift pallet, he learns his first lesson of what it means to have money: the rich often endure boredom.

He is confused by his feelings. Already today he has done more, seen more, said more than he has often managed in a whole week in Bejucal. Even as he considers what is happening, the surging of the boat rocks him to sleep.

The crack of a parrot's caw tumbles him awake. He slips to his feet from the bales on which he has slept. The parrot, perched on a rail of the gunnel, squawks off to a tree overhanging the bank of the river. The branch bobs under its weight.

José Antonio is hungry. He doesn't know how long he has been asleep, but it is still morning. A dream nags at him until it fades like something big just beneath the surface of water, a *pirarucu* maybe, going deeper. He peels a banana.

It goes on like this, the sleeping, the eating, the jungle and its river closing behind them, until José Antonio would believe they have been traveling a week, a month, whatever he was told.

Over the next days, the boat fills its holds, and the deck grows impassable with bales of textiles, cages of croaking macaws, tin vats of tortoises clambering over one another, tubs of something that looks like human fingers floating in vinegar. The nooks where one might doze away the afternoon under a canvas awning are filled with loose cargo. But José Antonio hardly notices. He paces the bow, cramped as it is, like the caged ocelot or the little peccary leashed to a cleat.

He grows impatient to arrive and fulfill the vow he has repeated as a prayer for nearly as long as he can remember. But always nagging him through the ten thousand nights — no, more — he knelt before the Virgin was how to carry out his promise to avenge his mother, how with his father fled and no means to follow? How, without help, could he track the murderer across that wilderness of years? How could he hunt a beast that had hidden itself in a thicket of time, whose black hair had turned to ash, whose handsome face sagged under a mask of wrinkled age, whose fierce eyes had dulled to tarnished coins? But it is all unfolding now, the path he could not see, like the brown river snaking silently through the impenetrable jungle all the way to Puerto Túrbido.

José Antonio will not be lulled again, not by the thrum of engines beneath his feet, not by the lassitude of a damp breeze, not by the sway of a loose-rigged boom. The lethargy of the jungle — the plodding gait of the *ai* slung along the underside of a dripping branch, the tapir's shamble through giant cane grass, the slumber of the anaconda — yields to the wariness of prey, the watchfulness of predator. He is alert, straining to see beyond the next bend.

Eventually, the next bend reveals a stand of huts, tottering on stilts sunk in the muddy wastes of the lapping river. Then, farther on, children peer from tin sheds in a clearing.

The jungle thins. Trees shrink to bush. Bush droops to brush. Brush crumbles to burned plains. Fires smolder across the horizon.

People emerge from the smoke. At first, one or two straggle out of shadow. Then the shadow thickens into a knot of human figures. Suddenly the whole plain is writhing with creatures, moving in aimless circles and dark with soot.

On both sides of the river, the mud banks are stamped with footprints, littered with refuse. The boat glides on.

Mud hardens into rude walls, rises into raw houses. Incinerators, like huge tree trunks, spire beneath the dense foliage of their yellow smoke. Foam bubbles halfway across the river wherever a factory squats on the bank. Rusted warehouses, barges lining their wharves, fill the spaces between.

The captain slows his vessel as it approaches a complex of whitewashed buildings and docks. Signaling with one long shrill of his whistle followed by one short blast, he waits for an echo from the harbormaster, then comes about and eases his boat against the wharf of a two-story shed.

Longshoremen are already on board, hefting cargo on their shoulders, before José Antonio can bid the captain farewell and make his way down the gangplank.

He follows the wharf along the river past warehouse after warehouse until it swings into the harbor itself. Jutting from the murky orange sunset behind them, the cathedral's three steeples, flanked by the cupola of the old colonial garrison and the little dome of the city hall, tower over the masts and the smokestacks of ships at anchor.

For the first time since his journey began back in Bejucal days and days ago, he is afraid. The welter of people, the clanging of sounds, the labyrinth of buildings — he stands confused in the church's vast plaza and doubts himself. Seeking refuge through the small wooden entrance set into one of the enormous carved doors of the cathedral, the man kneels before the statue of the Blessed Mother crushing the serpent Satan under her heel. Banks of candles flicker at her feet. José Antonio prays for guidance and, lifting his eyes, recognizes the snake: it is a bushmaster. The knowledge calms him; he realizes, whatever Puerto Túrbido may look like, he is still in the jungle.

5

The other great square of the city, the Plaza of the Peace of December the Third, is only a short walk from the widow's house in which José Antonio has taken a room.

Awaking at dawn, the man sits upon his bed until eight, when Señora Machado serves breakfast to her boarders. She is young to have lost a husband, he thinks, peeling a mango the woman has offered him from a blue bowl.

As she has instructed, he follows the Boulevard of the Revolution the few blocks to the plaza, about which all the government offices assemble like ornate stools around a flowered carpet, or so it looks to him as he regards the squat buildings bordering the square.

The Office of the National Lottery is on the second floor of the National Bank. Though the façade of the bank is gilded, the man is disappointed to discover at the top of a rear staircase that a simple door with a milky pane is the threshold to his future. Entering, José Antonio is surprised to join others, Indians and country folk like himself, milling about a vestibule fenced off from the main office by a gated mahogany railing.

Two clerks, each at his own desk, argue quietly with the people who sit across from them. One man, his back to the crowd in the vestibule, pounds the desk. The clerk speaking to him lifts both hands as if offended and closes the ledger lying between them. The angry man hunches his shoulders; even at a distance, it is obvious he is apologizing and cajoling the clerk to reopen the book. The young clerk, with a disdainful snort, relents. José Antonio notices that, against the far wall beneath a large window, the chief clerk drinks from a delicate cup and watches his two subordinates.

The waiting area grows more crowded. An hour passes before José Antonio finally swings open the mahogany gate and stands before a desk. The clerk gestures for him to sit and asks for his ticket. When he reaches behind his neck and lowers his knife in its sheath onto the desk, he sees fear blanching the young man's face. He doesn't like the clerk, the way the fellow made another man beg just an hour ago. So he holds the sheath in one hand and slowly draws the blade with the other. The clerk's frightened chatter is silenced abruptly when José Antonio pounds the lip of the sheath in his fist against the desktop. Raising the sheath, he reveals a crumpled blue ticket.

The nervous laugh as the pale hands of the clerk smooth the paper pleases José Antonio. He is getting his bearings in this stone jungle.

The clerk, comparing the ticket to his ledger, suddenly bends closer to the page. Excusing himself, he retreats to the desk of the chief clerk, where he waves the blue paper and whispers excitedly. He returns and tells José Antonio his superior will handle the case.

"Señor," he exclaims as the man stands and begins to walk toward the back of the room, "you are forgetting your knife."

José Antonio smiles and in one motion the knife disappears into its sheath and the sheath disappears over his head and down his back beneath his shirt.

The clerk scurries behind him, holding the ledger open to a particular page.

The old man shakes hands gravely. "Señor López, God smiles on you."

"And on you, señor."

"Perhaps, my friend. You see, we have an unusual circumstance here. The ticket you presented to my assistant, it bears a winning number."

José Antonio nods. "Your letter said so."

"Ah, we send many such letters. But from the secondary drawing."

"What secondary drawing?"

The old man smiles at his assistant. "It's true, no one ever reads the regulations."

"Regulations?" José Antonio repeats.

"On the back of the placards. They all have it. It's required. But never mind that. We're not talking about you, Señor López. The secondary drawing, that's for all those poor devils." The chief clerk waves vaguely toward the crowded vestibule. "A hundred pesos, two hundred pesos, perhaps five hundred for the lucky ones. They come all this way, and for what? Enough to get back home — maybe."

"That's their fortune?"

"No, my friend, that's their fate."

José Antonio sighs. "And me, what's my fate?"

"Why, a fortune." The old man grins. Then glancing at the ledger, he corrects himself. "A small fortune."

"How much?"

"We'll have to calculate that. It's a percentage of the third level. Minus the fees, of course."

"Fees?"

"Administrative fees. It's all spelled out in the regulations."

The assistant clerk computes the figures and presents his tally to the chief clerk, who examines the calculations before initialing them. Drawing a sheet of blue letterhead from a drawer, the old man copies the number, folds the page in half, and slides it across the desk to José Antonio.

Opening the blue sheet, he is surprised. Yes, it is more than he has ever had before, but he would not call it a fortune. He could buy a house with it, he guesses, a nice house, even here in the capital. If nothing changed, he could live a long time on it, for the rest of his life probably, in Bejucal. But the unimaginable riches promised on the placard in Doña Ananá's cantina, they must have gone to someone else. Still, his prize is enough to do what he has come to do.

José Antonio nods and starts to slide the paper back across the desk, but the old man stops him. "You must sign it as a receipt. Diaz will take you downstairs to the bank for the money and the other paperwork." The chief clerk stands and extends his hand. "I congratulate you, Señor López."

José Antonio nods again.

"Just one more thing," the chief clerk confides as if to save the man from an embarrassment. "It is the custom for a lottery winner like you to tip poor civil servants like us for this good fortune."

"Is that in the regulations, too?"

"Regulations?" The old man laughs. "Ah, very good, señor. I see we understand each other." He motions to his assistant. "Don't worry. Diaz will advise you when you get downstairs."

Despite Diaz's advice to leave the money in an account at the bank, José Antonio insists on taking his winnings with him in the woven bag from San Ignacio Falls, which he emptied of his clothing last night for this very purpose. He also ignores the young man's outraged remonstrations when the lottery winner declines to share a single peso of his wealth with the clerks of the Office of the National Lottery.

6

The young widow, cleaning beans for dinner at the kitchen table, listens sympathetically to José Antonio's story. He does not mention the lottery winnings he has hidden in his room upstairs behind the cornice of the heavy armoire, nor does he describe Elena's murder. But the woman learns he was orphaned of his mother and abandoned by his father at the age of five, raised by a great-aunt, and left to fend for himself after her death. He tells Señora Machado that he has come to Puerto Túrbido to track down his father and make peace with the old man.

The widow's melancholy sigh, José Antonio understands, is not for him but for her own young son, Enrique, whom she pets each time the child tugs at her skirt from under the table where he plays with a wooden rabbit.

"But how am I to find him?" her boarder asks as she dotes on the boy.

The child has distracted her from their conversation. "Who?"

"My father."

"You need a detective, Señor López. A professional. You must ask Dr. Hidalgo. He will know where to go. Tonight at dinner, ask him where."

"It sounds as if you need a detective to find a detective."

The woman's laugh is soothing as water over stones.

Dr. Hidalgo, unfortunately, does not know any detectives, but one of his patients is a lawyer. The next morning, the lawyer recommends one of his clients, a former policeman recently released from prison. "A temper, yes, it's true. But a more honest man you'll never meet. In court, no excuses, no alibis. He stands up and tells the judge, 'Sure I killed him. He was a pain in the ass.' How do you like that? Right there in the courtroom. Luis Menéndez, that's the man for you. Honest as the day is long."

By the time José Antonio returns to the widow's house at sunset, Menéndez has agreed to find Juan López. He is touched that a grown son would seek a father who abandoned the family. Between his old friends on the force and his new friends from prison, he is confident that he can track down the old man. It may cost a bit — "Everybody has one hand out," the former police officer complains, shaking his head — but he has no doubt he'll turn up the missing father.

His landlady greets José Antonio at the door. "What's this?" she wonders, pointing to the stuffed blue crocodile in his hand.

"For your little fellow," he explains shyly.

"Come." She smiles, taking his arm. "Dinner is ready."

As he lies in his bed after supper and Dr. Hidalgo's stories about patients' afflictions, he realizes it is finally in motion, the vengeance he has sworn. He throws off the covers, kneels on the worn rug, and repeats the vow he hasn't uttered since his last night in Bejucal, praying before the picture of the Virgin while Maciza watched him from the bed.

Falling asleep, José Antonio rehearses the scene he has imagined night after night as far back as he can remember.

He knocks at the door. His father answers. He drives his knife into the man's belly.

The one thing that changes, the one thing of which he remains uncertain, is what he should say as the blood pools beneath the figure dying at his feet. Should he declare, "I am the son of the woman you murdered"? Perhaps he should simply curse his father. Or should he say nothing, letting the old man die without explanation, without a word?

As always, he falls asleep without deciding.

When he next meets Menéndez, the detective has no firm leads but remains optimistic. "It's only a matter of enough time," the former policeman assures José Antonio, "and enough money." Menéndez himself has scoured the last three years of records in the notarial archives but has found no reference to a Juan López of the right age and with the correct birthplace. When his client prompts him, he admits it would go faster if he could hire assistants to examine the bills of sale, the tax assessments, the census records.

"By all means," José Antonio agrees. "Hire whoever you need. The money doesn't matter. The only thing I care about is finding my father."

"I wish I had a son like you," the detective sighs.

Each time Menéndez consults with Juan López's son, the operation to find the old man grows. Now there are retired policemen in Guadajierno, in Santa Maria, even on the western islands who are working on the case. The lawyer was right; Menéndez is an honest man, always ready with a receipt for each expense José Antonio reimburses. Once, the detective comments on the ready cash his client provides. "My inheritance," the man explains. "My mother's money." Satisfied, Menéndez does not bring up the subject again.

Señora Machado mentions the money, too, but indirectly, when she protests the many gifts her boarder has showered on young Enrique. She knows José Antonio does not work, and yet he does not seem a rich man.

"The money came too late in life to change me," he stammers, looking down at his shuffling feet.

The widow thinks she has embarrassed him. "No, Señor López, don't apologize. The poor would not hate the rich if they were all like you."

José Antonio takes long walks but never exhausts the stones of the city, which stretch, it sometimes seems, all the way to the horizon. Aware of the looks his rough clothes draw, he begins to dress like a townsman. One afternoon, alone in the house with Señora Machado — "Alma," she insists — he asks the woman how to knot the tie he has bought to go with his new collared shirt and linen jacket. The woman has very small shoulders, he notices, as she fiddles with the cloth around his throat. He thinks of the brown, muscled back of Maciza, of her broad shoulders. The man touches the young widow's pale face, and she presses her cheek against his hand.

From then on, they make love by daylight in his room after the other boarders have left for work and while the boy naps. Their discretion is useless, though. Neither can hide the tenderness for the other. Soon, the whole household accepts the arrangement. The Indian girl who helps with the cleaning never interrupts them when the door is closed. And as for the others, Dr. Hidalgo advises the aging roomers that it is physically unhealthy for a young woman, especially a young mother, to be — he chooses his word carefully here — alone. He approves of José Antonio not only for having taken his advice in the matter of the detective but also for listening attentively in the evenings to the stories about his practice.

One afternoon, Enrique runs into the parlor, where José Antonio reads the newspaper while Alma sips her tea. The child asks the name of a bird singing in the tree outside the window. When the man explains it is a canary, Enrique wonders, "But what is it singing about, Papá?" José Antonio glances at the child's mother, who offers him a sad smile and nods her resignation to what she cannot change.

Now it has been six months since José Antonio first saw the steeples of the cathedral over the harbor. The reports have filtered in from all over the country, nearly fifty of them. A pickpocket in Aldora reports a Juan López, a tobacconist, to Menéndez, but this López turns out to be an immigrant from Spain and ten years too young. Another Juan López is located on the coast in a fishing village; the age is right, but his right hand has been twisted into a deformed claw since his birth in, it is eventually confirmed, the same village where he still works in the icehouse. The detective counsels further patience.

But Menéndez mistakes his client for a man of the city. José Antonio has not been patient; he has been hunting his father as one hunts in the jungle. The man has seemed to the detective deferential, almost passive, perhaps even indifferent. Offered files to peruse, José Antonio thumbs through a few sheets, sighs, hands the folders back with a shrug. What the ex-policeman takes for boredom, though, is the stillness of a serpent as its cloven tongue tastes the scent in the breeze. Each morning José Antonio has sharpened his knife against the little whetstone he carries in his pocket. In the afternoon, with Alma still dozing amid the tangled sheets, he has eased the leather thong and sheath from the mahogany bedpost, slipped it over his head, and returned to the streets. Prowling until evening, he has sought his elusive quarry in strange neighborhoods, following unfamiliar streets to the slums on the outskirts of the city and beyond to the outlying shanties, tireless and keen as a jaguar trailing prey. And he has ended each day on his knees, promising the Virgin he will not fail.

By the end of the first year, Menéndez has reported to José Antonio on two hundred leads. None pans out. So the detective casts a wider net. Now his agents (as he begins to call them when he seeks payment for their services from his client) send dossiers on a Joaquim López in Plato Negro, a Juan Lopata in some mountain village ten kilometers from Titalpa, even an Englishman named John Loping, an engineer who is building a bridge in the Apulco Valley.

José Antonio still offers the same vow each night beside the bed in which he sleeps alone for the sake of propriety, but he begins to consider the possibility that his father never will be found. He himself has crisscrossed the city, pressing pesos into the palm of anyone who will listen to his story about the abandoned son seeking a lost parent. He has been blessed to God by hundreds of simple folk for his devotion to the old man. "If only my son . . . ," one after another has complained to him, almost never finishing the sentence. But even in a great city like Puerto Túrbido, the stone streets eventually powder into muddy lanes, and the muddy lanes finally dissipate into fields that fringe the jungle. After a year of his long prowls through the capital, people begin to recognize him. There is no one left to whom he can tell his story. Maybe, he allows himself to think, the old man is dead.

Though he will admit to no relief at the idea of laying his vengeance to rest, it does please him to think of opening a store with the money that remains, perhaps an ice cream parlor — a year ago, he didn't even know frozen custard existed, but now he grows cranky if he misses his scoop of chocolate after his siesta. And it pleases him to think of Alma as his wife, Enrique as his son, himself as the master of the house.

He makes up his mind to propose to his landlady, to adopt her child. He even begins to plan the wedding. The man has discharged his duty to his mother, he insists to himself. What more could he have done? He tells Menéndez he has had enough, to cancel the search. But before he can offer the woman the ring he has purchased with his dwindling winnings, the detective visits one Sunday morning after Mass with the news that Juan López, the father of José Antonio, has been located.

7

"All this time and he was right here under our nose." The detective shrugs. "And you know, we had him in our files since the beginning and didn't even realize it. Can you imagine? Report number eight. But the birthdate was entered in reverse. Not 1854 but 1845. That's how we missed him."

José Antonio remembers the file from the very first group. He even asked Menéndez to take another look; it seemed a close match, number eight. But no, the detective had assured him at their next meeting, number eight could not be his father. And then there were so many others to look at, the ex-convict had explained. He had a lead on a fellow in the south who met the description almost perfectly. It would cost a bit more to check it out, he had admitted, but he felt certain this was the Juan López they were seeking. When the fellow in the south turned out to be left-handed, Menéndez had seemed even more disappointed than José Antonio.

"So how did you find your mistake?"

"Fate, Señor López, divine intervention. I was boxing up the files after you told me to shut down the search, and the contents of number eight somehow slipped from my hand to the floor. There, next to each other on the tiles, were the copy of the subject's birth certificate and the page of my notebook where I had recopied the date. Somehow, my eyes fell upon the discrepancy."

José Antonio studies Menéndez. "You've checked it all out?"

"You won't believe this. Your father is in an apartment, not ten blocks from here. He goes by another name — Juan Sánchez he calls himself — but that's just his mother's name he uses. It's there on the birth certificate, the maiden name."

"The whole time he was right here? In this neighborhood?"

"I tell you, señor, the world is a handkerchief." The detective sighs. "He was clever, though. It was simple to go from Juan López y Sánchez to just Juan Sánchez. Nothing fancy, just a small thing, but now no one in this whole city knows who he really is. No one but you and me." The detective smiles, permitting himself a professional's pride in the job he has done. "I guess he must have been ashamed of abandoning his wife and child."

As Menéndez passes his client the file, he lays a final reckoning on top of the manila folder. "The last reimbursements," he explains. Then he clears his throat. "And, of course, I've added the bonus you promised in the beginning for actually finding your father."

José Antonio suddenly understands the detective's scheme with the disgust of a man who, emerging from the waist-deep muck of a swamp, discovers a swollen leech battening on his thigh. Menéndez has bled him dry. And he is absolutely certain the former policeman has known all along where the old man could be found.

"You'll get what I owe you," José Antonio promises, examining the bill, "when you take me to my father."

The detective hesitates.

"Tonight at nine. Where shall we meet? The fountain at the great plaza?"

Menéndez, unhappy but anxious not to jeopardize the last of the money, repeats, "Tonight at nine, at the fountain."

"Yes, my friend, tonight," José Antonio assures him, ushering the man out of the house.

When Alma and her boarders sit down to their Sunday dinner an hour later, José Antonio watches the woman laughing at a joke. He regrets that today is the Sabbath. Though the household will retire to their rooms for a siesta after the big meal, Alma will not slip into his bed while the others sleep this afternoon. She is ashamed to lie with him on a Sunday.

Alone in his room, having burned his father's file in the little fireplace, José Antonio slowly draws his knife across the small whetstone, over and over again, as he loses himself in memories, some more recent than others.

Just before nine o'clock, the sheath of the knife invisible beneath his old shirt from Bejucal, Juan López's son follows a flowered path to the great fountain at the center of the Plaza of the Peace of December the Third. As he approaches, rain that has threatened all day begins to fall, chasing the young couples, followed by stern old aunts, from the stone benches of the plaza to the cafés beneath the porticoes of the buildings surrounding the square. The drops, clapping like tiny hands against the water in the vast stone pool, remind José Antonio of home. He puts on the straw hat that hangs from a cord round his neck.

Menéndez is not late. "I almost didn't recognize you, dressed like this. You look like one of those peones from the country."

"It's for my father. This is how he remembers me."

The detective shrugs and leads his client down a quiet side street away from the plaza. The houses they pass have walls burnished with the brown clay of the earliest architecture of the capital. It is a kind of slum, this neighborhood people call the "old city." The rain picks up.

Menéndez turns his collar against the shower. "Tell me, señor, why was it so important, finding the old man?"

"I promised my mother," José Antonio explains, "never to forget my father."

"A good woman," the detective nods. Then he points. "There, across the street."

The two men hurry into the hallway of the shabby building. The front door is jammed open with a wooden shim.

"These people," Menéndez complains, shaking his head. "Too stupid to close a door even in the rain." Then he realizes whom they are visiting. "I didn't mean your father. I meant the old bitch, the one who lives down here." He points to the door beside the mailboxes to their right.

José Antonio notes to himself that Menéndez has been here before.

They climb the stairs to the second landing. The detective knocks roughly at a scarred door.

"Who's there?" The voice is reedy. Even through the wood, José Antonio can hear the wheeze between each word.

"The police, Señor Sánchez." Menéndez winks at his client. "We've found something that belongs to you."

"It's unlocked," the voice manages between wracking coughs.

"You're about to meet your father," the detective whispers, turning the knob.

The door swings open on the room, its walls shuddering with candlelight.

Juan López lies in his bed. He is a small man, nothing like his son. The voice rattles before it speaks. "What have you got of mine?"

The body in the bed is wasted; the face, sunken. Consumption, José Antonio realizes, remembering the wretched death of a consumptive Dr. Hidalgo described one evening.

The old man wheezes, waiting for Menéndez's answer.

The detective puts a hand on his client's shoulder. "Your son, Señor López."

Menéndez pauses, like a boxer who has just landed an unexpected punch, but the old man does not flinch. "I don't have a son," López growls between breaths.

"Papá? It's me, Papá, José Antonio."

"You?"

José Antonio nods. "My mother sent me."

"That whore —" But the word turns into a cough he can't stop.

"Choke on your insult, you murderer."

López recovers his breath, little by little. "Water," he begs. "For the love of Christ, a glass of water."

Ignoring the trembling hand stretched out to him, José Antonio walks around to the other side of the bed, so Menéndez fills a glass from the pitcher on the nightstand.

As his father laps it up, rattling breaths between sips, José Antonio leans over and barely utters, "You are going to die, Papá."

A cough — no, a laugh — bursts from López's lips, spewing water over his covers. The old man peels the damp sheet from his chest. Stains of yellow sputum blotch the undershirt he wears. "Of course I'm going to die," he manages between breaths. "And stop calling me 'Papá.' I'm not your father."

"You are Juan López, no? The husband of Elena Altiérrez?"

"Oh, yes, all that. But not the father of José Antonio López. He is a bastard, that boy."

José Antonio wavers. "Then who is my father?"

The old man tries to shrug but starts coughing again. "Some Indian," he chokes out, then calms himself with deep breaths. "Why do you think a man kills his wife? He looks at his boy and sees nothing of himself. And his woman, the bitch, she mocks him with it." He laughs to himself. "Of course he takes a knife to her."

"Gentlemen, please," Menéndez interrupts, "I can see you have things to discuss. I should go." But the ex-convict stands there, waiting. José Antonio looks up from the bedridden old man. "There's just the matter, señor, of the final reckoning . . ."

"Oh, yes, forgive me. I still owe you something, don't I?"

The detective nods as his client comes around the bed.

José Antonio knows how things kill only in the jungle. No slow toxin drips from the fangs of a jungle snake; already the mouse is being digested before it is even swallowed. And the monkey, pricked by a dart, plummets dead from its branch to the damp leaves matted about the trunk of the tree. So when he draws the knife from behind his back and drives it, all in one motion, into the heart of the man who has cheated him of nearly all his lottery winnings, the fat body slumps across the bed without a moan of protest.

José Antonio turns back to his father.

"I can't move," López coughs. The heavy corpse has pinned his withered legs to the mattress. Then, grasping the situation, he sneers, "Go ahead. Kill me, you son of a whore."

But José Antonio takes his father's skeletal hand and wraps it around the hilt of the knife still buried in Menéndez's chest. The old man struggles to extricate his bloody hand from beneath the body pressing against his own.

"They'll come in the morning, won't they, someone, the old lady downstairs, with your breakfast?" José Antonio explains as he wipes his hand on the blanket. "And what will you tell them, Señor Sánchez, about this former police officer murdered in your room with your own knife? It is yours, you know. It's the knife I pulled from my mother's belly."

The old man is defiant. "I'll tell them about you, you bastard."

"You'll tell them you are Juan López, the murderer of Elena

Altiérrez? Killing a young mother — that's even worse than this. Would you rather be executed for her murder? Either way, it's justice, isn't it?" José Antonio leans over and blows out the candle on the nightstand. "You think about it, Papá. You think about it all night until they come for you in the morning."

"You can't leave me like this," the voice wheezes pitifully in the dark.

"Isn't this how you left me?" the dark answers.

8

Sometimes in the jungle, surrounded by vegetation higher than the eyes, one nonetheless senses the path home. It requires no compass, no landmarks, only an ear to listen to what one already knows.

Monday at two o'clock, Alma climbs the stairs to José Antonio's room, taps twice, and softly opens the door, expecting to find her lover awaiting her afternoon visit. Though he has missed breakfast before, out early on one of his walks, he has always come home for their siesta.

But on the bed, his city clothes are laid out like a corpse on its bier. Above the linen pants, within the linen coat, the collared shirt is drawn closed with the tie she once taught the man to knot. As she bends to touch the cloth, Alma sees the tie has been threaded through a diamond wedding ring and the shirt pocket is stuffed with hundred-peso notes bound by a letter she will stain with her tears.

Already the steamer on which José Antonio has booked passage inland is leaving behind the smoking plains on the outskirts of Puerto Túrbido. As he sits in the bow on the case of whiskey he has bought for the fiesta with the last of his winnings, it salves his heart to see the brown brush unwither into green jungle.

MICHAEL CONNELLY

Two-Bagger

FROM *Murderers' Row*

THE BUS was forty minutes late.

Stilwell and Harwick waited in a six-year-old Volvo at the curb next to the McDonald's a block from the depot. Stilwell, the driver, chose the spot because he was betting that Vachon would walk down to the McDonald's after getting off the bus. They would begin the tail from there.

"These guys, they been in stir four, five years, they get out and want to get drunk and laid in that order," Stilwell had told Harwick. "But something happens when they get off the freedom bus and see the golden arches waiting for them down the block. Quarter Pounder and fries, ketchup. Man, they miss that shit in prison."

Harwick smiled.

"I always wondered what happened with real rich guys, you know? Guys who grew up poor, eatin' fast food, but then made so much money that money doesn't mean anything. Bill Gates, guys like that. You think they still go to McDonald's for a grease fix every now and then?"

"In disguise maybe," Stilwell suggested. "I don't think they drive up in their limos or anything."

"Yeah, probably."

It was new partner banter. It was their first day together. For Harwick it was also his first day in GIU. Stilwell was the senior partner. The *veterano*. They were working one of his jackets.

After forty-five minutes and no bus, Stilwell said, "So what do you want to ask me? You want to ask me about my partner, go ahead."

"Well, why'd he bug?"

"Couldn't take the intensity."

"Since I heard he went into special weapons I assume you're talking about your intensity, not the gig's."

"Have to ask him. I've had three partners in five years. You're number four."

"Lucky number four. Next question, what are we doing right now?"

"Waiting on the bus from Corcoran."

"I already got that part."

"A meth cook named Eugene Vachon is on it. We're going to follow him, see who he sees."

"Uh huh."

Harwick waited for more. He kept his eyes on the bus depot a half a block up Vine. Eventually, Stilwell reached up to the visor and took a stack of photos out from a rubber band. He looked through them until he found the one he wanted and handed it to Harwick.

"That's him. Four years ago. They call him Milky."

The photo was of a man in his early thirties with bone-white hair that appeared to be pulled together in back in a ponytail. His skin was as white as a new lampshade and his eyes were the light blue of washed-out denim.

"Edgar Winters," Harwick said.

"What?"

"Remember that guy? He was like an albino rock star in the seventies. Looked just like this guy. He had a brother, Johnny. Maybe he was the albino."

"Missed it."

"So what's Milky's deal? If you're on him, he must be Road Saints, right?"

"He's on the bubble. He was cooking for them but never got his colors. Then he got popped and went to The Cork for a nickel. He's got to crack an egg now if he wants in. And from what I hear, he wants in."

"Meaning whack somebody?"

"Meaning whack somebody."

Stilwell explained how the Gang Intelligence Unit kept contacts with intelligence officers at prisons all over California. One such contact provided information on Vachon. Milky had been protected by incarcerated members of the Road Saints during his five-year stay at Corcoran State Penitentiary.

As a form of repayment for that protection as well as a tariff for his admittance to formal membership in the motorcycle gang turned prison and drug organization, Vachon would perform a contract hit upon his release.

Harwick nodded.

"You're the resident expert on the Saints, so it goes to you. Got that. Who is the target?"

"That's the mystery we're going to solve. We're going to follow Milky and see if we can find that out. He might not even know himself right now. This could be an in-house thing or a subcontract job the Saints took on. A tradeoff with the blacks or the *eMe*. You never know. Milky might not have his orders yet. All we know is that he's been tapped."

"And we're going to step in if we get the chance."

"*When* we get the chance."

"*When* we get the chance."

Stilwell handed the whole stack of photos to Harwick.

"That's the Saints' active membership. By active I mean not incarcerated. Any one of them could be the target. They're not above going after their own. The Saints are run by a guy named Sonny Mitchell who's a lifer up at Ironwood. Any time anybody on the outside acts up, talks about changing the leadership, maybe bringing it outside the walls, then Sonny has him cut down. Helps keep people in line."

"How's he get the word from Ironwood to Milky over at Corcoran?"

"The women. Sonny gets conjugals. He tells his wife, probably right in the middle of giving her a pop. She leaves, tells one of the wives visiting her man in The Cork. It goes like that."

"You got it down, man. How long've you been working these guys?"

"Coming up on five years. Long time."

"Why didn't you ever rotate out?"

Stilwell straightened up behind the wheel and ignored the question.

"There's the bus."

Stilwell had been right. Milky Vachon's first stop after getting off the bus was the McDonald's. He ate two Quarter Pounders and went back to the counter twice for ketchup for his french fries.

Stilwell and Harwick went in a side door and slipped into a booth positioned behind Vachon's back. Stilwell said he had never met Vachon but that he needed to take precautions because it was likely Vachon had seen his photo. The Saints had their own intelligence net and, after all, Stilwell had been assigned full time to the gang for half a decade.

When Vachon went to the counter for ketchup for the second time, Stilwell noticed that there was an envelope sticking out of the back pocket of his blue jeans. He told Harwick that he was curious about it.

"Most of the time these guys get out, they want no reminders of where they've been," he whispered across the table. "They leave letters, photos, books, everything behind. That letter, that must mean something. I'm not talking sentimental. I mean it means something."

He thought a moment and nodded to himself.

"I'm gonna go out, see if I can set up a shake. You stay here. When he starts wrapping up his trash come on out. If I'm not back in time I'll find you. If I don't, use the rover."

Stilwell called sheriff's dispatch and had them contact LAPD to send a car. He arranged to meet the car around the corner from the McDonald's so their conference wouldn't be seen by Vachon.

It took almost ten minutes for a black and white to show. The uniformed officer pulled the car up next to Stilwell's Volvo, driver's window to driver's window.

"Stilwell?"

"That's me."

He pulled a badge out of his shirt. It was on a chain around his neck. Also hung on the chain was a gold 7 about the size of a thumbnail.

"Ortiz. What can I do for you?"

"Around the corner my partner's keeping an eye on a guy just off the bus from Corcoran. I need to shake him. He's got an envelope in his back pocket. I'd like to know everything there is to know about it."

Ortiz nodded. He was about twenty-five, with the kind of haircut that left the sides of his head nearly shaved and a healthy inch of hair on the top. He had one wrist on the top of the wheel, and he drummed his fingertips on the dashboard.

"What was he up there for?"

"Cooking crystal meth for the Road Saints."

Ortiz picked up the rhythm with his fingers.

"He going to go easy? I'm by myself, in case you didn't notice."

"At the moment, he should be easy. Like I said, he just got back on the ground. Just give him a kick in the pants, tell him you don't want him on your beat. That ought to do it. My partner and I will have your back. You'll be safe.

"Okay. You going to point him out?"

"He's an albino with a ponytail. Like that Edgar Winters guy."

"Who?"

"Never mind. You can't miss him."

"All right. Meet back here after?"

"Yeah. And thanks."

Ortiz pulled away first and Stilwell watched him go. He then followed and turned the corner. He saw Harwick standing on the curb outside the McDonald's. Moving north on foot a half a block away was Vachon.

Stilwell pulled to a stop next to Harwick, and his new partner got in the Volvo.

"I was wondering where you were."

"Forgot to turn on my rover."

"Is that the shake car just went by?"

"That's it."

They watched in silence as the black and white pulled to the curb next to Vachon and Ortiz stepped out. The patrolmen signaled Vachon to the hood of the cruiser and the ex-convict assumed the position without protest.

Stilwell leaned across to the glove compartment and got out a small pair of field glasses and used them to watch the shakedown.

Ortiz leaned Vachon over the hood and patted him down. He held him in that position with a forearm on his back. After checking him for weapons and coming up empty, Ortiz pulled the white envelope out of Vachon's back pocket.

With his body leaned over the hood, Vachon could not see what Ortiz was doing. With one hand Ortiz was able to open the envelope and look inside. He studied the contents for a long moment but did not remove them. He then returned the envelope to the man's back pocket.

"Can you see what it is?" Harwick asked.

"No. Whatever it was, the cop looked at it in the envelope."

Stilwell continued to watch through the field glasses. Ortiz had now let Vachon stand up and was talking to him face to face. Ortiz's arms were folded in front of him, and his body language suggested he was attempting to intimidate Vachon. He was telling him to get off his beat. It looked pretty routine. Ortiz was good.

After a few moments Ortiz used a hand signal to tell Vachon to move on. He then returned to his car.

"All right, you get back out and stay with Milky. I'll go talk to the cop and come back for you."

"Gotcha."

Ten minutes later the Volvo pulled up next to Harwick at the corner of Hollywood and Vine. Harwick climbed back in.

"It was a ticket to a Dodgers game," Stilwell said. "Tonight's game."

"In the envelope? Just a ticket to the game?"

"That's it. Outside was his address at Corcoran. With a return that was smeared. Not recognizable. Postmark was Palmdale, mailed eight days ago. Inside was just the one ticket. Reserve level, section eleven, row K, seat one. By the way, where is Vachon?"

"Across the street. The porno palace. I guess he's looking for —"

"That place has a back door."

Stilwell was out of the car before he finished the sentence. He darted across the street in front of traffic and through the beaded curtain at the entrance to the adult video arcade.

Harwick followed but at a reduced pace. By the time he had entered the arcade Stilwell had already swept through the video and adult novelty showroom and was in the back hallway, slapping back the curtains of the private video viewing booths. There was no sign of Vachon.

Stilwell moved to the back door, pushed it open, and came out into a rear alley. He looked both ways and did not see Vachon. A young couple, both with ample piercings and drug-glazed eyes, leaned against a dumpster. Stilwell approached them.

"Did you just see a guy come this way a few seconds ago? White guy with white hair. An albino. You couldn't miss him."

They both giggled and one mentioned something about seeing a white rabbit going down a hole.

They were useless and Stilwell knew it. He took one last look around the alley, wondering if Vachon had merely been taking precautions when he ducked through the porno house, or if he had seen Stilwell or Harwick tailing him. He knew a third possibility, that Vachon had been spooked by the shakedown and decided to disappear, was also to be considered.

Harwick stepped through the back door into the alley. Stilwell glared at him, and Harwick averted his eyes.

"Know what I heard about you, Harwick? That you're going to night school."

He didn't mean it literally. It was a cop expression. Going to night school meant you wanted to be somewhere else. Not the street, not in the game. You were thinking about your next move, not the present mission.

"That's bullshit," Harwick said. "What was I supposed to do? You left me hanging. What if I covered the back? He could've walked out the front."

The junkies laughed, amused by the angry exchange of the cops.

Stilwell started walking out of the alley, back toward Vine, where he had left the car.

"Look, don't worry," Harwick said. "We have the game tonight. We'll get back on him there."

Stilwell checked his watch. It was almost five. He called back without looking at Harwick.

"And it might be too late by then."

At the parking gate to Dodger Stadium, the woman in the booth asked to see their tickets. Stilwell said they didn't have tickets.

"Well, we're not allowed to let you in without tickets. Tonight's game is sold out and we can't allow people to park without tickets for the game."

Before Stilwell could react Harwick leaned over to look up at the woman.

"Sold out? The Dodgers aren't going anywhere. What is it, beach towel night?"

"No, it's Mark McGwire."

Harwick leaned back over to his side.

"All right, McGwire!"

Stilwell pulled his badge out of his shirt.

"Sheriff's deputies, ma'am. We working. We need to go in."

She reached back into the booth and got a clipboard. She asked Stilwell his name and told him to hold in place while she called the stadium security office. While they waited, cars backed up behind them and a few drivers honked their horns.

Stilwell checked his watch. It was forty minutes until game time.

"What's the hurry?"

"BP."

Stilwell looked over at Harwick.

"What?"

"Batting practice. They want to see McGwire hit a few fungoes out of the park before the game. You know who Mark McGwire is, don't you?"

Stilwell turned to look at the woman in the both. It was taking a long time.

"Yes, I know who he is. I was here at the stadium in 'eighty-eight. He wasn't so hot then."

"The series? Did you see Gibson's homer?"

"I was here."

"So cool! So was I!"

Stilwell turned to look at him.

"You were here? Game one, ninth inning? You saw him hit it?"

The doubt was evident in his voice.

"I was here," Harwick protested. "Best fucking sports moment I've ever seen."

Stilwell just looked at him.

"What? I was here!"

"Sir?"

Stilwell turned back to the woman. She handed him a parking pass.

"That's for lot seven. Park there and then go to the field level gates and ask for Mr. Houghton. He's in charge of security and he'll determine if you can enter. Okay?"

"Thank you."

As the Volvo went through the gate it was hit with a volley of horns for good measure.

"So you're a baseball fan," Harwick said. "I didn't know that."

"You don't know a lot about me."

"Well, you went to the World Series. I think that makes you a fan."

"I was a fan. Not anymore."

Harwick was silent while he thought about that. Stilwell was busy looking for lot 7. They were on a road that circled the stadium with the parking lots on either side denoted by large baseballs with numbers painted on them. The numbers weren't in an order he understood.

"What happened?" Harwick finally asked.

"What do you mean, 'what happened?'"

"They say baseball is a metaphor for life. If you fall out of love with baseball you fall out of love with life."

"Fuck that shit."

Stilwell felt his face burning. Finally, he saw the baseball with the orange seven painted on it. A dull emptiness came into his chest as he looked at the number. An ache that he vanquished by speeding up to the lot entrance and handing the lot monitor his pass.

"Anywhere," the monitor said. "But slow it down."

Stilwell drove in, circled around, and took the space closest to the exit so they could get out quickly.

"If we catch up with Milky here it's going to be a goddamn nightmare following him out," he said as he turned the car off.

"We'll figure it out," Harwick said. "So what happened?"

Stilwell opened the door and was about to get out. Instead, he turned back to his partner.

"I lost my reason to love the game, okay? Let's leave it at that."

He was about to get out again when Harwick stopped him once more.

"What happened? Tell me. We're partners."

Stilwell put both hands back on the wheel and looked straight ahead.

"I used to take my kid, all right? I used to take him all the time. Five years old and I took him to a World Series game. He saw Gibson's homer, man. We were out there, right-field bleachers, back row. Only tickets I could get. That would be a story to tell when he grew up. A lot of people in this town lie about it, say they were here, say they saw it . . ."

He stopped there, but Harwick made no move to get out. He waited.

"But I lost him. My son. And without him . . . there wasn't a reason to come back here."

Without another word Stilwell got out and slammed the door behind him.

At the field level gate they were met by Houghton, the skeptical security man.

"We've got Mark McGwire in town and everybody and their brother is coming out of the woodwork. I have to tell you guys, if this isn't legit, I can't let you in. Any other game, come on back and we'll see what we can do. I'm LAPD retired and would love to —"

"That's nice, Mr. Houghton, but let me tell you something," Stilwell said. "We're here to see a hitter, but his name isn't McGwire. We're trying to track a man who's in town to kill somebody, not hit home runs. We don't know where he is at the moment but we do know one thing. He's got a ticket to this game. He might be here to make a connection and he might be here to kill somebody. We don't know. But we're not going to be able to find that out if we're on the outside looking in. You understand our position now?"

Houghton nodded once under Stilwell's intimidating stare.

"We're going to have over fifty thousand people in here tonight," he said. "How are you two going to —"

"Reserve level, section eleven, row K, seat one."

"That's his ticket?"

Stilwell nodded.

"And if you don't mind," Harwick said, "we'd like to get a trace on that ticket. See who bought it, if possible."

Stilwell looked at Harwick and nodded. He hadn't thought of that. It was a good idea.

"That will be no problem," said Houghton, his voice taking on a tone of full cooperation now. "Now this seat location. How close do you need and want to get?"

"Just close enough to watch what he does, who he talks to," Stilwell said. "Make a move if we have to."

"This seat is just below the press box. I can put you in there and you can look right down on him."

Stilwell shook his head.

"That won't work. If he gets up and moves, we're a level above him. We'll lose him."

"How about one in the press box and one below — mobile, moving about?"

Stilwell thought about this and looked at Harwick. Harwick nodded.

"Might work," he said. "We got the radios."

Stilwell looked at Houghton.

"Set it up."

They were both in the front row of the press box looking down on Vachon's seat. It was empty, and the national anthem had already been sung. The Dodgers were taking the field. Kevin Brown was on the mound, promising a classic matchup between himself, a fastball pitcher, and McGwire, a purebred slugger.

"This is going to be good," Harwick said.

"Just don't forget why we're here," Stilwell replied.

The Cardinals went down one, two, three and left McGwire waiting on deck. In the bottom half of the first the Dodgers did no better. No hits, no runs.

And no sign of Milky Vachon.

Houghton came down the stairs and told them the ticket Vachon was carrying had been sold as part of a block of seats to a ticket broker in Hollywood. They took the name of the broker and decided they would check it out in the morning.

As the second inning started Stilwell sat with his arms folded on the front sill of the press box. It allowed a full view of the stadium. All he had to do was lower his eyes and he would see row K, seat one of section eleven.

Harwick was leaning back in his seat. To Stilwell, he seemed as interested in watching the three rows of sportswriters and broadcasters as he was the baseball game. As the Dodgers were taking the field again, he spoke to Stilwell.

"Your son," he said. "It was drugs, wasn't it?"

Stilwell took a deep breath and let it out. He spoke without turning to Harwick.

"What do you want to know, Harwick?"

"We're going to be partners. I just want to . . . understand. Some guys, something like that happens, they dive into the bottle. Some guys dive into the work. It's pretty clear which kind you are. I heard you go after these guys, the Saints, with a vengeance, man. Was it meth? Was your kid on crank?"

Stilwell didn't answer. He watched a man wearing a Dodgers

baseball cap take the first seat in row K below. The hat was on backward, a white pony tail hanging from beneath the brim. It was Milky Vachon. He put a full beer down on the concrete step next to him and kept another in his hand. Seat number two was empty.

"Harwick," Stilwell said. "We're partners, but we're not talking about my kid. You understand?"

"I'm just trying to —"

"Baseball is a metaphor for life, Harwick. Life is hardball. People hit home runs, people get thrown out. There's the double play, the suicide squeeze, and everybody wants to get home safe. Some people go all the way to the ninth inning. Some people leave early to beat the traffic."

Stilwell stood up and turned to his new partner.

"I checked you out, Harwick. You're a beat-the-traffic guy. You weren't here. In 'eighty-eight. I know. If you were here, you gave up on them and left before the ninth. I know."

Harwick said nothing. He turned his eyes from Stilwell.

"Vachon's down there," Stilwell said. "I'm going down to keep watch. If he makes a move, I'll tail. Keep your rover close."

Stilwell walked up the steps and out of the press box.

McGwire struck out at the top of the second inning, and Brown easily retired the side. The Dodgers picked up three unearned runs in the third off an error, a walk, and a home run with two outs.

All was quiet after that until the fifth, when McGwire opened the inning with a drive to the right-field wall. It drew 50,000 people out of their seats. But the right fielder gloved it on the track, his body hitting hard into the wall pads.

Watching the trajectory of the ball reminded Stilwell of the night in '88 when Kirk Gibson put a three-two pitch into the seats in the last of the ninth and won the first game of the series. It caused a monumental shift in momentum, and the Dodgers cruised the rest of the way. It was a moment that was cherished by so many for so long. A time in L.A. before the riots, before the earthquake, before O.J.

Before Stilwell's son was lost.

Brown carried a perfect game into the seventh inning. The crowd became more attentive and noisier. There was a sense that something was going to happen.

Throughout the innings Stilwell moved his position several times, always staying close to Vachon and using the field glasses to watch him. The ex-convict did not move other than to stand up with everybody else for McGwire's drive to the wall. He simply drank his two beers and watched the game. No one took the seat next to him, and he spoke to no one except a vendor who sold him peanuts in the fourth.

Vachon also made no move to look around himself. He kept his eyes on the game. And Stilwell began to wonder if Vachon was doing anything other than watching a baseball game. He thought about what Harwick had said about falling out of love with baseball. Maybe Vachon, five years in stir, was simply rekindling that love. Maybe he missed baseball with the same intensity he missed the taste of alcohol and the feel of a woman's body.

Stilwell took the rover out of his pocket and clicked the mike button twice. Harwick's voice came back quickly, his tone clipped and cold.

"Yeah."

"After the eighth you better come down here so we can be ready when he leaves."

"I'll be down."

"Out."

He put the rover away.

Brown let it get away from him in the seventh. St. Louis opened with two singles to right, spoiling the perfect game, the no hitter, and putting the lead in jeopardy with McGwire on deck.

With the runners at the corners Brown walked the next batter, bringing McGwire to the plate with the bases loaded. The Cardinals would gain the lead and the momentum if he could put one over the wall.

Davey Johnson trotted out to the mound for a conference with his pitcher, but the manager appeared to give only a quick pep talk. He left Brown in place and headed back to the dugout, accompanied by a chorus of applause.

The crowd rose to its feet and quieted in anticipation of what would be the confrontation of the night. Stilwell's rover clicked twice, and he pulled it out of his pocket.

"Yeah?"

"Do you believe this? We gotta send that guy Houghton a six-pack for this."

Stilwell didn't reply. His eyes were on Vachon, who had stepped away from his seat and was coming up the stairs to the concessions level.

"He's moving."

"What? He can't be. How can he miss this?"

Stilwell turned his back and leaned against a concrete support column as Vachon emerged from the stairs and walked behind him.

When it was clear, Stilwell looked around and saw Vachon heading toward the lavatory, making his way by several men who were rushing out in time to see McGwire bat.

Stilwell raised his rover.

"He's going to the bathroom just past the Krispy Kreme stand."

"He's had two beers. Maybe he's just taking a leak. You want me down there?"

As Stilwell replied, a huge noise rose from the crowd and then quickly subsided. Stilwell kept his eyes on the entrance to the men's room. When he was ten feet from it, a man emerged. Not Vachon. A large white man with a long dark beard and a shaved skull. He wore a tight T-shirt and his arms were fully wrapped in tattoos. Stilwell looked for the skull with halo insignia of the Road Saints but didn't see it.

Still, it was enough to slow his step. The tattooed man turned to his right and kept walking. Harwick's voice came from the rover.

"Say again. The crowd noise blocked you out."

Stilwell raised the radio.

"I said get down here."

There was another short burst of crowd noise, but it was not sustained enough to indicate a hit or an out. Stilwell walked to the lavatory entrance. He thought about the man with the shaved skull, trying to place the face. Stilwell had left his photos in the rubber band on the Volvo's visor.

It hit him then. Weapon transfer. Vachon had come to the game to get instructions and a weapon.

Stilwell raised the rover.

"I think he has a weapon. I'm going in."

He put the rover back into his pocket, pulled his badge out of his shirt, and let it hang on his chest. He unholstered his .45 and stepped into the restroom.

It was a cavernous yellow-tiled room with stainless steel urine troughs running down both sides until they reached opposing rows of toilet stalls. The place appeared empty but Stilwell knew it wasn't.

"Sheriff's department. Step out with your hands visible."

Nothing happened. No sound but the crowd noise from outside the room. Stilwell stepped farther in and began again, raising his voice this time. But the sudden echoing cacophony of the crowd rose like an approaching train and drowned his voice. The confrontation on the baseball diamond had been decided.

Stilwell moved past the urinals and stood between the rows of stalls. There were eight on each side. The far door on the left was closed. The rest stood half closed but still shielded the view into each stall.

Stilwell dropped into a catcher's crouch and looked beneath the doors. No feet could be seen in any of the stalls. But on the floor within the closed stall was a blue Dodgers hat.

"Vachon!" he yelled. "Come out now!"

He moved into position in front of the closed stall. Without hesitation he raised his left foot and kicked the door open. It swung inward and slammed against one of the interior walls of the stall. It then rebounded and slammed closed. It all happened in a second, but Stilwell had enough time to see the stall was empty.

And to know that he was in a vulnerable position.

As he turned his body he heard a scraping sound behind him and saw movement in the far reach of his peripheral vision. Movement toward him. He raised his gun but knew he was too late. In that same moment he realized he had solved the mystery of who Vachon's target was.

The knife felt like a punch to the left side of his neck. A hand then grabbed the back collar of his shirt and pulled him backward at the same moment the knife was thrust forward, slicing out through the front of his neck.

Stilwell dropped his gun as his hands instinctively came up to his torn throat. A whisper then came into his ear from behind.

"Greetings from Sonny Mitchell."

He was pulled backward and shoved against the wall next to the last stall. He turned and started to slide down the yellow tiles, his eyes on the figure of Milky Vachon heading to the exit.

When he hit the ground he felt the gun under his leg. His left hand still holding his neck, he reached the gun with his right and raised it. He fired four times at Vachon, the bullets catching him in a tight pattern on the upper back and throwing him into a trash can overflowing with paper towels. Vachon flopped onto the floor on his back, his sky blue eyes staring lifelessly at the ceiling, the overturned trash can rolling back and forth next to him.

Stilwell dropped his hand to the tile and let go of the gun. He looked down at his chest. The blood was everywhere, leaking between his fingers and running down his arm. His lungs were filling and he couldn't get air into them.

He knew he was dead.

He shifted his weight and turned his hips so he could reach a hand into the back pocket of his pants. He pulled out his wallet.

There was another roar from the crowd that seemed to shake the room. And then Harwick entered, saw the bodies on opposite sides of the room and ran to Stilwell.

"Oh, Jesus. Oh, Jesus."

He leaned over and studied Stilwell for a moment, then pulled out his rover and started to yell into it. He realized he was on a closed frequency, quickly switched the dial to the open band, and called in the officer down report. Stilwell listened to it in a detached way. He knew there was no chance. He dropped his eyes to the holy card he held in his hands.

"Hang in there, partner," Harwick yelled. "Don't go south on me, man. They're coming, they're coming."

There was a commotion behind him, and Harwick turned around. Two men were standing in the doorway.

"Get out of here! Get the fuck out! Keep everybody back!"

He turned back to Stilwell.

"Listen, man, I'm sorry. I fucked up. I'm so fucking sorry. Please don't die. Hang on, man, Please hang on."

His words were coming out like the blood flowing from Stilwell's neck. Nonstop, a mad torrent. Desperate.

"You were right, man. You were right about me. I-I-I lied about that game. I left and I'm so sorry I lied. You've got to stay with me. Please stay with me!"

Stilwell's eyes started to close and he remembered that night so long ago. That other time. He died then, with his new partner on his knees next to him, blubbering and babbling.

Harwick didn't quiet himself until he realized Stilwell was gone. He then studied his partner's face and saw a measure of calm in his expression. He realized that he looked happier than at any other time Harwick had looked at him that day.

He noticed the open wallet on the floor and then the card in Stilwell's hand. He took it from the dead fingers and looked at it. It was a baseball card. Not a real one. A gimmick card. It showed a boy of eleven or twelve in a Dodgers uniform, a bat on his shoulder, the number 7 on his shirt. It said, "Stevie Stilwell, Right Field" beneath the photo.

There was another commotion behind him then, and Harwick turned to see paramedics coming into the room. He cleared out of the way, though he knew it was too late.

As the paramedics checked for vital signs on his fallen partner, Harwick stepped back and used the sleeve of his shirt to dry the tears on his face. He then took the baseball card and slipped it into one of the folded compartments of his badge case. It would be something he would carry with him always.

THOMAS H. COOK

The Fix

FROM *Murder on the Ropes*

IT COULD HAVE happened anytime, on any of my daily commutes on the Crosstown 42. Every day I took it at eight in the morning, rode it over to my office on Forty-second and Lex, then back again in the evening, when I'd get off at Port Authority and walk one block uptown to my place on Forty-third.

It could have happened anytime, but it was a cold January evening, a deep winter darkness already shrouding the city at six P.M. Worse still, a heavy snow was coming down, blanketing the streets and snarling crosstown traffic, particularly on Forty-second Street, where the Jersey commuters raced for a spot in the Lincoln Tunnel, clotting the grid's blue veins as they rushed for the river like rabbits from burning woods.

I should tell you my name, because when I finish with the story, you'll want to know it, want to check it out, see if I'm really who I say I am, really heard what I say I did that night on the Crosstown 42.

Well, it's Jack. Jack Burke. I work as a photographer for Cosmic Advertising, my camera usually focused on a bottle of perfume or a plate of spaghetti. But in the old days, I was a street photographer for the *News*, shooting mostly fires and water main breaks, the sort of pictures that end up on page 8. I had a front page in '74, though, a woman clinging with one hand to a fire escape in Harlem, her baby dangling from the other hand like a sack of potatoes. I snapped the button just as she let go, caught them both in the first instant of their fall. That picture had had a heart, and sometimes, as I sat at my desk trying to decide which picture would best tempt a kid to buy a soda, I yearned to feel that heart again, to do or hear or see something that would work like electric paddles to shock me back to my old life.

Back in those days, working the streets, I'd known the Apple down to the core, the juke joints and after-hours dives. I was the guy you'd see at the end of the bar, the one in a rumpled suit, with a gray hat on the stool beside him. It was my seed time, and I'd loved every minute of it. For almost five years not a night had gone by when I hadn't fallen in love with it all over again, the night and the city, the Bleeker Street jazz clubs at three A.M. when the smoke is thick and the riffs look easy, and the tab grows like a rose beside your glass.

Then Jack Burke married an NYU coed named Rikki whose thick lips and perfect ass had worked like a Mickey Finn on his brain. There were lots of flowers and a twelve-piece band. After that the blushing bride seemed to have another kid about every four days. Jack took an agency job to pay for private schools, and that was the end of rosy tabs. Then Jack's wife hitched a ride on some other guy's star and left him with a bill that gave Bloomingdale's a boner. The place on Eighty-fifth went back to the helpful folks at Emigrant Savings, and Jack found a crib on West Forty-third. Thus the short version of how I ended up riding the Crosstown 42 on that snowy January night in the Year of Our Lord 2000.

The deepest blues, they say, are the ones you don't feel, the ones that numb you, so that your old best self simply fades away, and you are left staring out the window, trying to remember the last time you leaped with joy, laughed until you cried, stood in the rain and just let it pour down. Maybe I'd reached that point when I got on the Crosstown 42 that night. And yet, I wasn't so dead that the sight of him didn't spark something, didn't remind me of the old days, and of how much I missed them.

And the part I missed the most was the fights.

I'll tell you why. Because all the old saws about boxing are true. There's no room for ambiguity in the ring. You know who the winners and the losers are. There, in that little square, under the big light, two guys put it all on the line, face each other without lawyers or tax attorneys. They stare at each other without speaking. They are stripped even of words. Boxers don't call each other names. They don't wave their arms and posture. They don't yell, Hey, fuck you, you fucking bastard, you want a piece of me, huh, well, come and get it, you fucking douche bag . . . while they're walking back-ward, glancing around, praying for a cop. Boxers don't file suit or turn you in to the IRS. They don't subscribe to dirty magazines in your name and have them mailed to your house. They don't plant rumors about drugs or how maybe you're a queer. Boxers don't come at you from behind some piece of paper a guy you never saw before hands you as you step out your front door. Boxers don't drop letters in the suggestion box or complain to your boss that you don't have what it takes anymore. Boxers don't approach at a slant. Boxers stride to the center of the ring, raise their hands, and fight. That was what I'd always loved about them, that they were nothing like the rest of us.

Even so, I hadn't seen a match in the Garden or anywhere else for more than twenty years when I got on the Crosstown 42 that night, and the whole feel of the ring, the noise and the smoke, had by then drifted into a place within me I didn't visit anymore. I couldn't remember the last time I'd read a boxing story in the pa-per, or so much as glanced at *Ring* magazine. As a matter of fact, that very night I'd plucked a *Newsweek* from the rack instead, then tramped onto the bus, planning to pick up a little moo shoo pork when I got off, then trudge home to read about this East Hampton obstetrician who'd given some Jamaican bedpan jockey five large to shoot his wife.

Then, out of the blue, I saw him.

He was crouched in the back corner of the bus, his face turned toward the glass, peering out at the street, though he didn't seem to be watching anything in particular. His eyes had that look you've all seen. Nothing going in, precious little coming out. A dead, dull stare.

His clothes were so shabby that if I hadn't noticed the profile, the gnarled ear and flattened nose, I might have mistaken him for a pile of dirty laundry. Everything was torn, ragged, the scarf around his neck riddled with holes, bare fingers nosing through dark blue gloves. It was the kind of shabbiness that carries its own odor, and which urban pioneers inevitably associate with madness and loose bowels. Which, on this bus packed to the gills, explained the empty seat beside him.

I might have kept my distance, might have stared at him a while, remembering my old days by remembering his, then discreetly stepped off the bus at my appointed stop, put the whole business

out of my mind until I returned to work the next morning, met
Max Groom in the men's room and said, Hey, Max, guess who was
on the Crosstown 42 last night? Who? Vinnie Teague, that's who,
Irish Vinnie Teague, the Shameful Shamrock. Mother of God, he's
still alive? Well, in a manner of speaking.

And that might have been the end of it.

But it wasn't.

You know why? Because, in a manner of speaking, I was also still
alive. And what do the living owe each other, tell me this, if not to
hear each other's stories?

So I muscled through the crowd, elbowing my way toward the
rear of the bus while Irish Vinnie continued to stare out into the
fruitless night, his face even more motionless when looked upon
close up, his eyes as still as billiard balls in an empty parlor.

The good news? No smell. Which left the question, Is he nuts?

Language is a sure test for sanity, so I said, "Hey there."

Nothing.

"Hey." This time with a small tap of my finger on his ragged
shoulder.

Still nothing, so I upped the ante. "Vinnie?"

A small light came on in the dull, dead eyes.

"Vinnie Teague?"

Something flickered, but distantly, cheerlessly, like a candle in
an orphanage window.

"It's you, right? Vinnie Teague?"

The pile of laundry rustled, and the dull, dead eyes drifted over
to me.

Silence, but a faint nod.

"I'm Jack Burke. You wouldn't know me, but years ago, I saw you
at the Garden."

The truth was I'd seen Irish Vinnie Teague, the Shameful Shamrock, quite a few times at the Garden. I'd seen him first as a light
heavyweight, then later, after he'd bulked up just enough to tip the
scales as a heavyweight contender.

He'd had the pug face common to boxers who'd come up
through the old neighborhood, first learned that they could fight
not in gyms or after-school programs, but in barrooms and on factory floors, the blood of their first opponents soaked up by sawdust
or metal shavings in places where no one got saved by the bell.

It was Spiro Melinas who'd first spotted Vinnie. Spiro had been an old man even then, bent in frame and squirrelly upstairs, a guy who dipped the tip of his cigar in tomato juice, which, he said, made smoking more healthy. Spiro had been a low-watt fight manager who booked tumbledown arenas along the Jersey Shore, or among the rusting industrial towns of Connecticut and Massachusetts. He'd lurked among the fishing boats that rocked in the oily marinas of Fall River and New Bedford, and had even been spotted as far north as coastal Maine, checking out the fish gutters who manned the canneries there, looking for speed and muscle among the flashing knives.

But Spiro hadn't found Vinnie Teague in any of the places that he'd looked for potential boxers during the preceding five years. Not in Maine or Connecticut or New Jersey. Not in a barroom or a shoe factory or a freezing cold New England fishery. No, Vinnie had been right under Spiro's nose the whole time, a shadowy denizen of darkest Brooklyn who, at the moment of discovery, had just tossed a guy out the swinging doors of a women's shelter on Flatbush. The guy had gotten up, rushed Vinnie, then found himself staggering backward under a blinding hail of lefts and rights, his head popping back with each one, face turning to pulp one lightning fast blow at a time, though it had been clear to Spiro that during all that terrible rain of blows, Vinnie Teague had been holding back. "Jesus Christ, if Vinnie hadn't been pulling his punches," he later told Salmon Weiss, "he'd have killed the poor bastard with two rights and a left." A shake of the head, Spiro's eyes fixed in dark wonderment. "I'm telling you, Salmon, just slapping him around, you might say Vinnie was, and the other guy looked like he'd done twelve rounds with a metal fan."

Needless to say, it was love at first sight.

And so for the next two years Spiro mothered Vinnie as if he were a baby chick. He paid the rent and bought the groceries so Vinnie could quit his prestigious job as a bouncer at the women's shelter. He paid for Vinnie's training, Vinnie's clothes, Vinnie's birthday cake from Carvel, an occasion at which I was present, my first view of Irish Vinnie Teague. He was chewing a slab of ice cream cake while Spiro looked on, beaming. Snap. Flash. Page 8 over the lead line, UP-AND-COMER BREAKS TRAINING ON HIS 24TH.

He'd continued upward for the next four years, muscling his way higher and higher in the rankings until, at just the moment that he

came in striking distance of the title, Irish Vinnie had thrown a
fight.

There are fixes and there are fixes, but Irish Vinnie's fix was the
most famous of them all.

Why?

Because it was the most transparent. Jake La Motta was Laurence
Olivier compared to Vinnie. Jake was at the top of the Actors Studio, a recruiting poster for the Strasburg Method, the most brilliant student Stella Adler ever had . . . compared to Vinnie. Jake
LaMotta took a dive, but Irish Vinnie took a swan dive, a dive so obvious, so awkward and beyond credulity, that for the first and only
time in the history of the dive, the fans themselves started swinging, not just booing and waving their fists in the air, not just throwing chairs into the ring, but actually surging forward like a mob to
get Vinnie Teague and tear his lying heart out.

Thirty-seven people went to Saint Vincent's that night, six of
them cops who, against all odds, managed to hustle Vinnie out of
the ring (from which he'd leaped up with surprising agility) and
down into the concrete bowels of the Garden where he sat, se-
creted in a broom closet, for more than an hour while all hell
broke loose upstairs. Final tab, as reported by the *Daily News,*
eighty-six thousand dollars in repairs. And, of course, there were
lawsuits for everything under the sun so that by the end of the affair, Vinnie's dive, regardless of what he'd been paid for it, had
turned out to be the most costly in boxing history.

It was the end of Vinnie's career, of course, the last time he
would ever fight anywhere for a purse. Nothing needed to be
proven. The *Daily News* dubbed him the "Shameful Shamrock" and
there were no more offers from promoters. Spiro cut him loose
and without further ado Vinnie sank into the dark waters, falling as
hard and as low as he had on that fateful night when Douggie
Burns, by then little more than a bleeding slab of beef, managed to
lift his paw and tap Vinnie on the cheek, in response to which the
"Edwin Booth of Boxers," another *Daily News* sobriquet, hit the mat
like a safe dropped from the Garden ceiling. After that, no more
crowds ever cheered for Vinnie Teague, nor so much as wondered
where he might have gone.

But now, suddenly, he was before me once again, Irish Vinnie,
the Shameful Shamrock, huddled at the back of the Crosstown 42,
a breathing pile of rags.

"Vinnie Teague. Am I right? You're Vinnie Teague?"

Nothing from his mouth, but recognition in his eyes, a sense, nothing more, that he was not denying it.

"I was at your twenty-fourth birthday party," I told him, as if that were the moment in his life I most remembered, rather than his infamous collapse. "There was a picture in the *News*. You with a piece of Carvel. I took that picture."

A nod.

"Whatever happened to Spiro Melinas?"

He kept his eyes on the street beyond the window, the traffic still impossibly stalled, angry motorists leaning on their horns. For a time he remained silent, then a small, whispery voice emerged from the ancient, battered face. "Dead."

"Oh yeah? Sorry to hear it."

A blast of wind hit the side of the bus, slamming a wave of snow against the window, and at the sound of it Irish Vinnie hunched a bit, drawing his shoulders in like a fighter . . . still like a fighter.

"And you, Vinnie. How you been?"

Vinnie shrugged as if to say that he was doing as well as could be expected of a ragged, washed-up fighter who'd taken the world's most famous dive.

The bus inched forward, but only enough to set the strap-hangers weaving slightly, then stopped dead again.

"You were good, you know," I said quietly. "You were really good, Vinnie. That time with Chico Perez. What was that? Three rounds? Hell, there was nothing left of him."

Vinnie nodded. "Nothing left," he repeated.

"And Harry Sermak. Two rounds, right?"

A nod.

The fact is, Irish Vinnie had never lost a single fight before Douggie Burns stroked his chin in the final round on that historic night at the Garden. But more than that, he had won decisively, almost always in a knockout, almost always before the tenth round, and usually with a single, devastating blow that reminded people of Marciano except that Vinnie's had seemed to deliver an even more deadly killer punch. Like Brando, the better actor, once said, he "coulda been a contendah."

In fact he had been a contender, a very serious contender, which had always made his downfall even more mysterious to me. What could it have been worth? How much must Vinnie have been of-

fered to take such a devastating dive? It was a riddle that only deep-
ened the longer I pondered his current destitution. Whatever deal
Spiro Melinas had made for Vinnie, whatever cash may have ended
up in some obscure bank account, it hadn't lasted very long. Which
brought me finally to the issue at hand.

"Too bad about . . ." I hesitated just long enough to wonder
about my safety, then stepped into the ring and touched my gloves
to Vinnie's. "About . . . that last fight."

"Yeah," Vinnie said, then turned back toward the window as if it
were the safe corner now, his head lolling back slightly as the bus
staggered forward, wheezed, then ground to a halt again.

"The thing is, I never could figure it out," I added.

Which was a damn lie since you don't have to be a rocket scien-
tist to come up with the elements that make up a fix. It's money or
fear on the fighter's side, just money on the fixer's.

So it was a feint, my remark about not being able to figure out
what happened when Douggie Burns's glove kissed Vinnie's cheek,
and the Shameful Shamrock dropped to the mat like a dead horse,
just a tactic I'd learned in business, that if you want to win the confidence of the incompetent, pretend to admire their competence.
In Vinnie's case, it was a doubt I offered him, the idea that alone in
the universe I was the one poor sap who wasn't quite sure why he'd
taken the world's most famous dive.

But in this case it didn't work. Vinnie remained motionless, his
eyes still trained on the window, following nothing of what went on
beyond the glass, but clearly disinclined to have me take up any
more of his precious time.

Which only revved the engine in me. "So, anybody else ever told
you that?" I asked. "Having a doubt, I mean."

Vinnie's right shoulder lifted slightly, then fell again. Beyond
that, nothing.

"The thing I could never figure is, what would have been worth
it, you know? To you, I mean. Even, say, a hundred grand. Even that
would have been chump change compared to where you were
headed."

Vinnie shifted slightly, and the fingers of his right hand curled
into a fist, a movement I registered with appropriate trepidation.

"And to lose that fight," I said. "Against Douggie Burns. He was
over the hill already. Beaten to a pulp in that battle with Chester

Link. To lose a fight with a real contender, that's one thing. But losing one to a beat-up old palooka like —"

Vinnie suddenly whirled around, his eyes flaring. "He was a stand-up guy, Douggie Burns."

"A stand-up guy?" I asked. "You knew Douggie?"

"I knew he was a stand-up guy."

"Oh yeah?" I said. "Meaning what?"

"That he was an honest guy," Vinnie said. "A stand-up guy, like I said."

"Sure, okay," I said. "But, excuse me, so what? He was a ghost. What, thirty-three, four? A dinosaur." I released a short laugh. "That last fight of his, for example. With Chester Link. Jesus, the whipping he took."

Something in Irish Vinnie's face drew taut. "Bad thing," he muttered.

"Slaughter of the Innocents, that's what it was," I said. "After the first round, I figured Burns would be on the mat within a minute of the second. You see it?"

Vinnie nodded.

"Then Douggie comes back and takes a trimming just as bad in the second," I went on, still working to engage Irish Vinnie, or maybe just relive the sweetness of my own vanished youth, the days when I'd huddled at the ringside press table, chain-smoking Camels, with the bill of my hat turned up and a press card winking out of the band, a guy right out of *Front Page,* though even now it seemed amazingly real to me, my newspaperman act far closer to my true self than any role I'd played since then.

"Then the bell rings on Round Three and Chester windmills Douggie all over again. Jesus, he was punch-drunk by the time the bell rang at the end of it." I grinned. "Headed for the wrong corner, remember? Ref had to grab him by the shoulders and turn the poor bleary bastard around."

"A stand-up guy," Vinnie repeated determinedly, though now only to himself.

"I was amazed the ref didn't stop it," I added. "People lost a bundle that night. Everybody was betting Douggie Burns wouldn't finish the fight. I had a sawbuck said he wouldn't see five."

Vinnie's eyes cut over to me. "Lotsa people lost money," he muttered. "Big people."

Big people, I thought, remembering that the biggest of them had been standing ringside that night. None other than Salmon Weiss, the guy who managed Chester Link. Weiss was the sort of fight promoter who wore a cashmere overcoat and a white silk scarf, always had a black Caddie idling outside the arena with a leggy blonde in the back seat. He had a nose that had been more dream than reality before an East Side surgeon took up the knife, and when he spoke, it was always at you.

Get the picture? Anyway, that was Salmon Weiss, and everybody in or around the fight game knew exactly who he was. His private betting habits were another story, however, and I was surprised that a guy like Irish Vinnie, a pug in no way connected to Weiss, had a clue as to where the aforementioned Salmon put his money.

"You weren't one of Weiss's boys, were you?" I asked, though I knew full well that Vinnie had always been managed by Old Man Melinas.

Vinnie shook his head.

"Spiro Melinas was your manager."

Vinnie nodded.

So what gives? I wondered, but figured it was none of my business, and so went on to other matters.

"Anyway," I said. "Chester tried his best to clean Douggie's clock, but the bastard went all the way through the tenth." I laughed again.

The bus groaned, shuddered in a blast of wind, then dragged forward again.

"Well, all I remember is what a shellacking Douggie took."

Vinnie chewed his lower lip. " 'Cause he wouldn't go down."

"True enough. He did the count. All the way to the last bell."

Vinnie seemed almost to be ringside again at that long-ago match, watching as Douggie Burns, whipped and bloody, barely able to raise his head, took punch after punch, staggering backward, fully exposed, barely conscious, so that it seemed to be a statue Chester Link was battering with all his power, his gloves thudding against stomach, shoulder, face, all of it Douggie Burns, but Douggie Burns insensate, perceiving nothing, feeling nothing, Douggie Burns in stone.

"Stayed on his feet," Vinnie said now. "All the way."

"Yes, he did," I said, noting the strange admiration Vinnie still had for Douggie, though it seemed little more than one fighter's regard for another's capacity to take inhuman punishment. "But you have to say there wasn't much left of him after that fight," I added.

"No, not much."

"Which makes me wonder why you fought him at all," I said, returning to my real interest in the matter of Irish Vinnie Teague. "I mean, that was no real match. You and Douggie. After that beating he took from Chester Link, Douggie couldn't have whipped a Girl Scout."

"Nothing left of Douggie," Vinnie agreed.

"But you were in your prime," I told him. "No real match, like I said. And that . . . you know . . . to lose to him . . . that was nuts, whoever set that up."

Vinnie said nothing, but I could see his mind working.

"Spiro. What was his idea in that? Setting up a bout between you and Douggie Burns? It never made any sense to me. Nothing to be gained from it on either side. You had nothing to gain from beating Douggie . . . and what did Douggie have to gain from beating you if he couldn't do it without it being a . . . I mean, if it wasn't . . . real."

Vinnie shook his head. "Weiss set it up," he said. "Not Mr. Melinas."

"Oh, Salmon Weiss," I said. "So it was Weiss that put together the fight you had with Douggie?"

Vinnie nodded.

I pretended that the infamous stage play that had resulted from Weiss's deal had been little more than a tactical error on Vinnie's part and not the, shall we say, flawed thespian performance that had ended his career.

"Well, I sure hope Weiss made you a good offer for that fight, because no way could it have helped you in the rankings." I laughed. "Jesus, you could have duked it out with Sister Evangeline from Our Lady of the Lepers and come up more."

No smile broke the melancholy mask of Irish Vinnie Teague.

I shook my head at the mystery of things. "And a fix to boot," I added softly.

Vinnie's gaze cut over to me. "It wasn't no fix," he said. His eyes narrowed menacingly. "I didn't take no dive for Douggie Burns."

I saw it all again in a sudden flash of light, Douggie's glove float through the air, lightly graze the side of Vinnie's face, then glide away as the Shameful Shamrock crumpled to the mat. If that had not been a dive, then there'd never been one in the history of the ring.

But what can you say to a man who lies to your face, claims he lost the money or that it wasn't really sex?

I shrugged. "Hey, look, it was a long time ago, right?"

Vinnie's red-rimmed eyes peered at me intently. "I was never supposed to take a dive," he said.

"You weren't supposed to take a dive?" I asked, playing along now, hoping that the bus would get moving, ready to get off, be done with Vinnie Teague. "You weren't supposed to drop for Douggie Burns?"

Vinnie shook his head. "No. I was supposed to win that fight. It wasn't no fix."

"Not a fix," I asked. "What was it then?"

He looked at me knowingly. "Weiss said I had to make Douggie Burns go down."

"You had to make Douggie go down?"

"Teach him a lesson. Him and the others."

"Others?"

"The ones Weiss managed," Vinnie said. "His other fighters. He wanted to teach them a lesson so they'd . . ."

"What?"

"Stay in line. Do what he told them."

"And you were supposed to administer that lesson by way of Douggie Burns?"

"That's right."

"What'd Weiss have against Douggie?"

"He had plenty," Vinnie said. " 'Cause Douggie wouldn't do it. He was a stand-up guy, and he wouldn't do it."

"Wouldn't do what?"

"Drop for Chester Link," Vinnie answered. "Douggie was supposed to go down in five. But he wouldn't do it. So Weiss came up with this match. Between me and Douggie. Said I had to teach Douggie a lesson. Said if I didn't . . ." He glanced down at his hands. ". . . I wouldn't never fight no more." He shrugged. "Anyway, I wasn't supposed to lose that fight with Douggie. I was supposed to win it. Win it good. Make Douggie go down hard." He hesitated a moment, every dark thing in him darkening a shade. "Permanent."

I felt a chill. "Permanent," I repeated.

"So Weiss's fighters could see what would happen to them if he told them to take a dive and they didn't."

"So it wasn't a fix," I said, getting it now. "That fight between you and Douggie. It was never a fix."

Vinnie shook his head.

The last words dropped from my mouth like a bloody mouthpiece. "It was a hit."

Vinnie nodded softly. "I couldn't do it, though," he said. "You don't kill a guy for doing the right thing."

I saw Douggie Burns's glove lift slowly, hang in the air, soft and easy, drift forward, barely a punch at all, then Irish Vinnie Teague, the Shameful Shamrock, hit the mat like a sack of sand.

The hydraulic doors opened before I could get out another word.

"I get off here," Vinnie said as he labored to his feet.

I touched his arm, thinking of all the times I'd done less nobly, avoided the punishment, known the right thing, but lacked whatever Irish Vinnie had that made him do it, too.

"You're a stand-up guy, Vinnie," I said.

He smiled softly, then turned and scissored his way through the herd of strap-hangers until he reached the door. He never glanced back at me, but only continued down the short flight of stairs and out into the night, where he stood for a moment, upright in the elements. The bus slogged forward again, and I craned my neck for a final glimpse of Irish Vinnie Teague as it pulled away. He stood on the corner, drawing the tattered scarf more tightly around his throat. Then he turned and lumbered up the avenue toward the pink neon of Smith's Bar, a throng of snowflakes rushing toward him suddenly, bright and sparkling, fluttering all around, like a crowd of cheering angels in the dark, corrupted air.

SEAN DOOLITTLE

Summa Mathematica

FROM *Crime Spree*

SOMEHOW, no matter what the variables, the last customer always seemed to come in three minutes before closing.

It was uncanny: a chaos theorem that yielded takeout orders. There had been a time when Stephen Fielder, Ivan and Adele Stremlau Distinguished Professor of Applied Mathematics, would have been compelled to consider such a peculiar phenomenon in terms of statistical models and probability curves.

But Stephen Fielder, fry cook, only straightened his kink-riddled back and sighed. He put down his grill brick, wiped his hands on the last clean corner of his apron, and hauled himself up front to face the man squinting at the backlit menu marquee.

"Welcome to Bronco Burger," Fielder told him across the register. "Can I take your order?"

"Gimme the Bacon Double Bronco Buster," said the man. "And some fries. And a Diet Coke also."

"That's one Wrangler?"

"One what again?"

"Wrangler Meal Deal." Fielder pointed behind his head without looking at the board.

"Sure, whatever. Just make it a Diet Coke."

"Do you want to Chuckwagon-size that?" Wearily, Fielder waited with his finger poised over the color-coded keypad. When no answer came, he looked up to find the customer glancing around the empty store.

A thick fellow. Not tall. An oil drum, Stephen thought, in a wrinkled linen suit. The man wore the sleeves of his sport jacket pushed up to the elbows. If he noticed Fielder watching, he didn't show it.

"Chuckwagon-size that order, sir?"

The guy looked at him blankly.

"Look, it's a large fry and extra-large Coke. Thirty-five cents extra."

"Diet Coke," the man said. He now seemed to be checking the deserted seating area behind him.

"Sir?"

Finally the man rolled his stocky shoulders, turning to Stephen with a companionable grin. "So they got you holdin' down the whole place by yourself tonight, huh?"

In retrospect, Stephen Fielder would recognize that he probably should have heard warning bells then and there. But he was new to the late-night rhythms of the food service industry. He felt weary in his bones. It was midnight; he had raw hamburger in the creases of his palms. He only wanted to finish scraping the grill and go home.

But the kid with all the earrings was out back sweeping the parking lot; Veronica, the cute teen who worked the night shift drive-through window, camped in the break room, smoking cigarettes. Which made Stephen the only hand on deck.

So he shrugged and said, "Slow night. Will that be all, sir?"

"Sure," said the guy. "Pretty much."

Then he did something that caught Fielder by surprise. The man took a step toward the register, lifting his right hand as he moved. Fielder followed the slim gold bracelet dangling from the dark hairy overgrowth of the man's wrist.

So distracted was Stephen by the strange gesture, in fact, that he never saw the customer's other fist cross his jaw.

All Fielder saw was a blooming nova of cool blue light, followed by a hazy descending screen. He thought: *hey*.

Then he realized he was being dragged over the counter by the apron, which had somehow become tangled in the man's knuckle-bound grip.

"You two. Scramola."

Fielder heard the words as if from a great distance. His eyelids creaked open to a painful light. Stainless steel loomed up around him on all sides; dimly, Fielder realized he was prone on the greasy back-kitchen floor. He didn't remember being deposited there.

His workmates, David and Veronica, didn't need to be told twice. As they high-tailed it out the back door, Fielder lifted his pounding head. Eventually, he managed to raise himself enough to lean against the bun warmer. Only then did he look at his assailant, who picked stale curly fries from an unemptied fryer basket.

"Are you from the foundation?" It was a ridiculous question. Fielder realized he must still have been dazed by the punch. His jaw felt knocked off its hinges.

"Yeah," said the guy. He nodded right along, munching cold fries. "Sure. I'm from the We Stomp the Crap Outta Deadbeats Foundation. This is an outreach typa thing."

Fielder closed his eyes and probed his jaw gingerly. The room see-sawed around him. "I think there's been some kind of mistake."

"Yeah? I'd feel awful bad." The man produced a small black notepad from inside his jacket. "Fielder? Works at the Bronco Burger on Davenport, is what I got here. This is the Bronco Burger, right?"

Fielder nodded without speaking. The man pantomimed a sigh of relief by moving the back of one hand across his brow.

"I don't understand," Fielder said.

"I'm kinda gettin' that."

"I don't . . . what do want from me?"

"Me? Hey, I don't want anything. It's my boss." The guy gestured with the notebook. "He wants the money you owe him."

Fielder absorbed these words. Dookie Weber? He couldn't believe it. This guy worked for Dookie Weber?

"You work for Dookie Weber?"

"You're serious. I look like I work for a turdball like Dookie Weber to you?" The man placed a hand over his heart. "Hey. Ouch."

"Then I don't . . . I don't understand."

"Okay, see, here's how it is. Dookie Weber, like myself, works in the employ of a man named Joseph King. You've heard of Happy Joe King?"

Fielder shook his head. He honestly had not.

"Fair enough. But you're gonna want to remember the name, and I'll tell you why." The man crossed his arms and leaned back against a clean stretch of stainless steel. "Dookie Weber, I mentioned, works for Happy Joe King. Except Dookie's problem — his biggest one, anyway — is that lately he's been forgetting who he works for. And Happy Joe? He's none too happy, if you get what I mean. So Dookie Weber, let's put it this way, ain't working for

Happy Joe King anymore. And that's where Dookie's problem becomes your problem. You following?"

"I think I'm starting to."

"Atta boy." The man returned to his notebook. "Now I know what you prolly gotta be thinking, so don't worry. Happy Joe understands these things. You work with him, make an honest effort, he's actually a whole lot more flexible than a lot of folks give him credit. So let's you and me see where we are."

While Stephen sat, massaging his aching jaw with one hand, the guy who worked for somebody named Happy Joe King flipped a page in his notepad and ran a finger down the next. Soon he gave a low whistle.

"Took a bath on the playoffs, huh?"

Fielder closed his eyes and nodded.

The man flipped a page. "'Course, you ain't been doing too hot at the track, either."

Fielder sighed. "Not too."

The man flipped another page. He glanced at Fielder.

"I know," Fielder said. "I know."

"No offense, but you must be the unluckiest fuckin' guy I seen all year."

"You might say the numbers haven't been falling my way lately."

"You might say it a couple times." The guy flipped another page in his notepad, then closed it. "Okay. I can see we got our work cut out for us, here. Tell you what: you got some markers out at the casino that go back more than ninety days. We'll start there and work our way forward. That sound fair enough?"

"The casino?" The amount of information in this guy's notepad was beginning to fill Stephen Fielder with a deep sense of despair. "The Nugget?"

"No, the MGM Grand. Yeah, the Nugget. You know of another one on this river?"

"But Dookie had nothing to do with the casino."

"No," said the guy. "No, he didn't. But Happy Joe King, see, he does. And since he's consolidating the books, so to speak, it tends to put everything right there in one place, if you know what I mean. Certain patterns become visible where they might, otherwise, maybe not. Sorry to be the bringer."

Fielder didn't know what to say. So he just sat there.

"Hey," said the guy. "Chin up, partner. This is all gonna work out fine." He stepped forward, leaned over, and stuck out his hand. "Up we go."

Before Fielder could decline the offer, he felt himself being pulled to his feet. The room wobbled again. He blinked, suddenly enveloped by an invisible nimbus of cheap cologne.

"How you feeling? Chomper okay?"

"I think it's broken."

"Aww, come on. I didn't hit you that hard."

"If you say so."

The guy just chuckled, reaching inside his jacket to retrieve a pen. He scribbled something in the notebook, tore out the page, folded it once and stuck it in Fielder's shirt pocket.

"That's your number," he said. "We'll start out easy. That sound okay by you?"

"I . . ." Fielder had no words. "Yes."

"Then we're all set. I'll be back in a week." The guy grinned. Then he nodded darkly toward Fielder's pocket. "Have it, okay?"

Fielder wanted to look at the paper, but he didn't have the nerve. So he just nodded.

"Atta boy. I can see we're gonna get along fine."

Stephen nodded again. He felt a rough hand clap him on the shoulder.

"Now how about that burger?" the collector said.

The morning after began inevitably.

With telephone calls.

The first came from Fielder's brother-in-law, Ned, managing owner of six Bronco Burger locations citywide. Fielder let Ned harangue the answering machine while he fed Rhombus, the Labrador he'd owned since his undergraduate days.

Renee rang in by 8:30, close on her brother's heels.

Hello? Are you okay? Oh, no. Not Renee. The first words out of his ex-wife's mouth were, *I don't know what you've done this time, but you've definitely got a hell of a lot of nerve. I told Ned it was a terrible idea, hiring you.*

Stephen decided to let the answering machine take that one, too.

Finally, around 10:30, Fielder heard the answering machine pick up for the third time. By now he sat at the folding card table in the kitchenette, reading yesterday's newspaper and sipping today's first Stoli.

"Dad? You're screening, aren't you?"

This time, he snatched up the cordless receiver the minute he heard the voice on the other end of the line.

"Andrea?"

"Dad. What's going on? Are you okay?"

"I'm fine, sweetie. Aren't you supposed to be at school?"

"I'm between classes. And don't dodge me. What happened?"

"What do you mean?"

"My friend Derek told me you got beat up."

"Who?"

"Derek. You worked late shift together last night. He just told me some guy came in and clobbered you! Dad, is that *true?*"

Listening to her, Fielder felt something collapse in his chest. He thought it might have been the last of his pride. "The kid with all the earrings? I thought his name was David."

"Dad!"

Fielder sighed into the phone.

"Everything's fine, sweetie. Really. There was a guy, but it was nothing. Some lunatic, that's all."

"Derek said he heard the guy say you owed somebody money. Are you in some kind of trouble? Tell me the truth."

"I'm fine, Andie. Okay? Do me a favor. Tell your friend Derek to mind his own goddamned business."

"I'm coming over during lunch period."

"We're on opposite sides of town. Don't waste your gas."

"I'm coming over. Do you even have anything to eat in the apartment?"

"Andie . . ."

"Never mind. I'll stop and get something on the way." She paused theatrically. "Bronco Burger okay with you?"

"That's not funny."

"Who's laughing?" Andrea said, and hung up the phone.

For the next hour or so, Fielder sat at the crappy folding table, listlessly watching the ice cubes melt in his booze. At some point, Rhombus padded over and stood with his big doggy head in Fielder's lap. Fielder scrubbed him between the ears. They looked at each other. *So. What's new with you?*

When Andie finally knocked around 11:30, Stephen drew himself together and prepared himself to play the role of World's Most Disappointing Dad.

It was demoralizing, but Stephen could live with that. Since the divorce became official seven months ago, any moment he was able to spend in his daughter's company was a happy gift. Despite the mess he and Renee had made of the family, Andie just kept on growing into this extraordinary human being who never stopped impressing or delighting him. Stephen could live with her disappointment a thousand times more easily than her absence.

So he dumped the last of the Stoli down the sink, rinsed out the glass, stowed the bottle in the cupboard above the refrigerator, and hustled to the door.

Only it wasn't Andie.

"Stephen Fielder?" said the guy with the tool belt.

Fielder sighed, propping an arm on the edge of the door. "Now what?"

The guy pointed a finger at the manifest in his hand. "Fielder?"

Stephen recognized the cable company logo stitched on the guy's shirt. "Yeah. But I think there's been a mistake. My cable's working fine."

"Hey, great," said the dirty imposter, grinning cheerfully as he handed Stephen a fat business envelope embossed with the corporate seal of the university's law firm. "It's been a pleasure serving you."

Sometimes Stephen thought back to last year, just before the holidays, when one of his oldest friends had gone in for a routine physical that turned up brain cancer. *Jesus,* he'd thought then. *How do you handle a thing like that?* The poor damned guy had been dead by New Year's Day.

On the bright side, at least a cerebral lesion the size of a silver dollar was an explanation. Stephen had stopped seeking explanations for his own condition months ago. Each day he simply woke up, took a shower, dressed himself, and shambled off into the same waking dream his life had become — each day a vast Mobius treadmill that began where it ended and traveled nowhere in between.

Was this his mid-life thing? Fielder had heard of guys his age getting impotent or religious. He'd heard about guys who got earrings and sporty convertibles. He didn't know about any of that.

All Stephen Fielder knew was that one morning last November, he woke up to find he couldn't do math anymore.

It was a morning every bit like the last. All seemed normal; everything occupied its regular place. Except that when he went to warm up his oatmeal in the microwave, he just couldn't manage to decipher the keypad, somehow.

Later, standing in front of his undergraduate calculus seminar, he simply went . . . blank. Grease pen in hand, Fielder stood there in the echoing auditorium, staring at the empty whiteboard until one of the regular front-row students actually approached the stage to inquire gently if everything was okay.

The rest of that day was a warp in Stephen's memory. He remembered sitting in his office for three consecutive hours, unable to make heads or tails of the same scientific calculator he'd been using now for more than half his lifetime; the pressure-worn numbers and symbols inscribed on the keys appeared to him as impenetrable hieroglyphs.

He'd finally given up and turned to work. But his own research notes from the previous day mystified him.

Later, in the car on the way home, he'd tried quizzing himself with rudiments, just to get the juices flowing. But it was as if even the multiplication tables had simply fallen out of his brain while he wasn't looking.

Fielder had gone to bed early that night, somewhere between concerned and amused.

Because he *had* been working inhuman hours for weeks on end. He hadn't been eating well, and he hardly ever exercised. Hell, his marriage of twelve years had recently crashed and burned, and the smoke hadn't even cleared.

Stress, he'd begun to think. Sometimes you just didn't notice when your own levels crossed into the red zone. A good night's sleep could do wonders.

But then he woke up the next morning. And the next morning, and the morning after that. He was not restored. Two plus two did not equal four. And Fielder started to worry.

He made appointments with his physician, who found nothing wrong with him and wrote a referral to a neurospecialist. They threw the full battery of acronyms at him: PET, CAT, MRI. He was discovered to be thirteen pounds overweight but otherwise shipshape for a fellow his age.

Meanwhile, Fielder's amusement gave way to panic. On the recommendation of his physician, he began twice-weekly sessions with the nearest psychiatrist on his PPO list. The shrink prescribed a powerful test-market antidepressant that gave Fielder chronic diarrhea and made him dizzy all the time. But that was all.

Final diagnosis: *Nonspecific Acalculia.* Nonspecific Acalculia!

Translation: *Beats us, chum.*

Citing divorce complications, Stephen put in for emergency personal leave from work, letting his graduate assistants cover his classes for the remainder of the term. He was already scheduled to spend the following semester on a paid research sabbatical, funded by a prestigious annual fellowship sponsored by the university's Burkholder Foundation.

So he had time, Fielder had reasoned. Time to sort this thing out on his own.

Because no matter what else plagued him in life, he could not remember a time when numbers did not make sense. As a youth, Fielder had reveled in them. While the other guys in his class drew fart balloons in the margins of their textbooks, Stephen constructed elaborate Fibonacci sequences that went on for pages at a time.

As an adult, suddenly trudging toward middle age ankle-deep in the rubble of a wrecked marriage, numbers seemed to be the only thing in Stephen Fielder's world that still added up. They fit and resonated; they created mysteries and revealed unassailable truths. Unpredictable yet consistent, fluid yet fixed, intractable yet endlessly recombinant. People were somehow beyond him. But numbers he could understand.

And suddenly, inexplicably, just when he'd needed them the most . . . even the numbers had left him.

It was Gudder who said, "The essence of mathematics is not to make simple things complicated, but to make complicated things simple." For years, Fielder had used that quote in the introductory header of all his class syllabi.

But these days, the only quote he felt he understood was Darwin's: "A mathematician is a blind man in a dark room looking for a black cat which isn't there."

Fielder's world had become a dark, dark room. And all he had was a dog.

He began drinking heavily, late into the nights. He slept through most of his days. He couldn't work. And he found himself adrift, without strength to paddle, as the tide of his own malaise carried him farther and farther from shore.

The final slide began by accident. Or perhaps it was an inevitable point in some cause/effect chain. Fielder didn't know. Personally, Stephen Fielder had ceased to acknowledge order in the world.

All he knew was that one night, on a bender, he found himself at The Nugget, across the river. Only because the bar there stayed open two hours later than any place in town.

But it was here, amidst the color and lights and carnival noise, that Fielder experienced the kind of shimmering insight only clinical depression and vast quantities of alcohol can reveal.

For here — before him and above him, around him on all sides — was the essence of mathematics. Here was the complicated wonderment of odds and order. All reduced to the simplicity of a toss of dice, a spin of a wheel.

Stephen remembered sitting back on his stool, turning his face to the light, and experiencing a strange sense of peace.

Because if the odds still thrived in a place like this, by god, maybe there was still hope for him in this orderless world.

"That feels about right," said Happy Joe King's collector, hefting the envelope containing the five-hundred-dollar paycheck advance Fielder had secured from his ex-brother-in-law. "I don't guess I need to count it, huh?"

"It's all there." Stephen had asked Ned to count it in front of him, just to be sure.

"You know what? I trust you. Good faith goes both ways, am I wrong?"

"Trust is important," Fielder agreed.

"We speak the same language, my friend." The collector smacked Fielder on the shoulder. He wore the same suit as last week. "Future reference, you can call me Shorty. Nickname I sorta picked up on account of my height."

Fielder looked down at the parking lot. "Okay."

"Call me Shorty, but don't short me. That's what I always tell 'em." The collector's laugh sounded like a diesel engine shifting gears.

Fielder turned toward the Bronco Burger's back door, but a firm hand fell on his shoulder just as he began to move.

"Cool your heels a minute."

Stephen felt his blood chill. "It's all there."

"Easy, Professor. I got a little surprise."

Fielder tensed.

Shorty the collector just laughed again. "Buddy, you are one jumpy bag a nerves, you know that? You should learn to relax."

To Fielder's bewilderment, Shorty reached over to tuck the envelope full of cash into his apron strings.

"Let's take a little walk."

Fielder looked at Shorty and went numb.

"Don't worry, Professor," Shorty said. "I think your luck's about ready to change."

Shorty led him to a dark gravel lot in back of a secondhand furniture store. Amidst a shadowed clutter of scrap springs and broken wood frames sat a dusty black limousine. The big car's engine was silent, headlights off, dark glossy windows raised. Shorty opened one of the rear doors; no interior light came on.

"After you," he said.

Fielder didn't move.

"Will you calm down? I swear." Shorty nodded toward the open door.

"I should get back to the restaurant," Fielder said. "I think I left the broiler on."

"Get in the fucking car, Professor."

Fielder gazed at the dark portal waiting from him. He looked at Shorty. He released a ragged breath and sagged.

Shorty followed him in and slammed the door. Leather creaked beneath him as Fielder scooted over in the seat to make room. Shorty reached up and flicked a switch above their heads. On came an overhead light, yellow and blinding.

"You two smell like french fries," said the voice from the seat across from him.

The voice belonged to a slim man. Gray hair, impeccably trimmed, an angular face with shallow crow's-feet at the corners of the eyes. The man wore a western-cut suit with ostrich boots. He sat with one arm draped across the back of the seat, a drink in a cut-glass tumbler resting at his knee.

"Professor Fielder," the man said, leaning forward to extend a hand. "My name is Joseph King. How do you do?"

Fielder looked at Shorty, who tossed him a wink.

He shook the man's hand and said, "Mr. King."

"Call me Joe. My father was Mr. King, as the saying goes." King grinned and gestured toward a cabinet built into the side panel of the limo. "Care for a drink? Whatever you like, we probably have it around here somewhere."

"No, thank you." Stephen cleared his throat.

"Professor, I sense that you're uncomfortable. I'd guess you're probably wondering why we're all here."

"How do you people know I'm a professor?"

"Actually," said Happy Joe, "if I'm not mistaken, that verb is now past tense, isn't it?"

Suddenly Fielder felt supremely conscious of his filthy apron.

"I know a fair amount about this and that," Happy Joe King said. "For example, I know you are forty-four years of age. I know you fared poorly — let's face it — in a divorce settlement some months ago. You have one child, a girl, sixteen, name of Andrea, goes to Northeast High. Straight A's. College prep." Ice clicked against glass as King sipped his drink. "As for college, you were tenure track yourself, but are now in breach of your contract with the university here. I infer that you're too proud to let the utilities get shut off but not too proud to take a job flipping burgers for minimum wage. You're also being sued over some money. Burkholder Foundation, is it?" King glanced at Shorty.

Shorty nodded. "Right. Burkholder."

"I understand they're less than pleased with the product of some research they funded. Or lack thereof, as the case may be."

Stephen felt a cold knot behind his breastbone. "How do you know all of this?"

"Let's just say I make it a point to thoroughly background all potential employees."

"I'm sorry," Fielder said. "I don't understand."

"It would seem," said Happy Joe King, sipping again from his glass, "that you and I are in a position to help each other."

Fielder said nothing.

"On the one hand," King continued, "you've managed to accrue a somewhat unfortunate debt to me. On the other, it so happens that I find myself in need of a person with your specialized skills."

"You need a fry cook?"

Shorty laughed beside him. Even Happy Joe King seemed

amused. He crunched an ice cube. "I'm afraid those aren't the particular skills to which I was referring."

"Oh." Stephen sat, feeling like an idiot. He hadn't been trying to be clever. He truly didn't understand.

"Allow me to clarify. As you may know, I'm something of an entrepreneur. My holdings are — well, let's say my holdings are somewhat diversified. Being diversified, as they are, my professional success depends to a considerable degree on what some might consider a sophisticated accounting system. Don't misunderstand: I realize the workaday bookkeeping we're talking about here is a dip in the kiddie pool to a man of your training. But you'd be surprised how difficult it is to find qualified personnel in this area."

"Mr. King . . ."

"Professor. Please. I've told you: call me Joe."

"But I don't . . ."

"Bottom line," Happy Joe King went on, "this is what I'm able to do for you. I'm able to settle your unfulfilled obligation with the Burkholder people. I'm able to buy out the remainder of your contract with the university. Finally — and from your perspective, perhaps most importantly — I'm able to set aside your not-inconsiderable monetary arrearage to me. I'm able to offer all of these things in exchange for your exclusive service in the position of Chief Financial Officer of my various business ventures." King gestured with his drink. "I think you'll agree that I offer an extremely competitive benefits package."

For a long, echoing minute, Stephen just sat, smelling like french fries, staring at some vague point between himself and Happy Joe King. Shorty said nothing. Happy Joe King said nothing.

All Fielder could think to say was, "Don't you already have an accountant?"

"I did, yes. For many years." King's tone conveyed regret. "I'm sorry to say that your predecessor is no longer able to fulfill his duties due to health reasons."

"Health reasons?"

"He got something in his eye," Shorty explained.

Fielder looked at the collector. "He got something in his eye?"

Shorty shrugged. "Manner of speaking."

"The important thing," Joe King said, "is that your eyes are perfectly fine. And I don't just go around offering executive positions to every Tom, Dick, and Harry with a mark in the books. The important thing is that you have something to offer me. And that I have something to offer you. We can help each other." King raised his glass. "So. Professor Fielder. Can I get you that drink?"

It was as if Fielder's lips formed the words without his permission.

"I can't," he heard himself say.

Happy Joe King's eyes darkened. "Pardon?"

"I . . . Mr. King, I can't. I would. But I just . . . I just can't."

King glanced at Shorty again. He looked at Fielder. He did not look happy. "Forgive me for saying so, Professor, but that's a dumbfuck answer for a fellow in your position. I don't mind admitting I didn't expect such dumbfuckery from you. Shorty?"

"Yup."

"Did you?"

"I gotta say," Shorty said, sounding amazed, "no."

"You don't understand," Fielder said quickly. "It's not . . . I wouldn't . . . I'm just unable. Truly."

A quiet, awful minute passed.

"It's the numbers. I don't know how to explain it." He looked at King with a feeling of impending doom. "I'm not your man."

"That's unfortunate," Joe King finally said.

"I really am sorry."

King sat quietly. He swirled his drink. "Are you quite sure you wouldn't like to reconsider?"

"I don't . . . it's not that . . ." Fielder sighed. "I have a condition known as Nonspecific Acalculia."

"Forgive me, but what did you just say?"

"Says he has nonspecific genitalia," Shorty told him, then narrowed his eyes at Fielder. "You some kinda homo?"

"Acalculia," Fielder repeated. "It means that I can't . . ." He struggled, gave up. What was the use?

Happy Joe King said nothing.

"Mr. King," Fielder said, "please don't think the generosity of your offer is lost on me."

King nodded along, appraising him.

Fielder drew in a breath and forced himself to ask the question he didn't want Happy Joe King to answer. "What happens under these circumstances? Being the case that I'm unable to accept the . . . position?"

In reply, Joe King shrugged unimportantly, as if bygones were bygones as far as he was concerned. But he leaned forward to pluck the envelope from Fielder's apron strings.

"This feels light," he commented.

Fielder looked quickly to Shorty, who did not return his glance. "But it's all there. I swear it is. You can count it."

"I count five hundred."

"Yes. Five hundred. It's all there."

"The installment is eight."

"But I was told . . . Shorty said five." Fielder looked at Shorty again, desperate for aid. Shorty offered none. "Five. It's all there."

"Five? Yes," King said. "Last week, five. This week, eight."

"But that's . . ." Fielder's stomach did a queasy roll. "I don't understand."

"In an accelerated economy such as ours," King explained, "sometimes lending institutions — and that's, in a sense, how you can think of me from now on — are forced to raise interest percentages in order to keep expansion in line. It's a systemic necessity, Professor. Please understand, these are market forces we're up against. I don't make the rules."

Fielder felt himself deflating.

"Shorty?" said King.

"Yup."

"I'll need you to explain the matter of penalty fees to Professor Fielder. Bear in mind he has a condition."

As Shorty opened his door, and Stephen felt the collector's heavy hand descend on his shoulder, it was as if time stopped, then accelerated. He looked at Shorty, hoping unreasonably for some slim possibility of shelter, finding only hard, dutiful eyes.

Later, on the long but limp-free walk home to his building, Stephen told himself he'd made the only reasonable decision, under the circumstances.

First, there was only sick fear, accompanied by visions of compound fractures, in his very near future.

But several blocks after parting Shorty's company, a giddiness came upon Fielder. There arose within Stephen's breast a vague but euphoric tremor; a quick breath escaped him.

And as he walked on — moving between pools of sodium light cast by the streetlamps overhead, narrowing the distance to his apartment stride by lengthening stride — Stephen Fielder began to feel something he hadn't felt in as long as he could remember.

Lucky.

Maybe it was the delayed adrenaline rush of surviving a dicey situation. Maybe there was nothing like the hand of a professional motivator at your elbow to jolt you out of an unproductive frame of mind.

Fielder didn't know. He didn't know if night birds always sang like this in this part of town, or if he'd simply never noticed them before now.

All Stephen Fielder knew was that something important had happened this last half-hour. Something transformative.

Because people lost limbs, for heaven's sake. He understood that, now. Accidents maimed but did not kill. Careers in roaring environments slowly obliterated the ability to hear; viral infections robbed people of their eyesight. Awful diseases of the nervous and muscular systems impeded, immobilized.

Time and time again over the course of this strange affliction, Stephen had returned to thoughts of his friend with brain cancer. And for the first time, he realized he shouldn't have been thinking about his dead friend at all.

He *should* have been thinking about a French magazine editor he'd once read about.

The journalist's name was Bauby. Jean-Dominique Bauby. In the middle part of his life, Bauby had suffered a massive stroke that left him quadriplegic. And at forty-four — Fielder's very age — the man had written his own memoirs, nearly two hundred pages worth, by blinking his left eyelid.

Two hundred pages, all dictated in code. Character by character, one blink at time.

People survived. Plenty of people survived unimaginable horrors each and every day. And then they woke up and survived them all over again the day after that. People adapted; they overcame. They developed tools and engineered workarounds. They persevered and recalculated. They plugged in variable after variable until their personal equations finally produced a gain.

Fielder found himself awash in a tide of inspiration by the time he reached his apartment building. He was thinking in terms of visual recognition. How hard could it be to relearn the sight of a numeral? A symbol's unique lines and curves? He thought in terms of computer aid: spreadsheets, graphing applications, microprocessors with far more raw calculating power than any human mind. He thought of tools he'd once taken for granted. Marvels of human engineering designed for the express purpose of taking the complicated . . . and making it simple.

So lost in these thoughts was Fielder as he climbed the stairwell to his floor that it took him a moment to register that Rhombus waited for him in the hallway outside his door.

"Rhombie," he said, leaning down to scratch the dog behind the ears. "How did you get out here?"

Rhombus just looked up at him with soulful brown eyes. *Don't look at me. Ask them.*

That was when Fielder noticed that his apartment door stood ajar.

Four men waited for him inside. Two wore suits. One wore a sport jacket with jeans. One had doffed his sport jacket and draped it over the back of the couch, exposing a shoulder holster. Fielder noted the badge clipped to the man's belt.

"Professor Fielder," said one of the men in suits. He met Fielder at the door with one hand extended, the other flipping open an ID wallet. "Forgive the intrusion. My name is Special Agent Corrigan."

Fielder shook the man's hand robotically. Rhombus hung back, out in the hall.

Agent Corrigan pointed around the apartment. "That's my partner, Agent Klein. Detective Reese. Detective Carvajal."

The man in the shirtsleeves and shoulder holster raised his hand.

Fielder looked at them. "What are you doing in my apartment?"

"Professor Fielder," said Agent Corrigan, "it would seem we're in a position to help each other."

That night, Fielder dreamed he was playing checkers with Andie at a folding card table in an unfamiliar room. They were laughing and having fun together.

He was about to say, *King me!* when a door opened, and a team of Burkholder's lawyers jogged in. Fielder looked up, wondering how in the world they'd found him; the lawyers, all with matching briefcases, filed into a row.

Just as he was about to demand an explanation for this interruption of his personal time with his daughter, another door opened. Happy Joe King appeared with Shorty in tow.

They saw the lawyers. The lawyers saw them. Shorty snarled.

And all at once, a third door burst off its hinges; Agents Corrigan and Klein rushed into the room, sidearms drawn. Detectives Reese and Carvajal hustled in after them.

Fielder tried to stand out of his chair, but he couldn't move.

FBI!, shouted Corrigan, leveling his gun at Shorty across the checkers table.

Still snarling, Shorty reached inside his jacket and drew a gun of his own. *Back off, asshole,* he said. *The math man's ours.*

Fielder felt a hot salty lump in the back of his throat. He tried to speak. He tried again to stand. Andie looked at him, shaking her head. She said, *You've got a hell of a lot of nerve.*

At that moment, the row of lawyers simultaneously dropped to their knees, popped latches, and dove into their briefcases. They stood up armed with guns of all shapes and sizes.

Sorry, said one of the lawyers, suddenly crisscrossed over his suit with ammo belts. *But we'll be taking the professor with us.*

I'm not a professor anymore! Fielder wanted to shout. But his mouth was stuffed full by some unidentifiable wad. Looking down, he saw an empty Bronco Burger wrapper in his hands.

But before he could expel the foul obstruction, everybody opened fire.

Pinned down with Andie in the center of the triangle, Stephen noticed that the guns fired mathematics instead of bullets; numbers left muzzles in a flash of flame and floated slowly, as if weightless, across the room.

One of the lawyers riddled Agent Corrigan with a salvo of spinning sevens. Shorty capitalized on the vulnerability and shot the attorney in the neck with a nine. Klein hit the floor and rolled; Detective Carvajal covered him, snapping fraction after fraction over the lawyers' heads.

Andie watched the crossfire with an awe-dazed grin. *Dad! Look at this!* She reached up with an index finger and touched a passing greater-than/equal-to symbol, sending it spinning off course. *They're so beautiful!*

She never noticed the lawyer over her left shoulder, drawing down on Detective Reese. By the time she turned to see the discharge floating her way, it was too late for her to react.

Able to move at last, Fielder sprang up, lurching forward to shield his daughter.

Just as he reached her, arms outstretched, he took one in the shoulder. The force of the impact spun him around toward Happy Joe King.

Out of the corner of his eye, Fielder saw Shorty's gun buck, and he raised his hand defensively. But in the dream, somebody had turned off the slow motion, and he got a speeding pi in the face before he went down.

In the end, Fielder lasted almost two months before Shorty caught him wearing the wire.

It was a fluke. The collector had come to Bronco Burger to get Fielder for their weekly staff meeting in the back of Happy Joe's limo. On the customary walk to the parking lot of the used furniture store, Shorty made some joke and followed up with a quick play jab to Fielder's midsection. Stephen hadn't been paying attention, and he failed to juke away in time. Shorty's play fist brushed the transmitter device taped to Fielder's ribcage.

He reached again to check.

Then his face darkened, and the fist exploded into Stephen's belly for real . . .

. . . and when he could finally breathe again, Fielder found himself in the back of the limo — Bronco Burger shirt torn open, welts raising on the skin of his chest where the adhesive tape had been ripped away — facing Joseph "Happy Joe" King for what he knew would be the last time.

The old crook sat looking at the FBI-issue paraphernalia in his hand as though pondering some high-tech rune. Fielder could feel Shorty beside him, brewing like an electrical storm.

But Happy Joe just sat in silence for what seemed like ages.

At last, King spoke only two words: "How long?"

"A couple of months," Stephen admitted, for there was no use playing games at this stage. "Six, seven weeks maybe."

Joe King nodded. And Fielder couldn't be sure, but he thought he recognized the expression on the man's face. It was the look of a man who suspects he's in the process of losing something. Something he's always had.

Or maybe it was the look of a man on the verge of admitting to himself what he already knows he lost some time ago.

At last, Shorty could no longer contain himself. He erupted with a primal bellow of rage, and when the big gun in his hand connected with the middle of Fielder's face, Stephen felt his nose give way.

Cheek against the opposite window, pressed there by the muzzle of Shorty's gun at the hard bone above his opposite temple, Fielder gargled blood as the collector screamed at him, close enough to spray saliva in Stephen's ear.

"We trusted you!" Shorty shouted. "We trusted you, you miserable fuckin' fuck!"

Before he blacked out, Fielder saw Happy Joe King call off his collector with a slight shake of the head. Shorty roared again and gifted Stephen with one final, thunderous kidney punch.

Then chaos ruled.

Light flooded the world; doors came open, other doors slammed. Hard voices shouted commands. People appeared and scurried about; somebody had a megaphone.

Later, sitting in the open back end of the paramedic's rig, holding a bloody ice pack to his split lips and broken nose, Fielder saw Andie break free from a uniformed cop, cross the yellow tape, and sprint his way.

She'd told him she might stop in and see him tonight. Until that moment, their unofficial date had completely slipped his mind.

For some reason, the sight of his daughter brought the memory of a movie they'd rented together a year or two ago. Stephen didn't remember the name of the film. But it was all about how life as everybody knew it was really just a great elaborate computer program. And if you knew the program's secrets, you could bend its rules: jump higher, run faster, float in the air, that kind of thing. If you were truly special, you could figure out how to transcend the program altogether.

For some reason, Fielder thought about the pivotal moment in the movie where the hero finally reaches enlightenment. From that point on, the hero saw everything around him in terms of the endless datastreams that created the illusion.

And it occurred to Fielder that if he were the main character in that movie, this would be the point where he'd observe the bustling chaos of this scene before him and begin to see the underlying patterns, and all would be revealed.

He thought about Happy Joe King. Wondered if the patterns were any clearer to him.

He wondered if he was the only one who seemed to be missing the point.

And then he felt his daughter throw her arms around him, asking him in breathless tones if he was okay.

Fielder stroked her hair, grinned in spite of the pain, and told her he was fine.

Man Kills Wife, Two Dogs

FROM *Willow Springs*

THREE HARD RAPS on the door made Dudek drop his beer. Only the landlord ever knocked, and no way would he knock again. Not after that morning.

"The downstairs door was open," she explained.

He invited her into the room. She smelled like lilac. He figured her pearls for fake, though she wore them as if she didn't care. Strawberry blond hair brushed her shoulders and her purple pullover sweater. The reporter introduced herself, said she wanted to talk about the shooting.

"What do you want me to say?" Dudek said, hoping she'd hear how willing he was to say anything. The reporter didn't bite.

"Tell me what you saw," she said, "what you heard." Her voice reminded him of hot fudge pouring over mounds of vanilla. He said the first thing that came to mind.

"He came out with a cop on each arm. I tried to see his face. I mean, how does a guy look after he shoots his wife? I'll tell you. He was grinning. Like everything was blue sky and bird songs. He was in such a good mood, I thought of yelling at him, 'Hey, Mr. Tucker! You mind if I'm late on the rent this month?' Don't write that. It's a joke."

She grinned and watched him while scribbling on her notepad, her hard mahogany eyes unafraid to meet his. One hundred percent flirt. No question. Dudek could lock on a flirty smile through thirty feet of dark, smoky bar even when his heart pumped tequila instead of blood. In his own apartment, having downed only one can of beer, he felt as certain of the reporter's intentions as he did his own.

He got a rag from the bathroom to wipe up the spilled beer. He'd seen reporters on TV, always yak yak yakking — but not this one. Mostly she listened, frowning in sympathy, pooching her lower lip. "Ask me something," he wanted to say, but instead he turned the blinds and looked out on the grimy April afternoon. He thought she'd like that picture: the loner in a T-shirt and ratty trousers, staring out the window at a world gone to hell. On Dudek's street, that world was low-riders and rust-eaten pickups, and the house across the road where kids had hung a cheap nylon banner for the holiday. On it, a pink bunny gathered painted eggs and grinned, ignorant and idiotic, at the house where Dudek lived, where until about half past six that morning, Mrs. Tucker had lived, too.

"It kicks my ass that he picked Easter Sunday," Dudek said. "For Christ's sake, wait until Monday. You know what I'm saying?"

"For Christ's sake," she repeated, chuckling, so he laughed, too. He liked her freckles, sprinkled around her cheekbones like fairy dust.

Dudek made a show of sweeping crumbs off the couch, even beating a pillow with an open palm. "Have a seat," he told her while on his way to the kitchen. "Can I make you some coffee? Pop you a beer? Murder on Easter rates at least a six-pack."

"Sounds tempting, but I'm on duty," she said.

In the kitchen, he fished a can from the fridge, glad the reporter had turned down his offer when he noticed that can was the last one.

"You read our paper?" she asked as he sat near her on the couch. The newspaper lay slapdash over the coffee table he had scavenged from a neighbor's junk pile.

"It's the Tuckers'." He sipped his beer, folded the paper. He had read about two wars, a flood in China, and about people who wanted a state beach declared nude for one week a year. He was rooting for the nudies.

"So, when did you hear the shots?"

"I was making breakfast," he said, "boiling eggs, you know, because it's Easter. It was dark outside. Quiet. I can't sleep late. My old man was the same way, but he could blame smoker's cough. Me, I don't know. Anyway, the Tuckers. I'm hearing nothing from downstairs, which is strange, because I always hear them when they're at each other's throats. I mean, I used to hear them. Before. You'd think this morning they'd have been at it, too."

"What would they fight about?" she asked.

"Stupid things," he said. "Sad things. She called him fatso, though she was fatter. He hated that she didn't work. Some nights, I'd wake to him shouting, 'You ignorant witch!' or her yelling about how he was lousy with his hands." Dudek grimaced. "Stuff I didn't need to know. Some nights it sounded like they had fun hating each other that much."

Dudek swigged a mouthful, let it tingle his gums. Mornings after those fights, Dudek would listen carefully before leaving for work, waiting until he could hear either Mr. or Mrs. step out of their apartment. Then he would hurry down the stairwell that landed at their apartment door, wanting to see in their faces how they'd got through the night, how they'd changed from the day before, if something moved in or moved out. He didn't tell that part to the reporter.

She scribbled something and crossed her legs, her black pantyhose shimmering from the glare of the bulb on his ceiling. She had small feet, the reporter. And she wore black heels that came to a point like a knife. The heels were low, but he could imagine her in higher ones. He drained his beer and set the can between his feet next to the earlier empty, thinking she'd like it if he said something generous about the Tuckers.

"They loved the dogs. Two boxers. Purebreds. Frazier and Foreman. Cocky things. Big chests. God, they barked like maniacs."

"This morning?"

"All the time, but this morning . . . I'd never heard them bark like that before. Strangled. Half a howl, almost. You'll think I'm crazy" — he paused for effect — "but it was like they were begging."

He noticed her fingers as she wrote: mid-length nails, shiny with clear polish; no ring on the important finger. "When did the dogs start?" she asked.

"After the first shot. Like I said, I was at the stove." He told her how he'd stood there, the eggs knocking together, rattling the pot. The first bang. Jesus. He ran downstairs like an idiot. In his underwear, halfway down, he'd heard two more, the sound slamming through the walls to his spine. He turned back. One shot might be an accident. Three means something awful.

"Then?" she asked.

Silence. No barking. No nothing. He locked the door. Called the cops. "They were here in a few minutes," he said, though it had seemed longer as he waited, wondering if Tucker would come upstairs next. Dudek had sat in his living room, gripping the aluminum baseball bat he hid beneath his bed in case of trouble, trying not to throw up. Nothing Ms. Lilac-and-Fake-Pearls needed to know.

"When they brought her out she was on a stretcher," he said, "covered by a sheet. One of the wheels caught in a crack in the walk and they nearly tipped her. The dogs they brought out in garbage bags."

The reporter uncrossed her legs, but kept her knees tight together. She leaned toward him, and then placed the tip of her pen between her teeth, lips apart.

Jesus H. Christ, Dudek thought, and he laughed at his good luck.

"What's so funny?"

"Nothing, nothing. What else do you want to know?"

She thought a moment. "Why didn't he kill himself, too?"

"Seems dumb doesn't it? Maybe that's because when you hear about these things it's always murder-suicide. But Tucker walked out with that big grin. Maybe it's like a car alarm loud as hell in the middle of the night. You know how you want to shoot those things. You just want to shut it up. Nothing else matters."

"So, Mrs. Tucker was like a car alarm."

Dudek shrugged. "I'm no head shrinker. Just a neighbor."

"Did the Tuckers have friends or children?"

"None I ever saw."

"You didn't know them too well, then?"

"It's not like we bar-hopped together, but you live above people, you get to know something about them. They were nice enough, I guess. She read those true-life crime books. In summers she'd read on the porch, fall asleep in one of those scratchy lawn chairs, and snore. He watched the fights. As far as landlords go, he couldn't tell a wrench from pliers, you know? Cheap, too. You can tell he didn't like to spend money on the place."

She had stopped writing. She looked bored. Dudek chewed his lower lip.

"Our apartments have the same layout," he said. "My bedroom sits over theirs. The cops told me that's where he killed her, if you want to . . ." He pointed out of the living room, his face so dumb with faked innocence that she smiled.

Dudek had left his bed unmade, and dirty clothes shaped a hill in the room's far corner. "Maid's sick," he said, kicking underpants and T-shirts under his bed. Then he pointed at the floor. "Down there."

The reporter stepped around Dudek's dresser and his bed, her high heels clicking on the worn wood floor, and Dudek realized how eerie the room had become, how he'd avoided it all day. Suddenly, he couldn't help imagining Tucker, a few feet below, squeezing soft on the trigger, the jolt in his hand, the noise. Tucker must have blinked. When he opened his eyes . . . and what about Mrs. Tucker? Had he nudged her shoulder to wake her? Did he turn on the light? Tucker would have needed light. Unless he stood close enough to touch metal to scalp.

Dudek stopped rubbing his temples; he couldn't remember having started. "Blows my mind," he said. "Killing the wife and dogs on Easter. It's got a kind of poetry though, you know what I'm saying? Everybody's looking forward to a nice time. And bam! That's it. Tucker's waving his gun around shouting, 'Hey everybody, look at me! I'm in the shits big time! Forget spring. Forget that rising from the grave stuff. Let me give you a big wad of death.'"

"Why would he do that?" she asked.

"That's the big question, huh? Why would he put it in God's face that way, say 'Screw you, God!'" Dudek waved his middle finger at the ceiling. "Something must have made him that crazy . . ."

She wanted to know. She really did, he could tell — from her insistent voice, from her pale throat now flushed red — she wanted to brush against the ugliness and danger of that morning, feel the electric jolt that he'd stumbled into. She shouldered against the wall of his bedroom, hair tucked behind an ear to lay bare her smooth neck and delicate lobe pierced by a tiny, crystal stud.

"Well, I could've predicted it," Dudek said. He sat on the corner of his mattress, which sagged a few inches. "Early, before I even started breakfast, I heard the outside door of the house banging around, like someone wanted in. I went down, keeping quiet in case it was some thief. Brought my baseball bat just in case." He pulled it out from under the bed to show her. "I found Mr. Tucker at the landing, fully dressed."

She waited.

"It wasn't the first time he'd spent the night out," Dudek said. "'Happy Easter,' I said to him. He'd bent down to pick up the key they keep under the mat. I said, 'Happy Easter.'"

"'Happy Easter, Henry,' he said, and looked at the baseball bat. 'Watch out for the slider,' he said. Lots of laughs, that Mr. Tucker. He unlocked their door, then put the key back in its place. I could smell his breath."

When Dudek looked at the reporter, she stared back, writing without looking at her notepad. She tilted her head and asked the question with her eyes.

"Booze hound," he whispered. "Her, too."

She stopped writing. She looked as if she had heard that story before.

"They just weren't hobby drinkers," he insisted. "This was a career. You should see the liquor boxes stacked out back. Mr. Tucker used to miss work. And the dogs roamed loose everywhere. Come Tuesday, if he managed to get out their garbage, the bags of empties made Mount Everest on the sidewalk. Sometimes, they'd forget I owed rent. Fine with me, but you know . . ."

"And this is why he killed her?"

"Yeah. What? Murder on Easter Sunday, fighting, alcohol, that's not enough?"

"No," she said and scribbled something. "I mean, yes, of course it's enough. It is what it is. Well."

She handed him a business card, smiled, and asked him to call if he had anything else to say, and he nodded like it wasn't any big deal as she stepped out of his apartment and down the stairs in those pointy-heeled shoes. From the window, he watched her walk through the dusk to her car — a little Honda. She looked once more at the Tuckers' apartment and then slid into the driver's seat. Headlights on, zoom, she was gone.

In and out. That was Dudek's plan. He knew they'd have beer or some liquor, and they owed him. Mr. Tucker did at least, for raining murder down on the holiday. The man owed the whole block drinks.

The police had blocked the Tuckers' apartment, twisting yellow tape around a couple of rusty nails hammered into either side of the door frame. Dudek unwrapped the yellow tape, then found the key where Tucker had left it under the doormat. He rolled the deadbolt back into the door.

From where he stood he could see almost nothing, and the only light came from a low-watt bulb high above the stairway behind him. He waited for something to move or to make a sound, not surprised at how scared he was, but not having expected it either. A moment later, his eyes adjusted and he stepped inside. The room smelled sweet and coppery like a fresh pack of cigarettes, and he could hear the Tuckers' fridge humming from the kitchen. A clock ticked the time. From the darkness came a steady pulse of blue light, the display on a VCR. He knew there was a couch near the door; he'd seen it from the stairwell when passing their apartment as Mr. or Mrs. was on the way in or out, and he recalled that he'd never seen them together, never on the porch or walking the dogs; always he met them one without the other.

He felt the wall near the door for the light switch that would be in the same place as the one in his apartment, but then he worried maybe some neighbor would notice and call the cops. Burglars made a living like this, didn't they, raiding the homes of the recently dead? But that's not what he was doing, not really. Besides: quick in, quick out. The apartment would be dark again before anyone noticed.

When the lights flashed on, he expected to see a home wrecked by the violence of three murders, but it wasn't that way at all. He saw the couch, over-stuffed, with balding corduroy upholstery, and a coffee table with a wood laminate surface; on its top, an open TV guide from the newspaper, a coffee mug with coffee in it, a pen, and a few scraps of paper on which someone had written to-do lists: renew the termite policy, brake job, talk to Dudek about parking . . . He suspected that had pissed them off: parking behind them in that skinny driveway so they couldn't get their car out. In two of the room's corners were plaid doggie beds for Frazier and Foreman, their names embroidered on the pillows. On the eggshell-colored walls, framed prints — one of a barn in a wheat field and the other of toddling girls holding fistfuls of dandelions. A television and that VCR he'd noticed. A shelf with a few of Mrs. Tucker's books, but mostly a place for framed eight-by-tens of some kids in cowboy hats, posing and faking smiles in front of a photographer's background drape. In another photo, a thirtyish guy — who shared Mr. Tucker's pointed nose and pear-shaped ass — shook hands with Tommy Lasorda. So the kids lived in L.A. and that explained why Dudek had never seen them. Maybe they'd be flying in now to take care of things. Dudek supposed the police would have called them.

In the kitchen, he grabbed three beers, then changed his mind and took the whole six-pack in its paperboard carton. What difference did it make? Would Tucker junior take inventory? So what if he did? When Dudek shut the refrigerator door, magnets fell and along with them a Chinese menu and some photographs. He picked them up, started to put them back when he noticed — right at eye level — lottery tickets stuck to the fridge by a rubber magnet of Florida.

He leaned closer to read: five sets of numbers for April 7, the Wednesday after Easter. Hell, he thought, why not? He shoved the tickets into his pants pocket.

As he left the kitchen he looked down the hall to their bedroom. The door was shut. It's like those movies, he thought, where you want to yell "Don't open the door!" at the dumb babysitter but you want her to open the door, too, because you can't turn back, you have to know. Dudek wanted to see where it happened. It'd make a good story later on. So he set the six-pack on the seat of an easy chair and stepped down the dark hall.

Idiot, he thought even as he knocked. Embarrassed, he twisted the glass knob and shoved the door so it banged against the wall. Then he switched on the ceiling light, looking suddenly on an unmade bed, sheets blotchy and stiff, an explosion of blood against the yellow vinyl headboard, and more in two smears across the planks of the floor. The dogs. Mattress stuffing drifted from the stir of air that followed Dudek's hard push of the door. He shut his eyes, felt afraid, so looked again. Some blood had started to dry and it was brown on the wall, dark purple on the headboard, but still red where it soaked into the sheets and where it pooled thickest on the floor. He backed away, having seen enough, but stopped when he noticed cardboard boxes stacked along the nearest bedroom wall, so many boxes they covered the wall itself. There was a desk, too, and when he stepped closer, careful to avoid the smears on the floor, he saw above the desk a bulletin board with a chart tacked to it, high enough and far enough that it had stayed clean, untouched by the splattered blood. On the chart, in handwriting perfect and small like it came from a machine, Dudek read numbers, listed in series of six, no number over forty-five. Each series was marked with dates, some highlighted in yellow marker, others circled with red. Lottery numbers.

The clear packing tape — yellowed with age — shrieked as he peeled open a box. Shaking his head, he lifted out bundles of lottery tickets that he thumbed at the corners. Each bore that same picky script as on the bulletin board chart. Thousands of tickets, hundreds of thousands of numbers repeated over and over, twelves and twos, sixteens and thirty-sevens, loser after loser after loser, most with Xs through them but some circled, the ink long faded from red to pink. He tore open a second box dated on top "Aug. 76–Nov. 79," it too stuffed with lottery tickets, numbers circled or crossed out. Then another box — "Feb. 92–May 95" — and another. Dudek laughed. He felt sick, lightheaded, and he backed away from the boxes, wanting space between him and them as if the craziness that rattled the Tuckers had started with those boxes and could spread to him, too.

Shit! He remembered. Quick out. He grabbed the beer. Lights off, he locked the door, slid the key beneath the mat, and wrapped the yellow tape around the nails.

The Tuckers drank out of bottles. They bought fancy beers, dark like molasses, more bitter than Dudek liked, but beggars and choosers and all that crap. He shed his shoes and socks, turned out the lights, raised the blinds, and sat by the window to drink. Across the street, the colors on the rabbit banner washed gray in the dark, so Bunny's never-ending grin shined too bright, too happy. Dudek knew the rabbit couldn't mean it.

Between sips, Dudek heard now and then the lonely, panicked siren of a cop car, saw red lights flash and speed over the walls of buildings as far away as downtown. All those lights in all those rooms. He wondered if in one of them, or even two, someone was killing somebody. Odds were good.

He pulled the tickets from his pocket, creased them, then smoothed the fold. He read the numbers by the glow of a nearby street lamp, though he had to squint; the beer fuzzed his focus. Such bizarre patterns: a stray 12 among 31, 33, 36, 38, and 39. Another with 01, 02, 04, 05, 07, 08. Probably worthless, every last one. Dudek reminded himself to check them against the winning numbers in Thursday's newspaper, then slipped them into his wallet.

He opened another beer, then another, flipping the bottle caps toward his trash can and missing so the caps clattered across the

floor. He tried to think, but he couldn't fit the boxes, the numbers, the charts with everything else he knew — or thought he
had known — about the Tuckers. Then he remembered that guy
shaking Tommy Lasorda's hand. Poor sap. Now every painted egg
would remind the guy how his dad shot his mom. It was like Easter
backwards, what the old man did, passing around his pain and confusion like burned toast at the breakfast table, with Tucker junior
swallowing the biggest slice. Dudek imagined him on the plane,
pictured him in black with sunglasses on, thought of him landing
at Bradley International the next day and picking up a paper, looking for an obituary or something and seeing the reporter's story.
He'd read what Dudek had said. He'd read that his parents were
drunks, fighting all the time. Probably wouldn't be news to the kid,
but Tucker junior would know that everyone else in Hartford was
reading it, too.

And Tucker junior would be the new landlord.

Dudek chugged a mouthful, betting on eviction. Flush the security deposit. And what could he say? He could already imagine the
kid downstairs putting his parents' stuff in boxes. Dudek could see
himself sitting on the couch listening, not daring to walk downstairs, not even willing to flush the toilet, wanting just to disappear.
His stomach felt sour. That fancy beer. Too damn bitter.

His head felt mushy, so he leaned way back in his chair. Even in
the dark, he could make out the watermark that spread across
his ceiling. He remembered the torn screens on the back porch.
Dumps like this all over the city. Plenty of places to live. So it wasn't
the eviction that bothered him. And it wasn't the security deposit.
He'd never gotten one back anyway.

He set the beer down. Lousy sludge. He wondered if Tucker junior drank that stuff, too. Jesus, the kid would need something.
Dudek wondered if the reporter right now was writing what Tucker
junior would read, what Dudek had said, and he pictured her at
her desk. Long legs, heels, fake pearls.

Switching on a light, he found her business card. Maybe she'd
think he was being a nice guy. Concern for fellow man, you know?
She answered on the first ring. That hot fudge voice. Over the
phone, he liked it more.

He hesitated saying his name, then asked, "Would you mind not
using what I told you? It, well — it makes them look bad. Like

kicking dirt on them, you know? Haven't they had enough trouble?"

He bit the tough skin along his thumbnail while waiting for her reply. He thought he could hear her breathe in, about to say something, but then she didn't. He pictured her smoking. Tapping the cigarette against an ashtray. Didn't all reporters smoke? He liked that about her.

"I can't do that," she said. "I'm sorry, but I told you who I was, and you agreed to talk. Once you agree, what you say I can put in the paper. That's how it works."

"But think how this makes them look. What if they've got kids?"

"I can't worry about that, Mr. Dudek. Listen, there won't be a lot of what you said in the story, but I can't say I won't use any of it."

"That's shitty."

"You might have thought about that before you talked."

Dudek had turned in slow circles until the phone cord had wound around him. Now he circled the other way, unwinding. All wrong. He'd gone about this all wrong. Not the nice guy stuff. He remembered how her throat had flushed red. She liked the creepiness. Sure. What reporter likes sunshine and light?

"Okay," he said. "Look. There's stuff I didn't tell you. Stuff you wouldn't believe."

"Mr. Dudek, I'm on deadline."

"Wait. Let me tell you this. Lottery tickets. Boxes of them downstairs. They even kept track of the numbers. Wrote on every ticket. When I say boxes, I mean boxes. Like a warehouse. You should come by again. Check it out."

"Jesus. I don't know what game you're playing, but I'm done being part of it."

She hung up. Dudek kicked the table so the telephone spilled, the receiver flying from its cradle across the floor. "Bitch!" he said. What did she mean she didn't know the game? She knew the damn game! She'd played it, too, with her legs, her voice, her pen between her teeth. And she'd got what she wanted, hadn't she? And what about him? He could see himself again in his bedroom with that reporter, using the Tuckers as a pick-up line, and he wanted to reach out and squeeze his own throat.

Dudek grabbed another beer, the last one. He needed air, a walk, something.

The neighbors across the way had turned out their porch light, so Dudek couldn't see the rabbit banner anymore. Maybe they'd even taken it down. Easter was over. He stepped off the porch for a walk, but rain hit the back of his neck, so he turned around, finished the beer while sitting on the porch, and then chucked the bottle into the street just to hear it smash. That settled him a little, or maybe he was just buzzed. He couldn't tell. He just knew he felt better.

Dudek reached for his wallet. When he found the tickets, he flipped them over to the rules in fine print, then flipped them back to the numbers. All that mattered were the numbers. Maybe they weren't losers, after all. Hadn't the Tuckers studied this stuff?

Rainwater poured out of the gutters around the porch. Dudek's bare feet were cold, and he shivered. He wondered what time the Tuckers' paper would hit the doorstep. Maybe he could stay up that late, see what that bitch wrote hot off the presses. If he won the lottery, she'd call then, wouldn't she? Coo at him with that voice. He'd be generous. He could afford to be, a few million in a bank account. Start small with her, right? Dinner at Carbone's, some place ritzy like that. Get her interested. Then the day-long drives in his red Porsche, but only if she wore short skirts. "I've got standards," he'd tell her. Next thing you know, a strip of sand on some Caribbean island. He'd buy the reporter a string bikini, smear tanning oil on her back, and she'd get brown, brown, brown. They'd eat oysters and shrimp, and get blitzed on drinks with names bright as sunshine, and he'd fuck her till she hurt. Pretty soon word would get around the island that he was somebody, because he'd tip big. Ten bucks on a five dollar beer. That'd bring the women. He'd have his pick. The blonde with the full lips? The redhead with the silver hoop through her coppery belly button? The native girl? Oh yeah. The native girl. He'd drop that reporter's ass. Pay your way back, babe. That's shitty, she'd say. And he'd laugh and laugh.

A car flashed from the dark, splashing water over the sidewalk. Dudek's fists were clenched, squeezed so tight his fingertips had turned white. When he let them go, he saw that he had crumpled the tickets, each one a ragged ball in the palm of his hand.

Panicked, he unwrapped them, one by one, and with the flats of his fingers smoothed them against his thigh until he could read the numbers again.

BRENDAN DUBOIS

A Family Game

FROM *Murderers' Row*

THE JUNE DAY was surprisingly muggy and hot, especially out in
the baseball field behind the Morton Regional High School, where
there was no shade and the sun beat down so hard that Richard
Dow could feel its strength through the baseball cap he was wearing. The cap was yellow with a blue "P" in the center, just like the
caps of the dozen boys who were on the field or in the dugout this
day who played for the Pine Tree Rotary youth team. He stood by
first base, the team's assistant coach, and he looked over at the
scoreboard, kept current by a young girl using a piece of chalk almost the size of her fist. Pine Tree Rotary, 1; Glen's Plumbing &
Heating, 0. Two out, the bottom of the sixth. The game was almost
over. Just one more out.

He rubbed his hands together. A boy from Glen's Plumbing &
Heating was on third base. He didn't know his name. But he certainly knew the name of the boy pitching this afternoon's game:
Sam Dow, age twelve, who was one out away from earning Pine
Tree's first victory this season. They were 1 and 5, but nobody
on the team counted that solitary victory: it had been a forfeit,
when the other team — Jerry's Lumberyard — didn't make it to
the game because the coach's van had struck a moose on Route
Four.

"C'mon, Sam!" he called out, slapping his hands together. "One
more out, you can do it! Just one more out!"

Sam ignored him. Good boy. Focus on the hitter, standing there
with his helmet and blue and white uniform, bat looking so large in
his small hands. The attendance was good for a warm summer day

in Vermont, with a smattering of parents and friends and relatives in the stands behind home plate. Someone in the stands was smoking a large cigar, and a brief breeze brought the scent over, and Richard was surprised at the hunger he felt at smelling it. God, how long had it been since he had a really good cigar . . .

Richard looked over in the stands again, saw his ten-year-old daughter, Olivia, carefully keeping score in a large looseleaf binder. He waved at her but she, too, was ignoring her father, keeping focused on the job at hand. And that's what their mother Carla was doing this early afternoon as well, working at the local travel agency.

Sam wound up and the ball flew fast for a throw from such a young boy, and the batter swung just as Richard heard the satisfying *thump!* as the ball landed in the catcher's glove. The umpire did his sideways dance and said, "Strike!" and there were a few cheers and groans, but no jeers. The umpire today was Denny Thompson, the town's fire chief, and he had a good eye and for an umpire was pretty reasonable.

"C'mon, Sam," he whispered, "one more strike. You can do it." He rubbed his hands again, looked over at the few boys of Pine Tree who weren't on the field, now leaning forward on the badly painted green bench in the dugout. He could sense their anticipation, their youthful hunger, to feel — just once — what it would be like to win. That's all, pretty simple stuff, but for an eleven- or twelve-year-old boy, getting that first win meant everything. It had been a long time since Richard had been this young, but he remembered. He always remembered.

There. Another windup from his boy, the blur of the ball, and — *Crack!*

Richard snapped his head, tracking the flying ball, it was well hit, pretty well hit, but wait, it's arcing over, it's just a pop-up fly, great, a pop-up fly, that's it, it's going to happen, we're going to win, it's going to happen . . .

Then Richard noticed the slow-moving legs of the Pine Tree Rotary boy backing up in right field, one hand shading his eyes, the other hand holding up the open glove, his arm now wavering, trembling, moving back and forth like a semaphore signaler. Leo Winn. The youngest player on the team. Richard just whispered again, "C'mon, Leo, you can do it, buddy, just catch the ball, just like practice, nothing to it, nothing at all."

The ball plopped into his glove, and before the cheers could get any louder from the Pine Tree players and fans, young Leo, still moving backwards, tripped and fell on his back, the ball flying free into the freshly mown grass, the cheers and shouts now coming from the other team, as Pine Tree players and fans, including Richard, fell silent, as they lost once again.

After the ceremonial end-of-the-game lineup, when the players stood in line in the field and shook each other's hands, murmuring "good game, good game," Richard was in the parking lot of the school, one arm over Olivia's shoulder, the other over Sam's. Olivia was carrying the score book under her arm and said, "Sam, that was your best game ever. Three strikeouts and only one hit. And that was scored as an error."

"Yeah, I know, I know. I was there, okay?" Sam replied. "What difference does it make? We still lost."

Richard hugged his boy's shoulder. "You did well, Sam. Even Leo."

"Dad, he's no good," Sam complained.

"He's not as good as you, but he's still out there, practicing and playing," Richard said. "That counts for a lot. He could have given up a long time ago. But he didn't."

Sam didn't say a word, and Richard knew the poor guy was struggling over showing emotion at having lost yet again but determined not to say anything that could lead to dreaded tears pouring out. For twelve-year-old boys, sometimes showing tears was worse than anything else.

Olivia spoke up. "Look, there's the other team. Going out for ice cream."

"Well, we can go, too," Richard said, seeing the smiles and happy faces of the other boys, trooping into open car and minivan doors.

"Dad . . ." Sam said. "No, let's just go home. It doesn't count. They're going for ice cream 'cause they won. Losers don't get ice cream after a game like ours."

Richard was going to say something, but he noticed something going on over near the school's dumpster. He pulled out his car keys and passed them over to Sam. "Here, go in and get the car opened up. I'll be right along."

Sam said, his voice now not so despondent, "Can I start it up?"

"Yes, but move it out of park and I'll ground you till you're thirty."

His two kids ran ahead to his Lexus, and he dodged around the end of a pickup truck hauling an open trailer with a lawn mower on the back. There came a man's voice, loud and insistent, ". . . dummy, how in hell could you drop that ball? It was an easy out!"

Richard froze at what he saw. George Winn, landscaper in town — among other things, some legal, some not so legal — had his boy's T-shirt twisted up in a large fist and was shaking the poor guy back and forth. Tears were streaming down the child's face, and his ball cap was on the ground. George was huge, with a beer gut that poked out from underneath a dark green T-shirt and a beard that went halfway down his chest. The hand that was wrapped around the boy's T-shirt was stained with dirt and grease. Richard stepped forward. "Hey, George, lighten up, okay? It's just a game."

George turned, his face looking surprised, like he could not believe anyone would approach him for something so insignificant. "Hunh? What did you say, Dick?"

Richard hated being called Dick but let it go for now. "George, c'mon, it's just a game. Your kid did all right."

George let go of his son's shirt, and the boy quickly went over to pick up his hat. The older man stepped closer and Richard caught a whiff of beer. "You looking for trouble, Dick?"

Richard's hands seemed to start tingling, like they were being suddenly energized by the adrenaline. Richard recognized the sensation, tried to dampen it. "No, I'm just telling you that your kid's a good player. Hey, he's a trooper. Why don't you —"

George came over, punched a finger into Richard's chest, making him step back. "No, he ain't no trooper. He's a loser, writer-man, so back off. Unless you want to settle this right here and now."

A horn honked, and he recognized the tone. His kids were in the Lexus, urging him to hurry up so they could get home. A door slammed and he saw the small figure of Leo in the front seat of the truck. Richard stepped back, made sure his back wasn't turned to George.

"No, I don't want to settle this right here and now."

George snorted in satisfaction. "Good. Then why don't you go home to your kiddie books and leave me and my boy the frig alone."

Richard walked over to his Lexus as the truck backed up and roared away, the front right fender brushing his pants leg as it bailed out of the parking lot. He got to his Lexus and sat still for a moment as Sam talked more about the game and Olivia asked what he thought would be for dinner tonight, and it was like their voices were coming at him through thick cotton, for the only voice he could really make out was George's.

Dinner that night was the usual rolling chaos of dishes being prepared, voices being raised, the television set on, and the phone ringing, with boys and girls calling for Sam and Olivia — and was it a genetic quirk among children everywhere, Richard thought, that they always called at dinner time? — and he managed to give Carla a quick hug and kiss as she heated up a tuna fish casserole.

"Besides losing, how was the game?"

"Great," he said. "Sam pitched well. Got three strikeouts. Your day okay?"

"Uh-huh," she said, handing over a head of romaine lettuce to him. "Wash this up, will you?"

"Sure," he said, looking over at the trim figure of his blond-haired wife, her tight jeans and black flat shoes, and the light blue polo shirt that had white script on the left reading CENTRAL STREET TRAVEL. The casserole smelled all right, but he remembered a number of years ago, when Carla would prepare dishes like baked ziti and manicotti and a lobster fettucine . . . my, how good that had been. But all those food dishes had been left behind, years ago, when they had come to Vermont.

Olivia was at the kitchen counter, drawing a horse, and piped up, "I think Daddy almost got into a fight today."

That got Carla's sharp attention. "He did, did he?"

He started running the cold water, washing the lettuce leaves. "No, he didn't. It wasn't a fight; it was just a discussion."

"That true, Olivia?" Carla asked, her voice still tense.

"Dunno, mom," she said, still working on her horse. "The car doors were closed, but the other man was pushing his finger into Daddy."

"Oh, he was, was he?" she said, her brown eyes flashing at him. "I thought you said things went great."

"They did," he said, washing another leaf of lettuce.

"And who was this guy, and what was going on?" she demanded.

"Nothing much," Richard said, patting dry the leaves of lettuce on a stretch of paper towel. "We were just talking about the game and about sports dads. That sort of thing. He got a little heated up, and that was that. I just tried to remind him that it was just a family game. That's all."

"No trouble then," she asked.

He smiled at his demanding wife. "No trouble."

Some hours later he woke up in bed with Carla, staring up at the ceiling. He rolled over, checked the time on the red numerals of the nearby clock radio. It was 1:00 A.M. Time to go. He slowly got out of bed, sitting up and letting his feet touch the floor, hoping he wouldn't disturb his wife. But Carla was too good.

She gently touched his bare back. "What's up, hon?" she whispered, shifting closer to him in the darkness.

"Nothing much," he said, leaning over to a chair, picking up his pants and a pullover.

"Getting dressed?"

"Uh-huh."

"What's going on?"

"Gotta see a guy about something."

"Something bad?"

He reached behind him, stroked her face. "No, nothing bad. Just seeing a guy about something. No big deal. I'll be back in an hour or so."

"'Kay," she murmured. "You be careful, and you come back to us. *Capisce?*"

"*Capisce,*" he said, leaning over to kiss her forehead.

A half-hour later he was on the other side of town, at a small dirt park near the wooden covered bridge that spanned the Bellamy River. He shifted in his seat, wincing some at the uncomfortable feeling of the nine-millimeter Browning pistol stuck in his rear waistband. It was a quiet night, and he leaned his elbow outside the open window. The night sound of crickets and frogs were pleasant enough, but he remembered other night sounds as well. Traffic, always moving, always going. Horns and sirens and brakes squeaking. Music and the rattle-roar of the subway and people talking, shouting, laughing. And behind it all, the constant hum of an island filled with millions of people, always moving, always dealing, always doing something. That sense of energy, of being plugged in, of being part of something, God, he missed it as much as the faraway scent the day before of the cigar . . .

Lights coming across the bridge. The headlights flashed twice and then the lights dimmed as the car pulled up beside him. He stepped out and kept the hood and engine block between himself and the visitors.

"Richard?" came the familiar voice from the dark car. One Charlie Moore, and once again he wished he could be in a place where he would never hear that voice again.

"The same," he said, relaxing, bringing his hand to his side from where it had been, at the rear of his shirt.

"Glad to see you," he said. "Have a visitor here. Do you mind?"

"Do you care if I mind or not?"

A laugh. "Nope, I guess not."

The footsteps came toward his Lexus, and a voice cautioned, "Watch it, light coming on." He moved his head away and a small battery-powered lamp was turned on and was then placed on the hood of his car. In the small but bright light he made out the faces of two men, one familiar, the other a stranger. The familiar one said, "Time for introductions. Bob Tuthill, Department of Justice, please meet Richard Dow. Formerly known as Ricky 'the Rifle' Dolano."

Tuthill just nodded. He had on a dark suit, white shirt, and red necktie. His companion was dressed more comfortably, in jeans and a black turtleneck shirt. Richard said, "Charlie, what's going on?"

Tuthill spoke up. "What's going on is another trial, set to start in August."

"Where?"

"California. Two days, maybe three."

"Who are you guys after?"

"Mel Flemmi," Charlie said. "Used to be in your neck of the woods, then got into trouble in San Diego. The government needs to prove a pattern of criminal conduct, which is where you come in, testifying about what he did in Jersey. That won't be a problem, will it?"

"Nope," Richard said.

Tuthill shook his head. "Sorry, Ricky, that was —"

"Richard," he interrupted. "The name is Richard Dow. Go on."

Tuthill looked over at Charlie in exasperation and said, "What I was saying is that you answered too quickly. Saying there wouldn't be a problem is a given, 'cause you know where we've got you. Set up in this little piece of paradise is part of the deal, and so is your testifying when we say so. But I don't like the way you answered Mr. Moore so quickly. What I need to know is that we're going to have your full faith and cooperation in testifying against Flemmi. Understood?"

Richard folded his arms, feeling his breathing tighten, just like when he was face to face with that moron George Winn at the high school parking lot. He said, "Look, Mel Flemmi is an animal. I know enough about what he did so you guys could put him away until the next millennium, even without bringing up whatever he did in San Diego. So yeah, I don't have a problem with testifying against him. Little slug, his own teenage niece started doing drugs, started staying out late in the streets, and he whacked her, personally. So she wouldn't bring shame to his family. So that's the kind of guy he is, and so here's the story. I don't have a problem testifying against him. That good enough for you, Tuthill?"

A little smile came across the man's face. "Nice talk from someone accused of committing eleven murders in his career."

"Accused," Richard said. "Never convicted."

This time, Tuthill laughed and turned to Charlie. "What is it with these wise guys? Man, they flip and testify at the drop of a hat. The old-timers in my office, they said there used to be a time when guys like this would rather serve ten, twenty, or thirty years before being accused of being a rat. They getting soft or what?"

Richard tightened his arms against his chest. "I don't know about any 'they.' All I know is that I found out my boss was cooperating with clowns like you. So I cut my own deal, to protect myself and my family. Loyalty's a two-way street, and I'm not going to Leavenworth for life for some guy who wants to get free on my back."

Tuthill laughed. "Whatever. Moore, I'm ready to go back. Oh, Richard, one more thing."

"Yes?"

Tuthill leaned over the hood of the car. "Some of your compatriots over the years, they've embarrassed the department over side deals they had going on while they were in the program. Your job, what is it? A children's book writer?"

"That's what they gave me," Richard said.

"And the publicity problem . . . ?" Tuthill asked.

"You should know," Richard said. "I write under a pseudonym. The books are for two- and three-year-olds. Not much chance of many fan letters. There's no photo on the book jackets; they say the author lives in California. The locals, they don't care. This is Vermont. You could sacrifice goats to Lucifer in your spare time, and nobody'd care, as long as you don't keep your neighbors up with the noise."

"How charming," Tuthill said. "Which brings me to my original point. Other guys like you, they've gotten bored with their agreement. They've decided to get back to their original business, like loan sharking and gambling and breaking arms and legs. Which means sleazy defense lawyers get to jump all over their character, and whether or not their testimony is truthful."

"How interesting," Richard said.

"Wait, it gets better. So what I'm telling you is that your friggin' nose better be clean. No violence, no threat of violence, not even a parking violation. This trial is important, quite important, and I'm not going to let some stoolie killer like you spoil it for me. 'Cause if you do, you and your family will be moving. How'd you like to run a pig farm in the middle of Nebraska?"

Richard said, "I like it here. You won't have a problem."

"Good," he said. "Moore, I'm ready to head back."

"Sure," Charlie said. "I'll be right there."

When the sound of a car door being slammed reached them both, Charlie sighed. "Sorry. Young guy, new in his job, wants to make his bones. Sorry about all that yapping and such."

"Not your fault," Richard said, letting his arms relax.

"Still . . ."

"Yeah?"

"Listen well to what he said, Richard. Except for one little mark against your record since you moved here, you've done okay. Keep it that way, or he will transfer you out to a pig farm. Your wife, your kids, they've adjusted over the years here, haven't they. I don't think they'd like moving again."

Richard said, "You let me worry about my family. And that so-called black mark against my record, that was bogus, and you know it. Besides, I had only been out here a month. I was still adjusting."

Charlie laughed. "You broke the headlights on some guy's car with a baseball bat and threatened to do the same to his teeth. Doesn't sound too bogus to me."

Richard smiled. "He stole a parking space from me at the shopping center. Look, I've got the message, loud and clear. I'll be a good little boy."

"Okay," Charlie said. "Here, I've got two things for you." Charlie reached into his pocket and took out a computer disk, which he tossed over to Richard. He caught it with no problem.

"Your next book," Charlie said. *"Lulu the Seasick Sea Lion."*

"Marvelous. What's the other thing you've got for me?"

"This," Charlie said, handing over a plastic shopping bag, full and bulging. "Some souvenirs from your old haunts. Cheeses and sausages and pepperonis and spices and sauces. A little bit of everything. I figured you still missed some of that old-time food, don't you."

Richard was surprised at how much his mouth watered. "Yeah, you're right."

Charlie picked up the little lamp, switched it off. "Well, don't let it be said that the U.S. Marshall's Office doesn't have a little consideration. I'll be seeing you, Richard."

"Unfortunately, I think you're right," he said, now smelling the delicious scents coming up from the bag. His stomach began grumbling, and he hefted the bag a couple of times as he waited until the other car left the small lot. Richard waited until his eyes adjusted to the darkness, and then he walked a few yards to the beginning of the covered bridge. His feet echoed on the old wooden planks. He leaned over and heard the rushing of the Bellamy River below him, and then took the bag and threw it into the river.

He sighed, rubbed at his face. That was the only way. To follow the rules and survive, and never, absolutely never, dress or smoke or eat or do anything like you once did back home, because they were out there, still out there in the shadows, bent on revenge, and he didn't want to raise a single scent for their benefit.

He looked at the river for a couple of minutes, and then went back to his car and drove home.

At home he was in the upstairs hallway, heading to the bedroom, when he heard a murmuring noise coming from Sam's room. The door was ajar and he could make out a bluish light coming from inside. Sam was curled up on his side, his eyes closed, dressed in light gray pajama bottoms. On a dresser at the foot of the bed was a small color TV, and Richard made out a baseball game being played. He reached up to turn it off when a sleepy voice said, "No, Dad, don't . . . still watching it . . ."

"Sam, it's almost three in the morning."

"I know . . . The Red Sox are in Seattle . . . it's gone extra innings . . ."

Richard looked at a little graphic in the corner of the television picture. "Sam, the score is zero to zero, and they're in the eighteenth inning."

"Mom said I could watch the game till it was over."

Richard shut the little TV off. "And I'm saying it's just a game, okay? You need to get to sleep."

No answer. Just the soft noise of his boy, breathing. From the hallway light he made out posters of baseball players up on the walls, all of them Red Sox. He shrugged. He wished the boy would at least follow a winning team, like the Mets or the Yankees, but what could one expect. He bent down to kiss Sam's forehead.

"Just a game, son. Just a game."

In the morning, before she left for work and to bring the kids to a day camp, Carla brought him another cup of coffee in his small office, which was a spare bedroom when they had first moved in. He took the cup and sipped from it, and she said, "So. What went on last night?"

Other guys back then, they could spin stories to their wives about being solid waste management consultants, but he could not do that with Carla. She had entered things clear-eyed and agreeable, and not once had he ever tried to pull something over on her.

He put the coffee cup down on his desk. "A trip to California in a couple of months. Another testimony deal. Against Mel Flemmi."

She made a face. "Good. He sure deserves it. What else?"

"What do you mean, what else?" he asked.

Carla gently whacked him on the side of his shoulder. "There's always something else with the feds. What was it?"

He tried a casual shrug. "I've got to keep my nose clean, as always. That way, any defense lawyer won't be able to say I don't have the kind of character to testify truthfully."

"Keep your nose clean . . ." she said simply. "Does that mean not breaking some guy's headlights over a parking space?"

"It was my parking space, I'd just got here, and it won't happen again."

She leaned over, grabbed his ears, and kissed him firmly on the mouth. "Good. 'Cause it ain't no game, Richard. I like it here. The kids like it here. We can continue having a good life here. Don't do anything to screw it up."

"I won't."

"Good. Because if you do, I'll kill you."

He kissed her back. "I have no doubt."

For most of the day, he stayed in his office. He played twenty-three games of computer solitaire and another computer game involving shooting lots of fast-moving monsters — not surprisingly, he scored quite high — and he spent a while on the Internet as well, seeing the combined creativity of a number of women who could just barely dress themselves, and got an idea or two for next Valentine's Day.

Then, at about 3:00 P.M., he popped in the computer disk, called up a file called "Sea Lion," and printed out all thirty-three pages. He put the pages in an Express Mail envelope, drove to the post office, and sent the envelope to a publisher in New York City. Back home, he made another cup of coffee and waited for Carla and the kids to show up. "Man, writers have it easy," he said.

The next day was a practice one for the Pine Tree Rotary team, and he enjoyed seeing how enthusiastically all the kids took to the field — Patrick and Jeffrey and Alexander and his own Sam and even little Leo, chugging out there on his tiny legs, and all the others. They did some exercises to loosen up, and then some pitching and hitting, and some base running. He took it upon himself to spend some extra time with Leo, tossing up pop flies, and Leo managed to catch fifteen in a row.

Then he took Ron Bachman, the town auditor and the team's manager, aside. "Did you see how Leo's doing?"

"Yep," Ron said, making a note on a clipboard. "Not a single dropped ball. That's what happens when his dad's not around. Plays a lot better."

"So tell me, what's the deal with his dad, George? What's his problem?"

Ron looked up from the clipboard. "What do you mean, 'what's his problem?'"

"The way he goes after his kid, that's what."

"Oh, that," he said. "You know, George has got a lot of problems. Drinking and picking fights and being the son of the chairman of the board of selectmen, so he gets a lot of slack cut his way. He's a mean man who takes his frustrations out on his kid. Typical story. Unfortunately, it has to show itself here."

"Yeah," Richard said. "Unfortunately."

Two days later the team went on a field trip to Fenway Park in Boston, an hours-long drive that took three minivans and a number of other parents to act as chaperones. When putting kids in the vans, Richard made sure that Leo was in his van, and he glanced at the boy some while heading into Boston. He half-expected to see a haunted look in the boy's eyes, a troubled expression, but no, there was nothing like that there. Just the excitement of being in Boston and seeing the Red Sox play.

Richard took in Fenway Park as they found their seats. It was an old, tiny park, opened up in 1912, the same year the *Titanic* sunk on its maiden voyage. It had its charms, with the Green Monster out in left field and the intimacy of being close-up to the action, but Richard wasn't satisfied. It wasn't Yankee Stadium, it wasn't the House that Ruth Built, but he kept his opinions to himself.

All part of his new life.

As the game progressed, he enjoyed watching the kids almost as much as the game itself. They followed each pitch intensely and ate popcorn and hotdogs and drank sodas, and cheered when one of the Red Sox players rocketed a home run over the Green Monster, and booed when the opposing pitcher hit a Red Sox player with a fastball, causing both benches to clear. The game wasn't worth much — an early season bout with the Tigers that the Red Sox managed to lose, 4–3 — but it was still fun. He was glad to be here with his boy and was glad not to be in jail, and it even looked like Leo was enjoying himself, too, watching the game with wide eyes and grins, seemingly thousands of miles away from his father.

On the way back to Vermont, as Sam rode up front next to Richard, and with most of the boys in the rear seats, slumbering, he said, "Dad?"

"Yeah, Sam," he said, feeling a bit juiced after driving through real city streets for a change. Here was real traffic, intersections, lights, people moving in and out. Where they now lived, in Vermont, there were two traffic lights, and only a few hundred feet of sidewalk in the downtown. He liked driving in the city and rolled down his window as he drove, to hear the noises, smell the scents out there.

But now they were on a featureless stretch of asphalt, making the long drive back to Vermont.

"About the game," Sam said.

"Go on."

"When the Red Sox hitter got beaned by the pitcher, I was just surprised at how fast the other players came out of the dugout to go after the pitcher. And then, the other team . . . well, man, Dad, that fight started quick. Why do they fight like that? Couldn't it have been just an accident?"

"Maybe," he said, glancing at both sides of the narrow highway as they headed home, keeping an eye open for deer or moose on the side of the road, ready to trot across and wreck several thousand dollars' worth of vehicle parts. "But players like that, it's more than just that. It's a team thing. You stick up for a member of your team, no matter what. And when one of your team members gets hit, or gets in trouble, you help out. That's what happens."

"Oh," Sam said. "Like a family, right? Like you've said before, about me and Olivia helping each other out? Like a family?"

"Sure," he said. "Like a family."

He drove on a few more miles, and looked over at the drowsy face of his boy, remembered a time when he was much younger, and when they all lived in a neighborhood not unlike some of the streets they had passed through on the way to the ballpark.

"Sam?"

"Yeah, Dad."

"Besides the game, how did you like it?"

His son moved in his seat, like he was seeking a comfortable position to fall asleep in. "I dunno, what do you mean, how did I like it . . ."

"I mean the city. How did you like being in the city? You know, all those buildings, all those people. What did you think?"

Sam yawned. "It was too noisy, too dirty. I like it better back home."

"Oh."

He kept on driving, wondering if he should feel angry or glad that his son — his own boy, raised in New York! — should now hate big cities.

A few days later, the next to the last game of the season. Pine Tree Rotary was playing Greg's Small Engine Repair, and Richard was tired and hot and thirsty. The other team had jumped on the boys right away in the first inning, and the score was now 10 to 0. Even his boy, Sam, as good as he was, grounded out twice and struck out once. About the only bright spot in the lineup was poor little Leo, who was so small that he confused the opposing team's pitcher and managed to get on base twice through walks. Even though they were walks, Leo acted like Pete "Charlie Hustle" Rose himself — of course, before getting caught up in that gambling fiasco — and raced to first base, just so damn pleased to be there, out on the bases.

Last inning, and here was Leo. Richard checked his watch and was going to call out to the boy when somebody with a louder voice beat him to it.

"Leo!" the man bellowed. "You better get a hit or I'll be after you! That you can bet on!"

He shaded his eyes from the glare, knew who had shown up, like a shambling bear wandering into someplace he wasn't welcome. George Winn was at the fence, his fat fingers protruding through the open metal, shouting again. "Leo! You worthless player, you! Get a hit or you'll get one from me!"

Richard yelled out, "Leo, wait for a good pitch, guy, wait for a good one!"

But Leo, his legs trembling, his face red, swung at the first three pitches that came across the plate, and promptly struck out.

He ignored Olivia. He ignored Sam. He ignored the other coaches and players and strode right out to the parking lot again, where George was hauling his kid to his truck, the clothing of the boy's shirt clenched up in his fist. Richard called out, "George, you hold on!"

George spun around, moving surprisingly fast for such a large man. He propelled Leo forward with one hand and said, "Wait in the truck! Now!"

Leo ran ahead, and Richard came up to him, saying, "George,

you can't yell at your boy like that. He's doing the best he can, and yelling like that —"

And George stepped forward and punched him in the chest. Richard staggered back, the force of the blow bringing back hordes of muscle memories from times past, when he had faced down and put down bigger and badder guys than this, and his fists clenched up and he was spotting his move, what he should do to put this bullying jerk down, but thinking, now, he was thinking about Carla and the kids and —

The next punch struck his jaw, and then George grabbed him and he fell to the ground, and the kicks began, one after another, and Richard curled up and protected his kidneys and groin and face as much as possible, until there were other voices, other shouts, and the kicking and punching stopped.

Later that night, in bed, Carla was next to him, gingerly wiping down his face again with a wet cloth. Her face was hard and set, and he couldn't tell from one moment to the next whom she was most angry with, and he just kept his hands still and let her work and talk.

"You think I like having the children see you, their father, in a brawl right in their own school parking lot?"

It hurt to talk, so he kept his words to a minimum. "Wasn't a brawl. I didn't touch the guy."

"Well, he sure as hell touched you," she said. "Poor Olivia and Sam were crying so much, I thought they'd never stop."

"They're okay."

"Yeah, but you're not. And remember what those feds told you, about keeping your nose clean? Is this how you're doing that?"

"Didn't file a complaint," he said. "No cops."

She wiped him down again, and he winced. Even with the painkillers, it was going to be a long night.

"Doesn't matter," she said. "Word gets out. And poor Sam . . . he thinks the whole team should get together and go on over and burn down George Winn's house. He thinks they should stick up for you. Is that right?"

"Nope."

"You're damn right," she said, getting up from the bed, walking into the bathroom and back out again with a fresh washcloth. "But our family . . . that's something else. I don't like what happened, not one bit. Are you going to do something about it?"

He thought for a moment. "Yeah."

She wrung out the cloth over a small metal bowl. "Are you going to tell me?"

"Not yet," he said. "Not yet."

"When?" she asked.

"Soon," he said.

The next day, in his office, playing computer solitaire and wincing in pain as he moved the fingers on his right hand, the phone rang.

"Is this Richard?" came the vaguely familiar voice.

"It is," he said. "Who's this?"

There came a slight chuckle. "Let's just say it's one of the two gentlemen you spoke with the other night."

He sat up straighter in his chair. "You shouldn't be calling. It's not part of the agreement. It's not part —"

"Look, pal, here's the only agreement I care about, and that's that you testify in August, and that you stay out of trouble. Right now, you're batting five hundred, and I don't like it."

"I don't understand what you mean," Richard said.

"Wasn't there a fight yesterday? In the parking lot of a school? Right after a baseball game with your kid?"

He winced again as his hand clenched the phone tighter. "It wasn't my fault. He picked the fight, not me. There was no complaint filed with the cops."

Another chuckle. "Yeah, I heard you didn't even put up a fight. Man, you must really like that place to put up with crap like that. So here's the facts, one more time. You're right on the edge, my friend. Right on the edge. One more little problem, and I don't care whose fault it was, who threw the first punch, you're still coming out to testify. But you'll come back to that pig farm in Nebraska."

Richard didn't even bother replying, because the caller had already hung up.

He sat back in his chair, looked at the little computer mouse next to the computer, and in one flurry of motion, tore it from his desk and threw it across the room.

*

Two days after the phone call, he was in the kitchen when Sam came tearing through. He wanted to call out to Sam, to tell him to slow down, but instead he said, "Hey, bud. What do you have going on today?"

Sam went to the refrigerator, opened up the door, and started chugging down a couple of swallows of orange juice. His mother would never let him get away with doing anything like that, but he knew his father would. What a kid. Sam put the juice away and said, "Not much. Some fishing later with Greg over at the river."

"Want to catch a late-afternoon matinee?" he asked.

Sam smiled. "Just the two of us? What would Mom and Olivia think?"

"Mom's at work," he said, "and Olivia's over with some friends, staying through till dinner. I'll leave a note for your mom. It'll be fine. Come on, you've got a big day tomorrow. Last game of the season."

Sam slammed the door of the refrigerator. "When?"

"Right now."

"Cool, Dad," he said.

The movie theater was on the outskirts of town, in a little shopping mall, and the cool interior felt comfortable. He let Sam pick the movie, and it was a live-action film based on a popular comic book series Richard had never heard of. Most of the audience were kids about Sam's age, with a scattering of parents like himself, there to chaperone and make sure the little ones didn't walk out and sneak into an R-rated film. He sat in a row next to a guy he knew, some clerk at the hardware store named Paul, who was there with a boy of about eight or nine.

He checked his watch as the movie droned on with punches and gunshots and buildings blowing up. He looked at the smiling faces of the young boys, illuminated some from what was up on the screen. Smiling and young and full of energy and life. He wondered how Leo was doing, if he was dreading tomorrow's game, the last game of the year, the last chance to win one before the season was over, one more time out there in the field with his father watching and shouting at him.

One more time with his watch. Time. He leaned over to Sam and whispered, "I'm going to get some more popcorn. You want another drink?"

"Uh-huh," Sam whispered back, attention still focused on the screen.

Richard got up, stepped on Paul's foot — "Jeez, excuse me" — and walked out of the dark theater.

Later that night, he was in the living room, trying to judge which one of Olivia's drawn horses was the best one — "for a contest the library's holding, Dad, and the deadline is tomorrow!" — when the doorbell rang. Olivia looked up at him and then Carla appeared in the entranceway to the kitchen, slowly wiping a salad bowl from dinner. He looked down at Olivia and said, "Right away, squirt. Go see your mom."

"But, Dad . . ."

"Now, please," he said, and Carla added, "Olivia, listen to your father. He'll finish with your horses later."

He went to the door, wiped at his hair for a moment, remembered the many other times when he had answered evening doorbells like this one, so he wasn't surprised when he opened the door and saw the town's police chief there.

"Mr. Dow?" he said quietly. "Ted Reiser. Chief of police."

The chief was about ten years older than Richard, heavyset, with a black mustache and a chubby neck that spilled over the collar of his white uniform dress shirt. A gold star was in each of his collar tabs, and Richard thought the chief — who was boss of a whole six officers — looked slightly ridiculous.

"Sure," Richard said. "What can I do for you?"

The chief looked past Richard and said, "Can I come in for a moment?"

"Absolutely, come on in," he said, and the chief came in and took a seat on the couch, balancing his gold-brimmed hat on his knees. Richard sat down and said, "If you'd like, can I get you a drink, or —"

Reiser raised his hand. "Sorry, no. Look, I'm sorry, but this is an official call. I'm investigating something that occurred earlier today. Something I'm afraid that might involve you."

He made a point of folding his hands together and leaning forward in his chair. "One of my kids? Did they do something?"

The chief ignored the question, went on. "George Winn. I take it you know him."

"Sure. I coach his kid in the baseball league."

"You've also had words with him, plus one altercation. True?"

Richard nodded. "True. I try to help out his boy, and George thought the kid would work best under threats."

"But there was an altercation, nearly a week ago."

"I didn't hit him, not once. Can you tell me what's going on?"

The chief sighed. "George Winn was attacked and severely injured today. An intruder broke into his home, struck him from the rear. No description of the attacker, but I'm afraid I'll have to ask you what you were doing at about four forty-five P.M. today."

"Why?"

"Please, Mr. Dow. You were in a fight with him last week. I need to know this."

"Should I be getting a lawyer?"

That got the chief's attention. "Do you think you need one?"

"No," Richard answered.

"Then why don't you tell me where you were this afternoon."

Richard shrugged. "All right. I was at the movies with my boy Sam, at the River Mall theater. The picture started at three-thirty, got out at five-thirty."

"Do you have any proof?" the chief asked.

"Sure." He dug into his pants pocket, past his handkerchief and change. "Look. Ticket stubs for the both of us."

"Anybody see you at the theater?"

"Um, a kid named Larry who took my money."

"Anybody else?"

"Let's see . . . oh, sure. Paul, who works at Twombly's Hardware. He sat next to me. In fact, I stepped on the poor guy's toes when I left to get some popcorn about halfway through the movie."

The chief moved his hat in a semicircle. "Did you know what time it was?"

"Nope."

"And what time did you get back into the theater?"

Richard looked at the chief, tried to feel what was going on behind those unblinking eyes. "I'm sorry, what did you say?"

Now it was time for the police chief to lean forward. "You said you left the theater to get some popcorn. And what I want to know is, how long were you out there?"

"Two minutes, maybe three."

"And did anybody see you come back into the theater?"

"Yeah, Paul did, I'm sure."

"Oh, you are, are you," the chief said. "And why's that?"

Richard looked at the chief calmly. "Because when I tried to get past him and sit next to my son, I accidentally poured a cold drink on his head. That's why."

Another sunny day, hot but the air was dry, with little humidity. Richard was back at his position near first base, waiting. It was the bottom of the sixth inning and the score was tied, o to o, but his boy Sam was on third base. He rubbed his hands together, could feel the anticipation in the air, as the next Pine Tree Rotary batter came to the plate, little Leo Winn, holding his baseball bat strong and true.

The stands were nearly full, and there was Olivia, keeping score again with the large notebook on her tiny lap. Today Carla had taken the afternoon off and she was there as well, and he waved at them both, but neither waved back, as they were talking to each other. Maybe later, he thought.

He wiped his hands on his pants legs. It was a beautiful day, the best so far this summer, and there was the first pitch . . .

Thump! as the ball went into the catcher's mitt. Denny Thompson was umpiring again today, and he slowly got up. "Ball!" came the shout.

"Good eye, Leo, good eye!" Richard called out, and he looked up in the stands again, and sure enough, there was Leo's dad George, sitting there stiffly. Richard thought about waving at George but decided that would be pushing it.

Another pitch, and this time Leo swung mightily at it, and missed. Another *thump!* of the ball into the glove.

"Strike!"

Richard clapped his hands. "That's fine, Leo, that's fine. You're doing all right," and even his teammates in the dugout joined in, calling out to Leo, encouraging him, telling him to take his time, to swing at a good pitch. It was a good sound, a wonderful sound, made even better by the fact that no one was shouting insults, no one was shouting threats. Like he had mentioned the other night in the van to his son, sometimes a team was like a family, looking out for each other. Richard looked up in the stands again, and there was George, sitting still, sitting quietly.

He clapped his hands again, "Come on, Leo, the next one's yours!"

But of course, George had no choice, for George was sitting there, jaw wired shut, after somebody broke into his house and smashed his jaw with what the police believed to be a length of lead pipe. Funny how things happen, Richard thought, and then he looked over at Carla, and waved at her.

And she raised her arm and waved back, and even at this distance, he could see the slight pain in her eyes, for she had quite the workout the previous day, and wielding a lead pipe with such a slender arm could cause some soreness. He smiled as the other team's pitcher began his windup, remembered the meeting last week with the two feds, and how even to this day, they couldn't figure out why he had gotten away with eleven killings in his previous life. It was simple, really, if you looked at it as a game, as a family game, and he waved once more at his lovely wife.

The pitch flew by and this time, oh, this time, there was a powerful *crack!* as Leo swung his bat and the ball flew up and out, heading so far out into the sky, and the people in the stands began cheering as little Leo chugged up the baseline, his face so alive and excited, and true enough, this was just a game, but it was the best damn game in the world.

DAVID EDGERLEY GATES

The Blue Mirror

FROM *Alfred Hitchcock's Mystery Magazine*

"YOU KNOW HOW long a tail gunner's supposed to last in combat?" Stanley asked me. "Twenty-four minutes, on average. Me, I beat the odds, did my fifty missions, came back to the States, went on a bond tour." He shook his head ruefully. "Now the cancer's got me, I won't live out the year."

I'd known Stanley Kosciusko most of my life. He came from Fitchburg, just north of Leominster, where me and my brother Tony grew up. There were quite a few Poles up there, close to the New Hampshire border, and a fair number of Finns, oddly. The Poles had come originally to work in the paper and textile mills, the Finns to make furniture — Windsor chairs and dining room sets. Stanley had married a Finnish girl himself after the war. Maria Aho.

"You got to have an appreciation for life's little ironies, ain't it the truth?" he remarked.

Did his wife know? I wondered out loud.

"About the cancer, sure. This other thing, no." It was the other thing he'd come to talk to me about.

"I lied about my age," he went on. "Enlisted when I was seventeen. Wound up in a B-24 Liberator, flying out of Sicily bombing the Ploesti oilfields. Froze your ass off in those planes, but man, you'd sweat bullets when the German fighters came at you, Fockes and Messerschmitts. Anybody claims they weren't scared stiff is retarded or just plain crazy."

I was thinking about how old he was. Fifty-odd years since D-Day. Add it up, and Stanley was in his mid-seventies. He still seemed vigorous enough, but now that I knew what to look for, I saw the tightness around his eyes from holding in the pain, and a metallic cast to his skin, tarnished and dull. In the afternoon sunlight coming in my office windows I noticed he'd used some kind of rouge or blush to give his face the color it lacked. I figured that was harmless enough.

"Your dad was in the war, wasn't he?" he asked.

"Different war," I said. "Korea."

Stanley nodded. "I knew that," he said, as if it were important for me to understand he still had all his buttons. He'd dressed for the occasion, too, like he had to impress me.

Stanley was a retired auto body man. Tony and I had hung around his shop on Saturday mornings when we were kids because Stanley could fix anything. You could take him your bike or a broken kitchen appliance your mom was ready to throw out or a Lionel locomotive with a bad armature, and he'd make it work. He loved tools, not just what he used on the job, breaker bars and socket sets and orbital sanders, but old hand tools like rabbeting planes and Yankee drills, miter boxes and shake splitters, anything that had a purpose, because Stanley himself was purposeful. Me and Tony would hunt up objects in the abandoned mills and the local landfill just to have Stanley tell us what they were for. He'd examine a rusty, weathered thing, a spokeshave or a bit-and-brace with a corroded ratchet, and take it apart, clean it up, hone the bit or the blade, and put it back together so he could show you how well it suited your hand, you wanted to make a paper-tight join or dowel a table leg. He could repair a grandfather clock or a .22 rifle, and the trick was his curiosity, that certain knowledge that somebody else had made it, whatever it was, had designed it with a use in mind.

"I blame myself," Stanley said. "You have to own up to the responsibility for what you've done or haven't done."

"Cancer's not your fault, Stanley," I said.

"You think I don't know that?" He shifted his weight awkwardly, his suit making him self-conscious. "Jack, there's somebody looking to hurt me. Or my family, which amounts to the same thing."

His namesake was a Revolutionary War general who later went home to Poland and led a hopeless revolt against the Russians.

"Here's what I need you to do for me," he said. "I'm dying on the vine here. I got to have me a surrogate."

I could still see him breaking some Cossack's neck with his bare hands.

"See, if the damn Commies hadn't killed Stosh over in Vietnam, things'd be different," he said. "The way it is, I'm stuck with it. But me, I can't hardly lift a glass."

Life's little ironies. If somebody's going to be dead inside a year, what do you threaten him with? But more to the point, how do you turn him down when he asks you for help?

Here's the rest of what Stanley told me. I was explaining it to my brother Tony over a beer.

"Stanley junior died in Vietnam, right?" he asked.

"First Cav," I said.

Tony swung his wheelchair over to the sink. I'd just helped him move into this place, and he was still adjusting to being on his own. He'd resented being dependent, and once he was out of rehab he didn't need nursing care, but it was a big step all the same. He rinsed out his beer bottle and left it on the drainboard. "And there's a grandson?"

"Andy. Andy Ravenant. He took his stepfather's name after his mom remarried, but he and Stanley have always been close."

"Ravenant. Why's that name ring a bell?"

"You used to see his ads on late-night TV, after *Star Trek*. Raving Richie Ravenant. Sold rugs and wall-to-wall."

"Out in Lynn on the discount strip?"

"Next door to Adventure Car-Hop, home of the Ginsburger."

"He must do a pretty high volume," Tony said. "You'd think somebody would go after the carpet king, not Stanley."

"Except the stepdad's been dead for eight years, and Andy's mom lives in Florida."

"Puts a crimp in that line of inquiry."

"Assuming you were using Andy for leverage," I said.

"Unless it's the other way around."

I took my own bottle to the sink, rinsed it out, and got two more out of the fridge. I cracked the tops.

"Okay," Tony said, taking the beer I handed him, "why is who-ever-this-is bothering Stanley? If they've got a beef with the kid, what's it have to do with the grandfather? And how did Stanley get wind of it anyway?"

Stanley was seeing a specialist out at Beth Israel, off the Jamaica-way. He's coming out of the hospital, headed for where he'd parked on Brookline Avenue, and some greaseball — Stanley's description — starts giving him a hard time.

"Explain that a little better," Tony said. "This guy comes out of nowhere?"

"Apparently," I said. "Stanley's like, hel-LO, what's *your* story? Homeless vet, willing to work for food?"

"I take it *not,* unhappily."

The guy's trying to act smooth, but he's antsy, like he has someplace else to be and this is just a pit stop.

"Coked up?" my brother asked.

"Good observation," I said. "Except that Stanley wouldn't know what to look for. I'm reading between the lines. The dude was looking over his shoulder."

"Sorry," Tony remarked, smiling. "You were saying?"

According to Stanley, the guy couldn't seem to get to the point, or it was like he was talking in code. He kept using these veiled, oblique references as if they were supposed to make sense to Stanley, and Stanley finally gets fed up and just steps around him. The other guy is so frustrated with Stanley for, like, *willfully* refusing to understand that he calls after him he'll send him his grandson's tongue in a pickle jar.

"This is the first overt mention of Andy, right?"

"Right. The rest of it's been this sly jive-ass hinting around."

"I can see this going one of two ways," Tony said. "Or one of *one,* namely Stanley drop-kicking the guy to Chestnut Hill."

"Except that he's past seventy and he's on heavy medication and he doesn't know what any of it's about."

"So he suppresses his natural instinct to scrub the bricks with this yo-yo's face, not to mention that he's maybe no longer the man he once was, and he comes to you."

"Pretty much."

Tony pursed his lips. "Where do you start?" he asked.

"I start with Stanley's grandson."

"The kid."

"He's not a kid, exactly." In fact, Andy was close to my brother's age. He was thirty-one, an attorney. Criminal law, unglamorous but always in demand. He'd done a couple of years as a public defender in Suffolk Superior Court, and now he was in private practice, with an address downtown on Milk Street.

"You hoping that dog will hunt?" Tony asked.

"Andy's more likely to have enemies than his grandfather."

"Yeah, you'd think so," Tony said, but he seemed distracted by something, a thought hovering on the periphery.

"What?" I asked him.

"I can't put my finger on it," he said. "Maybe if I'd quit chasing after it, it would stop ducking out of sight."

The offices of Ravenant & Dwyer were at the bottom edge of the financial district, in the shadow of the Customs House tower. It was one of the oldest sections of town, built over again and again, but like the North End or Beacon Hill, you could still see an imprint of how Boston had once been laid out back in the eighteenth century when its commerce depended on shipping and the narrow, crooked streets led down to the harborfront. The traffic then would have been horse-drawn wagons and drays lurching over the cobblestones and the small businesses would have been ship's chandlers and jobbers, sailmakers' lofts, and rope factories. It remained a commercial district, outlets for wholesale plumbing supplies and the like at street level, and the tenants in the offices on the upper stories were a similar mix of tradesmen and professionals, but they offered a different range of services these days. Andy's law office was one flight up, the entry door sharing a small landing with a jeweler and an architectural drafting studio. I had a ten o'clock appointment.

I gave the receptionist my name and sat down to wait.

I'd waited all of forty-five seconds when Andy Ravenant stepped out of an inner office, came through the small wicket that fenced the receptionist off from clients, and stuck out his hand as I got to my feet. We shook hands.

"I remember you and your brother from my grandfather's body shop," he told me, smiling.

I had a vague recollection of his father, Stan Jr., but I didn't remember Andy at all. Of course, if I'd been seven or eight, I wouldn't have paid much attention to some four-year-old kid if I didn't have to. I decided not to say that.

He took me into his office. It was small and lined with law books — Massachusetts General Statutes, extracts from federal rulings, bound trial transcripts. We sat down.

"Okay," Andy said, leaning back and tenting his hands in front of his sternum. "What's got Papa Stan's bowels in such an uproar? He's been evasive with me."

"Did you know he was dying of cancer?" I asked him. I knew it was sudden, but I couldn't afford to spare his feelings.

Andy sat up abruptly, his face frozen.

I made an apologetic gesture. "He's told your grandmother about it, and he told me yesterday," I said. "I guess he hasn't gotten around to making it general knowledge."

"Jesus," Andy said softly. "I knew he was coming into town for treatments, but I didn't realize how bad it was. He's such a tough old bastard. You figure somebody like that's going to die standing up. He won't go for being an invalid."

"Yeah, that's the way I read it," I said.

"Why did he come to see you, Jack?"

"Somebody threatened him," I said. "In actual point of fact, they threatened *you*. Why they'd go after Stanley I don't know. It seems sideways, or backwards."

"What was it about?"

"The guy didn't say, that's the trouble."

"Who was this guy?"

I shrugged. "Some cretin, according to your grandfather. Stanley didn't give me much to go on, but it sounded like he was supposed to warn you off something."

"My particular client base, that could mean damn near anything," Andy said. He picked up the phone and punched one of the intercom buttons. "Hey," he said, "you got a minute?" He paused and then nodded. "Bring him along," he said to whoever was on the line, and hung up. "Let's check it out," he said.

There was a light tap on the door, and two people came into Andy's office, a man and a woman.

I got up to shake hands as Andy made the introductions.

The woman was Catherine Dwyer, Andy's law partner. Kitty was of medium height with thick, dark hair cut short and that luminous Irish complexion, like Spode porcelain. She was very trim in a silk pants suit, but she would have turned heads if she'd been wearing jeans and a baggy sweatshirt. I felt awkward and foolish all of a sudden, as if we were on a first date.

The guy was Max Quinn, a big beefy job with a white sidewall haircut. He looked like an ex-cop, which is what he turned out to be, a private license who did legwork for Ravenant & Dwyer.

"Jack Thibault," he said, grinning. "I hearda you. You're the hockey player's brother."

"That'd be me," I agreed.

"What's the pitch?" he asked.

Andy gave them a quick outline, nothing about the cancer, just the fact that someone seemed to be using his grandfather to get at him.

Both of them picked up on it without needing more.

"Current caseload, what do you think?" Kitty asked, turning toward Max Quinn.

He pulled a face. "There's that little squirrel Donnie Argent," he told her. "He's tight with those bums in Revere, or he'd like us to think."

"Ring of chop shops," Kitty explained to me. "Who else?"

"The dopers over in Charlestown," Max said.

"That's one of mine," Andy told me. "Kids just getting into the heavy. Too scared to roll over on their wholesaler and plead out."

"I don't blame them," Quinn said. "That'd be Chip McGill."

"Something there?" Kitty asked him.

He shrugged. "You know that neighborhood, they're like the freaking Sicilians — *omérta* — or, anyway, before the made guys started falling over their own feet, they were in a rush to rat each other out to the feds."

"Everybody dummies up," Kitty said to me. "Even these kids know better than to drop a dime on their connections."

"Who's Chip McGill?" I asked.

"Dealer," Quinn said. "Methamphetamine, mostly. Roofies, angel dust, some psychedelics. Party animal. Runs with a bunch of Hell's Angels wannabes, call themselves the Disciples."

"I thought they were out of Springfield," I said.

Quinn gave me a reappraising look. "Good call," he said.

"You figure they might be looking to open up a new market?" I asked him.

He nodded. "McGill's a local boy, grew up around Monument Square. Been in the rackets since God was a child. He cuts his overhead, he can get crystal direct from the source. It's a symbiotic relationship."

Symbiotic wasn't the kind of five-dollar word I expected to be in Max Quinn's vocabulary. It must have shown on my face.

He grinned. "It's what you get, you hang around with these college kids," he said.

McGill and the bikers sounded promising, and I said so.

"I see a downside to this," Kitty Dwyer said.

Quinn and I looked at her.

"If it doesn't have anything to do with McGill and Jack starts sniffing around him, it's going to raise a red flag," she said. "We could regret it."

"McGill's got no reason to think our clients are about to testify against him," Andy put in, "and we wouldn't want to give him one, but that's the lawyer in me talking."

"Makes our situation a little ticklish," Quinn observed.

He didn't actually seem that bothered by it. I figured his way would be to jam McGill up and take whatever came next.

Kitty thought the same, apparently. "You know, Max, a full frontal assault might be counterproductive," she commented.

"Shortest distance between two points," he said. "You got your Polish grandfather on the one hand, and you got Chip McGill on the other. I'd sooner take McGill off the board."

"So would I," Andy said. "I know we've got an obligation to those kids, Kitty, they're our clients, but if Chip McGill is trying to muscle Papa Stan, I vote we ask him about it."

"*Ask?*" Quinn didn't sound too thrilled.

"Feel him out, I mean," Andy said. "If he's got legitimate concerns, we put his mind at rest."

It sounded a little too much like a euphemism for me. Andy seemed to be giving Quinn the go-ahead to lean on McGill.

"Your grandfather went to Jack, remember. He didn't come to you," Kitty said. "Maybe he doesn't want us involved."

Quinn gave her a sleepy glance.

"Well?" Andy was looking at me. "What do you say to that, Jack? You want to fly solo?"

"Give me a day, maybe," I said.

"Max?" Andy asked him.

"No problem," Quinn said.

"Watch your step," Kitty Dwyer said to me.

Did she mean with Max or McGill? I wondered.

"You'll keep us in the loop?" Andy asked.

"Of course," I said.

Kitty walked me out, leaving Quinn and Andy together. She could have wanted a minute alone with me, and she seemed to be making up her mind whether or not to tell me something. We were out on the landing at the top of the stairs when she spoke up.

"It might be personal," she said.

"You mean, nothing to do with one of the law firm's cases?" I asked.

She nodded.

"Andy have any skeletons in his closet?"

"I'm not the one to ask," she said, which only suggested to me that she was.

"If you think of something, will you give me a call?"

"I was thinking I'd call you anyway," she said, smiling.

I wasn't quite sure what to make of that, but I was all too aware of her eyes on my back as I went down to the street.

I'd parked over by India Wharf. I was walking back along the waterfront toward my car when I passed an espresso bar with an outside deck and decided to get a cup of coffee. I went in and ordered a latte and took it out onto the deck, where I could sip it and look at the harbor.

It was Indian summer, late October, when the nights are crisp but during the day it can be almost balmy. The sky was nearly cloudless, and sunlight glanced off the oily water. Herring gulls swooped for floating trash and fought over it when they got something. A container ship moved down the channel, headed out toward the bay. It might be going up the coast to the Maritimes or south through the Cape Cod Canal to New York or the mouth of the Chesapeake.

There is a romance to ships, to cast off on a voyage and leave the land behind. The sea is a different place, with different rules, where the hopes and vanities of men have small effect. The kinds of problems I dealt with in my line of work usually boiled down to basic, base motivations. Envy. Lust. Greed. They might seem like primal forces of nature to the people they took possession of, but if you balanced them against the brute power of the North Atlantic, they stood for nothing.

It helped to put things in a healthier perspective. I thought about Stanley in the belly of a bomber, where life could be measured in moments, the flak and the German fighters, the odds against survival. I finished my coffee and turned away from the briny smell of the harbor, the moving water slopping at the pilings, and went inside to use the pay phone.

I called a cop I knew downtown. Frank Dugan owed me a favor, and I was lucky enough to catch him at his desk. There was an open case file on the Disciples, he told me, going back a few years.

"They're a pretty strong presence, the Springfield-Hartford corridor, out in the Berkshires, too," Dugan said. "A while back DEA and the state cops ran an operation against them, shut down a lot of their traffic, busted some cookers, but the gang bounced back. That's the trouble with speed. Doesn't take much to set up a lab once you figure a way to mask the odors."

"What about the recipe?"

Ingredients weren't that hard to come by, he explained.

"Basic pharmaceutical supplies, ephedrine, phenylacetone, hydrochloric acid. Thing to look out for, it's dangerous, cooking meth. You're working with volatile materials, you can blow yourself up. And then there's the fumes. That's a giveaway, the smell of acetone and ammonia, like nail polish or cat urine, plus you got your toxic slurry, four or five pounds of waste for each pound of product. Two ways to go. You stake out an industrial area with a lot of smudge and smut, or you go out in the boonies where the neighbors don't complain."

"So it's messy, and it stinks, and it's an explosive mix," I said. "Which makes it sound perfect for a crew of sociopathic losers like these outlaw bikers."

I could hear Dugan sucking on his teeth. "Far be it from me to step on your toes, Jack, but the Disciples are a seriously mean outfit. How'd you fasten onto this?"

"Guy name of Chip McGill, over in Charlestown," I told him. "I heard they were his new source for product."

There was an even longer silence this time around.

I waited him out.

"You sure know how to pick 'em," he said at last. "You're headed for a long walk off a short pier, you fish *that* water."

"Care to give me a little more detail?"

"Okay. Chip McGill's the type, he's burning the candle at both ends. He's a loose cannon, and sooner or later the Bunker Hill boys are going to take him out. I'm kind of surprised he hasn't already turned up in the trunk of a parked car out in the long-term lot at Logan."

Long-term parking at the airport was a favored method of putting a dead body on ice. It did double duty. First, the crime scene was stale by the time Homicide got to it, but there was a secondary benefit. A corpse left unattended swells with fluids and eventually bursts and putrefies. Nobody wants his family to see him like that. So it was an object lesson.

"Anyway, your little pal there, this McGill, he's a bad apple, take my word for it," Dugan went on. "He's got a sheet going back to juvie, he's done time for distribution, he's been pulled in on assault, conspiracy, murder. Whether it stuck to him or not, we're talking mainline hood here. He's been on the radar a while. Major Crimes wants him bad."

"I don't know as that's really my lookout, Frank," I said. "I just don't want to accidentally stumble into a rat's nest."

"You will be, you try to put the arm on this chump."

"Far as I know, McGill is in the background," I said, "part of the scenery."

"I think you're horsing me around, but I guess it's not for me to say," he remarked. "My advice would be to walk away."

"I'm not out to bust the guy's chops. All I want is a quiet word."

"Chip McGill is a nut job, and a speed freak on top of it," Dugan said. "Give him an excuse, he'll whack you out."

"Well, that's not very encouraging," I said.

"It's not supposed to be. The point is, all you have to do is wait about six months, and he won't be a problem."

"Yeah, I understood you the first time. Somebody with a bone to pick is likely to put the guy in the ground. Trouble is that I don't have six months to wait."

"Do what you gotta do," Dugan said.

"What about habits and habitat?" I asked him.

"He holds court at a joint called the Blue Mirror, by the Navy Yard. You know it?"

I was afraid I did.

"Most every afternoon between four and six. Happy hour."

"That's pretty deep in Indian Country," I said.

"I've been trying to tell you," Dugan said cheerfully and hung up.

*

Boston is a town known for its tough, parochial neighborhoods, Southie, Charlestown, the North End, Fields Corner and Savin Hill in Dorchester, and the neighborhood bars that cater to the locals are often like ethnic social clubs, friendly and familiar to initiates but suspicious of outsiders.

The Blue Mirror was in Charlestown, right outside the main gates of the Navy Yard, where the USS *Constitution* is berthed.

The yard's fallen on hard times since the seventies, deactivated with defense cutbacks, new keels being laid at Bath Iron Works in Maine and down at Norfolk and out on the West Coast in Puget Sound. Developers have had their eye on it over the years and now it's a National Historic Site, but as a shipbuilding facility and a port of call for bluewater sailors, it's been mothballed. Even when the yard was an active military installation, though, the Blue Mirror was off-limits to enlisted personnel.

There were rougher places, I'm sure, but you probably had to go to Belfast or Kingston, Jamaica, to find them. All the same, at four-thirty in the afternoon it looked pretty tame. A couple dozen vehicles were parked outside, vans, pickups, muscle cars, along with some choppers, low-slung panhead Harleys sporting ape-hangers and chromed valve covers. I went on in.

It took a minute for my eyes to adjust to the gloom. The room was long and low, opening up like a keyhole at the far end, where there was a small hardwood dance floor and a band was doing a sound check, testing levels. The bar itself ran along the near wall, probably thirty-five or forty feet, with two guys working behind the stick. The only lighting was a set of pinpoint spots down the back bar, the narrow focus putting the bottles on the shelves in high relief and making the liquor seem lit from within, like coals. Having the light behind them, the bartenders were in silhouette, so their faces were unreadable. The effect was a little sinister, but I guessed it might even be intentional, giving them the edge on a rowdy crowd when the clock edged last call.

They had Sam Adams on tap. I ordered a draft. Glancing down at the bar, I saw there seemed to be loose change scattered all over it, but when I tried to nudge a dime with my finger, I realized the coins were polyurethaned into the surface. It made me feel like a dope for falling for it, and it marked me as a stranger in a place where I wanted to be taken for furniture. I nursed my beer and looked around.

Given that it was a little shy of quitting time for a day job, the Mirror was pretty busy, and most of the people in there were guys. Not many of them were dressed like they'd come from work, either. Nobody in coveralls wearing a hammer holster or spattered with paint, anyway. Everyone seemed to be wearing aggressive casual, double-knits or Dockers depending on the age bracket.

I picked up my beer and wandered down the bar toward the bandstand. Tucked around the corner was a pool table, a quarter a game. The guy leaning over the table to break was wearing colors, biker leathers with an elaborate design on the back like an old Grateful Dead album. He broke open the rack but didn't make any balls, and when he straightened up, I could make out the gang insignia better. It looked like a representation of Leonardo's *Last Supper* but with Satan at the head of the table. Hitler, Idi Amin, and the Ayatollah were among his guests. Underneath, in Gothic script, was a legend that read THE DISCIPLES. I turned back to the bar, ordered a second beer, and asked for my change in quarters.

The girl the biker was playing pool with looked underage, strung-out sixteen, no more than a hundred pounds wringing wet, tie-dyed tank top and jeans she kept tugging up because she didn't have any hips for them to hang on to. But she had tattoos across her shoulder blades and enough piercings to set off a metal detector — ear clips and a stud in her lower lip and one at the outer edge of each eyelid, the extreme outer edge where it wouldn't scratch the sclera of her eyes if she looked sideways. She made five solids without breaking a sweat and then scratched with a cross-corner shot on the seven.

I stepped over and put my quarter up for the next game.

Neither one of them seemed to pay any attention to me. The biker was studying the way the table lay. He was shooting stripes, and he had two pockets safed, his balls hanging on the lip, duck shots, but in the way of her making a ball. He took a harder shot, banking one up and back, and made it. She thumped her cue on the floor, acknowledging a good call. He kept moving around the table, sinking his other six balls, and then blew the eight, slamming it too hard so it popped back out of the side pocket. The girl dropped the rest of the solids and sank the eight in a corner. She glanced over at me.

It was probably then that I made my first mistake. I'd assumed they were a couple, although the biker had a good twenty years on her. He had red hair pulled back in a shaggy ponytail, and you could see the streaks of gray in it. And he had kind of a Zapata mustache, drooping past the corners of his mouth. It showed white next to his chin. The mistake was that I spent more time on him than her. Young girl, but skinny as she was, I still should have been looking down the front of her shirt after I put my money in, the balls dropped and I racked, and she bent over the table to break. Anybody else would have.

Like a dummy I went for the target too quickly. The girl was running the table on me, and I stood back a little, just outside the edge of the light that picked out the balls on the green felt, making the colors pop. She made six balls before I got a shot, and then she left me safed behind one of her own high balls. I called a bank, made it by some miracle, and then blew a much easier shot on the four in the side. I stepped away from the table again, shrugging philosophically, and went to stand next to the redheaded biker. "Need to get my chops up, I guess," I remarked.

"Girl plays a mean stick," he said.

She took the eight on a long bank, back up in the corner, and he went over to the table to rack. I put another quarter up to play the winner.

The thing was, their concentration on the game wasn't fierce at all. The girl played deliberately but not as if anything were at stake. Her pride wasn't involved. She simply took each shot as it came and seemed to be playing more against herself than the biker. For his part, it didn't bother him if she had the better eye and control of the cue ball with English that would have made Minnesota Fats and Fast Eddie Felson give her a second look. He wasn't indifferent, or just humoring her, but he wasn't threatened by it.

I was watching him bridge to make a shot when I saw the jailhouse tattoo on the web of skin between his thumb and forefinger: 1%. It took me a minute to get it. One percent.

Back when Marion Brando made *The Wild One* and biker gangs were exotic, some square made the remark that motorcycles were ridden by family men and it was only that one percent that gave bikes a bad name. Now, anybody who's hung out with bikers knows they can be family men, for openers, but that's not the point.

Bikes have never lived down that outlaw image, and of course it's part of their appeal, especially riding a big Harley instead of a rice-burner, but Red was flaunting it. The colors, the attitude. Maybe he was for real, or maybe it was all show and no go. I had a funny feeling he was profiling, trying it on for size, and trying just a little too hard.

When he missed a shot and came back to where I was standing, leaving the table to the girl, I made a clumsy remark about speed. I wasn't trying for subtlety, mind you, but it was all too obvious what I was fishing for.

"You looking to score some flake?" He sounded almost bored with the transaction.

"Weight, not just a couple of lines," I said.

He nodded, not bothering to look at me, still watching the girl shoot pool. "I think you mistook me for somebody else," he said without glancing in my direction.

I shrugged. "I figured to cut out the middleman," I told him. "McGill steps on his product because he's trying to make up in volume what he uses himself. I've got motivated buyers but they don't like being cheated, and maybe it's time you found a new pipeline."

"Sing a different song, bro," he remarked edgily.

"He'll bring you all down, you don't jerk his leash," I said.

He looked at me finally, losing patience. "I'm trying to shoot a game here," he said. "You're rubbing up too close, and it's giving me a rash."

"You don't think Chip McGill's a loose cannon?" I asked. "How come he's trying to muscle Andy Ravenant, then? Seems like a good way to attract the wrong kind of attention."

I had Red's interest now, but I didn't think I'd struck a nerve. It was more puzzled curiosity, like how'd I come up with this angle and where the hell was I going with it.

"I hear Ravenant's defending a couple of neighborhood kids on a drug fall, but he can't plead them out unless they agree to burn Chip," I told him. "Think there's anything to it?"

"What in the name of sweet Jesus Christ is your game, pal?" he asked.

"I travel in a lot of weird company," I said. "I make connections. That's my stock in trade, putting things together. I'm what they call a rainmaker, seeding the clouds."

"You're a goddamn parasite," Red said.

"Whatever," I said. "I'm still in the market."

He leaned his cue against the wall. "Let's go out back for a taste, where we can talk more private," he said.

He went through the fire door behind him, and I followed. We were outside by the dumpster behind the building. His bike was on its kickstand there. He opened the saddlebags and felt around inside. It was still light out, the sky pearling toward dusk, the shadows long across parking lot. The girl came out through the fire door.

"Hey, darlin'," Red said.

"Hey yourself," she said. "I'm starting to flag."

"Got what you need," he said, straightening up with a small Baggie in his hand.

And that was my second mistake, if anybody's counting, to be watching him instead of watching my back, figuring her for a crank slut out to score a free pop. She kicked me so hard in the back of the knee that I went cross-eyed from the pain as my leg collapsed, and the two of them were on top of me like a snake on soap. She jerked the .40 Smith out of my waistband at the small of my back and wedged the muzzle into the base of my skull, notching the hammer back. The oily click sounded like a twig breaking. Red pinched the bridge of my nose between his knuckles and forced my head back, the gun digging into my spinal cord. I felt dizzy and ready to throw up. The girl giggled.

"No cop with any street sense would be that obvious," Red said, leaning down to stick his face into mine. "You take the cake for stupid, bud."

He had that part right. Stupid was my middle name.

"I ask myself, what's your stake in it? And what I come up with is, you're on your own. So what's this jive you're giving me about Chip McGill and the lawyer? My guess is you're running interference for somebody, so who sent you?"

My mind wasn't working fast enough to come up with a plausible answer. They say the prospect of an imminent hanging is supposed to sharpen your faculties, but a psychopathic meth groupie holding a gun to my head had filled it with white noise.

My tank was dry, and I was sucking air.

"Now, darlin', you best let me have that thing," Red said. "I think you're liable to pop a cap on this old boy afore I even have the chance to loosen his tongue."

He might have put his thumb between the hammer and the frame as he slipped the gun away from her, but I wasn't breathing any easier. She could have shot me by accident, or just to see which way my brains went on the pavement. Red was likely to shoot me on purpose, if I couldn't talk him out of it.

"Care to set my mind at rest, bro?" he asked me.

He'd let go of my nose and the Smith wasn't cutting into my neck anymore, but I was scared to tell him nothing and just as nervous about saying something dumb.

"I can't *hear* you," he crooned, leaning close again like a father confessor.

"Hear *this?*" another voice inquired, and the next sound was unmistakable, the slide on a pump shotgun being racked.

Red went absolutely still.

"We'll do this by the numbers," the new guy said. I'd heard his voice before, but I couldn't place it. "Point the weapon away from your body and safe it." Red uncocked the Smith. "Good. Now put it down and back away. You too, girlie. I got no compunction about taking you off at the knees."

I felt them give me some room. I glanced around.

"You're looking a little the worse for wear, Jack," Max Quinn said to me, grinning. He was holding a Mossberg pump at port arms, relaxed and obviously enjoying himself. "You able to walk?"

I picked up my gun and got carefully to my feet. I had to favor my left leg to get it to hold my weight.

"Now, about these two," Max said. I had some ideas on that score, but what I wanted to do was likely to see me pulling eight to ten at MCI Cedar Junction.

"No?" Max asked. He shrugged. "Well, in that case, we'll take our leave of you lovely people," he said to Red and the girl. "I'd think it right intelligent if you'd just lie down on the pavement until we left."

The girl hadn't even looked at me while this whole business was going on, but Red was watching me with a hostile squint.

"I meant *now*, people," Max said. They got down and assumed the position.

I limped toward my car, and Max backed away behind me, the

shotgun held down next to his leg, where it was less conspicuous.

The lights were coming on in the parking lot.

He leaned down to the window when I got behind the wheel. "This probably isn't the place to talk," he said.

"I'll call you," I said. "Thanks."

"No sweat," he told me.

I watched him cross the street to where he was parked and put the shotgun in his trunk. He'd probably had me under surveillance from the time I walked into the bar. I wasn't going to look a gift horse in the mouth, but it seemed a little too convenient.

Max gave me a wave as I drove away and climbed into his own car. I went home to pack my sore knee in ice and brood about how big a dope I'd been.

"So you figure the bikers are a red herring?" Tony asked the next morning.

"I don't know," I told him. "I think Quinn set me up, yes, but that doesn't mean they're not dirty."

"Quinn just wants to make himself look good?"

"Pulling my chestnuts out of the fire? That's one way of looking at it. Or he could be using me as a stalking horse, get them looking in the wrong direction."

"Andy Ravenant?"

"Yeah, something's hinky," I said. "But I don't see how it connects to the Stanley problem."

We were driving out to the hospital in Ayer to see Stanley. He'd collapsed the day before while I was busy getting myself washed, dried, and folded. He wasn't home — he was out cruising junkyards or something, up in apple orchard country — and the paramedics got him to the closest ICU. Once he was stabilized, he'd probably be moved into town to Peter Bent Brigham if things still looked bad.

"Any other irons in the fire?"

I shook my head. "I was hoping Stanley might come up with something else I could use," I said. "Only trouble is, I've got nothing to give him in return."

The hospital was fairly new, built sometime in the early seventies, I guessed. It was on a rise north of town, set off from neighbors, with a view through the trees to a small pond. A lot of the country villages beyond 495, the outer beltway, have become bed-room communities for the high-tech industries along Route 128, but Ayer is an anomaly. It sits outside the main gates of Ft. Devens, and for a good sixty years or more it's been a company town sup-ported by the army presence. Now there was talk of closing down the post. There was still a squadron of Ranger choppers based out there, and some logistical and support operations, but there was no longer a captive population of enlisted dependents, and the rental market was going down the tubes. Not a bad thing consider-ing how local landlords had gouged the GIs with inflated rates. And the used-car dealers out on the Shirley road no longer had such easy prey. But the downside was that the bottom had fallen out of the tax base, and maintaining a decent hospital was suddenly a squeeze.

Tony wasn't crazy about the hospital scene in any case. He'd spent too much time helpless on his back after he'd gotten creamed on the ice, but he was still game to go in and visit Stanley. I got his wheelchair out of the back seat, unfolded it, and helped him lever himself out of the front seat and into it. I was awkward about it, but Tony had long since gotten over any embarrassment.

"How's your leg?" he asked.

I had an Ace bandage wrapped around my knee, but the tendon was still badly swollen and it felt like I had a lemon wedged behind the joint. I couldn't bend my leg, and I couldn't put any weight on it, either. Not that I didn't feel foolish, since it was my own fault.

"Shouldn't have turned your back on a woman," Tony said.

"Don't get me started," I told him.

"I didn't mean it that way," Tony said. "It's not about sex, or gen-der, or whether she's a victim herself. I only meant you shouldn't take anything for granted."

The thing about being brothers us that you figure you're always in competition one way or another, but then they somehow man-age to sneak under your radar.

We made our way through the automatic doors into the lobby.

Stanley was down the hall in a private room. We startled Maria when we went in. I realized she'd dozed off sitting next to Stanley's bed, and it took her a moment to gather her wits.

Tony unbridled the charm. He had a gift for it, an effortless in-terest, because it was genuine. He rolled his wheelchair over next to Maria, not so close he was crowding her space, but making himself available. I didn't hear what he said to her, but she smiled bravely and took his hand.

Stanley seemed to be just coming to, floating in a sea of painkillers and barely breaking water. I had the feeling he was losing buoyancy. He made an effort to focus.

"Hey," I said, leaning in close so he'd recognize me.

"Jack," he whispered, hoarsely. "Who's that with you?"

"My brother Tony," I told him.

He nodded, smiling, his eyes fluttering closed. "Always liked having you two come around," he murmured. "Liked having kids at the shop. Reminded me of Stosh. Kept me alive during the war, knowing I had a boy I had to come home to." His concentration was drifting, the drugs in the intravenous drip clouding his thoughts. He'd cut his moorings and was headed out to sea. "The Blue Mirror," he muttered indistinctly.

I thought I'd misheard him. "What?" I asked, too sharply.

Tony had caught it. He swiveled around.

Stanley was in a reverie. "That's what we used to call it, the Adriatic," he said, so softly I had to bend over the bed.

"The blue mirror. On bombing runs into Rumania. Before you had to worry about the fighters. It looked beautiful, but it was hard as iron if your plane went down. I used to write letters to my son in my head, but I always forgot them by the time we got back."

I glanced at Tony.

"I always forgot," Stanley whispered, sinking back into the pillows, exhausted.

I straightened up.

Tony caught my attention, and belatedly I went over to pay my respects to Maria. I always feel awkward in situations where I have to pretend everything's swell. I get claustrophobic and look for an early avenue of escape. Tony smoothed us out of it, covering our retreat.

We were just ducking out the door when Stanley revived long enough to say something else. "Bees," he said, and fell back.

"Bees?" I asked Tony. I was driving him home, and he was sunk in his own thoughts. I figured he was brooding about the transience of human endeavor and Stanley in particular, but I'd missed a turn in the road while Tony had taken it.

"Guy name of Creek Fortier, you remember him?" Tony asked.

That was going back a ways. "Big guy with a beard, kind of rough around the edges but basically shy?"

Tony nodded. "Rode a thousand-CC Vincent," he said.

"Right," I said as the details started coming back to me. "Used to pull into Stanley's shop once in a while, looking to cannibalize scrap. I remember the bike, a Shadow or a Lightning he'd restored. Why, what about him?"

"He was in Vietnam with Stanley's son Stosh."

I didn't know where Tony was going, but I was willing to hitch a ride.

"Fortier came back, but Stan junior didn't," I said. "You're thinking what?"

"I'm wondering if Creek Fortier weren't a kind of surrogate son," Tony said. "A way for Stanley to hang on to Stosh."

"It's a reach, isn't it?"

"Well, yeah," Tony said, "but I knew there was something floating around in my head that I couldn't put a name to. The kid, Andy, he would have been four or five years old at the outside, so you and me, we were too grown up to pay him any mind, right? He was underfoot, we probably treated him like the measles."

I'd thought the same thing when I saw Andy in his office. When you're in third or fourth grade, you don't want some "baby" dragging on your coattails.

"Here's how I remember it, though," Tony went on. "Creek Fortier always had the time to humor Andy whenever he came by Stanley's. It was like he was more comfortable on a kid's level than he was with adults."

"You see something unhealthy there?"

"No, that's not what I'm getting at," Tony said. "There was something *simple* about him, in the old-fashioned sense, like he was a case of arrested development."

"Post-traumatic stress disorder?" I suggested.

Tony nodded. "Yeah, shell-shock, battle fatigue, whatever you want to call it. Stanley was always very protective, looked out for him, treated him gently."

"Walking wounded," I said.

"More than that," Tony said. "I mean, not just being a good Christian. We both know Stanley's a decent guy. I'm thinking he appointed himself Creek's guardian angel, ran interference for him, paid off his bad debts. Basically assumed the burden, in other words."

"Stanley lost a son, and Creek Fortier stood in for him."

"I hadn't thought about it for years," Tony said. "Fortier had a place out in the sticks, up by Pepperell or Townsend, near the New Hampshire line. Worked on bikes, raised his own vegetables. Stanley used to say he was a pioneer, born in the wrong century."

"You've got a better memory than I do," I told him.

"It's what Stanley said that brought it back."

"Which?" I asked him.

"Creek Fortier cultivated bees," Tony said.

I called Andy Ravenant's office with a couple of questions, but Andy wasn't there and Max Quinn hadn't clocked in at all. I wanted to talk to Max, not least to thank him, although I wanted my ducks in a row first because I wasn't certain just where he stood. Then the receptionist put me on hold, and when the phone was picked up again, it was Kitty Dwyer on the line.

"How'd you make out?" she asked me.

I didn't know that I was any more ready to talk to Kitty than Max, but you can't script every encounter. "Well, there's good news and bad news," I told her, shifting mental gears. "I got my tail caught in a crack but maybe I pushed some buttons. I don't know for sure. Max bailed me out of a jam anyway."

"*Max?* How so?"

"One of those things," I said. "You needed to be there."

"You mean more background than you want to go into over the phone?"

"I mean I'm not ready to confide in you, frankly," I said.

"Meet you for a drink after work?"

I hesitated and then took the plunge. "Sure," I said.

"Sun's already past the yard-arm," Kitty said.

That was true. I hadn't gotten back to town until three in the afternoon. "I think I take your meaning," I told her.

"Let's close up shop, then," she said.

We met at a bar in the financial district, busy enough with suits stopping on their way home that we didn't attract any attention and just loud enough for personal conversations not to be overheard. It was a good choice. Too many people think a meeting should be held in a deserted place; it's actually the reverse. Kitty knew a crowd gave better cover, and the ambient noise made a wire unreliable.

"So?" she asked as we put our drinks on a corner table.

I shrugged. "You guys gave me the bait, and I took it," I said. "I don't know how deep Ravenant and Dwyer is in, but you're in deep enough to be worried about it."

She didn't fence. "I don't want to be disbarred," she told me, "but I don't want to put Andy in the hot seat."

"Is it that narrow a choice?"

"Most of our choices come down to self-interest," she said.

"That's open to definition," I said. "What about Max?"

"What about him?"

"How'd you recruit his services, for openers?"

"He came to us from the states. Max had good connections."

"Inside, you mean."

"He's got a lot of markers to call in."

"Cops and private dicks don't get on that well as a rule," I said. "Then again, a lot of private dicks used to be cops."

"The old blue network," she said.

"Did he leave the state police under a cloud?"

"How do you mean?"

"You know what I mean, Kitty," I said. "Did he take early retirement? Was he being investigated by Internal Affairs? Did he cut corners? What?"

She rolled her eyes. "Max is *sui generis,*" she said. "He worked a lot of undercover, drug stings, bribery, payoffs, you name it. He made enemies. But he made good busts, arrests that stuck. Andy was a PD, remember, but he respected Max."

I understood what she meant. A public defender would smell out a dirty cop. "Andy knew Max from before?" I asked her.

"Sure," she said.

I was trying to make something compute and couldn't do the math.

"What exactly is bothering you, Jack?" Kitty asked.

"Max steered me in the direction of the bikers, and then he was there to save my bacon when I ran into grief."

She didn't wonder what kind of grief I'd run into. "What's the problem with that?" she asked. "He's using you as a blind? We're defending a couple of kids on a trafficking rap. If we can make a case for intimidation, witness tampering, the whole nine yards, maybe we can buy them a little less time. Max Quinn is just doing his job."

"Who are you trying to convince?" I asked her. "This isn't a summation in front of a jury."

She hadn't touched her drink. She fiddled with the stem of her glass.

"I don't feature it, either," she admitted.

"What's his game, then?"

"Oh for Christ's sake, Jack, stop jerking me around," she said, fiercely. "You know goddamn well what he's up to, and he doesn't give a rat's ass if he takes us down, too."

I was startled by her vehemence and realized there were tears welling up in the corners of her eyes. I didn't think she was acting, either.

She swallowed, gulping down her sorrow. "Max is using *you*? How do you think *I* feel?" she demanded.

Probably like crap, I thought. "Confused," I said.

"You are *not* a lot of help," Kitty said, scrubbing her eyes angrily on her sleeve.

Up until then I hadn't wanted to be.

"This isn't going the way I'd hoped," she muttered.

"Me, either," I told her.

"Well, that's a small relief," she said.

I didn't know what to make of that remark.

"You want me to put it into words, don't you? Okay," she said. "You think Max Quinn is using his job at Ravenant and Dwyer as leverage. So do I. He's collecting proprietary client information to make a case against Chip McGill for the states. It'll never stand up in court, if it comes out, because the evidence would be tainted and none of it admissible, but he can set them up, all of them, McGill and the bikers, and the state police can tell a judge we have a confidential source, somebody inside, and the judge will go along with it."

"But how much does Max know?"

"Not enough, obviously. That's where you come in."

"Working under attorney privilege for Ravenant and Dwyer."

"Which could put me and Andy both in the toilet."

I saw that. How could you claim to be oblivious? You were either unscrupulous or incompetent.

Kitty sighed. "This is a no-win situation," she said.

"Looks that way," I said. "Max is working from a stacked deck. But even if all of this is true, what's his handle on Andy? Or are you saying that Andy could have been in on it from the get-go, that he's a party to it?"

"I don't believe that."

"Don't believe it or can't bring yourself to?"

She gave that a moment's thought. "No, it's not wishful thinking," she said finally. "I don't believe it because it's not in Andy's character. It runs counter to what *he* believes in. The practice of law may he adversarial, but you hope it all balances out, on average."

"Okay," I said.

I must have sounded unconvinced. "Jack," she explained, "Andy Ravenant is a straight arrow. Not a Boy Scout, but a guy who honors the law, even if it's an imperfect instrument. And that's as much a weakness as it is a strength in this trade. The point is, he wouldn't countenance unlawful means even if they led to a desirable end."

"Okay," I said again, smiling this time. "Let's make sure we're reading off the same page, here. We both figure Max Quinn sees Chip McGill as a target of opportunity, and helping Major Crimes take him out would put Max in solid with the AG's office and the old blues. The fact that you guys are defending a couple of kids who might be persuaded to rat McGill out gives Max an angle, and the fact that Andy's grandfather is involved makes for a strong pressure point, although you don't think Andy will fold."

"I *know* so," Kitty said.

I didn't have quite her confidence, but I let it go. "Does Andy have power of attorney for his grandfather?" I asked her.

"I couldn't tell you even if I knew," she said. "Why?"

"Stanley's in intensive care," I told her. "He might be on his way to the back exit."

"Oh my God," she said, shocked. "That's why Andy isn't at the office. He should have said something."

It occurred to me why he hadn't, and Kitty worked it out in the next heartbeat.

"He didn't want Max to know," she said, staring up at me.

I was already standing, fishing for my wallet. I dropped a ten on the table and put my glass on top of it.

Kitty was right behind me as I made for the door. "What is it?" she demanded, catching up with me on the sidewalk.

"I don't think Andy's at the hospital with Stanley," I told her. "You have a cell phone?"

She pulled it out of her handbag as we hoofed it down the block to my car. I unlocked the passenger door, and Kitty climbed in, reaching across the seat to unlock the driver's door as I limped around.

"I don't know the number," I said as I got behind the wheel. "It's a listing in Ayer. See if you can get through to Admitting."

Kitty was already punching up directory assistance.

I pulled out into the traffic, headed for the expressway. It was the wrong time of day and we'd be fighting rush-hour on the Mystic Bridge approaches, but I figured the McGrath & O'Brien was our best bet to get to Route 2. It was the same road I'd traveled that morning with Tony.

"You want to know whether Andy's there?" she asked me.

"No harm in asking," I said, jumping an intersection, "but I want to find out where the EMTs picked Stanley up. If you can get directions, that's a plus."

The Central Artery was gridlocked. I inched along until I could take the Storrow Drive exit.

"Stanley's only visitor is his wife," Kitty told me, her hand over the phone for a second. I heard her tell the nurse on duty she was an insurance adjuster looking for time and mileage on the emergency call. "Right," she said, listening, and noting it all down on a legal pad. She disconnected with a thank you.

Traffic along the river was moving faster. I could pick up Route 2 in Cambridge.

"Pepperell," Kitty said. That's where Stanley was picked up. "Volunteer fire department, ambulance on call. I've already got the number; you want me to give it a shot?"

I should have known Stanley wasn't just joyriding. He'd been on his way to see the beekeeper.

"Try my brother first," I said. I gave her Tony's number.

She started to explain who she was when he answered; I interrupted impatiently. "Ask him how the hell we're going to find

Creek Fortier," I said. "Tell him I screwed up, and we're behind the clock."

"He heard you," Kitty told me, listening to Tony. Then she laughed. "You got that right," she said into the phone.

We were past the Magazine Street railroad trestle, closing on Soldiers Field Road and the Eliot Bridge. I was shifting back and forth between lanes, picking every gap I could, leaving some exasperated commuters behind me, giving me the finger.

"He'll have it for us," Kitty said, speaking to me with exaggerated calm as if she were talking a kitten off a ledge. "Tony wants to know how soon you think we're going to get there if we survive the ride?"

"Forty-five minutes, an hour, if we're lucky." I let my foot off the gas incrementally. "Make that an hour and a half." It was sort of an apology to Kitty for being so abrupt.

"Okay," she said to Tony and flipped the cell phone closed. "He says to be cool, Jack."

"I'm working on it," I said, but I was stirred with unease and a sense of urgency.

My brother used a livery service out of Lexington on a regular basis. They had handicapped-accessible vans, and a fleet of cabs to cover the suburban area beyond Route 128, and they bid on school bus contracts, filling in between assigned stops. If you were too far off the beaten track or had a special-needs child who wasn't being mainstreamed, Tony's taxi guys would carpool you, mileage paid by the state. Their dispatchers knew every secondary road in Middlesex County, including this poverty pocket outside the 495 loop. Tony was passing us directions.

"Stanley's been helping Creek Fortier out ever since Vietnam," I explained to Kitty. "He's lent him money he never expected to be paid back, given him tools, kept him afloat. I don't mean Fortier's a *user*, but Stanley was a soft touch because Creek was a link to his dead son, something Stanley wouldn't want to let go of. My guess is that Stanley cosigned a mortgage for this property Creek's got, and when Creek didn't keep up the payments, Stanley took title or something like that. Creek's on the dim side, I hear. Or not of this world, anyway, which Stanley wouldn't take as a handicap. And he wouldn't want to see Creek lose the place. He must have told Andy to make sure the land got transferred to Creek's name, but he didn't tell Andy the punchline, which is that he was dying. Andy got curious."

I glanced over at her. "I guess that's an occupational hazard. Besides, you don't want to see your grandfather make foolish moves when he's getting along in years. That's why Chip McGill put the heat under Stanley. He thought Andy was trying to roust him because, like any paranoid, he made it for a conspiracy."

"When all it is is miscommunication," Kitty suggested.

"All it is is Stanley trying to protect this guy."

"From the rigors of the modern age," she said.

"Yeah, well, my guess is that Creek Fortier has been lured into the modern age in a big way," I said. "I think it's the biker connection. Creek builds custom bikes. So long as people leave him alone to raise bees and build bikes, he's got no kick with the twenty-first century. Stanley insulated him, but with Stanley gone he'd be on his own. If he didn't think about it, somebody might have suggested it to him."

She was ahead of me. "Chip McGill," she said.

I stood on the gas to get around a pickup loaded with drywall. Kitty dug her feet into the floorboards as we swerved back into our own lane. "Creek was in the biker loop," I told her. "I don't mean he's a card-carrying member of an outlaw club, but gear-heads know about each other. It's word of mouth. So a Disciple comes by to talk bikes, and they hit it off. The guy sees an opportunity. Here's a reclusive motorcycle freak living out in the sticks, no near neighbors. Kind of a Luddite even, except when it comes to tuning bike engines."

"Which is what? Basically his only real social skill?"

"Exactly. And the Disciples persuade him his interests lie in diversification, expanding his horizons."

"Including?"

"Better living through chemistry," I said.

Her cell phone beeped. It was Tony. I'd slowed down coming into Groton. Kitty, the phone to her ear, pointed me up a back road north that led along the Nashua River, a tributary of the Merrimack. The narrow blacktop followed the contours of the hillsides that supplied the watershed and crossed the river on a covered bridge, coming into the foot of the village.

Pepperell is another one of those settlements that time forgot after the mills closed. It was as if the waters of a great flood had lapped at its doorstep and then left it high and dry. It was a dry town, literally. You couldn't buy liquor there.

"Got it," Kitty said into the phone. She glanced at me. "We go through town past the elementary school and take a right-hand fork at the Congregational Church," she said.

I followed her instructions.

"Bald Hill Road," Kitty said. "Okay." She turned in her seat. "He's starting to break up," she told me. "We're getting out of range."

Cell coverage overlapped, but we were in a blind spot.

"I'm losing you," Kitty said to Tony. "Say again." She listened, had him repeat it a third time, and then broke the connection. "We look for a side road up here on the left," she said to me. "Unpaved but graded. There should be horse barns and a riding ring maybe half a mile in. A mile or so past that, there'll be a split-rail fence and a dirt driveway and kind of a shed. I didn't quite get that, but it's the best I could do."

We took the turn we thought we were supposed to, and half a mile in we passed the horse barns. There was nobody there. After a mile point two by the odometer there was a little lean-to up against a split-rail fence. Inside the lean-to was a shelf with jars of honey for sale and a coffee can where you left the money on the honor system. The property was heavily wooded, and we couldn't see a house from the road. I drove past slowly and pulled up a hundred yards farther along.

"You thinking to go in on foot?" Kitty asked me.

"That's the plan," I said.

"And this is where you tell me to wait here, right? With a cell phone that doesn't work and no idea what's going on."

I'd already had second thoughts about bringing Kitty along, but she was right. "You weird with guns?" I asked her.

"No more than the next girl."

I took out the Smith, checked the magazine, and tucked it away in the small of my back. I reached under the seat and got the compact nine out of its spring clip. I worked the slide, safed it, and held it out to Kitty. "Point it, snap the safety off, squeeze the trigger," I said, showing her what I was talking about. "Don't use it unless they get close and you can hit them square in the upper body, no chance of a miss."

She nodded and took the gun. "Combat nine millimeter, double-action-only, pre-Brady double-stack, thirteen rounds. I've got a concealed carry permit, Jack," she said. "My mistake, I left my own gun in my other pants."

I was going to remark that she wasn't wearing pants, she had on a navy jacket and a skirt that showed off her legs, but I figured I'd embarrassed myself enough already. She tucked the nine in the waistband of her skirt, under her jacket and behind her back, the same as I had. "What are we likely to run in to?" she asked me.

"Maybe just an emotionally disabled vet," I said. "Maybe your partner come to warn him —" I held up my hand when Kitty started to protest. "Or come to explain things to him," I went on. "Or we could be about to step into the deep end of the pool, and land in the heavy. Are you ready for that?"

"No," she said.

I sighed. "Neither am I," I told her.

"Might as well get to it, then," Kitty said. "It won't get any easier if we wait."

We stepped out of the car into the lingering late-afternoon light. The hum of insects buzzed in the grass, and birdsong sounded in the near distance. We walked back to Creek Fortier's drive and started up it. The maples had turned, their leaves scarlet and bronze, the poplars lemon yellow, the birches dusty gold. It was quiet under the trees. The leaves smelled dry and spicy.

The road opened out into a meadow, and we stopped at the edge of the trees. There was a small clapboard farmhouse, and a shop building in back. Beyond the buildings was an apple orchard, untended but with beehives spaced between the trees, square boxes up on platforms, the orchard left for the bees, not for the apples. Fallen fruit lay on the ground, fermenting.

"Do bees hibernate?" Kitty asked.

"I think they go dormant in the winter, if they don't die," I said. "Maybe you have to take them in, like tomato plants or geraniums."

"You're full of vegetable lore," she remarked, smiling.

I was looking at the open ground we had to cover. We'd be exposed to the house if anyone was watching for us. There were a couple of big bikes out back by the shop, and three cars — a GTO, vintage muscle; a '53 Ford clunker; and a new Audi. "That's his car, the Audi," Kitty said.

"Andy's?"

She nodded.

I blew out my breath, trying to think.

"Suggestion?" Kitty asked.

"Sure," I said.

"What's to keep me from simply going over there?"

"And your story's what?"

She shrugged. "I'm just some yuppie twit from Boston," she said. "A leafpeeper looking for local color."

"Andy won't give you away, you walk in on them?"

"Andy's a trial lawyer, and a good one," she said. "He can improvise."

I didn't have anything better.

"You flank the house," Kitty said, and off she went.

Flank? I thought. She sounded like a platoon sergeant. I let her get out in the open where she could be seen and worked my way around the meadow, keeping under cover of the trees.

Kitty was halfway to the house, and then she paused for a second, leaning down to straighten her heel or pick a stone out of her shoe. She didn't look in my direction.

I froze where I was, wondering if she was trying to send me a signal, but I didn't see that anything had changed. The place was completely still except for a few late-season cicadas sawing in the tall grass, and the air felt hot and somnolent.

Kitty went on up the drive, approaching the house without any obvious apprehension, like somebody who'd run out of gas and needed to use the phone.

I'd stopped circling, watching her.

She went up onto the small porch and peered in the windows, and then she went around back toward the shop.

I waited to see if something happened, but nothing did.

Kitty came back out front and made a shrugging gesture, her hands out at her sides. I hobbled across the grass, favoring my bad leg. "Nobody home, tiddley-pum," she said.

The sun was just below the tree line, the light taking on a metallic quality, sharp and coppery. A slight breeze lifted the leaves of the maples. There was the scent of water, a stream or a spring nearby, and something else, not acrid but steely, like a whiff of ammonia.

"What *is* that?" Kitty asked, sniffing the wind. "It smells like nail polish remover."

"Acetone," I said. It was very faint, though. From what Frank Dugan had told me about cooking meth, I'd expected more of a piercing odor.

"They're here, then," she said.

Did she still think Andy was an innocent bystander in this?

I didn't ask her out loud.

We went through the orchard, moving carefully.

"Are bees territorial?" she asked me.

"I don't know," I said. "Social insects, mated to their hives. They kill intruders, but beekeepers work around them all the time and don't get stung."

I wished I knew what I was talking about. The bees were everywhere under the apple trees, but they seemed sleepy, headed home with dusk. You could brush them aside gently, and they'd go on about their business. We were no more than objects in the way, and they went around. There was nothing angry about them.

"Jack," Kitty said, stopping short.

A few trees off the path a bunch of bees were swarming, confused and without any apparent purpose, rising in a cloud and then settling again, like moths. It was uncharacteristic.

I ducked under the branches and went closer. The bees were agitated and uncertain. I didn't want them any more worked up.

He lay his length on the ground, staring at the sky. I hadn't seen him in over twenty years, but I knew it was Creek Fortier. The bees kept lighting on him, almost plucking at his hair, his clothes. I'd never seen anything like it. I couldn't credit them with a dog's intelligence or loyalty, but there it was. They seemed to be trying to coax him up. With the back of his head blown off, I didn't think he'd rise to the occasion.

I backed away. "We got big trouble," I murmured to Kitty.

"Who is it?" she asked.

"It's not Andy, it's Creek," I told her.

She looked relieved.

"We should go to the car, and to town, and get some backup," I said.

"Not if Andy's down there," she said.

"We're in over our heads," I said.

"You, maybe," Kitty said, turning away.

Below the orchard the ground sloped off to a brook overhung with poplar and birch. We moved into a stand of trees to our left and worked our way down to the water. From there we made our way downstream, using what cover we could, and found what we were looking for.

"Like a moonshiner's," Kitty whispered to me.

It was a small shed built on a platform over the brook with outside ductwork to a hood on the roof and a tangle of copper piping that went under the surface of the water. It was a distillery, in effect, to condense and filter the residue, disguising the smell. Creek's work, I figured.

"A peculiar genius," Kitty remarked.

I nodded. "But why did they kill him?" I asked.

"They're closing down," she said.

Which made sense if the operation was compromised, but how sure of that were they?

We made our approach to the shed incrementally, move and then crouch, move and crouch, trying to make as little noise as possible. The running water chuckled in the stream bed loudly enough that we weren't heard. When we got next to the little outbuilding, we hunkered down outside the windowless plywood sheathing. Nobody had raised an alarm.

Whoever was inside wasn't listening for trespassers. They were too intent on something else. There was an indistinct murmur of voices and then an involuntary whimper and ragged, heavy breathing. What it sounded like was an interrogation, and a painful one.

Kitty and I probably had the same thought at the same time: Andy was being tortured.

We ducked around the corner of the shed and took up our positions on either side of the plank door, both of us with guns up, cocked and locked, fingers alongside the trigger guards. There was another sharp whimper of pain.

I nodded to Kitty, stepped back, and kicked the door open. We were inside before anybody had time to react.

Everything stopped for maybe a long three count, all of us taken by surprise.

Three guys, one tied in a chair. The guy in the chair was battered and bruised, but it wasn't Andy. It was the redheaded biker from

Charlestown. Andy was standing behind him with a pair of bloody pliers in his hand. The third guy was in front of the chair, caught in a half crouch, looking over his shoulder at us. I knew he was Chip McGill.

Sometimes things slow down, like it's happening under water, but this was sudden and abrupt. McGill snapped out of his crouch, coming up with a stainless autoloader in his right hand. It was incredibly stupid of him, and he made the same mistake I'd made in back of the Blue Mirror, not watching the girl. Kitty shot him twice in the chest with the nine, punching two holes in him you could have covered with a quarter. He was dead when he hit the floor.

Andy jumped back, and Kitty shifted her aim. I thought for a second she was going to shoot Andy, too.

"Oh God, Kitty," Andy bleated, dropping the pliers. "Look what he made me do."

Kitty wasn't having any. "Shut up," she said tiredly. "Don't give me any more reason to hate your guts." But at least she lowered the gun.

They'd wired Red's wrists together behind his back, and I had to use the pliers to get it off. I tried not to think about what else they'd been used for. "DEA," he croaked, rubbing his hands together to bring back the circulation. "Working undercover with the state police."

Well, at least he'd gotten my gun away from the speed freak before she killed me with it, I remembered.

We started back up toward the house. Red needed my help, which I didn't wonder at. He was in bad shape. Kitty seemed to have gone numb, too, which I didn't wonder at, either. It was a delayed reaction from shooting McGill. You don't shake it off that easily.

We were still below the orchard when Andy took it into his head to make a run for it. He just suddenly bolted, pumping his legs through the tall grass, plowing uphill. None of us had the energy to chase him, and there wasn't much point in shooting him. How far was he going to get, after all? Maybe he thought he could outrun his disgrace, his life in a shambles.

"Andy," Kitty called after him wearily.

But he didn't look back. He charged recklessly through the orchard, flailing at the aroused bees.

"Oh Jesus," Kitty whispered.

I didn't quite get what was happening. I saw Andy stumble and find his feet and then stumble again and go down.

Kitty had stopped where she stood, stricken.

Andy managed to stand again, his angry shouts turning into a terrified wail. The air around him was thick with insects, and bees had settled on him like a carpet, so many they obscured his shape. He fell a last time and didn't get up.

The clamor of bees subsided in the gathering twilight, and the light breeze rustled through the maples.

We made a wide circle around the orchard, not speaking. If any of us had thoughts, we kept them to ourselves.

Stanley died two days later. He'd gone into a coma and hadn't come out of it. Maybe it was for the best, since he didn't have to learn about his grandson.

Andy had cut himself in on McGill's racket early when Creek Fortier had come to ask his advice, not daring to bring it up with Stanley. I'd guessed right about that part at least.

Stanley had held the paper on Creek's land, intending to put it in trust with Andy as trustee. The part I'd guessed wrong about was why Chip McGill had gone after Stanley. It was insurance, plain and simple, in case Andy got cold feet. McGill thought like a thug, which he was. What nobody figured out until afterward was that Andy had already decided he'd throw McGill over the side. If the Disciples thought McGill were a liability, they'd take him out for their own protection. Andy just needed a credible story, one that would sell on the street, and he had it in the case he was preparing, the townies who had bought product from McGill. If word got out they were going to plead down in exchange for giving him up, he was dead meat. His big name in the neighborhoods wouldn't buy him a pass.

Why had Andy gone bad? Maybe somebody had finally met his price, but that doesn't really explain it. Kitty Dwyer believed in him right up until she saw him with the pliers in his hand.

And that's where my own thinking led me. Andy had gotten tired of living up to other people's expectations. He stepped over the line because the line was there. They say in the trade that the dealer always gives you the first taste for free.

*

Then there was Max Quinn.

I knew that Kitty had terminated his contract with Ravenant & Dwyer, and by an unhappy coincidence I met him a couple of days later, lugging his files out of the office. I was there to take Kitty to lunch.

Max put the box he was carrying down on the tailgate of a station wagon parked in the loading zone and looked me over with bland venom. "You queered me good, pal," he said, smiling.

The smile was for show. "Not my intention," I said.

"Well, the good Lord save us from honest intentions," Max said. He leaned back and rested his elbows on the carton. "You ever stop to think I had those vermin in the palm of my hand and I was ready to close my fist? I coulda had every one of the bastards, and what do *you* have to show for it? Chip McGill on a slab and a dead lawyer." He shrugged. "'Course, I guess a dead lawyer ain't the worst thing. You take the bitter with the sweet." He smiled that crocodile smile again.

"I'm not arguing," I said. "But our interests weren't the same. You were looking for it to go your way. My client wanted a different outcome."

He snorted. "Your *client*," he said. "Jesus, you take the prize. Your client is *dead*, for Christ's sake. He had one foot in the grave when he hired you. You should of showed me some professional courtesy, for openers. Not to mention that I saved your ass from a whipping."

"I wasn't forgetting," I said.

"Me, either," Max said.

"You had a personal axe to grind," I told him, "and you were looking to buy chips so you could get back in the game."

"Is *that* what you think?" Max shook his head. "You stupid s.o.b."

"Don't push it," I said.

"I have an axe to grind, yeah," he said hoarsely. "You want to know what it is? My daughter Olivia died on speed. She took a hot-shot. And those bikers are out there peddling methedrine cut with rat poison. You'd *better* goddamn know I've got an axe to grind."

"You were on the task force, state police, and DEA," I said, finally seeing the forest for the trees.

"Now we're playing catchup hall."

There was nothing I could say. I tried anyway. "I'm sorry about your daughter," I said.

"Sorry don't do the trick, pal," he said, and turned away.

I remembered what Stanley had said about flying over the Adriatic during bombing runs. It had looked so beautiful, like a blue mirror, but was hard as cement if you hit it going down. It was an appropriate metaphor.

Enemies are like that.

Max could smile his crocodile smile and pretend to carry on a civil conversation with me, like bygones were bygones, but he'd be looking for a chance to drop me in a hole, the deeper the better. It was a brute fact like the bright blue ocean below, unyielding as stone. I'd done Max an injury, and it didn't matter that it was an honest mistake. He wasn't going to give me room to make another.

JOE GORES

Inscrutable

FROM *The Mysterious Press Anniversary Anthology*

KNUCKLES COLUCCI wasn't known as Knuckles because they dragged on the ground when he walked. Far from it. Oh, his jaws were blue enough, his nose was Roman, his eyes were mean, his lips had that Capone twist. But he was physically slight, not bulky. So while maturing into a classic Mafia soldier, and then graduating to Armani suits and Ferragamo shoes — which he invariably wore with parrot-bright aloha shirts — Knuckles needed some sort of physical edge. Thus the habit, in his youth, of carrying a set of brass knuckles as an equalizer.

Those days were long past. Now Knuckles was a frightener. He never demanded of some poor fool the vigorish due a local loan shark. He never broke knees or cut off thumbs. He wasn't an enforcer. He *warned* people. Once.

If the warning was ignored, he killed them.

On this particular Wednesday he had flown first class from Detroit to San Francisco. A boring flight because today would be just a warning. He walked through the jammed, noisy, jostling airline terminal and down two escalators. The first took him past the luggage area, where he had no luggage to pick up. He never brought anything more lethal than sinus breath onto any of the numerous commercial flights that his profession demanded. He'd taken three falls in his thirty-nine years. If he took another he wouldn't get up again, so he wasn't about to take it.

The next escalator took him to a long slow-moving walkway. In the underground parking garage a bright-eyed kid in his twenties fell into step with him on the angle-striped pedestrian walk.

"Nice flight?" Knuckles merely grunted. The kid handed him a set of Lexus keys. "The red one," he said, and turned off to lose himself among the endless rows of cars.

The Lexus was nestled between a hulking, sullen SUV and some sort of canary-yellow Oldsmobile convertible. Knuckles pulled on thin rubber surgeon's gloves, unlocked the door, got in. There was a black violin case on the passenger seat. He unsnapped it, raised the lid, looked inside, grinned thinly, and closed and resnapped it. He set it upright in the bucket seat and snugged the seat belt about it, then followed the EXIT signs out of the labyrinth. His nose was already tingling from the exhaust fumes trapped in the garage. Too many freaking people. Kill 'em all.

"I need a frozen Milky Way," said Larry Ballard.

He was a tall, athletic blond man in his early thirties, with a surfer's tan, a hawk nose, and cold blue eyes that just saved his face from true male beauty. He was also a repo man for Daniel Kearny Associates at 340 Eleventh Street in San Francisco.

"Nobody needs a frozen Milky Way," Bart Heslip pointed out.

He too was very well conditioned, early thirties, shorter, thicker, plum black, and with the shaved head currently in favor among African American males. After winning thirty-nine out of forty pro fights, he had quit the ring to become a repo man for DKA.

"I've been working out really hard," explained Ballard. "My blood-sugar level is way down."

"We can't have you going hypoglycemic before you win that black belt," said Heslip. "Ray Chong's it is — *after* you take me back to my car in Pacific Heights."

Above the door of the narrow Eleventh Street storefront sandwiched between a tire repair shop and an auto supply store run by Persians in turbans was the legend PEKING GROCERY STORE — CHINESE DELICACIES in English letters and Chinese characters.

The owner, Ray Chong Fat, was anything but. Ray was skinny and stooped, with a thin face, not much chin, a long upper lip, and lank black hair. As always, he wore a highly starched white shirt, the cuffs rolled up two turns over his skinny wrists, the collar two sizes too big for his scrawny neck.

Ray was a widower with seven, count 'em, *seven* daughters. And not even one lousy little son. One daughter in grad school, two in college, two in high school, one in elementary school, one just about to enter kindergarten. Seven daughters meant a lot of expenses, which meant a lot of hard work for Ray.

But he was a satisfied man, whistling tunelessly to himself as he stocked the shelves with assorted cans of exotic fruit: rambutan canned with pineapple; soursops; jackfruit in syrup; and of course Chinese lychees.

The rest of the narrow store was jammed with Chinese yams and cabbage; mandarins and mangoes and pawpaws and star fruit; dried and salted squid; frozen ducks and fish, frozen candy bars and ice cream bars, green tea and chow mein noodles and dried rice noodles and sweet rice candies, all redolent with the smell of strange spices. The shelves in the back room bulged with rental videos, all in Chinese and most shot in Hong Kong. Romance and martial arts were the favorites.

The front door jangled its little bell. The familiar salt-and-pepper team from down the street came in.

"Hey, got riddle," exclaimed Ray in his high-pitched singsong voice. "Why Chinese so smart?"

"I don't know, Ray," said Ballard. "Why are they?"

"No blondes." Ray went off into gales of high hee-hee-hee-hee laughter. Heslip shook his shaved head.

"It's what I always tell you, Larry. Inscrutable."

Two jokes and a riddle later, they headed for the door. A slight man was getting a violin case out of a red Lexus when they emerged. Ballard waved the frozen Milky Way after him.

"Not my idea of the third violin at the symphony."

"Maybe it isn't a violin in the case," chuckled Bart.

The bell tinkled. A short, swarthy man with a nose as big as a parrot's was coming up the aisle toward Ray. The man wore a very expensive suit and carried a violin case. Ray wreathed his lean face in a welcoming smile full of prominent teeth.

"Yessir, yessir, help you, sir?"

"Yeah, you freaking slope, you can help me," said Knuckles.

Ray Chong Fat's eyes became flat and stupid.

"No savvy," he said.

Knuckles set his violin case on the counter.

"Know what I hear? I hear some Chinaman is running an unsanctioned Asian card club for the really high rollers in this town once or twice a month, on the weekends."

"No savvy," said Ray Chong Fat.

"I hear this freaking Chink's got a game planned this weekend. I hear a certain gentleman in the South Bay don't like that shit, get my drift?"

"No savvy." A drop of sweat ran down Ray Chong Fat's nose.

Knuckles Colucci unsnapped the violin case. He opened it. "Take a look at that," he said.

Ray Chong Fat looked into the case. He paled.

"Yeah, you savvy that okay, slope," said Knuckles. He closed the case, resnapped it, waggled a finger under Ray's nose. "Don't do it no more," he said.

"I need a beer," said Bart Heslip.

It was nine-thirty that same night, and he and Ballard, working in tandem, had scored two repos each.

"Nobody needs a beer," Larry Ballard pointed out.

"This is thirsty work."

"Okay. Ray'll be open for another half-hour at least."

But Ray Chong Fat's store had the CLOSED sign out, even though light still glowed from the back room. They rapped on the glass and rattled the door. In this neighborhood, even DKA had alarms on the doors and heavy mesh screens on the ground-floor windows. Ray had neither.

"How many years have we been coming here and he's never been closed before ten o'clock?" asked Ballard.

Bart said softly, "Maybe it *wasn't* a violin."

Ray's door was no proof against their lockpicks. They were half-way down the length of the store when the door of the back room opened and Ray came out. Even in the dim light he looked drawn and wasted.

"Go 'way! We closed."

"After you tell us what's wrong."

Over green tea and delicate almond cakes in the video room, they got the story out of him. The little man with his threats and the violin case with anything but a violin inside.

"It's easy," said Bart. "Just cancel the game."

"Two year ago, number three daughter real sick, 'member?"

"We remember." They had gotten up a cash donation at DKA.

"Go to Chinese Benevolent Association, borrow money. Lots of money." He opened his arms wide. "Big interest."

"Not so benevolent?" suggested Bart.

Ray nodded morosely, sipped tea. They ate almond cakes.

"Man come, say I gotta run weekend Asian card club to pay off loan. If I won't, he say they do things to my daughters."

"They needed a front," said Larry. "At least the loan —"

"Never get loan paid off. Only pay off interest."

"You know the guy with the violin case?" asked Bart.

Ray shook his head vigorously.

"Know who *sent* the guy with the violin case?"

"Somebody in South Bay." Ray started wringing his hands with the theatricality of true emotion. "What I do?"

"You hold the game and save your daughters," said Ballard.

"Then man with violin come back and kill me."

The two repo men looked at each other.

"No," said Heslip.

"Why is sex like insurance?" asked Rosenkrantz.

"The older you are, the more it costs," said Guildenstern.

"Their jokes are worse than Ray's," said Bart Heslip.

It was six A.M. Thursday. He and Larry were with the two bulky SFPD homicide cops in the upstairs conference room at DKA, where they had total privacy because nobody could get up the stairs without making noise. The cops had insisted on this since they were outside department regs just being there.

Rosenkrantz was bald as Kojak and Guildenstern had hair that looked fake but wasn't. It was rumored in the department that even their wives called them by their nicknames.

When they did good cop/bad cop, Guildenstern was always the bad cop. He had the eyes for it. He said, "You guys been talking for ten minutes and you ain't given us anything we'd be ashamed to tell our mothers."

"Only thing could embarrass your mothers is that they *are* your mothers," said Heslip.

Guildenstern looked at Rosenkrantz. "He being profound?"

"Just nifty," said Rosenkrantz.

"Just careful," said Ballard. "If you try to take down the game, our guy's family gets hit."

"And if he holds the game, he gets hit. We got that part of it."

Rosenkrantz was suddenly angry. "The mayor and the D.A. are always telling us there ain't any Mafia in San Francisco. Asian gangs fighting for power, maybe. Chicano gangs fighting over turf, perhaps. Black gangs fighting over drug money and rap music, could be. But —"

"But no Mafia action," said Guildenstern. "These days, local guys who are connected have only bookkeepers on their payroll. They need something done, they make a call and somebody gets on a plane out of Chicago or Detroit or even Cleveland."

Rosenkrantz took it up. "The threatener picks up his hardware at the airport on the way in, does what he does, leaves his hardware at the airport on the way out. We got a lot of names and reputations, but we can't get nothing on nobody."

"You're saying the guy with the violin case isn't local?"

"Tell us about him," suggested Rosenkrantz.

They did. The cops exchanged glances.

"Knuckles Colucci out of Detroit," said Guildenstern.

"Mean as a snake," said Rosenkrantz.

"Call the undertaker for your pal," said Guildenstern.

"Who hired him?"

The two big cops heaved themselves to their feet. "South Bay? Let us worry about that," they said almost in unison.

"Who runs the Chinese Benevolent Association?"

"Let us worry about that, too."

"You'll let us know when Colucci leaves home again?"

Rosenkrantz said, "What's the most important question to ask a woman if you're interested in safe sex?"

"What time does your husband get home?" said Guildenstern.

Larry and Bart descended the back stairs to the big back office that office manager Giselle Marc shared with the mainframe computer and the teenage girls who sent out legal notices and dun letters after school. Giselle was a tall, lithe blonde in her early thirties whose brains were even better than her long and wicked legs. This early she was alone in the office.

"Well?" asked Ballard.

"Every word," said Giselle with an almost urchin grin. She held up the tape recorder she'd had plugged into the intercom that Heslip, at her suggestion, had left open in the conference room. "Was that a yes or a no on Colucci from those guys?"

"A yes," said Ballard. "No, there'd have been no joke."

"If you think you're leaving me out of this, you're crazy."

"Never crossed our minds," fibbed Heslip.

They had been listening to the tape for about ten minutes when behind them O'B said, "Ahem."

Patrick Michael O'Bannon, in his early fifties, with guileless blue eyes in a leathery drinker's face splattered with freckles, was as devious as a two-headed snake. He was also the best repo man around save Kearny himself. He pulled up a chair and sat down.

"Now, you got a couple of holes in your plan . . ."

None of them thought about letting Dan Kearny, their boss, in on things. He'd just say no, then he'd take over their operation and run it himself. He did it every time.

The Chinese Benevolent Association was up a flight of creaky wooden stairs from an aged Buddhist temple on Old Chinatown Lane, a little stub of an alley just below Stockton Street. There was nothing to tempt the casual tourist or, indeed, any Caucasian to try the street door. It just bore a set of Chinese characters that spelled out God knew what.

Yet on this particular Thursday midday, two bulky white men came tramping up the stairs and into the reception room. It was hung with bright silk tapestries and there were delicate carved ivory figurines on inlaid tables. There was a hint of incense on the air. On the walls were numerous photos of association leaders shaking hands with local and national politicians.

A pert, pretty Chinese girl was making her fingers fly over the keyboard of a very modern computer. She looked up when they entered, finding a smile for them.

"May I help you?"

When they just walked past her toward the door in the back wall, she dove for the buzzer under her desk. But by then they were already into the next room, where a white-haired Chinese gentleman sat behind a desk arranged so no window overlooked it. A heavyset thug was coming out of his chair on their side of the desk even as he reached for his armpit.

Guildenstern put a big hand on the man's face and pushed. He pushed with stunning, unexpected strength. The thug went backward over his chair. Rosenkrantz was holding out his badge for the older gentleman to see.

"Rosenkrantz and Guildenstern, SFPD Homicide," he said.

The old man spoke sharply in Mandarin. The thug righted his chair, sat back down, and ceased to exist for them.

"Mr. Li?" asked Rosenkrantz.

"I am Fong Li," admitted the white-haired man gravely. His English was accented but elegant. He had a long, narrow, lined face with a thin aristocratic nose. His eyes were dark but benevolent, like his association. In any country of the world, in any race, at any time, he would have been a patriarch.

Rosenkrantz sat on a corner of the desk. "Ray Chong Fat."

"Ah so," said Fong Li, much as Ray Chong said, "No savvy."

"Guy came around and threatened him with death if he held your Asian card game this weekend."

"I am desolated that I have no information of this event for the honored gentlemen," said Fong Li.

Guildenstern turned from a table under the window with a delicate Chinese urn in one paw. "This one of them Ming vases?"

Fong Li went very still. He said very softly, "I can make inquiries and discover whether this game of which you illustrious gentlemen speak might be canceled."

"We don't want it canceled," said Rosenkrantz.

Surprise actually flitted across the Chinese man's august features. "Then I am sure that Mr. Chong Fat need not run —"

"We want Ray to run it this weekend," said Guildenstern.

Sudden comprehension illuminated Fong Li's face. "Ah so," he said again, with a very different inflection.

"But after this weekend, he don't have to ever run another one," said Rosenkrantz. "And he don't owe you any money. The books are balanced, the slate is wiped clean. Anything ever happens to him, or his daughters, anything at all . . ."

Fong Li bowed gracefully. "This insignificant person would not wish to insult such brilliant men as yourselves, but —"

"I said we were Homicide. We don't care about gambling."

A delighted Fong Li beamed. Rosenkrantz stood. Guildenstern carefully set the Ming urn back on the table.

"Nice vase," he said, making the word rhyme with *base.*

Two-Ton Tony Marino took his nickname from the heavyweight boxer Two-Ton Tony Galento, who had once gotten himself creamed by Joe Louis. Tony didn't weigh quite two tons, but even so he was built like a watermelon. When the phone rang in his Detroit office on the following Monday afternoon, he picked up without hesitation: The place was swept twice daily for bugs.

"Yeah, Marino."

"Tony. Leone in San Francisco. The *scemo* Chinaman held the game last Saturday night. So Knuckles'll have to come back out." Leone gave a sudden gross chuckle. "Blood on the chop suey by Wednesday, right?"

They said laconic goodbyes and hung up. Tony was a little offended. Leone had no real class. You didn't say things like that. Things got done, bing bang boom, they were over. Nothing personal. You never talked about them before or after.

He dialed the phone. When a machine answered, he told it, "Knuckles, on Wednesday you gotta make that West Coast delivery."

Shoehorned with the technician into the closed van parked on a side street in the South Bay town of Milpitas near the Summitpointe Golf Course, Guildenstern asked Rosenkrantz, "What's the leading sexually transmitted disease among yuppies?"

"Headaches," said Rosenkrantz.

"I think that's what we'll be giving our boy Leone."

"I especially liked the part about blood on the chop suey."

"Conspiracy to commit?" suggested Guildenstern.

"At least," agreed Rosenkrantz.

It was Wednesday again, and Knuckles was flying first class from Detroit to San Francisco. He was feeling good. No dry run today. The real thing. At SFO he went through the jammed, noisy, jostling terminal and down the two sets of escalators to the moving walkway. As he started along the angle-striped pedestrian walkway in the vast echoing underground garage, a tall elegant blonde with breathtaking thighs fell into step with him.

"Nice flight?" she asked. Her voice was soft, caressing.

"My name is Knuckles Drop-Your-Pants," Knuckles said with his most winning smile. She handed him a set of keys.

"The gold Allante," she said, and was gone among the endless rows of cars before he could think up another zinger.

He sighed, pulled on his thin rubber gloves, unlocked the Allante, got in. He knew damn well he would never be able to buy anything like that in his entire life. The black violin case was on the passenger seat. He unsnapped it and raised the lid. Yeah.

But as he was setting it upright on the bucket seat there was a knock on the window. The blonde. She had a cell phone up to her ear and was gesturing at him to roll down the window.

"Open the trunk." As she spoke she reached through the open window for the instrument case. "Hurry, there's no time."

She tossed the case into the trunk, slammed the lid, came back to slide into the front seat next to him.

"Terrorist bomb threat. They're searching all the cars with single men in them, so our only chance is to get you and that hardware out of here before they bottle up the garage." When he did nothing, she yelled angrily at him, *"Move it!"*

Knuckles had no experience of a woman like this. He put the car in gear, followed the arrows toward the exit as if on automatic. Just before the ramp down to the ticket booths, a hard-eyed red-haired man in his fifties stepped out in front of the car and held up a badge wallet with a freckle-splotched hand. He came around to Knuckles's side of the Allante.

"FBI. We're going to have to take a look in your trunk."

"You got a warrant?" demanded the suddenly strident blonde. "This is harassment! My husband has just picked me up from a seven-hour flight and I'm not going to have you getting filthy pleasure from pawing through my underwear looking for drugs."

"It isn't . . ." The redhead stopped and sighed and stepped back. "And they wonder why," he muttered under his breath. He gestured wearily. "On through, the pair of you."

Once they were on the exit road from the airport, she told Knuckles to pull over at the Standard station. She got out.

"Open the trunk. I'll get your case for you." She recited a phone number. "Remember it."

She retrieved the violin case, slammed the trunk lid, put the case back in the car, and finally leaned in his open window.

"If the heat's still on here at the airport when you're finished, call me and report," she told him.

This was the kind of thing Knuckles understood. He'd make damn sure the heat would still be on at the airport.

"If it is, maybe you and me can —"

"Sure. Whatever you want, Knuckles. Leone said to treat you right." She gave him a suddenly wicked, even debauched smile. "You'll be staying over at my place."

A freaking dream come true. Yeah! Do the Chink, call the blonde, then do her. All night. Paradise on a platter. In a feather bed, rather.

Knuckles turned the dead-bolt knob on the front door and flipped the OPEN sign over to CLOSED. Only when he was going down the aisle did he see that there were a couple of customers with the dead man. On the killing ground that was how he always thought of his prey: the dead man.

One customer was a tall blond guy with a hawk nose, the other a shorter, wider jig with a shaved head. Sexual excitement rippled through Knuckles. His first triple-header! Tonight he'd give that freaking blonde a ride she'd *never* forget.

All three men were eating ice cream cones, for Chrissake! Goddamn pansies, maybe. He set his violin case on the counter.

"I told you I'd be back," he said roguishly to the Chink. He opened the case, reached in. "The back room. All of you."

"Or?" said the jig.

"Or this," said Knuckles, and brought up from the violin case — a violin. He gaped down at it.

The Chink stuck an ice cream cone into his left eye. He yelled and clawed at the icy mess, and the white guy kicked him explosively in the balls. Pain shot through his entire being. As he coiled down on himself, mouth strained open in a rictus of pain, the black guy caught him with a terrific right cross that knocked three teeth right out of his head.

Knuckles Colucci came around sitting behind the wheel of the gold Allante in a no-parking zone at SFO's domestic terminal. His savaged mouth was bleeding and his groin was pure pain. Beside him on the other bucket seat was the violin case.

It was the blond bitch who had made the switch, of course. She'd had a second violin case in the trunk, and after the redheaded federal agent had been bluffed out . . . No! Not an agent. Part of the con. He'd been hidden by a pillar from the ticket-takers in the booths. No terrorist bomb. Nothing. But *why?*

Later for that. Get out of here, fast. He somehow pulled himself
together enough to reach for the ignition keys.

There were no ignition keys.

Both front doors opened. Two hulking men, one bald and the
other with a thatch of sandy hair, peered in at him.

"Knuckles Colucci, you are under arrest for attempted murder,"
said the bald one. He was opening the violin case.

"With a freakin' violin?" asked Knuckles hoarsely.

"No, with this," beamed the bald man. His hand came out with
a stubby machine pistol wearing a silencer as long as it was. "Looks
to me like an Ingram M11 using a .380 ACP. Heard it was your
weapon of choice, Knuckles, 'cause it'll just fit in a violin case.
Frilled barrel with a wire screen, a baffle —"

"And two spirals to decelerate the gases so the gun doesn't make
any noise at all," said the one with hair, slipping the cuffs on the
dazed Knuckles's wrists.

The bald one put his nose down and sniffed. "It's been fired, too.
The report I got said he shot up the Chinaman's place pretty
bad . . ."

"You know, Knuckles," said the other one, shaking his head,
"you're a real birdbrain, aren't you?"

All five of them were feasting at the House of Prime Rib on Van
Ness Avenue. It just seemed the kind of occasion to saw at slabs of
blood-rare beef two inches thick and to hell with diets and cholesterol and a size six dress.

Ballard raised his glass. "To Ray. For shooting up his own grocery
store."

"All that fun, and it's covered by insurance," said Bart.

"You make a hell of a Feeb," Giselle was saying to O'B.

O'B pulled down the lower lid of his right eye. "And you make a
hell of a con woman. You hit him with everything all at once, never
gave him a moment to think . . ."

They all drank. O'B, who was facing the door, gestured. Rosenkrantz and Guildenstern were threading their way through the tables. They came up and looked over the company with benevolence. Rosenkrantz spoke first.

"Hear about the blonde who got an AM radio?"

"It took her a month to figure out she could play it at night," said
his partner.

Giselle, as the only blond woman present, said, "What's SFPD Homicide's version of the Miranda warning?"

"You have the right to remain dead," said Larry Ballard.

"Have a seat, gents," suggested Bart Heslip.

Guildenstern shook his head and chuckled.

"We got an all-nighter going. Knuckles is in a cage downtown and squawking like a parrot, trying to get a deal. He's giving us everything he ever knew about anybody in the mob."

"Witness relocation?" asked Giselle.

"Four-time loser? No chance. We don't need him anyway. The feds are busting Two-Ton Tony back in Detroit right now — he took the conspiracy across state lines. He can buy the local heat but he can't buy the feds. He's going down."

"Leone?" asked Bart.

"We got him on tape talking about blood and chop suey. He'll get a five-spot at Q, be out in two — but by then somebody'll have eaten his lunch down there in the South Bay."

Ray Chong Fat asked almost timidly, "Mr. Li?"

Guildenstern said, "What do you call someone who's half-Apache and half-Chinese?"

"Ugh-Li," said Rosenkrantz. He clapped Ray on the shoulder. "Seems he made a bookkeeping mistake. You're all paid up with him forever, and you don't have to run any more games."

Ray looked at him for a long time. There was a great deal in the look. Then he said, "Chinaboy cook at dude ranch. One ranch hand, every day he come in, say, What's fo' dinner?' Chinaboy say, 'Flied lice.' Pretty soon, ranch hand always asking, 'Flied lice? You got flied lice fo' dinner?' Every day. So Chinaboy get book, study English. Next time ranch hand come in, say, 'Flied lice? Flied lice?' Chinaboy say, 'We have a very great sufficiency of fried rice — you plick!'"

Rosenkrantz beamed down at the others.

"What d'you think he means by that?" he asked.

"If you stand by the river long enough," said Ballard, "the body of your enemy will float by."

"Huh?" said Guildenstern.

JAMES GRADY

The Championship of Nowhere

FROM *Murder on the Ropes*

GENE MALLETTE and the kid named Sandy were wildcatting a double shift on an oil derrick fifty-five afternoons before Independence Day. Drill and generator motors pounded May's prairie air. Sandy laughed about something and smiled. Then a drill chain broke, whipped like a silver tie around his neck, and rocketed him to the top of the fifty-foot rig. His body swung there while pipes clattered and a driller screamed and all Gene could think about was Sandy's teenage face smeared oil black except for his happy eyes and the glint of white teeth.

The chain unraveled with a spin and Sandy crashed to the derrick floor.

Gene and another guy rode to town in back of the flatbed truck with Sandy's body laid at their boots. There'd been a spring snow two weeks before, so the truck didn't kick up much dust from the dirt road. The earth smelled damp and good. He heard the foreman in the truck cab say maybe the drought was over. They saw a skinny deer grazing by the walls of a deserted sod house. They saw the blue misted Sweet Grass Hills rising from the yellow prairie between them and Canada. Those three volcanic crags would have been mountains anyplace else but here in Montana. The foreman drove to the Shelby undertaker parlor. As they lifted Sandy off the truck, Gene heard the mortician's hand jingling silver dollars for those happy eyes.

"I'm done," said Gene, and walked to the boarding house.

He put a shower and a tub soak on his tab. Sat at the dinner table with other boarders and ate stew he didn't taste. Walked out to the sidewalk to sit on a bench, watch the people and cars around the Front Street speakeasies, and make himself think about nothing, nothing at all.

Least I got that, he thought.   ·

Just before sunset a rancher named Jensen staggered out of a speakeasy called the Bucket of Blood, walked to a roan horse cinched to one of the new electric light poles, pulled out a silver pistol, and shot the horse smack between the eyes. The roan plopped to the ground so hard it snapped the cinch. Jensen pumped slugs into the beast, filling the town with the roar of the gun. He had gone through a full reload of the revolver and had its cylinder swung open for more bullets when the black Ford with a big white star painted on each of its front doors pulled up behind the dead horse. Texas John Otis unfolded his grizzly bear body to climb out of the car, sheriff's badge on the left lapel of his black suit, a dead German sniper's ten-inch broomstick handle Mauser in his right hand. Sheriff Otis ripped the shiny revolver away from Jensen and slammed the Mauser against the rancher's skull.

"You dumb son of a bitch!" roared the Sheriff. "You shot your own damn horse!"

But by then Jensen lay draped unconscious across that bloody roan.

Gene turned away and saw her walking toward him.

He'd seen her before, back in '06 when she was nine and he was fourteen. Her white father moved her and her kid brother off the Blackfeet Rez to educate in Shelby instead of being sentenced to an Indian boarding school. Gene'd seen her every day when he was a high school senior. She'd skipped a grade so she was a shy freshman who wore her black hair like a veil. Gene just knew she wouldn't talk to him. Then he couldn't talk to her while she was still in high school and he was a graduated adult doing a man's job as a gandy dancer building railroads to bring homesteaders out West and ship the loot of the land back East. He'd seen her almost every week, often trying to corral her wild brother. Gene had seen her at the train depot the day he shipped out to the Marines for the Great War against the Kaiser. That day, damned if he wouldn't before he died doing what had to be done, he'd gone up to her, said: "Goodbye." She'd flinched — then lanced the gloom with her smile. When he came home from Europe with no visible scars, he'd seen her in the Shelby cemetery putting flowers on the influenza graves of the homesteader she'd married who'd been old enough to be her dad and the baby girl she'd let that dreamer father. After bloody California, as Gene's parents and their ranch died, he had seen her move to town when the great winds of 1920 ate the homestead she'd tried to keep going while working the schoolmarm job her husband had been white enough to let her get and the town had been Christian enough to let her keep for the full year of widow's black. Gene had watched as she waitressed at the Palace Hotel where she lived in the back room, sometimes with her brother when he was in town trying to find dollars for ivory powder he pumped into his arm. And Gene'd seen her sad smile two months earlier when he'd asked her out. She'd whispered: "I got nothing that's worth it for you." He'd seen her not believe him when he swore she was wrong, seen her walk away so she wouldn't see tears fall she couldn't catch.

But that night, he saw her and knew she was walking toward him.

She blocked the red ball of the setting sun as she drew near. They were together inside a crimson lake. He could barely breathe and the water of this moment turned her walk into a slow swim toward him, her hair undulating out from her shoulders, her dress floating around her calves. He remembered forever that dress was the blue of morning sky. She wore no makeup on her skin, which was the color of milked coffee. The scent of purple lilacs came with her. Gene felt like Sandy spinning free of the chain that hung him high above the earth as he fell into her midnight eyes.

He knew he said "Hello Billie" and she said "Hello Gene."

Maybe they tried to say more, but they couldn't, not until she said: "I need your help. I need you to meet with some men. They sent me to get you. They want you to do something. It might save me, but it won't be anything but trouble for you, no matter what they promise. But I had to come. I had to ask. I had to do that much. I'm sorry."

All of a sudden it was night. Lights came on throughout the town. The glow from the street lamp on the corner yellowed her skin.

"Is it a long walk?" said Gene.

"I've got their car."

The license plate on the Ford bore the county ID numbers from

Butte, two hundred miles to the south, the only place rougher than Shelby in the whole state. Butte was a smokestack city of 60,000 people, tough Bohunk miners digging up the richest hill on earth for Irish robber barons who ran the place with Pinkertons, dynamite and satchels of cash they spent to fight off Wobbly labor organizers and Ku Klux Klan Catholic haters and reform meddlers from back East. On a good day, Shelby only had 1,200 people crowded into its prairie valley, busted-out honyockers who'd believed the Iowa newspapers' lies about homesteading, ranchers like Jensen and cowboys who cut barbed-wire fences whenever they rode up to one, Basque sheepherders who couldn't converse with two-legged creatures, Blackfeet and Gros Ventre and even Cheyenne stepped off their scrub reservations hunting for hope or honor or a last resort hell of a good time, railroad men, shopkeepers, and saloon tenders and border runners and streetwalkers and roughnecks like Gene had become who were trying to cash in on the Great North Country Oil Strike of 1921 that had filled every hotel hallway with dime-a-night cots.

Gene liked the no-nonsense way Billie drove, shifting when she had to, not afraid to let the engine whine and work it up a steep grade rather than panic-shift to high, stall, and maybe die. She drove them east, out of town past the railroad roundhouse and the mooing slaughterhouse pens, up and over the rim of the valley. Lamps of the town winked away in the Ford's mirror. Somebody'd shotgunned a million white stars in the night overhead. The sky shimmered with green and pink sheets of northern lights, and the yellow cones of the car headlights showed only a narrow ribbon of oiled highway.

"This road goes all the way to Chicago," said Gene.

"We can't," said Billie. "I can't."

She drove into the night.

"Why me?" he asked.

"Because of who you are. What you can do. California."

"Because I'd come if you asked."

"I don't know what to say about that."

"We never did."

"No." She steered the car toward a farmhouse. "We didn't. Neither of us."

She stopped the car in the dark yard beside a Cadillac Gene thought he recognized.

"I'll take you back right now, if you want," she said.

"Will you stay with me?"

He saw her head shake.

"Then let's go," said Gene as he got out of the car. "They're waiting."

Her brother opened the farmhouse door. He wore a frayed white shirt unbuttoned at the collar, loose pants, and a pencil pusher's black shoes that were as dull as his droopy eyes. His right hand that pumped Gene's was strong enough to deal cards at the Palace Hotel but not much more, a weak grasp that whispered he was a man who couldn't cover his bets.

"Zhene Mallette!" he slurred. "What d'you say, what d'you know, good ta see you!"

"How you doing, Harry?" said Gene, though he knew enough to know that answer and sent all the question's sincerity to the man's sister. Gene's fingers brushed Harry back into the living room where the two men who mattered waited, and though he silently prayed otherwise, he sensed Billie step into the farmhouse behind him and shut the door.

The Cadillac in the yard belonged to the pudgy Shelby banker standing by the table supporting a bottle of pre-Prohibition whiskey and glasses. The brass nameplate on his desk in the bank read PETER TAYLOR — VICE PRESIDENT. He had a knotty head of not much hair and reminded Gene of a grinning toad who never said no to another fly.

"Good evening, Mr. Mallette," said Taylor. "Thank you for coming."

"Wasn't for you," said Gene.

"We know," said the other man, the one Gene had never seen. Least, he'd never seen that particular black-haired city-suited man who hadn't bothered to get up off the couch — or to either fill his hand with the .45 on his lap or hide the gun. Gene'd seen those eyes and that set of face once in the trenches, another time in a Tijuana cantina, a third time ringside at a smoker in Fresno, and the last and worst time in a set of chains headed through the work camp to the scaffold at San Quentin. Wasn't that the man was tough, though Gene knew he could take a beating and then some, it was that he'd crawl up off any floor you knocked him down on to tear your heart in two and suck in the sound of ripping flesh.

"Please," said the banker, "have a chair. Call me Peter."

"Never figured on calling you at all."

"Life adds up like we don't expect. Please, sit down. There, beside the woman."

"Where should I sit?" said her brother, but his words went into the night as *didn't matter*.

Gene eased himself into the folding chair closest to the couch and acted as if his legs weren't coiled springs. Banker Taylor settled into an easy chair and filled glasses with whiskey. Harry Larson strutted to the folding chair close to Gene, grandly lowered himself but misjudged his balance and almost crashed to the floor. By the time he got himself stable, his sister stood behind him, a hand on his shoulder. The man on the couch didn't move.

"Nice night for a drive." Gene sent his words to the banker, kept the man on the couch in his gaze. "But that whiskey is illegal. Seems like a man in your position would be more careful."

"Laws like Prohibition are for people who fear man's nature." Taylor held a whiskey toward Gene. When Gene didn't take it, Taylor sat the glass on a milk crate near Gene's legs. "Wise of you not to drink, given the opportunity in front of you. As for what's legal, a man like you who's served time in a prison work camp can't be sanctimonious."

"Your friend on the couch there would know more about prison than me."

"Never been," said the man on the couch. "Witnesses never make it to the trials."

Banker Taylor extended a glass of whiskey to the black-haired man. "Gene, you'll find that Norman here — pardon my manners, this is Norman Doyle — Mr. Doyle is a lucky man."

Doyle took the whiskey glass with his left hand; the butt of the .45 faced his right.

"You don't need a glass, do you, Harry? You took care of yourself as soon as your sis left for town. Your vice is still legal, though the politicians are going to fix that, too. And you, Wilemena — or should I call you Widow Harris? You know, Gene, she's been without a man for a long time. A broke-in mare without a saddle for the itch. I don't think we'll give her a glass. She's a woman, plus whiskey and Injuns don't mix, even if they are breeds."

"Get to it," snapped Gene.

"How you doing in the market?"

"What?"

"The stock market," said the banker. "Everybody plays the market these days. Going up, up, up. Going to make everybody a millionaire. How you doing in the stock market?"

"You know I'm not that kind of guy."

"You mean you can't be. 'Cause you don't have the money. So how you going to get rich? This is America. Everybody wants to get rich. Can't get a good car or the woman you want if you don't have silver dollars to jingle. Are you going to get what you want, what you need, by roughnecking other people's oil out of this God-forsaken ground?"

"I get by."

"And that's all you're getting. By. Passed by. Till one day the wind just up and blows you away like you were never here. Forgotten. But tonight, you're a lucky man. If you got the guts to be who you are and do what you can do better than any man in this state."

"Tell me."

The banker said: "You're a boxer."

Harry Larson blurted out: "Everybody knows, Gene! We all heard. You're the best!"

Billie squeezed her brother's shoulder and he shut up.

"I gave that up," said Gene. "I'm not ever going back in the ring."

Doyle said: "Yet."

"California rules don't matter up here," said the banker. "What that judge said —"

"It isn't about that."

"Maybe you don't have the guts for it anymore," said Doyle.

"It's not guts," said Gene. "It's the stomach."

"Killing a man should be no big deal for a war boy like you," said the man with the gun.

"I didn't kill him. We fought. I hit him. He went down. He didn't get up. He died."

"Oh." Doyle smiled. "So *you* didn't do it. What happened? Did some angel come down to the canvas and snatch his soul?"

"I don't know. Angels don't tell me their secrets. The only reason the night court judge called it reckless misadventure was to keep the locals from lynching me. Banning me from boxing in the state and sticking me in the work camp for ninety days got me out of town. When I got out, nobody cared anymore. Except me. I went home. So what's my boxing to you?"

"It's what it is to our whole damn town," said the banker. "We got us a heavyweight championship of the world going to be fought here. Jack Dempsey against Tommy Gibbons."

"That's just a joke going around," said Gene.

"Yes, it started that way. A joke. A telegram from a civic leader that was a publicity stunt to get Shelby a little free fame. As if anything is free."

"Who cares about fame."

"Be a modern man, Gene. Modesty is over. Useless. So is reality. Image is everything. What's true for a man is true for a town. This is a dirt road nowhere, but so what? If it can become famous, a celebrity, then riches and the happy-ever-after good life will surely follow."

"That's a load of crap."

"Maybe, but it's the way things work nowadays. The joke telegram was going to get us a few newspaper stories back East, a publicity stunt. But Dempsey's manager Jack Kearns called the bluff, agreed to his boy fighting for the championship in Shelby. Nobody out here wants to be a back-down kind of guy. So now this 'joke' thing has grown a life of its own, a bigger one every day. Dempsey's been guaranteed a hundred thousand dollars. Now accountants are estimating a total cash gate of a million to a million point four."

"What does that have to do with me?" Gene nodded his head to take in Billie. "With us?"

"We're going to heist the fight."

"*What?*"

"I don't believe the million-dollar-gate hype," said the banker. "But figure it's half that, and figure our plan will get us half of that half. A quarter of a million dollars split up among we five won't make us famous, but these days, that much cash will still buy us some sweet years."

"You're nuts!"

"No, I'm the inside man. If these locals knew the strings I've been pulling the last few years, they'd lynch me. I've been a public naysayer on this fight, but a whisper here, a question phrased just so, and suddenly people get an idea they think is their own. That's how I put this in place, that's how we'll take it."

"To make it work," said the toad, "we all need to be insiders. I inspired the idea that to perfect our glorious Dempsey-Gibbons fight, we need a preliminary bout: the heavyweight championship of Shelby. That'll put us all on the inside. That's how we'll rip it off."

"You want me to be your man in that prelim fight. Your boxer."

"Don't care if you win," said the pudgy banker in the lantern-lit farmhouse. "Don't care if you lose. All we care about is that you fight, that you make it go the distance, and that you climb out of the ring alive with enough left in you to do the job."

"Getting out of the ring alive seems like a good idea," said Gene.

"We're good idea men," said the banker. "The question is whether you got the guts and the smarts to be one, too. You can say no, walk out of here right now. If you're dumb enough to tell anybody what's what, we'll call you crazy and a liar. They'll believe us, not you."

"This hard world is hell on liars." The black-haired man reclined on the couch, made a show of keeping his eyes on Gene and the .45 automatic on his lap.

"How is it on crazies?" said Gene.

"Depends." Norman Doyle didn't smile.

"What if they have to carry me out of the ring?"

Doyle said: "Don't bother to wake up."

The hophead beside Gene looked at nobody.

"So what's it going to be?" said the banker. "Yes or no?"

"Never happen." Gene shook his head: "Forget about whether the heist would work, the crime thing isn't what I do."

"Then you can say goodnight and leave," said the toad. "Your Billie girl will drive you back to that charming boarding house. Say goodbye to her, then, too. She'll be leaving town.

"You see," continued the toad, "there've been expenses. Bringing Doyle up from Butte. Guaranteeing debts Harry incurred 'round the state. He was the one who knew of your fondness for his sister. She's a hell of a woman. A fine worker. But schoolmarming and waitressing won't settle Harry's debts. Bankruptcy foreclosure from the people Harry owes is permanent. So if our scheme 'never happens,' then Doyle will drive her to Butte so she can work buying her brother's lifeblood a few dollars at a time in an establishment whose proprietor I happen to —"

Gene was on his feet, the folding chair spinning behind him before he knew it, but not before Doyle'd filled his hand with the .45.

"You did this whole thing!" he told the banker.

"Let's say I brought elements together for a successful business venture," said Taylor. "Now you choose. What do you want that business to be?"

The black hole of the .45 watched Gene's heart. The banker watched his eyes. Harry Larson slumped with his face in his hands.

His sister stood behind him. Gene saw her soft cheek he'd never touched now scarred by a wet line.

Must have been deep into the twenty-first century before he said: "Who do I have to fight?"

"Doesn't matter," said Doyle.

"No," said Gene, "I guess it doesn't. How long do I have to get ready?"

"Seven weeks and change. You fight on the Fourth of July."

"That's not enough time."

"Make it be," said Taylor. "Inspired local sponsors 'found' Doyle to manage you. The mayor's sending an offer. Accept it. Also, cultivate your mustache: in your pictures, that's what we want people to see and remember, for your sake. Tomorrow, Billie will fetch you out to the old Woon ranch. The four of you will live there while you train."

"One of you might be able to run away for a while," said Doyle. "I'd catch you, but you'd have a while. But the three of you . . . easy pickings."

"I have enough running to do for the fight," said Gene.

"Good," said Taylor. He raised his whiskey glass: "And good luck . . . champ."

She drove him back to town. They didn't talk. The envelope with the offer from the mayor was in his mailbox. Gene scrawled *OK,* signed his name, and gave the clubfooted desk clerk two bits to deliver it. Gene settled his tab through the morning and stretched out on his last honest bed. Trains clattered through town on the tracks fifty yards from where he lay, but he let them go without him to clean forests and seaside towns.

Billie picked him up after breakfast. The highway snaked through erosion-farmed prairie spreading sixty miles west to the jagged blue sawtooth range of the Rocky Mountains. That highway beneath heaven's blue bowl sky led to Mexico. She turned left off that oiled route, put the Rockies at their backs as they followed a graveled snake trail. The farmland became hilly with the breaks for the river named Marias after some woman in Meriwether Lewis's life. Gene thought Lewis was damn lucky to be able to do that for her.

The peeling Woon house and barn stood against the horizon at the end of the road.

"There's two bedrooms upstairs, one down, and a room in the barn," said Doyle as he came off the front porch to where Gene and Billie parked. "I got the downstairs where I can hear the screen doors creak. You're upstairs, palooka, the woman, too. Hophead is in the barn."

Doyle led them into the barn, where the oven air was thick with the scent of hay and manure. Flies buzzed. A black horse whinnied from a stall. A heavy punching bag hung down into the open other end from one beam, while another dangled a speed bag. Dumbbells waited on a table next to boxing gloves, rolls of tape, and five pairs of canvas shoes.

"Taylor guessed about your size," said Doyle. "We'll get other stuff if you need it."

"I've got my own shoes and gloves for the fight." Gene picked up a pair of sneakers. "These'll work in the meantime."

From ten feet away, Doyle said: "So what now?"

"You got a knife?"

Doyle's right hand snapped like a whip to drop a switchblade out of his sleeve. Light flashed between him and Gene, and with a *thunk* the knife stuck into a stall wall. "Help yourself."

So I gotta watch out for that, too. Gene pulled the knife from the barn wood and cut his pants into shorts. Tossed the knife to the dirt in front of Doyle's shined shoes. Gene took off his shirts, changed his work boots for the new sneakers, said: "Time to train."

Working the oil rigs had kept him strong with endurance. That was crucial, but he'd need explosive power, too. He spent an hour working with dumbbells while telling Harry how to construct a flat bench for chest presses. He put a ten-pound weight in each hand to shadowbox. When his arms were on fire, he put on training gloves and moved first to the heavy bag, then to the speed bag. Gene's arms were so heavy that even if he'd had his old timing, the twenty-minute display of *tap tap miss* he gave the watching Doyle, Billie, and Harry would still have been pitiful.

"Seems you're working it backward," said Doyle. "Skill stuff should come first."

"Find out what skill you got when you're at your worst." Sweat covered Gene's bare chest. "Then you know how much further you've got to make yourself go."

" 'Pears to me you'll be lucky to make it out of this barn."

"I might not be the only one."

" 'Least you talk like a fighter." Doyle spit. "Woman: I'm hungry. Go make lunch."

"Make your own lunch," said Gene. "I need a spotter for road work and I don't fancy your company or figure Harry can handle the heat."

"Your job ain't to figure, palooka."

"Fine. You explain to Taylor how you chose to screw up me getting ready."

"I explain nothing to nobody." Doyle'd taken off his suit jacket so his white shirt showed dampness around the leather straps of the .45's shoulder holster.

But you won't push things too far, thought Gene. *Not yet.*

Doyle said: "I'm going to the house."

As he walked away, Gene told Billie what he needed.

She bridled the black horse. Didn't even look for a saddle. Swung herself up on its back, her dress swirling, hiking up past her knees. Her feet were bare, as were her legs that gripped the naked flanks of the black horse. Harry draped glass jars of water on each side of the quivering animal's neck. Billie tapped her heels against the animal, and he carried her out of the barn, her round hips split evenly along the beast's spine and rocking with the rhythm of each step. When she got into the sunlight, she turned back, gave Gene a nod.

Gene ran.

Out of the barn, through the yard, along the gravel road. Dust filled his panting mouth. Rocks stabbed the soles of his feet. He followed a wagon trail along the crests of the river breaks. A quarter mile and the house vanished behind rises and dips in the land. He dropped the strong set of his shoulders. Heard the *clump clump* of the horse behind him, the rattle of the glass water jars. A half-mile and he vomited, staggered, and would have fallen but somehow she was down on the ground beside him, holding him up as he wheezed and gasped and the world spun in bright explosions of light.

She poured water over him, made him wash his mouth and drink. "Can you do it?"

"Have to, don't we?"

Billie touched his sweaty chest. His slamming heart made her hand twitch. "Thank you."

"Have to run ten miles a day by end of next week."

She got back on the horse. He stumbled along for another three minutes before he turned around and made his mind see him running back to the house. He wouldn't let Doyle see him have to be carried back. Billie made Gene eat four scrambled eggs for lunch. Hosed him off behind the house. Laid him down on the bed upstairs while she unpacked his suitcase with his clothes, the canvas bag with his still supple ring shoes, blue satin trunks, and those blood-smeared black gloves. Before dinner she held his ankles while he did sit-ups until his midriff cramped at ninety-seven and he thrashed out of her control on the barn's dirt floor. He sparred with the heavy bag and the speed bag and lost both times. She watched for the five minutes he hung swaying from a pipe by both arms to stretch out and give himself a whisker longer reach. She couldn't tell that he'd tried to finish with a set of pull-ups and failed. Hosed him down again. Dinner was whatever and he ate it all, including the nighttime-only bone-building milk that could cut his wind. Upstairs, in only his underpants, he lay helpless while she sponged his face in the pickle brine he'd made Doyle get from town. Some trickled in his eye, but she was fast and put her hand over his mouth so his scream stayed muffled in the bedroom walls. She eased both of his hands into other bowls of brine: working the rigs had toughened their flesh, but every trick mattered. The brine stung in the dozens of cuts on his hands. He was too tired for pain.

"Would he do it?" said Gene. "Your brother. Make you . . . let them force you into . . ."

"Harry would hate that but he already hates himself. He'd shoot up and believe it was a trick of fate he couldn't help and can't help, something that'll go away if we just get through it."

"What about you?"

She turned away. "My mom died. My baby died. My brother's all I've got left to lose."

"There's you."

"You're the only one who cares about that." She shook her head. "Besides, they wouldn't just kill Harry, they know he wouldn't care. So they'd kill me, too, to prove the point to the world. At least if the two of us are still alive . . . we've got that."

She turned back to him. "You know that . . . whatever you want from me, you can have."

"I don't want anybody to hurt you. I don't want you to ever have to cry."

Billie left the bedroom. He lay there with his hands in the bowls of brine. *If the house catches fire, here's where I'll die.* The bedroom door opened and she came in carrying a roll of blankets and a pillow. She made a bed for herself on the floor, took his hands out of the bowls, pulled a blanket over him, but then he was gone into a sleep beyond rest.

The next day was worse. And the day after that. Bone-thumping soreness. Muscles of rubber, lungs of fire. Half the time he couldn't think straight as he lifted weights, tried not to trip and kept failing as he jumped rope. He'd hang from the pipe first thing every morning, drop down to bend and twist every way he could before Billie bridled the horse, filled the water bottles, and followed his stumbling run across the prairie. Heavy bag, speed bag, more rope, shadowboxing, then another run before dinner. Brine sponges and soaking. And always Doyle watching, hanging around, eating across from him and Billie, and when he wasn't on the needle, brother Harry, who kept trying to joke, who talked of what a fight it would be, of how all Gene's road work was building them streets of gold, a highway to heaven.

On the fifth night at the farm, Taylor sneaked out to see them.

"They found your opponent," said the pudgy banker. "Eric Harmon. He's got twenty pounds of muscle and two inches on you, and he's only two years out of high school. Won the Golden Gloves down in Great Falls, and he's got glory in his eyes."

"He can have it," said Gene.

"That's right. As long as you don't let him finish you off getting it."

Taylor left them a radio and left them alone.

Training the next day was hell. And the next. Nights while he soaked his hands, Billie read Sinclair Lewis to him as music played on the radio downstairs where Doyle smoked and watched the door. Gene could read just fine, but her voice was magic. He'd ask her questions. Knew she answered him with the truth, perhaps saying it for the first time in her life without qualification. About how her father bought her mother. About how Billie always knew she never belonged, not white, not Indian, not a man with power, not a woman with respect. How freedom only came when she lost herself in a book or at a movie or in a song on the radio. Or sometimes on a horse, galloping over empty prairie. How the only time she ever felt real was when she was teaching and some kid's face lit up as he got it, whether "it" was the Pythagorean theorem or the glories of Rome. How she took pity on the fatherly man who begged to marry her, gambled that he'd at least keep her safe. How he gave her baby Laura, who fiercely stirred her soul. How daughter and husband died coughing while Billie watched.

Gene answered her questions, too. About how after the blood of Belleau Wood he'd rotated to England, where a sergeant gave him a choice of boxing or the front. The ring seemed saner. Learning to slip and bob and weave, combinations and counters and timing.

"And I found out that while I could do a lot, I was only truly good, really good, born in the blood special good for one thing: boxing."

"Then knowing and having that makes you lucky."

"You'd think so, wouldn't you," he said.

She said nothing. Blew out the bed lantern and lay down on her floor.

The next morning he ran clear and cool in his head, heard the horse trot to keep up behind him. He went three hills farther than he'd ever gone before and ran back without stopping. Took only one jar of water from Billie. He used heavier weights, did more sit-ups, made the jump rope sing and swirl. Slipped on training gloves. The heavy bag hung in the sunlit barn. Gene glided to it on feet that didn't stick to the earth. He felt the rhythm of a breeze. Feinted once, twice —

Hit the heavy bag with a right jab that shook dust off the barn beam, a great slamming *thwack* that made the horse jump in his stall.

Gene turned and grinned at Billie. Saw her want to smile back, and that was something, almost enough. The heavy bag cried in pain for half an hour of his punches. He worked the speed bag like a machine gun. Doyle came out of the house, the leer gone from his face. Harry pranced around the barnyard like a chicken chirping: *What'd I tell you! What'd I tell you!*

And Gene breathed as a boxer.

That night Billie blew out the lantern on the bedside table, but instead of lying down on her floor, she stood there looking at him on the bed as moonlight streamed through the open window. The breeze stirred her hair and her long white nightshirt.

"You lied to me," she said.

"That's one thing I'd never do."

"You said you were only truly good at one thing, at boxing. But you're the best in the world there ever could be at this. At risking everything to save me. No one could do that better and there's sure no one who would ever want to."

The bed floated in front of the light of her eyes in that shadowed room.

"Do you think we're going to get out of this alive?" she whispered.

"Or die trying."

But she didn't laugh. Said: "Either way, just once, for one thing, I want to choose."

"That's what I want for you, too."

She lifted the nightshirt off over her head like a white cloud floating away to let her bare skin glisten with the lunar silver glow. The bed squeaked as she knelt on it, as she lay beside him. He'd never been so afraid of doing the wrong thing. She took his right hand and pressed it on her breast, filled it with her round, warm, stiffening flesh, and he felt her heart slamming as hard as his as she said: "Everything I can, I give to you."

"But do you want to?" he whispered.

Her breath came quicker, shallower, like she was running. Her long legs stirred against his. He pulled back, her face held away from his, her lips parted but unable to reach him, and he held her away until he heard her whisper *Yes!* she whispered *Yes!* she told him *Yes!* and as her bare leg slid up his thighs he moved into their kiss.

In the morning Gene found the edge. That knife line border where strength and hunger meet. That fury place when you sink into your eyes and your spine steels. You no longer walk, no longer run: you are a tight wind with legs like thunderclouds and lightning bolt arms. The smile on your skull is death and your mouth's coffee-metal-salty taste for blood doesn't care whose. He devoured ten miles of road with the scent of her on him, her hips bouncing up and down on the black horse. He shadowboxed in the barn with her watching everywhere and not there at all. Bare-fisted, slew the heavy bag with his favorite three-punch staccato rhythm and whirled without losing cadence to make the speed bag sing, then spun to snatch a horsefly out of the air with his right jab. He was totally in the moment of that hay-stinking, dusty, oven horse barn even as he was absolutely in eternity's every four-cornered canvas ring. Pain simply didn't matter. He was a boxer.

"Clean up," said Doyle. "We're all going to town, show the yokels we're for real."

Doyle drove and made Gene sit up front with him. Harry was a wire in the back seat beside Billie. She wore that blue dress.

Shelby'd been full before the fight announcement. Now Gene felt like he was in a beehive swelling with hot air from the beating of a million wings. The town had six dance halls for workers who'd flooded in to hammer up the eight-sided, 40,000-seat wooden arena rising like a toothpick skeleton on the edge of town. On the prairie across the tracks from the fight site stood an encampment of Indian tepees. Cars jammed Main Street. People stared and pointed. Men took it upon themselves to clear a slot for them in front of the movie house, holding up traffic, beckoning Doyle into the parking spot. When they got out of the car, hands appeared from everywhere to shake Gene's, to touch him on the back, the shoulders. The crowd stared at the Larsons, who followed in the wake of the fighter and his trainer, knew these merely local half-breeds were now somehow sacred, too. Fans smiled a dark hunger. An oilman's blond daughter whose eyes Gene had never marked now pulled at the gladiator with her sapphire gaze.

Harry jumped out front: "Let us through! Let Gene through!" They entered a barbershop. A white-shrouded half-clipped customer leapt out of his chair, and Doyle nudged Gene to obey the barber's plea to take that throne.

"On the house for you two boys," said the barber. "On the house."

"What two boys?" said Gene.

The back room curtain opened and out came a husky giant whose muscles bulged his shirt sleeves. Eric Harmon said: "Me and you."

The good part of Gene, the old part, the real part, wanted to say:

You were here first, Eric. Take the chair. But the boxer he was now smiled and leaned back for the barber's clip.

"I won't be long," said Gene. "Then you can have your turn."

"Don't I know it," said Eric.

Only the *snip snip* of scissors sounded in the barbershop as Eric leaned against the wall. Doyle sat, nodded for Billie and Harry to sit, too. Two other customers pretended to read magazines. On the street outside the window, none of the shoulder-to-shoulder crowd moved; all of them faced every which way they could to keep that glass in the corner of their eyes.

"Is that okay?" whispered the barber after he spun Gene around to look in the mirror.

"Looks damn fine," said Gene. "I look damn good, don't I?"

Thought: *Please Billie, know I don't mean it!*

"Never thought of you as a pretty boy," said Eric.

"I never thought of you at all." Gene got out of the chair, tossed the barber a quarter. Told the scissors man: "You do such fine work, think I'll hang around and watch."

Eric shook his head and took the chair. The white sheet whipped around him. Gene noticed the barber's shaking hands.

"Careful there, Pete. Don't nick our boy and make him red out too soon."

"Doesn't matter if he uses the razor," said Eric. "I don't bleed easy."

"We'll see." Gene looked across the room. "Mind if I put on your radio?"

The barber didn't break his concentration as he cut the younger man's hair, and Gene walked over, tuned the radio to some hot New York jazz. Gene turned the volume up.

Gene said: "I got to wash up. But not as much as some."

Then he walked through the curtain to the sink and the bathroom. The sound of radio jazz blanketed the room outside the curtain. Nobody could hear anything from the washroom. Gene turned on the water and didn't look around as he heard the curtain swing open, get pulled shut.

"Think we gave them enough show, Eric?" Gene took a towel off the rack, turned around, drying his hands. The younger fighter stood watching him. At least two inches. At least twenty pounds.

"This isn't a show for me," said Eric. "We never met, not really, but I know who you are, seen you around. Always kind of admired you. So you should know this isn't personal."

"At least you're that smart."

"This is about winning. About who's a champion. And that'll be me. I'll fight you fair, but I'll beat you."

"Eric, don't kill yourself over —"

"California was a long time ago. Not long for people out there in the street, but for guys like us who have to climb into the ring, damn near the weight of forever ago. I got no feelings for what you did, except sorry for you and the guy who fell."

"I knocked him down."

"You'll have to do more than that to me. This is my only chance to prove I'm somebody."

"No it's not."

"Sure it is. Just look at you."

Then the younger man stuck out his hand. When they shook, he didn't try to crush Gene's fingers, and Gene suddenly loved him for that.

"Give me a good fight," said Eric. "I want to know I won something hard."

Gene didn't know what to say. Let him leave with silence. Gene gave him time to get clear of the barbershop, swept open the curtain, and there stood Sheriff John Otis.

"'Pears I didn't have to hustle down here after all." Texas John's eyes pulled back from Gene to take in Billie, trembling Harry. Doyle. "Don't see no trouble to put down."

"Could have been," said the barber. "Why —"

"My law ain't about 'could be.' 'S about what I see with these two good eyes." Those two good eyes rode Doyle. "Though just 'cause I size up a son of a bitch doesn't mean I'll give him what he deserves. But when he makes his wrong play, I drop the curtain."

"Just like you were in a movie, huh?" said Doyle. "Not out here in the real world."

The sheriff laughed, and his suit coat *coincidentally* opened with his swinging arms. Gene saw the Colt Peacemaker holstered on Texas John's hip like it had been in his Ranger days. Saw the wooden stock for the Mauser slung under Otis's right arm, knew that thousand-yard sniper automatic hung near the sheriff's heart.

"This ain't the real world. This is Shelby."

"Imagine that," said Doyle.

"Don't have to," answered Texas John. "I'm here. And we got phones and everything. And when I called around about a curly-haired fancy-dancy with a Butte license plate who claims to be a boxing manager, the boys down there wondered how you ended up in an honest game."

"Just lucky, I guess."

"Luck is a fragile thing," said Doyle. "Be sure to watch it close. You can bet I will."

The sheriff told Gene: "You in with some fine people, Home-town."

His black cowboy boots shook the barbershop as he tromped out to Main Street.

"We're back to the ranch," said Doyle.

Great by me, thought Gene. Every day his training ran him like a growing steel tiger. Every night he lay beside Billie. He needed less sleep and more of her. She gave him all she could reach. She'd ask questions, care about his answers.

"What was the hardest thing to learn about boxing?" asked Billie.

"Making yourself pull down into the fighter's crouch where you could hit and where you could get hurt. Getting past the terror. Your mouth all dry, your stomach heaving in and out, and you look across the ring and see that steely stare coming back at you and you hope he doesn't see your stomach fluttering and then you see his and it's jumping like mad, too, and oh Christ, any second they'll ring that bell."

He told her how easy it was to forget to keep your guard up. How his favorite combination was a lightning left-left-right, and when you throw the left jab, how you had to remember to bring it back at eye level, quick and straight. How after the second left, your dance had to move your left foot four inches to the left so your shoulders squared up and gave your right jab the snap that created power. How the uppercut was easy, go pigeon-toed and corkscrew your punch. How the hook took him months to learn, how he practiced a million times with each fist until he could keep his elbow up and whip it out tight and close, just eighteen inches of loop — two feet and it's an arm punch, a pillow, a joke, a nothing and left you only with how lucky you were in dodging the others guy's coming-in cannonball.

"But besides being good at it, what do you like about boxing?"

Took him all the next day to find the answer. That night they lay like spoons in the darkness, his face brushed by the perfume of her hair, her bare spine pressed against the mass of his chest, the two of them alone on the white sheet of their starlit bed.

"In the ring," he whispered, "what's happening is real. True. Even the feints, the fakes, and the cheats. You use every single bit of yourself and find more you didn't know was there. No chain is gonna whip out of the sky and hang you dead and dropped before you know it. You're not gonna need to shoot your own damn horse. You know exactly who you are. Where you are. It's a fight. You're a boxer."

She said nothing.

Then told him: "This here with you is the closest I've got to that."

Told him: "You say the one special thing you can do is boxing. The one special thing I can do is make you love me."

Billie curled into a ball, away from him and into him at the same time, her head pulling away on the sheet from his kisses even as her round hips pushed back against his loins, pressed against him, rubbing, and Gene gave himself to her.

Nine nights before the fight Doyle threw open their door, stood backlit in the entrance as Billie jerked the sheet over her nakedness and Gene sneaked one bare foot down to the floor.

"Wake up and dress, palooka. I need a driver."

"That's not my job."

"The hophead's too shaky, so it's either you or the woman. If it's her, the coming back to you will take a good while longer. That's okay with me."

Gene made the time as midnight when he drove Doyle away from the farmhouse.

"They say a woman weakens a boxer," said Doyle. "Steals his legs. His wind."

"Only way to find out is to get me a sparring partner. Why don't you volunteer?"

"You'd like that, wouldn't you, punchy?"

"I'm just doing the job I said I'd do."

"No. Tonight you're driving. Like I say you'll do."

Doyle made him take a back road into Shelby. Music came from the joints on Front Street. Doyle had him park on an alley slope up

from the drop-lit rear door of Taylor's bank. "Shut off the lights
and engine, but keep your hand on the starter."

"We meeting the man?"

"Might say that if you weren't supposed to keep shut up." Doyle
bent over to hide the strike of a kitchen match that let him check
his watch: ten minutes to one. Doyle puffed out the blue flame. Sul-
phur smoke soured the darkness. He eased out the passenger door,
flapped his suit coat so it was loose.

"When I come running, you start the engine. Keep the lights
out." Doyle crept to a shed where the shadows hid him from the alley below, stood there like a rock.

Gene knew time in three-minute increments. In the middle of
the sixth round, way down the slope, between two Main Street
buildings, Gene spotted the hulking figure of a man walking toward the alley. The man stepped out of the passageway: Sheriff
Otis.

From that distance, the car with Gene was an innocent shape,
one of the new vehicles crowding into town for the oil rigs or the
railroad spur they were building for the chartered trains from back
East. Even if the ex-Texas Ranger spotted the car, its engine was off,
its doors were closed. Shadows cloaked Doyle. Sheriff Otis walked
along the flat stone wall of a building and into the cone of light
dropping down over the bank's rear door. Otis wrapped his
gun hand around the bank's doorknob to be sure it was locked
tight.

Gene barely heard Doyle's whisper: "Draw!"

Saw the shadowed man's solo hand clear his suit coat and snap
straight out toward Otis.

Saw the flash of the pistol and heard its roar as a blast of crimson
graffitied the bank's cement wall below the doorknob and Otis
flipped into the air and crashed to the alley.

Doyle leapt into the car and they sped to the back road south.

"Got the son of a bitch just like I wanted!" yelled Doyle.

"Sucker shot!"

"Depends on which side of the trigger you're on. Besides, I could
have put the pill through his black heart, but instead he'll get to
gimp around and play the local hero."

"What makes you so kind?"

"A dead lawman brings heat from everywhere. A cripple is a
joke."

"Hope he doesn't bleed out."

They hit a bump.

Doyle said: "Those are the risks you take."

Three nights later, six days to the fight, Taylor drove out, told Doyle: "Perfect job. The town fathers gave a local guy the badge. Otis is parked in his house on the east end, sitting on the porch with his gun on his lap, his leg cemented up, watching the trains go by, and cursing like a son of a bitch. Somehow everybody's talking about two guys with Texas accents who blew into town and now can't be found anywhere. Almost like they never existed, but they must have been the ones. A man's past come back to haunt him. Happens all the time."

"Will he walk again?" asked Gene.

"Who cares?" said Doyle. "The law dog's not gonna be there to figure what he can't see, he's not gonna be able to run after no robbers."

"You will have to run," said the toad to Gene. "In all the confusion, our locals won't piece it together but, quick enough, they'll take it to the real lawman. He'll figure your part, especially since he already's got a lead on Doyle. But Doyle's good shot bought you half a day at least.

"After the heist, this is the first place they'll look. Doyle'll plant a burned map of Mexico in the trash ashes. But you go east to that farm where we met. Cut up the cash. Hide my share in the lockbox under the living room floor. Harry, leave the money you owe. Doyle will peel off extra bills for expenses. There'll be scissors, hair dye. A razor for your mustache, Gene. If you're banged up from the fight, there'll be a sling for your arm and doctor's papers about a farm accident. Only lie when you have to. A close trim, a henna, and Billie'll look respectable. The shed has a change-up car. Alberta plates. Harry knows the bootlegger trail into Canada. The four of you'll hit that whistle-stop depot at Aden before the evening papers. Doyle'll have train tickets to Vancouver for Mr. and Mrs. Louis Dumas. Doyle figures he'll like New York: Anybody can be anybody there. Harry, you can help Doyle drive to the big time or he'll let you out on the way, your choice."

"What about you?" said Gene.

"I stay here to keep messing with the minds of our friends and neighbors. A year from now, I regretfully leave this paradise for a better job. Six months later, I vanish a free man."

"What's to stop us from keeping all the money?" said Gene. "You won't go to the cops."

"You're too smart to risk running from my insurance men plus hiding from the law." Taylor smiled. "Besides, you and the Larsons are fundamentally honest people. A banker learns how to judge that real quick."

That moonlit night as she floated on his chest, Billie whispered: "Would Doyle double-cross our banker?"

"No. Not as long as it's all working. They're both too clever for that."

"What about us?" whispered Billie.

"Yeah." A breath made his chest rise and fall. "Any way you look at it, what about us."

On the first day of July the thermometer said it was 92 degrees in the shade. Doyle was gone; Harry was stoned. After his morning run and workout, Billie stretched Gene out on their bed, rubbed him down, lay beside him like every morning. They napped. Something woke Gene before the ticking alarm clock. The window glowed like molten white gold. He shielded his eyes and shuffled to the edge of the fluttering curtains.

Out there. By the barn. Doyle closing the trunk of his Ford and carrying a shovel back into the barn where maybe it hadn't been hanging that morning.

That night, Gene told Billie: "Tomorrow I need you to go to town. With Doyle. If Harry comes, even better, but you've got to get Doyle away from here and keep him away for at least half a day. Say it's for supplies or whatever, but you've got to get me free of him." She nodded in the darkness, and he hated them both for the creeping fear.

The next day, the second day of July, two days before the fight, he watched as Billie drove away from the farm toward Shelby. With Doyle. Doyle alone.

Gene ran to the barn, found Harry slumped on a stool. Harry sat in that manure oven, his shirt sleeves buttoned tight on his wrists, flies crawling untroubled on that face where the eyes clung to open above a slack-jawed smile. Gene said: "What kind of man are you?"

"Wasted," answered Harry.

"Can you still lie and do it good enough to save your sister?"

Harry stared at ghosts standing witness. Licked his lips, told Gene: "I'm the kind of guy who says *whatever* and then believes it's true. Believing a lie helps sell it. So you're telling me that for once in my stupid life, what I gotta do is just be myself? Even I can't screw that up."

Can't do it like Billie, thought Gene as he saddled the black horse while lecturing her brother: "If Doyle beats me back, tell him I took the horse to ride out my crazies. Sell him that. If I get back first, we got to get this horse in his stall like he never left it."

As he galloped away, Gene didn't look back at the man slumped in the barn door.

Way he figured it with Billie's talk about the Pythagorean theorem, from the barn on the ranch south of Shelby to the farmhouse east of that town was just under fourteen miles. But that was one way, and across fenced rolling prairie and farmland where somebody might see him.

Somebody, but not Doyle. He'd be busy. In town. With Billie.

Gene boot-heeled the horse's flanks. *Not for nothing. Not all this for nothing.*

Misted indigo humps of the three Sweet Grass Hills rode a horizon of blue sky. Fields of wheat Gene and the horse charged through were losing green to gold, baking to an early harvest in the ninety-five-degree heat. The horse reeked of wet sweat. *Would Doyle's nose pick up that scent rubbed on a man? When he got back. With Billie.* A circling hawk watched Gene cut the first of many barbed-wire fences. *I'm just like an old-timer now,* he thought as he rode through the savaged fence. *What was it like for them? Fields of horse-belly-high buffalo grass instead of sodbuster-ruined scrub and wheat planted for starving Boston urchins. What was it like for Billie's people who rode this endless open with a hundred million buffalo?* Gene heeled his horse.

He spotted the farmhouse. Nobody else had seen him, though he'd seen a wagon ferrying a Hutterite family in their religion's strange black pants, homemade checkered shirts, and plain faces. They'd ignored a frantic horseman who galloped past them, cutting fences before they were even out of sight. They'd tell no one outside their colony what they'd seen: nothing outside their community of God mattered.

Gene sat in the saddle on the heaving horse. Watched the farmhouse for ten minutes. Saw nothing move. He made the horse trot forward.

"Hello?" he called. No answer. He reined in the horse by a garage window. Gene peered inside: dusty sunlight showed him a coupe with Alberta license plates. And only two seats.

Took him one loop around the farmhouse to spot what he hadn't found at Woon's ranch. Behind a shed was a freshly shoveled solo hole in the earth, six feet long and four feet deep, its dirt pile waiting beside that gaping maw.

Call me a lucky man, thought Gene. *Not many people get to see this.*

Doyle, you lazy bastard. Four feet isn't deep enough for even one in this coyote country.

From the saddle, he nudged open the shed door and saw three sacks of quicklime.

Gene pulled the door shut, then jerked the reins and kicked the frothing horse home.

In a gully a mile from the Woon barn, the horse staggering beneath him, Gene glanced over the ridge toward the highway: two cars turned off that main road toward the ranch.

"Go!" he kicked his boot heels. The exhausted black beast stumbled through the rocky gully circling Woon's ranch. If Gene rode low and kept the horse's head down, maybe no one driving up in a car would spot him. He risked a scouting peek over the sage-brushed ridge.

Saw Doyle's Ford and the toad Taylor's Cadillac closing in on the ranch.

From the barn ran Harry, stumbling into the path of the cars so they had to stop, had to not get to the ranch as he waved his arms and ranted like a man poisoned with monsters.

"Hya!" Gene charged the horse through the gully, around the back of the ranch, up out of its shelter, and into the barn as car engines whined closer. Gene rode the white-foamed black horse into the open stall, flipped off the saddle and almost ripped the teeth out of the wheezing horse's mouth as he stripped off the bridle, let it fall to the stall floor as car engines stopped. Gene raced toward the mass of sunlight filling the barn door —

Out, charging toward the two cars emptying of Doyle and Taylor and caught-a-ride Harry. And Billie. Gene yelled: "Where the hell have you been!"

"In town!" called Billie. Her face told him the truth: "Just in town."

Gene whirled to Taylor: "Why the hell are you here?"

"The town dispatched me to brief you on their plans." The toad smiled. "And I'll tell you ours. All that sweat: you've been working out. Good. But rest now. Hot out here. Let's go inside."

Gene snapped: "The barn?"

"I'm no animal," said Taylor, and led everyone into the house.

Sitting in the Woon living room, Gene told Taylor: "Sounds like we ain't going to have a fight. The radio says the chartered trains from back East have all canceled. No money, no fight, nothing for us to steal. Dempsey's boss Jack Kearns says —"

The toad lunged across the room to scream at the sitting boxer: "The fight is happening! Don't you say that! The fight is happening and we're . . . we're . . ."

"You're wound tight," said Gene. "Just as tight as one of the real boosters."

"Worry about you!" Taylor's hands shook. "You got to fight fifteen rounds and still be workable! Don't worry about Kearns! The fight's going to happen! They're meeting in a bank right now getting seed money! People will show up with cash they owe for tickets! And the chartered trains! They're going to run full speed from St. Paul and Chicago and fifty dollars ringside! They're bringing all that money so we can take it! Nobody's going to keep it from us!"

Gene shrugged. "You're the boss."

Saw Doyle staring at the trembling toad.

"Yes," said Taylor. "Yes I am. And this is how it works.

"Under that wooden arena are four rough dressing rooms, one for each fighter. And a collection room for all money coming through the gate. By the sixth round of the Main Event, accountants figure ninety percent of the gate cash will be in. To get it to the bank, they'll send a posse in the seventh round. Kearns will make Dempsey take it that long so people get their money's worth. Everybody knows Dempsey can put Gibbons away, so they will all be glued to the ring for the first rounds, for the quick knockout. Guards will be on the gates leading down into the dressing rooms and collection area. But inside there'll only be fighters, their trainers, a couple counting room clerks — and all that cash.

"You've got to take Eric the full fifteen rounds so you'll have an excuse to still be inside when the Dempsey fight starts. Change fast. Pillowcase masks and gloves go inside with you. Soon as the crowd roars with the bell starting Round One, you three run to the count-

ing room, muscle inside, tie up the clerks, grab the cash, walk out
with everything stuffed in your gear bags. Billie picks you up out
front during the fifth round while the posse is still at the bank.
You're gone before anybody knows anything is wrong."

"No killing," said Gene.

"I'm not a necktie fool," said Doyle. "We got handcuffs and tape
strips for the clerks. Shouldn't be more than two of them. I'll be
gun man, you truss them up, Harry scoops up cash."

"You know the rest of the plan," said Taylor.

"Yes," said Gene, "I do."

"So," said the banker to Gene as he stood to leave: "How you
gonna do in the fight?"

"Swell."

"Glory," said Doyle. "Ain't it great."

That night Gene and Billie made love for the last time before the
fight.

"We have to beat everybody," Gene whispered to her. "Even
Harry, and we have to clue him in as much as we dare. We have to
do the holdup. Not let anybody die. Get to the car. Then take over
Doyle, wrap him up. Drive out east to Texas John's, dump the
whole true thing on him, and convince him ours was the only way.
If we turn in the cash plus the guy who shot him and stole it, we got
a chance. Maybe Doyle will rat on Taylor, too, buy himself a deal.
The men Harry owes won't go after you two: you're not worth it to
be roped in as accessories. I'll do time if I have to. No matter what,
you'll be free."

"You mean from all this."

"From all that you want free of."

"It's a terrible plan."

"Yes," he said. "I know."

Heaven moved aside and let the noon sun boil down on a bull's-
eye boxing ring that Fourth of July, 1923, a black-roped canvas
square centered in the heart of an octagonal sloping wooden arena
on a sallow dust prairie. Gene wore those bloodied black gloves,
blue satin shorts, and his second skin shoes. For a long count he existed alone in the hollow, dry breeze, floating in slow motion,
bouncing on the balls of his feet, jabbing air that was as thick as invisible molasses. He lived in the belly of a blazing whiteness. He
heard his rasping breaths, his cannon heartbeat. Then gravity's

roar rocketed him back to a box of glory in Shelby, Montana, to Doyle and Harry wearing corner-men's white shirts and bow ties and sweating at their post, and Gene knew everything had gone terribly wrong.

"Nobody's here!" he yelled to Doyle. "Look out at the stands! Like three rows of people! Maybe three hundred at most! Empty bleacher seats stretching all the way up to the sky!"

Toad Taylor bobbed outside the ring beneath their corner, a ridiculous straw skimmer knocked off-center above his crimson face as he shook both hands in the air and hissed at them: "They're coming! The charter trains! Don't believe them when they say they didn't go! We stopped the rumors about no fight! We did! So they have to go! They have to be here! Plus the crowds outside! Thousands of them! You're just the throwaway! The time filler! The real people will be here! They'll bring the big money! They have to! They must! This is the heavyweight championship of the world!"

But not for Gene.

Or for Eric Harmon, younger, taller, heavier muscled, and abruptly materialized in the opposite corner. The sheen on Eric looked like the boy had oiled himself, but Gene knew it was sweat: Eric would not cheat. Eric's eyes were bullets. As their gloves fell away from the referee's handshake, Gene felt Eric drop benevolence he'd cradled for a lifetime.

Then rang that bell.

A whirling fury charged across the ring to Gene, gloves hooking and jabbing and feinting fast, so fast, trees falling on his raised arms as Gene backpedaled, saw flashes of sky and flesh flung his way. Eric connected with a right hook Gene blocked with his shoulder. Gene spun —

Hit the canvas and bounded up before the referee could count two. The bell rang.

"He's killing you out there!" screamed Doyle in the corner as he sponged Gene's face.

"He's trying."

"The fight's gotta last!" Doyle glared into Gene's face. "Decide how you want to die."

Ding!

Gene took the ring and meant it. Eric rained blows at him. Gene slipped a punch and fired his jab back along the younger man's arm in a blow that shook Eric's face. But Gene pulled the last two punches of his combination. Eric didn't care. Round Two, Three, Four, Five. Eric matched each ticking second of the clock with a punch, a move, a charge.

Round Six Eric bloodied Gene's mouth. Not much. A trickle of salty wet inside his cheek. The bell rang. Gene went to his corner. If Doyle or Harry said anything, he heard them not. He swallowed. When the bell rang, a new beast pranced out to meet Eric.

All fights have a rhythm, a jazz that is the two combatants and the fight itself, a music that shimmers beyond the sum of its parts into a set with its own time and place and fury. Often individual elements of a fight so dominate that the jazz is muted or lost to naked eyes and souls. But even then, the jazz is there. The true boxer senses that jazz in his bones, a feeling he can't create alone but one that he can slip into, and through it, become it. And command.

Round Seven came the jazz, and the jazz was Gene. Eric's punches hit him and hurt, damaged and didn't matter. Gene's jabs slammed into the bigger man on time, in rhythm. Gene's mind cut a deal with the jazz to play long enough to keep the set alive as Gene's gloves smacked the meat of a young man. Here the ribs. There a hook to the face. Left-left-square up right *bam!* Over and over again. Round Seven. Eight. Nine. Ten. Eric fought with everything he had and more, but in this music *that* was his sound, his damning sound: Eric was a fighter fighting. Gene was a boxer. Force against finesse. Strength against science. Work against art. Eric had a heart full of prayers but the angels' chorus was jazz.

Round Eleven. Blood ran from Eric's ears and nose. He threw off the referee. *Come on!* his gloves beckoned Gene. *Come on!* Round Twelve. Thirteen. Gene danced him into a clinch.

"You can have it!" whispered Gene. "I'll take a dive in the fifteenth! Don't make me do this!"

Eric pushed off him and wildly swung-missed. Spit out his mouthpiece. Through broken teeth yelled: "Hell wi' you! I'm real!"

The low punch Eric threw might have hit home in Round One, but now Gene slid back and let it fan. Without thought, Gene's right counter slammed his opponent's jaw. Eric hit the canvas so hard Gene bounced. *Stay down!* Gene willed. Eric staggered up on the seven count.

Round Fourteen. Eric stood in the center of the ring like a heavy bag absorbing punch after punch from Gene, who for a fury blind minute couldn't stop. Then he backed away, only bobbed back in close when it looked like the referee would call it.

Fifteen. Final round. Strings down from the sky plucked Eric off his corner stool and puppeted him toward Gene. Blood and sweat trickled down both of Eric's arms to drip on the canvas. His guard didn't rise above his belt. Gene tapped his face twice. Eric staggered back —

A roar from the soles of his shoes tore through the state. Eric charged, his arms swinging slow wild haymakers like a baby, his eyes drowned by gore streaming from his splattered forehead as he yelled: "W're are 'ou? 'Hre 'ou? Fight me! Fight me!"

No one should lose like that. Gene snapped up a perfect guard, danced in. As softly as he dared, Gene hooked a right into the staggering man's cheek and felled him to the canvas.

The referee stood there, not bothering to count ten. The last bell rang.

Gene knew the referee raised his hand. Knew Harry gave him water, wiped him down. Knew the mayor bounded into the ring and hung a gold-painted brass medal around his neck. Men carried Eric out of the ring. Gene saw his chest move and knew that boy's hands still clung to life inside bloodied boxing gloves. And as Gene staggered between the ropes Doyle held and saw an arena overflowing with empty seats, he knew that now began his real fight.

Momentum pulled him to the arena corridor. As they walked past the stands, Gene saw a man pass a Mason jar to the only other two people sitting in the row. Gene knew the Mason jar didn't hold the concession stand's lemonade. Going down the corridor's ramp, Gene and his crew met a squad of trainers and corner-men coming up with night-haired Jack Dempsey.

Dempsey hit Gene with eyes that were black ice and saw everything about him, the sheen of sweat, the glint of brass around his neck, the blood splattered on Gene's chest. *I'm taller than him,* thought Gene as they drew close. That flicker of arrogance whispered to Dempsey. His gaze jabbed Gene's soul and Gene knew: never had a day that good, never will.

The paltry paid crowd roared when they saw the true champion emerge into the sunlight.

The lone guard on the door to the walled-in area for the dressing and other rooms told Gene's crew: "Not a single chartered train came! And everybody else is still hanging outside!"

"Nothing changes!" hissed Doyle as they hurried to the pine-planked sweat chamber the promoters grandly called a dressing room.

Inside, door closed. Harry threw a bucket of water over Gene, wiped him with a towel. Kept muttering: "Great fighter, you're a great fighter, great fight. Not me, you. 'S' thing to be." From a duffel bag, Doyle pulled pillowcases cut for masks and money hauling, his .45 shoulder rig, a suit jacket. He tossed revolvers to Harry and Gene.

"Don't worry, Champ. They ain't loaded."

Gene said: "If the trains didn't come —"

"We take what's there!" said Doyle. "You better pray there's enough!"

Gene had only his shirt left to button when a thunderous *creak!* rolled through the wooden arena. The room around them bent and screamed. From outside came a great roar. Three would-be holdup men ran into the dungeon of rooms built under the area. The dim hall was empty. They ran to the corridor door. No guard. They hurried up the ramp into a blast of sunlight. Dempsey and Gibbons danced in the ring for Round One, but the great rolling-herd roar of a thousand voices caught even their attention.

In they came from every entryway. Men in suits and straw hats, work boots and denim. Women in long skirts and yellow scarves. Umbrellas and pocket flasks. Clothes ripped by the barbed wire and turnstiles they'd torn down to storm inside for free. Damn the big money they'd never have: no one would keep them from their championship.

"Look!" Harry pointed to a corridor a hundred feet away. A toad of a man, his straw hat askew, hopped back and forth in front of a stampeding phalanx, his hands outstretched to hold them back, screaming so loud that even Gene and his crew heard him: "Go back! You didn't pay! You've got to pay! Everybody's got to pay!"

Laughter drowned him out as he spun into the ranks of wild-faced men and cackling women. Gene lost sight of Taylor as the crowd swirled. The banker popped out, pressed against a railing as elbows and shoulders slammed his back. The toad's face was a purple moon with craters for eyes and the scream of his mouth. Taylor's hands clutched his chest like he'd been punched, clawed at his throat fighting a strangler. A well-wisher poured amber liquid from a pocket flask into the uptight banker's maw. Taylor choked, gurgled. He flopped over the rail as the crowd surged into the arena. Revelers plucked the banker from the rail and dragged him along until he sprawled into a hatless toad heap on a bench, reeking of bootleg whiskey like he was dead drunk, but Gene knew the toad was just dead, that he'd bake in the sun until the cleaning crew and newspaper eulogies told about an innocent casualty of championship fever.

"Gone." Harry trembled as he stared at the chaos. "'Sall gone to crazy!"

"Come on!" yelled Doyle as the crowd of twelve thousand gate crashers scrambled in and the bell rang the end of Dempsey-Gibbons Round One. "We've got a job to do!"

"No good," muttered Harry as Doyle marched them back down inside the bowels of the arena, past the unguarded corridor door. "Nothing's no good 'less you're a fighter."

"Shut up!" snapped Doyle as they hurried back to Gene's dressing room.

Harry plucked at Doyle with a trembling hand: "No good, you're no good, this is all gone no good and we know what you're going to do!"

Shut up, Harry! willed Gene.

Harry chose to fight for the first time in his life. He jumped on Doyle: "Get him now, Gene! Don't wait!"

Doyle threw Harry into Gene. Gene shoved Harry back toward Doyle as that man's right hand whirled. A heartbeat before the crowd outside roared the start of Round Two, Gene heard *snick* and saw light flash in the dim wooden cavern. Crimson misted the air between Harry and Doyle. Harry spun to show Gene his new wet red collar. The inertia of the switchblade slash turned Harry all the way around to face Doyle again. Doyle pushed the dying man aside. Harry fell between wooden beams to lie underneath the arena until the demolition crew found him two weeks later, long after insects and animals finished with his flesh. The law chalked up his bones to a worker who'd gone missing after cops ran two Wobbly labor organizers off the construction site, one of those tragic industrial accidents that happens all the time.

Doyle stabbed at the boxer but Gene still had the jazz. He batted the knife out of Doyle's hand with a left slap and slammed his right fist straight into the killer's jaw. Fifteen rounds earlier, that punch might have put Doyle out for good; now it dropped him out but breathing.

Finish him — No! Gene dragged the moaning man to his dressing room, threw him inside, and slammed the door: no lock. He wedged the knife in the doorjamb and snapped off the blade.

Doyle won't be out for long. The wedged door won't hold him long. *Think! Won't let us get away, we're witnesses, 'n' he doesn't need no other reason than rage.*

But first he'll go to the money. Try to feed his money hunger first, then revenge.

Gene ran to the counting room. *Get there first! Tell them Doyle'd gone crazy! Killed Harry! Was going to hold them up.* With a clerk, maybe two, maybe guns with bullets, they could ambush Doyle and the clerks would be witnesses to Gene's story, to his being a hero, to him and Billie being innocent, safe, fr —

The counting room door stood ajar.

The crowd roared as Gibbons split open an old cut over Dempsey's eye in Round Four.

A short guy in a good suit stood in the counting room. Four chairs behind the long table were empty. Notebooks and tills were strewn everywhere. But no silver dollars. No stacks of greenbacks. The short guy stared at the big man in the doorway whose hand dangled a revolver.

"If you've come for money, you're too late," said the short guy. "Someone beat you to what little of it they had. Got them to give it up to him. Then once the bust-in riot started, the clerks knew it was over and they all left to see the big fight."

"You're Dempsey's manager. Jack Kearns."

"Guilty. And with that gun in your hand, you're a man looking for trouble."

"Doesn't have any bullets."

"A man with a gun and no bullets is a man who's *in* trouble." Kearns squinted. "I saw you fight, Mallette. You held back. Got size, speed, strength, technique. But give it up. You got no future as a real champ. Inside you there's no killer."

"You'd be surprised."

"Not likely. What did they promise you for winning?"

"Wasn't about the money."

"For you, probably not. But how much to be the champ of this town?"

"A thousand."

"They cheaped you. You'll never get it anyway. This crazy day cheated them, too. They'll all go bust." Kearns held a fold of bills toward Gene. "Every winner deserves a purse. Five hundred, and keep this between you and me. Call yourself lucky to get it and get gone before your half-assed manager comes looking for his cut."

Gene didn't know what to do. Put the money in his pocket. Kearns took the revolver from Gene. Broke open the cylinder and clucked at the empty slots for bullets. "You're too honest for your own good."

He took a flat .25 automatic from his back pocket and disappeared it in Gene's hand. "An honest guy needs iron that works. This one's ready to go, though it won't damage anybody who's not kissing close."

Kearns walked toward the door. The crowd outside roared when Gibbons connected with a combo that stung the champion and then danced around the ring to escape a furious Dempsey.

"Mr. Kearns!" said Gene. "Who got all the money from the fight?"

"Gee kid, beats me."

Then he was gone. Outside, the crowd roared. Gene fled the counting room. Saw the door to his dressing room shake. Out of the door crack fell a knife blade.

Gene ran. Made it out of the roaring arena. A naked yellow eye baked the oiled air. He muscled his way through a dirt street jammed with crazed strangers. Two Martin boys set off a string of Chinese firecrackers. A man and two women sat on an overturned sausage peddler's cart, stuffing themselves with meat tubes they plucked from the ground. A tuxedoed redhead bounced off Gene and staggered away, his eyes whirling in his head. A cowboy shot his Peacemaker into the air and no one flinched.

Where are you, Billie? Got to be here! She's got to be here!

Firecrackers. A horse screamed and a fat woman laughed. The cowboy fired his pistol.

Car horn, was that a —

"Gene! Over here!"

Billie waved from the Ford's running board. Gene shoved his

way to their getaway car that was pinned against the curb by a deserted truck. Parked vehicles jammed every road.

She grabbed Gene to be sure he was alive and real. "Where's Doyle? Where's . . . ?"

"All gone wrong. No heist. Doyle killed Harry. He —"

Glass exploded in the car window.

Doyle: near the arena. He stood on a wobbly overturned pushcart, his gun hand shaking as he lined up for another shot over the sea of heads who didn't give a damn.

Gene grabbed her hand, held on to his life, and plunged into the mad, milling crowd.

"One chance!" he yelled as he dragged her behind him. Every bone in his body wept. His legs shook. Lemonade he grabbed from a kid didn't cool the fire in his throat. "We got one chance! Get to Texas John! Not crooks! We're targets 'n' only he can save us!"

"His house is two miles across town!" But she ran with him.

By the time they'd fought their way to Main Street, Billie was more carrying Gene than running with him. They looked back and saw only the sea of people in their wake.

"Still there," gasped Gene. "He's still there somewhere. Won't stop. We can't stop."

The crowd became a solid wall of flesh at the east end of Main Street, an audience to the volunteers battling a ball of fire that had once been a tailor shop.

"Railroad tracks!" gasped Billie. "Nobody's there! We can go quicker along them!"

"But not straight to John's! That's maybe three football fields north of his house —"

"Only hope," she told him as they staggered to the steel rails. Hundreds of parked freight cars squatted on the tracks, diverted there for the passenger charters that hadn't come. A metal *clang!* shuddered the wall of boxcars beside them as the locomotive a thousand yards away got a clear track signal. Steel wheels creaked a slow revolution.

Gene pressed Kearns's close-in gun into Billie's hands. Shoved Kearns's money into her dress pocket. "Get on train! Can't make it farther. Can't run no more."

"Yes, you can!" Billie grabbed his shirt. "Look! You can see Texas John's house from here! Just up that hill!"

"Can't get up that hill 'fore Doyle catches us. You know he's out there, hell-hound smelling us. He won't stop until he gets his blood. Till he gets me. But you: hop on this freight, open boxcar comin' up. Hide. Taking care of me will slow him down. He'll see me, stop for me. Enough so you can go. Get free."

"You can get away!" cried Billie.

"No. I can only do what makes me special. You said it. I save you. Only special you can do is make me love you. Let me be special and love you and get you on the train. You be special and do it. Don't let us both die as nothing."

"Too late," she said, looking past him, wrapping her grip around the pistol.

Doyle stood a hundred yards down the tracks.

Billie raised her gun —

Gene covered her hand with his: "That won't work until he's close enough to kiss."

The barrel of her automatic swung down along Gene's ribs. Billie hid the gun behind her.

"You have to let him get real close," said Gene. "He'll like that. Do that. For you. Not for me. He'll never let me get close to him again. But I won't just stand here and take it."

He stepped away from her grabbing hand. Took two steps forward as Doyle strolled toward him. Doyle stopped when he was about the same distance away as a sucker shot to a bank door. But instead of night, he had a broad daylight aim, though the sky had suddenly gone gray with rain clouds as Dempsey threw everything he had at Gibbons, yet had to settle for a clinch finish at the final bell, a decision victory instead of a knockout.

The freight train groaned and inched forward.

Gene Mallette brought both hands up in fists and dropped into the stance of a boxer.

Heard Doyle laugh and saw that man's solo hand clear his suit coat and snap straight out.

A crimson rose blew out Doyle's left ear and sprayed red on a passing boxcar. Doyle fell to the chipped rock track bed as the *crack!* of a German sniper's Mauser from a front porch on a hill a thousand yards away whispered to Gene above the rumble of the train.

No second shot came from the man who used to have a badge

and who knew what his eyes saw. Gene stared at the house on the hill: whatever had happened up there was over. He and Billie went to the dead man. A million angels dropped tears on them as she helped Gene throw Doyle and the guns through open doors of crawling boxcars. Gene almost fell under the steel wheels, but she grabbed him and held on. The train rumbled toward the mountains and the ocean beyond. Gene ripped the medal off his neck and threw it onto the last boxcar out of nowhere.

CLARK HOWARD

The Cobalt Blues

FROM *Ellery Queen's Mystery Magazine*

LEWIS GOT OFF the Harrison Street bus, turned up the collar of his old surplus Navy watch coat, and walked, head down against the cold March wind, to the Cook County Medical Center down the street. Chicago, he thought, was a lousy place for a guy to have to spend the last weeks and months of his life. He should have moved out to Arizona or down to Florida a long time ago, like most of the rest of the old gang he had grown up with did. At least he could be lying out in the sun while he died.

At the big, sprawling medical complex, he made his way to the Radiology Building and entered the foyer. He paused a moment to turn down his collar, catch his breath, and pull a tissue from his pocket to dry his watery eyes. On his way to the elevators, he looked up at the lobby clock and saw that it was 8:52. As usual, he began making the mental bet he made every Thursday morning. Would he be the first to arrive and sign in? The second? Or the third? There were three of them that had the nine o'clock appointment: himself, a skinny white guy named Potts, and a sullen black man named Hoxie. The radiology technician had three come in at once because there were three phases to the treatment, and he could have a patient in each phase as the morning progressed.

Because Lewis was an obsessive gambler, his mind, without conscious direction from him, invariably broke everything he did in life down to odds for or against. So when he stepped onto one of the elevators and reached past two Hispanic orderlies to press the button for five, he started trying to decide how it would be today: Would he be first, second, or third? The rule he applied was that he had to make up his mind before the elevator door opened on five. That was the only fair way to do it. Otherwise, he might see one of the other two in the hall upstairs. Then there could be no bet. Just like if he encountered one of them in the lobby. No bet.

The elevator stopped on three and the orderlies got off. The door closed and the car started again. Since he was now alone, Lewis said aloud, "Okay, one, two, or three? What's it gonna be?"

This was important to him. This, in his mind, might tell him whether he was going to have a winning day or a losing day. To a confirmed gambler, every day was a new beginning, a fresh start, another chance to hit it big. Yesterday never mattered. A gambler that looked back on what he lost yesterday was a fool. The same as a gambler who planned what to gamble on tomorrow. Yesterday was over, tomorrow wasn't here. There was only today.

The elevator stopped on five. A split instant before the door opened, Lewis decided. Second. He would be second today.

On five, he walked down a long corridor to a door with a sign above it that read: OUTPATIENT RADIOLOGY. Taking a deep breath, as if he had a fortune bet on the moment, Lewis opened the door and entered the waiting room. In a glance he saw that Potts, the skinny white guy, was already there, slouched down in a corner chair, leafing through one of a dozen outdated magazines spread about the room. Hoxie, the sullen black man, sat in an opposite corner, looking straight ahead, not moving, as if he were in a trance.

Lewis cursed under his breath. He had lost. Disgruntled, he signed in at the reception window and found a place to sit that was well away from either of the other two. Controlling his annoyance at this unlucky turn of events, he took off his heavy coat, pulled a racing form from one of its pockets, and began to reevaluate bets he had made earlier that morning in the day's lineup at Calexico Downs.

An hour before catching a bus to the hospital that morning, Lewis had been knocking impatiently on the door of a basement apartment on the near Northwest Side, in the neighborhood where he had grown up, once all Irish and Italian, now mostly mixed black, Hispanic, and Asian. He had to pound on the door three times, the cold wind whipping at his ankles, before his friend Ralph opened the door.

"What the hell, you going deaf?" Lewis complained peevishly. "I'm freezing out here."

"You're lucky I'm letting you in at all," Ralph replied without rancor. He closed and triple-locked the door behind Lewis. "This ain't no Vegas casino, y'know. It's a business. We got reg'lar hours. Especially on Thursdays and Fridays, which is count days."

The two men retreated into what had once been a basement apartment but had been converted into a neighborhood betting parlor, where bets were taken not only on daily lineups from seasonal racetracks around the country, but also on baseball, football, basketball, and hockey games, as well as major boxing matches. The parlor was owned by Cicero Charley Waxman, who was nicknamed after the Chicago suburb where Al Capone had once had his headquarters. Waxman had two dozen similar locations, all of which were illegal but much more popular than the state-owned off-track betting sites, because the former accepted wagers on *all* sports, the latter only horse racing.

The parlor where Lewis gambled was managed by his friend Ralph, one of the gang he had grown up with, and the only one other than Lewis who was still around. Ralph had started as an errand boy for Cicero Charley while still in elementary school, and over the years had grown into gambling-parlor middle management. Even though his net income depended on the earnings of the parlor, he constantly nagged Lewis about his gambling problem.

"Why the hell don't you give it a rest for a few days, Lew?" he griped now. "Go out and buy yourself a decent overcoat instead of laying bets every day."

Lewis threw him a derisive look and did not even bother to respond to such an absurd suggestion. The day Lewis did not lay a bet would be the day when all racehorses, boxers, and football, baseball, basketball, and hockey players were dead. At a counter next to the betting cages, Lewis spread out a Green Sheet racing form and began filling out a wagering slip.

"So how's the gallbladder treatment going?" Ralph finally asked, seeing that Lewis was ignoring his advice.

"Slow," said Lewis. "The stones are shrinking, but slow."

Lewis had not told anyone what was really the matter with him; the thought of someone feeling pity for him was nauseating. Ralph

thought he was going to the hospital every Thursday morning for
some kind of treatment that shrank and dissolved gallstones. That
was the reason he let Lewis in early to bet on Thursdays. The parlor
normally opened at ten.

Standing across the counter from each other, the two men were
acutely but not uncomfortably aware of the marked differences between them. Both forty-six, Ralph now had a wife, two teenage
daughters bound for finishing school, a two-story colonial home in
an upscale suburb, two sedans, and a recreational utility vehicle.
Lewis lived alone in a shabby little kitchenette in a tenement building in the same neighborhood in which they had grown up. He had
no family, no regular job, and wore secondhand clothes from St.
Malachy's Thrift Shop.

Over the years, Ralph had tried to interest Lewis in bettering
himself. Just a month earlier he had talked to Cicero Charley Waxman about giving Lewis a janitorial contract for all of Waxman's
gambling parlors. "It'll put you on easy street, Lew," his friend had
promised. "You hire a dozen welfare mothers to do the work, see,
and you pay them in cash so they don't have to declare the income.
All you gotta do is supervise them. I know guys that would cut off a
toe for a setup like that."

But not Lewis. He shied away from steady employment like a two-
year-old resisted discipline. When he had to work — emphasize
had to, as in riding out a losing streak — he took a temporary job as
a dishwasher or a trucker's helper, or delivered advertising fliers
door-to-door, whatever — as long as it was not permanent. Lewis
wanted nothing in his life that was permanent. Especially now.

"Did I tell you Debbie finally got her braces off?" Ralph asked
now, as Lewis continued to fill out his wagering slip. From his wallet, Ralph extracted a wallet-size photo of his eldest daughter. Lewis
looked at it, seeing a girl who resembled Ralph too much to ever be
pretty, but who did have, after thousands of dollars of orthodontics,
a near-perfect smile.

"She's a looker," Lewis lied. "You're a lucky man, Ralph." Inside,
he shuddered at the mere thought of such responsibility.

As they were standing there, another knock sounded on the outside door and Ralph went over to answer it. He admitted two men,
both very large, wearing hats and overcoats, each carrying two
large suitcases. As they walked past Ralph, one of them asked,
"Count room unlocked?"

"Yeah, go on in," Ralph said. "I'll be with you in a minute."
Returning to the counter, Ralph took the wager sheet, tallied it up, validated it in an automatic stamping machine, and shook his head in sad resignation as Lewis counted out sixty-five dollars and gave it to him.

As Lewis made the bets, an old, familiar thought surfaced in his mind: *Maybe today will be the beginning of a winning streak that will give me enough money to get the hell out of cold, dirty Chicago and go live where it is warm and sunny for the rest of my life.*
What was left of it.

The following Thursday, he walked from the elevator to the outpatient radiology waiting room, again betting with himself that he would be the second of the three patients to arrive. When he got to the door and was about to open it, he paused, hearing a quiet voice inside. He did not think it was either of the other two patients, because they never talked. Opening the door, he went in and saw at once that Potts, the skinny white guy, sitting alone in a corner, appeared to be talking quietly to himself. When he glanced up and saw Lewis, he stopped at once. *A nut,* Lewis thought as he signed in. At that moment, Hoxie, the black man, came in, looking angry as usual, not speaking to either of them, and sat down as far away as possible.

Just as Hoxie sat down, the waiting room door immediately opened again and two uniformed, armed men brought in a younger man, his wrists cuffed to a waist chain, wearing an orange jumpsuit stenciled on the back with large black letters: ISP. Illinois State Prison. The radiology technician met them in the waiting room and escorted them directly into the treatment room.

Lewis, Potts, and Hoxie exchanged curious looks, but none of them commented about it.

A little while later, the young man was brought back through again, and this time the three regular patients were prepared and all got a better look at him. He was pretty ordinary in appearance, his only outstanding feature being a head of thick, curly black hair that, Lewis and the others knew, he would soon lose if his radiation treatment was above the neck. Potts, when Lewis had first seen him, had healthy blond hair combed straight back. Because he was undergoing radiation treatment for a brain tumor, he was now bald as an egg. Lewis, who had cancer of the pancreas, and Hoxie, cancer of the esophagus, were both radiated below the head and had kept their hair, such as it was. As if to make up for the hair loss, however, Potts did not have the other debilitating side effects; he experienced a temporary loss of taste, but that was mild compared to the vile nausea, vomiting, and fatigue suffered by Lewis and Hoxie.

After his original diagnosis, Lewis had gone to the medical section of the main public library and researched his illness. He concluded that he had a one-in-five chance of living five more years. When he had subsequently learned in conversations with the radiology technicians the types of cancer Potts and Hoxie were dealing with, he had, out of curiosity, returned to the library and researched their illnesses. Potts he put at eight-to-one to reach five years, Hoxie at nine-to-five.

Lurking somewhere in the back of his mind, Lewis had a vision of a huge national pool made up of cancer patients between the ages of forty and sixty. If each one put in a hundred bucks, the last patient still living would become a very wealthy person. He doubted, however, that the American Medical Association would approve such a plan. Doctors only approved of taking chances with life and death, never money.

The following Thursday, Lewis was the first patient to arrive, and the first to go in for treatment after the young convict had been treated and taken away. While he stripped to the waist, and as the radiology technician adjusted the Cobalt-60 applicator for his treatment, Lewis surreptitiously looked down at the technician's desk. As he expected, there was a new clipboard there, in addition to his and those of the other two regular patients. He was able to quickly read that the young prisoner's name was Alan Lampley, age twenty-eight, residing in the Joliet Correctional Center south of Chicago, diagnosis lymphatic leukemia. Lewis was not familiar with that particular type of cancer, so he could not put any odds on it.

"Ready, Lewis?" the technician asked, coming out of the little control room where he was protected from radiation.

"Sure thing," Lewis replied.

Lewis stretched out on the leather treatment table. He stared at the ceiling as the technician began painting a design on his upper torso with water-soluble orange dye. When he was finished, he carefully placed leather pads filled with lead all around the outside of the pattern, to deflect the radiation from those parts of the body where it was not needed. The radiation itself would come from the Cobalt-60 applicator, which the technician had adjusted following instructions from a radiologist-oncologist as to the diameter and filtration of the cobalt beam and the target distance at which Lewis was lying. That beam was generated by radioactive cobalt pellets sealed in a stainless-steel cylinder mounted behind shields jacketed with sheet steel and carried by a mechanical arm to an open port through which it would be aimed at Lewis.

It continued to amaze Lewis that such a powerful beam could penetrate his body without pain, without heat, without any sensation at all — yet that same ray would — could — *might* — destroy a malignant cancer that was trying to destroy him. The doctor had explained it to him, of course. The radiation beam did not affect ordinary body tissue; it merely passed through it. Radiation affected only what would *absorb* it: cells, cartilage, bone — and tumors.

When the technician finished preparing Lewis, he retreated to his safe room and presently activated the Cobalt-60 applicator. Lewis closed his eyes. But instead of dozing, as he usually did, he found himself wondering what Alan Lampley had done to be sent to prison.

On the next treatment day, after Alan Lampley had been taken through the waiting room by his guards, Lewis spoke up to the others and announced, "I know what he done."

Potts and Hoxie, startled at the sound of his voice, jerked their heads around to stare at him. "He killed a guy," Lewis said.

"Man, how do *you* know?" Hoxie challenged.

Now Lewis and Potts stared at Hoxie. Neither of them had ever heard him speak before. His voice matched his demeanor: angry; it cracked like a whip.

"I looked him up in the library," Lewis said.

"The *li*-brary?" Potts said incredulously. He had a slow, Southern drawl, lazy-like. Lewis and Hoxie looked at each other in surprise. Both of them had the same thought: *redneck*. There had been an influx of them recently, Southerners coming north looking for high-paying factory jobs. It happened every time crops failed.

"Yeah, the library," Lewis confirmed. "I got his name off the chart in the treatment room. Alan Lampley. Then I looked up his trial in the old newspapers down there at the library. He was in a couple stories four years ago. Killed a drug dealer."

Hoxie snorted derisively. "Poor little white boy junkie got carried away, huh?"

"He wasn't the junkie," Lewis said. "It was his sister. The dealer who got her hooked on crack put her on the street to hustle for him to support her habit. This kid Alan came looking for her; they were both from some little town in Indiana somewheres. When he found them in an apartment where she was living with the guy, the sister was so humiliated that she ran into the bedroom, got the dealer's gun from a drawer, and blew her brains out right in front of both of them. The dealer panicked and tried to beat it, but Alan picked up the gun, ran after him, and shot him four times as he was getting into his car."

"Good for him, by God," Potts drawled.

"I suppose," Hoxie said, glaring at both of them, "that the dealer was a black man."

"Paper didn't say," Lewis told him. "But what difference does it make?"

"I'll *tell* you what difference it makes," Hoxie said, jabbing an accusing finger at both of them. "If he had killed a *white* dude, he wouldn't be here taking no treatments; he'd be waiting on death row to get the needle."

Potts grunted disdainfully, looking down at the floor, shaking his bald head. Lewis just shrugged and said, "Maybe, maybe not. Works out about the same, anyway. The kid got fourteen years for second-degree murder. Far as he's concerned, it's still a death sentence."

"Oh, yeah?" Hoxie said, his voice almost a growl. "Why's that?"

"He's got it in the lymph glands," Lewis explained. "I seen on his chart that he's getting megavolts that go three inches under the skin. That means it's prob'ly spread too far to stop. I read up on all this cancer stuff at the library. Even money he ain't got six months left."

Hoxie started to say something, reconsidered, and looked away. His fixed, dark countenance seemed to soften a little, and he blinked rapidly several times. Potts sat up straight instead of slouching. Lewis chewed on the inside of his mouth. Alan Lampley's mortality had somehow synchronized with their own.

None of them said anything further until the young prisoner's treatment was over and his guards brought him back out. Lewis and the others then looked at him with new interest; he was a person now, with a story as well as a dread disease.

When Potts rose to go in for his own treatment, he impulsively paused at the door and asked, "How long you fellers got after your treatment before you get sick?"

Lewis shrugged. "I got about three hours."

" 'Bout four for me," Hoxie said. "Why?"

"Well, I don't get real sick, you know, but I start to lose my taste after two or three hours. So what I do is, I go down Harrison Street 'bout three blocks, toward the lake there, and around the corner on Ashland Avenue is a little bar called Billy Daly's Place. I like beer, see — nice, cold, draft beer. An' I only have a little while to drink it before my taste goes. So I was just thinking, if you fellers want to mosey on down when you get done here, I'll buy you a pitcher of beer. What d'you say?"

Lewis and Hoxie exchanged looks. Lewis sensed that it was up to him to speak first; Hoxie's expression was again almost hostile.

"I wouldn't mind." Lewis said. He and Potts looked at Hoxie, who glared back at them. "Come on, man," Lewis said quietly. "We're all the same inside — especially now."

Hoxie nodded curtly. "I be there."

Billy Daly's Place was one of those Chicago neighborhood taverns that opened at eight A.M. to accommodate people who had to have one or two drinks to steady their morning shakes so they could go to work. Those who worked nearby were back in at lunchtime to steady their afternoon shakes.

When Lewis arrived, Potts was at a small table in the back, almost finished with his first pitcher of cold draft. By the time Hoxie got there, Potts was well into his second pitcher, and Lewis was working hard on his first. When the bartender put a glass and pitcher in front of Hoxie, he reached for his wallet, but Potts held up a hand and said, "Hey, no, I already paid for one pitcher apiece for you fellers. After that, you're on your own."

As men who drink together for the first time invariably do, they got around to telling each other about themselves. Potts, who had drunk the most, got around to it first.

"I come up to Chicago from a little town in Tennessee to find work. I had a good job down there in a paper mill, but some Japa-

nese land group bought up all the property and closed down the
mill. They was supposed to be going to develop some kind of industrial complex: said there'd be good jobs for ever'body. That was two
years ago; they ain't developed nothin' so far. I went on unemploy-
ment for six months, then picked up odd jobs here and there for
another six. But with a wife and three kids to take care of, things
just kept gettin' tighter and tighter, so finally I got on the bus and
come on up here. Got me a pretty decent fac'try job with Motorola.
Moved into a ratty little kitchenette so I'd be able to send home
enough money ever' week to take care of my family. I was riding the
bus down twice a month to be with 'em for a weekend. Ever'thing
seemed to be going along fine — then I started having what they
call focal seizures, where my arms and legs would start shaking like
I was freezing to death. Fac'try doctor sent me for a MRI scan and
they found a brainstem glioma. They put me on a anticonvul-
sant drug and started radiation. I collect disability pay, but it ain't
enough to send anything home. So me and my wife worked it out
for her and the kids to go on state welfare by saying I'd abandoned
my family. Now they get along pretty good — but I can't come
around in case somebody was to see me there. So here I am: got no
job, got no family, got no hair, and ain't got no future to speak of."
He grinned crookedly. "Like the feller once said: Life's a bitch —
and then you die."

"Man, ain't that the truth," Hoxie enthusiastically agreed. "A
year ago, I had it knocked, you know? Me and my old lady had just
got divorced after thirty-two years of marriage. It had got down to
the point where we couldn't stand being in the same room with
each other. I tell you, she had turned into the meanest damned
woman that ever drew breath. Never happy. Nothing pleased her.
She could find things to complain about before they even *happened*.
Like she'd say, 'I know what you're gonna do next Wednesday. You
gonna go out with those no-good friends of yours.' Next *Wednesday*
she's complaining about, and it ain't even *here* yet.

"Anyway, I finally had enough of it; I moved out and we got divorced. I took early retirement from my job at the post office, and
that was when I *really* started living. I got a little place of my own,
got a new TV, new stereo, new set of wheels, and — best of all — I
started running around with this little fox in her second year of *college*. She had one of those father-complex things, you know; had to
have an older man in her life. 'Course, everybody said I was having

a midlife crisis; tru'f is, I was having a *ball*. Only thing was, I started getting these damned sore throats all the time, and my voice would go hoarse." Hoxie smiled widely. "This young fox of mine, she say it sounded sexy. After a while, though, it didn't *feel* sexy. When I went to the doctor about it, I found out why."

Hoxie sat back and sighed wearily. "Now the young fox is gone, the apartment's gone, the new wheels are gone, my daughter and her husband have the TV and the stereo, and I got a room in their basement where I'm welcome to stay as long as they's the beneficiaries on my life insurance." He raised his beer glass in salute. "Like you said, life *is* a bitch."

Hoxie fell silent then, and he and Potts sat looking at Lewis with expressions that said: *Okay, man, what's your story?* It took Lewis a few moments but he finally caught on. All he could really say, however, was that the only effect cancer had on his lifestyle was that he had to get his Thursday bets down early, and he'd begun to brood about dying in a cold climate.

"That's it?" Hoxie said incredulously. "Hell, you might as well not even *have* cancer."

"That's fer sure," Potts agreed. "I've knowed people with the flu had their lives more messed up than you."

"Well, excuse the hell out of me," Lewis said, annoyed. "Sorry I don't have something worse to tell you. Hope I ain't ruined your day."

Potts and Hoxie exchanged glances and then suddenly burst out laughing.

"You know what this reminds me of?" said Hoxie. "The day I tol' my daughter and son-in-law about my diagnosis. Know what my fool son-in-law said? He said it was too bad I couldn't have a *respectable* disease like sickle-cell anemia. Said cancer was a white person's disease!"

"You think that's bad," Potts told him, "listen to this. I was feeling kind of down about a month ago, so I went to see this Baptist preacher, thinking maybe he could console me a little, jack up my spirits, you know. Guess what the idiot said. He told me to thank God I had a disease like cancer instead of something *impure* like AIDS. Said AIDS was the Lord's way of punishing the homosexuals of the world, but that cancer was for *decent* folks. An' he was *serious*, too!"

Lewis loosened up then and joined in the laughter, although

normally he was not the laughing type. He tried never to show *any* emotion; he did not consider emotion appropriate for a gambler. But with these two men, it did not seem unfitting in any way. Despite the conspicuous differences among the three of them, along with the fact that it had taken them more than two months to even say "Good morning" in the waiting room, Lewis now began to feel at ease with them and sensed that each one of them felt the same with him and with each other. All of a sudden, it seemed as if they had been friends for a long time.

When their laughter subsided, and before they could order more beer, Lewis began to feel sick and said he had better leave; he needed to be back in his apartment before the intense nausea hit him. Hoxie said he would leave, too, since his own nausea was imminent. Potts decided he would leave with them, saying, "No sense in drinking it if you can't taste it."

It was then that Potts suggested that they meet there again Saturday afternoon to have a few pitchers and watch the Bears game on the bar's big-screen TV. Lewis and Hoxie, to their mutual surprise, readily agreed to the plan.

On his way home on the bus, with the numbers and odds and calculations in his mind beginning to spin about from the buzz of the beer, Lewis inexplicably blocked them out and again began thinking of Alan Lampley. Lewis had thought it was bad to have to spend the last months of his life in cold and dirty Chicago, but what must it be like to have to spend them locked in a prison cell?

The three of them began to meet at the bar several times a week: Wednesday nights before their treatment; Thursday afternoons following treatment; Monday evenings to watch a preseason Bulls game. They began to talk about Alan Lampley. Casually, at first, wistfully.

"Too bad that boy can't join us for beers," Potts said at one point.

"Yeah," said Lewis. "Hell, big spenders like us, we'd even buy for the guards."

Another time, Hoxie said, out of the blue, "Damn shame, kid that young having to deal with cancer *and* prison."

"Yeah, it ain't like he killed some upright citizen," said Lewis. "All's he done was ice a drug dealer."

"It ain't right," said Hoxie.

"They call that justice?" Potts demanded.

"Don't confuse justice with the law," Lewis said sagely. "Them's two different things."

On Thursdays now, when the guards brought Alan in, the three began bobbing their chins at him, nodding, giving him a wink. Potts even stood up one day to talk to him, but one of the guards got between them and said to Alan, "Just keep moving, Lampley." To Potts, the other guard said, "Sorry, the prisoner isn't allowed to talk to anyone except medical personnel."

But they knew that Alan had recognized their overtures of friendliness, understanding, even commiseration, because he began to nod back their greetings, and even grin a little. The little signals they passed to him seemed to say: *You're not alone.*

In the bar, the three new friends, after a pitcher or two, began to daydream of helping Alan. "If I was to win me the lottery," Potts said, "you know what I'd do with part of it? I'd hire the bes' damn criminal lawyer in the city to try and get that boy paroled or something, so's he could die in some real nice place."

"Yeah," Lewis said drily, "like us."

"If *I* was to win the lottery," Hoxie said, "I wouldn't mess with no lawyers. I'd hire me three or four real tough street dudes to jump them guards and turn that boy loose. Give him enough money to skip out to South America or someplace."

"Now *that's* a good idea," Lewis allowed.

"Only thing bad about it is ain't none of us gonna win no lottery," Potts said glumly.

"Seems like," Hoxie said, "I always be reading how some group or organization or something be trying to get some worthless piece of shit off death row 'cause he's got a low IQ, or his mama whipped his ass too much when he was a kid, or *something*. But don't nobody seem to be helping this boy. Leastwise, nobody we know of."

"People don't help other people 'cause they've usually got something to lose by doing it," Lewis said. "Only time people *really* go out on a limb for somebody is when they got nothin' to lose."

"You mean people like us?" Potts asked.

Neither Lewis nor Hoxie answered.

For a long time, nobody said anything. But they all knew what the others were thinking.

They got down to it the next time they met, when Potts said, "I wish there was some way *we* could help the kid."

Without consciously realizing it, that was what Lewis had been waiting for.

"We could," he said simply.

"What do you mean?" Hoxie asked. "How?"

"Get the jump on those two guards. Be easy. They ain't expecting no trouble from three sick guys like us. We could take 'em down with no problem, let the kid go, and use them shackles they got on him to chain up the guards and the radiology tech in the scan room. Before anybody knew what was happening, we could all be out of the hospital and gone."

"Yeah, but gone where?" Potts asked. "The hospital knows who we are, where we live — hell, we'd be caught before lunchtime."

"Not if we had an escape plan," Lewis said.

Hoxie frowned, but with interest. "What kind of escape plan?"

"I ain't sure," Lewis admitted. "But it'd have to be a plan where we could all get out of the country. Go to someplace where we couldn't be extradited. And where we could still get our treatments. Like Argentina."

"Lewis, good buddy, you are dreaming," Potts said. "An escape plan like that would take a whole hell of a lot of money."

"Well," Lewis said quietly. "I just happen to know where we can get our hands on a whole hell of a lot of money."

He told them about the four suitcases of cash that he saw being brought into the betting parlor run by his friend Ralph every Thursday morning. Hoxie's eyebrows went up.

"Man, are you talking about sticking up one of them parlors that's owned by Cicero Charley Waxman? If you are, that ain't too smart."

"Who's Cicero Charley Waxman?" Potts asked.

"Bigtime rackets boss who runs the gambling on the North Side," Hoxie told him. "We steal from him, he'll have his hoods after us like fleas after a junkyard dog."

Potts shrugged his skinny shoulders. "So what? Look, if we busted this kid loose, we'd have the Chicago cops and the Illinois state police after us anyways. A few hoodlums wouldn't make no difference."

"He's right," Lewis said. "If our escape plan worked, we get away from everybody. If it didn't, what's the difference who catches us? We go to jail or we get killed. We're dying anyways." Lewis leaned forward with his elbows on the table and lowered his voice. "Look, I'm gonna be straight with you guys. I want those four suitcases of dough as much for myself as I do for the kid. I don't know if I'm gonna beat this cancer or not — just like you guys don't know if you'll beat yours. But if I don't beat it, I'd like to spend my last days in someplace clean and warm; maybe some little beach village not too far from a city where there's a modern hospital where I can get my treatments —"

"You know, I got the same feeling," Hoxie admitted. "I'd like to have a way to get the hell out of my daughter's house. I don't want to die in no basement room. That little beach village sounds mighty good to me."

Lewis and Hoxie looked at Potts. The Southerner nodded slowly. "I guess I got a reason, too. I'd like to have my wife and kids with me when I go. Somebody to say goodbye to besides strangers." He blushed slightly. "No offense."

"Looks like we all understand each other," Lewis said.

They sat back and raised their beer glasses in a silent toast.

They met in Lewis's shabby little apartment the following evening and, over pizza and beer, began to make plans.

"First thing in the morning," Lewis said, "we go downtown to the federal building and get passports. Then we gotta figure some way to get a gun —"

"I can cover that," Hoxie said. "My son-in-law gots a thirty-two-caliber Saturday-night special he keeps in a drawer nex' to his bed. It's a little gun, but he had it chromed and it looks bigger."

"Just one gun all we need?" Potts asked.

"Yeah, the other two guys can keep their hands in their pockets like they got guns, too," Lewis said. "Anyway, we'll take guns off the guys carrying the money. They're bound to be strapped."

"Okay. What else?" Hoxie asked.

"Plane tickets," said Lewis. "I checked out the airlines this morning. There's an Argentine Air flight from here to Buenos Aires at nine o'clock every night. One-way fare is eleven hundred and eighty bucks, first class."

"First class!" said Potts.

"Certainly," Lewis confirmed. "We'll be in the money; you don't think we're gonna fly coach, do you?"

"Where we gonna get the money to buy first-class tickets?"

"We don't need no money. The airline will hold the tickets at the airport until two hours before flight time; we pay for them when we check in. But we do need a little front money for a few other things."

"Like what?" Hoxie wanted to know.

"We need to rent a car. We need to rent a motel room out near the airport. And we need to buy some clothes for the kid; we can't have him running around in that orange jumpsuit. Either of you guys got a credit card?"

"Not me," Hoxie said glumly. "My daughter canceled mine. She gives me an *allowance* now, like I was some kid."

"I got a Visa card," said Potts. "I don't use it much; just for groceries and stuff when I run short of cash."

"What's the credit limit on it?"

"Five hundred."

"That ought to be enough. You got a driver's license?"

"Yeah. Tennessee license."

"That'll do. We'll rent the car at the airport the night before, and drop it off when we go to catch the flight."

"We taking the kid with us?" Potts asked. Lewis shook his head.

"Can't. He won't have no passport. We'll give him a fourth of the money and then he's on his own." Hoxie and Potts exchanged cheerless looks. Lewis shrugged. "It's the best we can do for him."

For a long moment then, the three men were silent: looking at each other, looking down at the remains of the pizza, sipping beer that was turning warm, drumming silent fingers. It was a brief time of limbo, a heavy interval in which any one of them could have hesitated just a hint, looked even a trace tentative, and maybe the whole unlikely scheme would have broken to pieces in their minds and evaporated like some juvenile plan to steal a math test the night before the exam. But none of them faltered.

"Well then," Potts drawled, "when do we do it?"

"A week from Thursday," Lewis said. "We should have everything set up by a week from Thursday. We'll do it then."

When a week from Thursday came and Lewis's friend Ralph opened the parlor door to let Lewis in to make his early bets, the parlor manager was surprised to find Lewis accompanied by two men he had never seen before. "What the hell?" he said, holding the door only partly open.

"These are a couple of guys I go to the hospital with," Lewis explained. "Just let 'em stand inside out of the cold while they wait for me, okay?"

"Damn it, Lew, I shouldn't even be letting *you* in before the place opens," Ralph complained. "Now you're taking advantage by showing up with two guys I don't even know —"

"They're *okay*," Lewis assured him, gently shouldering his way in and gesturing for Potts and Hoxie to follow. "They'll wait by the door, you won't even know they're here, Ralph. Come on, let me get my bets down . . ."

Reluctantly, Ralph closed and locked the door behind them. Walking around the betting counter, he studied Lewis curiously. There was something different about him. Suddenly it dawned on Ralph what it was.

"Where's your racing form?" he asked. It was the first time in twenty years that he could remember seeing Lewis without a racing form either in his hand or sticking out of a pocket.

"I, uh — guess I forgot it," Lewis said. He tried to sound casual, but he knew at once that he had blown the ploy; the nervousness that he heard in his own usually sanguine voice betrayed him.

Ralph glanced at Potts and Hoxie, who were just inside the door, watching intently. His eyes narrowed suspiciously. "All right, Lewis, what's going on?" he demanded.

Lewis locked eyes with him but did not answer. Ralph wet his lips. Swallowing, he moved one hand to reach under the counter. There was a red telephone under there that was Cicero Charley Waxman's hotline. Just taking it off the hook without saying anything was enough to send a quartet of thugs from the neighborhood to check out the problem.

Before Ralph could get to the receiver, however, Lewis reached over and grabbed his arm. "Keep both hands up on the counter, Ralph," he said quietly.

Hoxie walked over and drew his son-in-law's chromed revolver. "Do what the man say," he ordered.

Ralph looked at Lewis in utter disbelief. "Are you out of your mind, Lewis?"

Before anyone could say anything else, another knock sounded at the door. Lewis quickly pulled Ralph around the counter. He jerked his head at Hoxie and the black man hurried to stand behind where the door swung open. Potts stood with him.

"Open the door, Ralph," Lewis instructed, nudging him toward it.

"You're crazy," Ralph muttered.

"Open it."

Ralph did as he was told, and immediately through the door came a pair of burly men, each carrying two suitcases. Before it could register with them what was happening, Potts slammed the door behind them and locked it, and Hoxie stepped out to face them with the revolver leveled.

"Put the bags down and stay real still!" Lewis snapped, all nervousness dissolved from his voice by adrenaline.

"Do what he says," Ralph told the men. "He's crazy. Don't make trouble."

The couriers remained still while Potts relieved each of them of an automatic pistol and fished around in their coat pockets until he found the keys to the suitcases.

"All right, get in that closet," Lewis then ordered. "You too, Ralph."

It was a small closet behind the counter, the door usually open, with shelves on which the parlor kept pads of betting slips, boxes of ballpoint pens, rolls of calculator tape, cartons of disposable coffee cups, and other supplies. There was hardly room for all three men to squeeze in together. As Ralph followed the two couriers in, he shook his head in pity at Lewis.

"You've bought yourself a lot of trouble, Lewis, for a few thousand bucks."

"A *few* thousand, huh?" Lewis smirked.

"That's what I said, smart guy. A *few*. What, did you think you and your friends were going to get rich here today?"

"Four suitcases full of money," Lewis pointed out. "A week's take from all of Cicero Charley's parlors —"

"That's not parlor money," Ralph said evenly. "That's football-game parlay-card money from all the cigar stores and candy stores and bars. Ninety-five percent of it is minimum bets. You've got yourself four bags of mostly dollar bills, Lewis. Maybe twenty, twenty-five thousand, maximum." Ralph pointed a stiff finger at him. "But you got a million bucks' worth of grief from Cicero Charley."

A stunned look on his face, Lewis guided his friend into the closet and closed the door. Turning, he found Hoxie and Potts staring at him with sick expressions. Stepping over to Potts, he took the suitcase keys out of his hand.

"Do the door," he said to Hoxie.

The black man shoved the revolver into a coat pocket, drew a ball-peen hammer from under his belt, and from another pocket got out a handful of four-inch carpenter nails. As he proceeded to nail the closet door shut, Lewis knelt and unlocked one of the suitcases. It was filled with sheaves of cash held together by rubber bands. Checking half a dozen of them, he found that Ralph had been telling him the truth: there were occasional fives and tens mixed in the currency, but the vast majority of the bills were singles.

"We done stepped in something soft now," Hoxie said, looking down from his hammering.

"What the hell we gonna do?" Potts asked, his voice breaking as he stood there incongruously with a large automatic pistol in each hand.

"For now, we're gonna follow the plan and get out of here," Lewis said. He bobbed his chin at Hoxie. "Finish the door." To Potts, "Get the car." He himself tore all the phone wires out of the wall, including the hotline.

Moments later, Potts pulled up in a rented Buick and opened the trunk. Lewis and Hoxie carried the suitcases out one at a time and loaded them. Then they all crowded into the front seat and Potts drove off.

"We got two decisions to make," Lewis said tensely. "One: Do we follow our plan to spring the kid — or do the three of us make a run for it now? Two: If we do spring him, do we give him part of the money or just cut him loose?"

"Making a run from here ain't gonna give us much of a head start," Potts reasoned. "We started this because we were sorry for the kid. If we don't go ahead with that part of it, we'll really feel like fools. I think we ought to spring him."

"Me too," Hoxie agreed. "But I *don't* think we ought to split the dough with him. We gon' need it a lot worse'n him. I mean, Cicero

Charley ain't gon' be after *him*. I say give him the clothes we bought him and a few hundred bucks. Let him take his chances."

Lewis thought it over for a few moments, then concurred. "Sounds fair to me. Head for the hospital."

They parked in the visitors' lot of the Cook County Hospital complex and unobtrusively made their way to the Radiology Building. When they got upstairs to Outpatient Radiology, they entered and signed in as usual, then took separate seats in the familiar waiting room as they always did. From past experience, Lewis had already calculated that the odds were five to four that they wouldn't have to wait more than fifteen minutes. He was right; they only had to wait eleven.

When the two prison guards walked in with Alan Lampley between them, they proceeded, as usual, directly to the treatment room door. As they were about to enter, Lewis nodded to Potts and the lanky Southerner jumped to his feet and drew one of the guns taken from the money couriers.

"Don't shoot or I'll move!" he ordered. The guards, Alan Lampley, Lewis, and Hoxie all looked at him with mixed expressions. Potts swallowed and said, "I mean, don't *m-m-move* or I'll shoot!"

"Take it easy, mister," one of the guards said. "Nobody's moving."

Hoxie quickly stepped up behind the guards and disarmed them. "We gon' be able to open a gun shop pretty soon," he muttered.

Just then, the door to the treatment room opened and the radiology technician came out. Potts turned the gun on him. "Hand it! Put your holds up! Damn it, I mean *hold* it and put your hands up!"

The technician froze. Alan Lampley looked around incredulously. "What's going on?" he asked.

"You'll find out in a minute," Lewis told him. "All right, everybody into the treatment room. Move it!"

In the treatment room, Lewis searched the guards, found keys, and unlocked Alan Lampley's cuffs and waist chain. "Get out of that jumpsuit," he said. To the technician, he said, "Take off that lab coat and your pants. Hurry up!"

In less than five minutes, Lewis and the others had the two guards and the technician, in his underwear, handcuffed and chained to the floor-mounted Cobalt-60 X-ray machine in the treatment room.

"You won't get away with this," one of the guards warned.

"Five to two you're right," Lewis agreed. He turned to his cohorts and their liberated prisoner. "Okay, let's go. Straight down to the fire stairs at the end of the hall."

Six minutes later, they were in the rented Buick, driving off the parking lot.

From the rear seat, where he sat with Hoxie, Alan Lampley said, "You guys are crazy. You just got yourselves in a hell of a lot of trouble."

"We thought you'd consider it a favor," Lewis said wryly. "So you wouldn't have to spend your last six months or so in prison."

"I don't have six months," Alan said. "They figure three at the most."

"Well, three, then," Potts said, glancing back over his shoulder from the driver's seat. "Wouldn't you rather be out than in?"

"Sure, I would," Alan admitted. "But not for the trouble you guys are into now. I mean, why'd you do it? You don't even know me, or anything about me —"

"Yeah, we do, son," said Hoxie. "We know why you're in jail; about your sister and that drug dealer an' all."

"Anyway," said Lewis, "we're doing it for ourselves, too. We pulled a stickup this morning to get enough dough so we could *all* live out what time we got left in a little style. On'y thing is, we didn't get as much as we figured. But we can still give you enough dough to get out of town, maybe go out to Las Vegas or L.A. or someplace and at least die a free man."

"Canada," Alan said. "I want to go to Canada."

Lewis grimaced. "What the hell for? It's cold up there. Don't you wanna go someplace warm?"

"I've got an uncle in Canada," Alan explained. "He went up there years ago to avoid the draft during the Vietnam War. He's got a little badger ranch up near Moose Jaw, that's in Saskatchewan. Raises badgers and harvests their hair like people shear sheep for their wool. They use the hair to make expensive shaving brushes. If I could get up to my uncle's ranch, I know he'd let me stay there and look after me for the time I've got left."

"Wouldn't work," Lewis said, shaking his head. "You couldn't get there without no ID of any kind: no driver's license, no passport, nothing. You'd never get in."

"I'd get in, all right," Alan promised. "I've been up there and gone on fishing trips with my uncle. There's places in the Grasslands National Park on the Montana border where you can just walk into Canada like you were crossing the street. You just get me a Greyhound bus ticket to Shelby, Montana. I'll take it from there."

Lewis and Potts exchanged looks, and Hoxie nodded to them in the rearview mirror. "You got a deal, kid," Lewis said.

In the motel room they had rented, about a mile from O'Hare Airport, Alan showered and dressed in the new clothes they had bought for him while Lewis and the others opened the four stolen suitcases, dumped all the money on one of the beds, and set about counting it.

"Throw all the ones on the other bed," Lewis said. "I'll start putting them in hundred-dollar bunches with rubber bands. You guys sort the bigger bills."

"That ain't gonna be hard," Potts cracked.

While they were counting, Alan finished getting ready and came into the room. He looked distressed. "I can't do this," he said. "I can't let you guys go on with this plan. It's not fair. I'm going to get away and you guys are going to get caught and go to prison. Then in three months or so, I'm going to be dead and they're going to be bringing *you* guys in from Joliet for radiation treatments — and *you're* going to die in prison." He shook his head determinedly. "It's all wrong. Look, if I give myself up, maybe they'll go easy on you. Maybe you'll just get probation."

The three men who had freed him exchanged glances, each in his own way moved by Alan's concern.

"Look, Alan," said Lewis, "it's nice of you to feel that way about us, but the fact is, it ain't only you and us and the cops that are involved in this thing. See all this money here? We stole it from Cicero Charley Waxman, a mobster — and Cicero Charley don't grant probation. If he catches up with us, we're dead — and he'll catch up with us just as easy inside prison as out."

"Maybe easier," Hoxie amended.

Potts went over and draped an arm around Alan's shoulders. "What he's saying, old buddy, is that we're up to our necks in this thing. Ain't no way out for us now. We got to play it right to the end. It just might turn out that the only thing we get out of this is knowing we helped you get away. You take that away from us an' it could turn out that we done it all for nothing. You don't want to do that to us, do you?"

"No," Alan shook his head, "I don't."

"You best get on up to that little badger ranch then," Hoxie told him quietly. "That way we get *something* out of it."

"All right," Alan said, lowering his eyes. He looked like he might cry.

Lewis guided Alan over to one of the open suitcases, which was now neatly packed with bundles of currency. "There's three thousand dollars in one-dollar bills, another fifteen hundred in fives and tens, and here" — he handed Alan a separate bundle — "is another five hundred in mixed bills to put in your pocket. Potts is going to drive you over to the Greyhound terminal near the airport. He'll go in and buy you a ticket on the first bus leaving; it's safer for him to do it, 'cause there won't be no pictures of us out yet. Then you take the ticket and get on the bus. Wherever it takes you, you can start out from there for Canada. Eight to five you'll make it."

Alan shook hands with Lewis and Hoxie, and left with Potts.

Lewis and Hoxie went back to counting dollar bills.

When Potts returned, Lewis and Hoxie were watching television.

"We made the evening news," Lewis told him.

"Made it bigtime," Hoxie added. "Lead story."

"They got a picture of the kid on there, but none of us yet. We got the city cops, state police, and FBI after us. They got the feds in on it 'cause they say we're prob'ly gonna leave the state and that's something called 'Interstate Flight.' How'd the kid do?"

"Good," said Potts. "Got him on a bus to Omaha, Nebraska. He said he can make Montana easy from there, then just walk into Canada through the woods." Potts looked at one of the beds, which was piled with bundles of money. "All counted, huh?"

"All counted," Lewis confirmed. "My friend Ralph estimated it pretty close. Total take was twenty-three thousand six hundred and twelve dollars. Minus the five grand we gave the kid, leaves us with eighteen thousand six hundred twelve. That comes to sixty-two hundred and four bucks apiece."

"Damn poor wages," Hoxie muttered, "considering we got all that law *plus* Cicero Charley after us."

"Yeah, sixty-two hunnerd ain't gonna get us far," said Potts.

"We could still make Buenos Aires," Lewis pointed out. "At least we'd be out of the country, and each have five grand to last us down there."

"Count me out," Potts said. "I got my wife and three kids to think about. Only reason I went in on this was I figured to have enough money to send for them, so's they could be with me when I die. Since that ain't worked out, I'll prob'ly just send my share of the dough to them and go on the bum around the city here until I get picked up."

"Hell, you can send them my puny little share, too," said Hoxie. "I'll go on the bum with you. Anything to get out of my daughter's basement."

"There is one other thing we could do," Lewis said quietly. He was sitting with his eyebrows knitted together in a frown, looking like a cross between James Cagney and an owl. "I don't know if you guys would go for it or not."

"Well, let's hear it. I mean, we ain't never let you down yet, have we?" Potts said drily.

"Yeah, tell us all about it," Hoxie declared. "Hell, we wouldn't be where we are today if it wasn't for you, my man."

"I thought of something while we was counting all them dollar bills," Lewis explained. "It was something my friend Ralph said to me one Thursday morning when he let me into the parlor early to lay my bets. He said I was lucky he was letting me in at all — especially on Thursday. Because Thursdays and Fridays was count days. Thursdays *and Fridays*. If the chump change from parlay cards comes in on Thursdays, the serious money from track and sports betting must come in on Fridays. I picked the wrong day for us. The big bucks should be delivered in the morning."

Hoxie looked askance at him. "Lewis, are you saying what I think you're saying?"

"Next thing you know," Potts said, "you'll be wanting to hold up a bank."

"I thought about that," Lewis admitted, "but with the security and alarms and all, I figured it was nine to five we'd get caught."

"And you think we *won't* get caught if we rob the same place to-morrow that we robbed today?" Hoxie asked incredulously.

"That's exactly what I think," Lewis said. "Right now, Cicero Charley thinks he's lucky that we hit him on Thursday. Ralph's already admitted to him that he let me in on Thursdays only. Cicero Charley's got no idea I even know that Friday is a count day, too. Plus which, by now he already knows from the news what else we done, springing the kid, and he knows the law's after us. Right now, he figures we're running for our lives. He wouldn't think in a million years that we'd hit him again tomorrow."

"That friend of yours, Ralph, ain't gonna open the door again," Potts pointed out.

"He won't have to. Look, we got guns. We take down the couriers on the sidewalk, after they get out of their car. We can do this in two minutes, be in our own car, and be gone. We'll slash their tires so they can't follow."

Potts leaned forward, a look of intense interest on his thin face. "What do you think the odds are, Lewis?"

"Eight to one, our favor," Lewis said confidently.

"Hmmm," Hoxie said, "that high?"

"Absolutely."

It only took a moment for them to decide.

"I'm in," Potts said.

"Me too," Hoxie added.

Lewis smiled.

Potts telephoned out for pizza and beer, and when it was delivered, the three dying men began planning their second stickup.

STUART M. KAMINSKY

Sometimes Something Goes Wrong

FROM *The Mysterious Press Anniversary Anthology*

"YOU SURE?"

Beemer looked at Pryor and said, "I'm sure. One year ago. This day. That jewelry store. It's in my book."

Pryor was short, thin, nervous. Dustin Hoffman on some kind of speed produced by his own body. His face was flat, scarred from too many losses in the ring for too many years. He was stupid. Born that way. Punches to the head hadn't made his IQ rise. But Pryor did what he was told and Beemer liked telling Pryor what to do. Talking to Pryor was like thinking out loud.

"One year ago. In your book," Pryor said, looking at the jewelry store through the car window.

"In my book," Beemer said, patting the right pocket of his black zipper jacket.

"And this is . . . ? I mean, where we are?"

"Northbrook. It's a suburb of Chicago," said Beemer patiently.

Pryor nodded as if he understood. He didn't really, but if Beemer said so, it must be so. He looked at Beemer, who sat behind the wheel, his eyes fixed on the door of the jewelry store. Beemer was broad shouldered, well built from three years with the weights in Stateville and keeping it up when he was outside. He was nearing fifty, blue eyes, short, razor haircut, gray-black hair. He looked like a linebacker, a short linebacker. Beemer had never played football. He had robbed two Cincinnati Bengals once outside a bar, but that was the closest he got to the real thing. Didn't watch sports on the tube. In prison he had read, wore glasses. Classics. For over a year. Dickens. Hemingway. Steinbeck. Shakespeare. Freud. Shaw, Irwin, and George Bernard. Then one year to the day he started, Beemer stopped reading. Beemer kept track of time.

Now, Beemer liked to keep moving. Buy clothes, eat well, stay in classy hotels when he could. Beemer was putting the cash away for the day he'd feel like retiring. He couldn't imagine that day.

"Tell me again why we're hitting it exactly a year after we hit it before," Pryor said.

Beemer checked his watch. Dusk. Almost closing time. The couple who owned and ran the place were always the last ones in the mall besides the Chinese restaurant to close. On one side of the jewelry store, Gortman's Jewelry and Fine Watches, was a storefront insurance office. State Farm. Frederick White the agent. He had locked up and gone home. On the other side, Himmell's Gifts. Stuff that looked like it would break if you touched it in the window. Glassy-looking birds and horses. Glassy, not classy. Beemer liked touching real class, like really thin glass wineglasses. If he settled down, he'd buy a few, have a drink every night, run his finger around the rim and make that ringing sound. He didn't know how to do that. He'd learn.

"What?"

"Why are we here again?" Pryor asked.

"Anniversary. Our first big score. Good luck. Maybe. It just feels right."

"What did we get last time?"

The small strip mall was almost empty now. Maybe four cars if you didn't count the eight parked all the way down at the end by the Chinese restaurant. Beemer could take or leave Chinese food, but he liked the buffet idea. Thai food. That was his choice. Tonight they'd have Thai. Tomorrow they'd take the watches, bracelets, rings to Walter on Polk Street. Walter would look everything over, make an offer. Beemer would take it. Thai food. That was the ticket.

"We got six thousand last time," Beemer said. "Five minutes' work. Six thousand dollars. More than a thousand a minute."

"More than a thousand a minute," Pryor echoed.

"Celebration," said Beemer. "This is a celebration. Back where our good luck started."

"Back light went out," Pryor said, looking at the jewelry store.

"We're moving," Beemer answered, getting quickly out of the car.

They moved right toward the door. Beemer had a Glock. His treasure. Read about it in a spy story in a magazine. Had to have it. Pryor had a piece-of-crap street gun with tape on the handle. Revolver. Six or eight shots. Piece of crap, but a bullet from it would hurt going in and might never come out. People didn't care. You put a gun in their face they didn't care if it was precision or zip. They knew it could blow out their lights.

Beemer glanced at Pryor, keeping pace at his side. Pryor had dressed up for the job. He had gone through his bag at the motel, asked Beemer what he should wear. Always asked Beemer. Asked him if he should brush his teeth. Well, maybe not quite, but asked him almost everything. The distance to the moon. Could eating Equal really give you cancer. Beemer always had an answer. Quick, ready. Right or wrong. He had an answer.

Pryor was wearing blue slacks and a Tommy Hilfiger blue pullover short-sleeved shirt. He had brushed his hair, polished his shoes. He was ready. Ugly and ready.

Just as the couple inside turned off their light Beemer opened the door and pulled out his gun. Pryor did the same. They didn't wear masks. Artist's sketches were for shit. Ski masks itched. Sometimes Beemer wore dark glasses. That's if they were working the day. Sometimes he had a Band-Aid on his cheek. Let them remember that or the fake mole he got from Gibson's Magic Shop in Fayetteville, North Carolina. That was a bad hit. No more magic shops. He had scooped up a shopping bag of tricks and practical jokes. Fake dog shit. Fake snot you could hang from your nose. He threw it all away. Kept the mole though. Didn't have it on now.

"Don't move," he said.

The couple didn't move. The man was younger than Beemer by a decade. Average height. He had grown a beard in the last year. Looked older. Wearing a zipper jacket. Blue. Beemer's was black. Beemer's favorite colors were black and white. That was the way he liked things. The woman was blond, somewhere in her thirties, sort of pretty, too thin for Beemer's tastes. Pryor remembered the women. He never touched them, but he remembered and talked about them at night in the hotels or motels. Stealing from good-looking women was a high for Pryor. That and good kosher hot dogs. Chicago was always good for hot dogs if you knew where to go. Beemer knew. On the way back, they'd stop at a place he knew on Dempster. Make Pryor happy. Sit and eat a big kosher or two, lots of fries, ketchup, onions, hot peppers. Let Pryor talk about the woman.

She looked different. She was wearing a green dress. She was pregnant. That was it.

"No," she said.

"Yes," said Beemer. "You know what to do. Stand quiet. No alarms. No crying. Nothing stupid. Boy or a girl?"

Pryor was behind the glass counters, opening them quickly, shoveling, clinking, into the Barnes & Noble bag he had taken from his back pocket. There was a picture of Sigmund Freud on the bag. Sigmund Freud was watching Beemer. Beemer wondered what Freud was thinking.

"Boy or girl?" Beemer repeated. "You know if it's going to be a boy or a girl?"

"Girl," said the man.

"You got a name picked out?"

"Melissa," said the woman.

Beemer shook his head and said, "Too . . . I don't know . . . too what everybody else is doing. Something simple. Joan. Molly. Agnes. The simple is different. Hurry it up," he called to Pryor.

"Hurry it up, right," Pryor answered, moving faster, the B&N bag bulging, Freud looking a little plump and not so serious now.

"We'll think about it," the man said.

Beemer didn't think so.

"Why us?" the woman said. Anger. Tears were coming. "Why do you keep coming back to us?"

"Only the second time," said Beemer. "Anniversary. One year ago today. Did you forget?"

"I remembered," said the man, moving to his wife and putting his arm around her.

"We won't be back," Beemer said as Pryor moved across the carpeting to the second showcase.

"It doesn't matter," said the man. "After this we won't be able to get insurance."

"Sorry," said Beemer. "How's business been?"

"Slow," said the man with a shrug. The pregnant woman's eyes were closed.

Pryor scooped.

"You make any of this stuff?" Beemer asked, looking around. "Last time there were some gold things, little animals, shapes, birds, fish, bears. Little."

"I made those," the man said.

"See any little animals, gold?" Beemer called to Pryor.

"Don't know," said Pryor. "Just scooping. Wait. Yeah, I see some."

Beemer looked at his watch. He remembered where he got it. Right here. One year ago. He held up the watch to show the man and woman.

"Recognize it?" he said.

The man nodded.

"Keeps great time," said Beemer. "Class."

"You have good taste," the man said.

"Thanks," said Beemer, ignoring the sarcasm. The man had a right. He was being robbed. He was going out of business. This was a going-out-of-business nonsale. The man wasn't old. He could start again, work for someone else. He made nice little gold animals. He was going to be a father. The watch told Beemer that they had been here four minutes.

"Let's go," he called to Pryor.

"One more minute. Two more. Should I look in the back?"

Beemer hesitated.

"Anything back there?" Beemer asked the man.

The man didn't answer.

"Forget it," he called to Pryor. "We've got enough."

Pryor came out from behind the case. B&N bag bulging. More than they got the last time. Then Pryor tripped. It happens. Pryor tripped. The bag fell on the floor. Gold and time went flying, a snow or rain of gold and silver, platinum and rings. And Pryor's gun went off as he fell.

The bullet hit the man in the back. The woman screamed. The man went to his knees. His teeth were clenched. Nice white teeth. Beemer wondered if such nice white teeth could be real. The woman went down with the man, trying to hold him up.

Pryor looked at them, looked at Beemer, and started to throw things back in the bag. Wait. That wasn't Freud. Beemer tried to remember who it was. Not Freud. George Bernard Shaw. It was George Bernard Shaw with wrinkled brow who looked up at Beemer, displeased.

"An accident," Beemer told the woman, who was holding her husband, who now bit his lower lip hard. Blood from the bite. Beemer didn't want to know what the man's back looked like or where the bullet had traveled inside his body. "Call an ambulance, Nine one one. We never shot anybody before. An accident."

It was more than five minutes now. Pryor was breathing hard trying to get everything. On his knees, scampering like a crazy dog.

"Put the gun away," Beemer said. "Use both hands. Hurry up. These people need a doctor."

Pryor nodded, put the gun in his pocket, and gathered glittering crops. The man had fallen, collapsed on his back. The woman looked up at Beemer, crying. Beemer didn't want her to lose her baby.

"He have insurance?" he asked.

She looked at him, bewildered.

"Life insurance?" Beemer explained.

"Done," said Pryor with a smile. His teeth were small, yellow.

The woman didn't answer the question. Pryor ran to the door. He didn't look back at what he had done.

"Nine one one," Beemer said, backing out of the store.

Pryor looked both ways and headed for the car. Beemer was a foot out the door. He turned and went back in.

"Sorry," he said. "It was an accident."

"Get out," the woman screamed. "Go away. Go away. Go away."

She started to get up. Maybe she was crazy enough to attack him. Maybe Beemer would have to shoot her. He didn't think he could shoot a pregnant woman.

"Joan," he said, stepping outside again. "Joan's a good name. Think about it. Consider it."

"Get out," the woman screamed.

Beemer got out. Pryor was already in the car. Beemer ran. Some people were coming out of the Chinese restaurant. Two guys in baseball hats. From this distance, about forty yards, they looked like truckers. There weren't any trucks in the lot. They were looking right at Beemer. Beemer realized he was holding his gun. Beemer could hear the woman screaming. The truckers could probably hear her too. He ran to the car, got behind the wheel. Pryor couldn't drive, never learned, never tried.

Beemer shot out of the parking lot. They'd need another car.

Not a problem. Night. Good neighborhood. In and gone in something not too new. Dump it. No prints. Later buy a five-year-old Geo, Honda, something like that. Legal. In Beemer's name.

"We got a lot," Pryor said happily.

"You shot that guy," Beemer said, staying inside the speed limit, heading for the expressway. "He might die."

"What?" asked Pryor.

"You shot that man," Beemer repeated, passing a guy in a blue BMW. The guy was smoking a cigarette. Beemer didn't smoke. He made Pryor stop when they'd gotten together. Inside. In Stateville, he was in a cell with two guys who smoked. Smell had been everywhere. On Beemer's clothes. On the pages of his books.

People killed themselves. Alcohol, drugs, smoking, eating crap that told the blood going to their heart that this was their territory now and there was no way they were getting by without surgery.

"People stink," said Beemer.

Pryor was poking through the bag. He nodded in agreement. He was smiling.

"What if he dies?" Beemer said.

"Who?"

"The guy you shot," said Beemer. "Shot full of holes by someone she knows."

The expressway was straight ahead. Beemer could see the stoplight, the big green sign.

"I don't know her," Pryor said. "Never saw her before."

"One year ago," Beemer said.

"So? We don't go back. The guy dies. Everybody dies. You said so," Pryor said, feeling proud of himself, holding G. B. Shaw to his bosom. "We stopping for hot dogs? That place you said? Kosher. Juicy."

"I don't feel like hot dogs," said Beemer.

He turned onto the expressway, headed south toward Chicago. Jammed. Rush hour. Line from here to forever. Moving maybe five, ten miles an hour. Beemer turned on the radio and looked in the rearview mirror. Cars were lined up behind him. A long showroom of whatever you might want. Lights on, creeping, crawling. Should have stayed off the expressway. Too late now. Listen to the news, music, voices that made sense besides his own. An insulting talk show host would be fine.

"More than we got last time," Pryor said happily.

"Yeah," said Beemer.

"A couple of hot dogs would be good," said Pryor. "Celebrate."

"Celebrate what?"

"Anniversary. We've got a present."

Pryor held up the bag. It looked heavy. Beemer grunted. What the hell. They had to eat.

"Hot dogs," Beemer said.

"Yup," said Pryor.

Traffic crawled. The car in front of Beemer had a bumper sticker: DON'T BLAME ME. I VOTED LIBERTARIAN. What the hell was that? Libertarian. Beemer willed the cars to move. He couldn't do magic. A voice on the radio said something about Syria. Syria didn't exist for Beemer. Syria, Lebanon, Israel, Bosnia. You name it. It didn't really exist. Nothing existed. No place existed until it was right there to be touched, looked at, held up with a Glock in your hand.

Gluck, gluck, gluck, gluck, gluck.

Beemer heard it over the sound of running engines and a horn here and there from someone in a hurry to get somewhere in a hurry. He looked up. Helicopter. Traffic watch from a radio or television station? No. It was low. Cops. The truckers from the Chinese restaurant? Still digesting their fried wonton when they went to their radios or a pay phone or a cell phone or pulled out a rocket.

Cops were looking for a certain car. Must be hundreds, thousands out here. Find Waldo, only harder. Beemer looked in his rearview mirror. No flashing lights. He looked up the embankment to his right. Access drive. The tops of cars. No lights flashing. No uniforms dashing. No dogs barking. Just *gluck, gluck, gluck.* Then a light. Pure white circle down on the cars in front. Sweeping right to left, left to right. Pryor had no clue. He was lost in Rolexes and dreams of french fries.

Did the light linger on them? Imagination? Maybe. Description from the hot-and-sour-soup-belching truckers? Description from the lady with the baby she was going to name Melissa when Joan would have been better? Joan had been Beemer's mother's name. He hadn't suggested it lightly.

So they had his description. Stocky guy with short gray hair, about fifty, wearing a black zipper jacket. Skinny guy carrying a canvas bag filled with goodies. A jackpot piñata, a heist from St. Nick.

Traffic moved, not wisely or well, but it moved, inched. Music of another time. Tony Bennett? No, hell no. Johnny Mathis singing "Chances Are." Should have been Tommy Edwards.

"Let's go. Let's go," Beemer whispered to the car ahead.

"Huh?" asked Pryor.

"There's a cop in a helicopter up there," Beemer said, moving forward as if he were on the roller coaster ride creeping toward the top, where they would plunge straight down into despair and black air. "I think he's looking for us."

Pryor looked at him and then rolled down his window to stick his head out before Beemer could stop him.

"Stop that shit," Beemer shouted, pulling the skinny dryness inside.

"I saw it," said Pryor.

"Did he see you?"

"No one waved or nothing," said Pryor. "There he goes."

The helicopter roared forward low, ahead of them. Should he take the next exit? Stay in the crowd? And then the traffic started to move a little faster. Not fast, mind you, but it was moving now. Maybe twenty miles an hour. Actually nineteen, but close enough. Beemer decided to grit it out. He turned off the radio.

They made it to Dempster in thirty-five minutes and headed east, toward Lake Michigan. No helicopter. It was still early. Too early for an easy car swap, but it couldn't be helped. Helicopters. He searched this way and that, let his instincts take over at a street across from a park. Three-story apartment buildings. Lots of traffic. He drove in a block. Cars on both sides, some facing the wrong way.

"What are we doing?" asked Pryor.

"*We* are doing nothing," Beemer said. "*I* am looking for a car. I steal cars. I rob stores. I don't shoot people. I show my gun. They show respect. You show that piece of shit in your pocket, trip over thin air, and shoot a guy in the back."

"Accident," said Pryor.

"My ass," said Beemer. And then, "That one."

He was looking at a gray Nissan a couple of years old parked under a big tree with branches sticking out over the street. No traffic. Dead-end street.

"Wipe it down," Beemer ordered, parking the car and getting out.

Pryor started wiping the car for prints. First inside. Then outside. By the time he was done, Beemer had the Nissan humming. Pryor got in the passenger seat, his bag on his lap, going on a vacation. All he needed was a beach and a towel.

They hit the hot dog place fifteen minutes later. They followed the smell and went in. There was a line. Soft poppyseed buns. Kosher dogs. Big slices of new pickle. Salty brown fries. They were in line. Two women in front of them were talking. A mother and daughter. Both wearing shorts and showing stomach. Pryor looked back at the door. He could see the Nissan. The bag was in the trunk with George Bernard Shaw standing guard.

The woman and the girl were talking about Paris. Plaster of? Texas? Europe? Somebody they knew? Nice voices. Beemer tried to remember when he had last been with a woman. Not that long ago. Two months? Amarillo? Las Vegas? Moline, Illinois?

It was their turn. The kid in the white apron behind the counter wiped his hands and said, "What can I do for you?"

You can bring back the dead, thought Beemer. *You can make us invisible. You can teleport us to my aunt Elaine's in Corpus Christi.*

"You can give us each a hot dog with the works," Beemer said.

"Two for me," said Pryor. "And fries."

"Two for both of us. Lots of mustard. Grilled onions. Tomatoes. Cokes. Diet for me. Regular for him."

The mother and daughter were sitting on stools still talking about Paris and eating.

"You got a phone?" Beemer asked, paying for their order.

"Back there," said the kid, taking the money.

"I'm going back there to call Walter. Find us a seat where we can watch the car."

Pryor nodded and moved to the pickup line. Beemer went back there to make the call. The phone was next to the toilet. He used the toilet first and looked at himself in the mirror. He didn't look good. Decidedly.

He filled the sink with water, cold water, and plunged his face in. Maybe the sink was dirty? Least of his worries. He pulled his head out and looked at himself. Dripping-wet reflection. The world hadn't changed. He dried his face and hands and went to the phone. He had a calling card, AT&T. He called Walter. The conversation went like this.

"Walter? I've got goods."

"Jewelry store?"

"It matter?"

"Matters. Cops moved fast. Man's in the hospital maybe dying. Church deacon or something. A saint. All over television with descriptions of two dummies I thought I might recognize."

"Goods are goods," said Beemer.

"These goods could make a man an accessory maybe to murder. Keep your goods. Take them who knows where. Get out of town before it's too late, my dear. You know what I'm saying?"

"Walter, be reasonable."

"My middle name is 'reasonable.' It should be 'careful' but it's 'reasonable.' I'm hanging up. I don't know who you are. I think you got the wrong number."

He hung up. Beemer looked at the phone and thought. St. Louis. There was a guy, Tanner, in St. Louis. No, East St. Louis. A black guy who'd treat them fair for their goods. They'd check out of the motel and head for St. Louis. Not enough money, without selling the goods or going to the bank, to get a new car. They'd have to drive the Nissan, slow and easy. All night. Get to Tanner first thing in the morning when the sun was coming up through the Arch.

Beemer went down the narrow corridor. Cardboard boxes made it narrower. When he got to the counter, the mother and daughter were still eating and talking and drinking. Lots of people were. Standing at the counters or sitting on high stools with red seats that swirled. Smelled fantastic. Things would be all right. Pryor had a place by the window where he could watch the car. He had finished one hot dog and was working on another. Beemer inched in next to him.

"We're going to St. Louis," he said behind a wall of other conversations.

"Okay," said Pryor, mustard on his nose. No questions. Just "Okay."

Then it happened. It always happens. Shit always happens. A cop car, black and white, pulled into the lot outside the hot dog place. It was a narrow lot. The cops were moving slowly. Were they looking for a space and a quick burger or hot dog? Were they looking for a stolen Nissan?

The cops stopped next to the Nissan.

"No," moaned Pryor.

Beemer grabbed the little guy's arm. The cops turned toward the hot dog shop window. Beemer looked at the wall, ate his dog, and ate slowly, his heart going mad. Maybe he'd die now of a heart attack. Why not? His father had died on a Washington, D.C., subway just like that.

Pryor was openly watching the cops move toward them.

"Don't look at them," Beemer whispered. "Look at me. Talk. Say something. Smile. I'll nod. Say anything."

"Are they coming for us?" asked Pryor, working on his second dog.

"You've got mustard on your nose. You want to go down with mustard on your nose? You want to be a joke on the ten o'clock news?"

Beemer took a napkin and wiped Pryor's nose as the cops came in the door and looked around.

"Reach in your pocket," said Beemer. "Take out your gun. I'm going to do the same. Aim it at the cops. Don't shoot. Don't speak. If they pull out their guns, just drop yours. It'll be over and we can go pray that the guy you shot doesn't die."

"I don't pray," said Pryor as the cops, both young and in uniform, moved through the line of customers down the middle of the shop, hands on holstered guns.

Beemer turned and so did Pryor. Guns out, aimed. Butch and Sundance. A John Woo movie.

"Hold it," shouted Beemer.

Oh God, I pissed in my pants. Half an hour to the motel. Maybe twenty years to life to the motel.

The cops stopped, hands still on their holsters. The place went dead. Someone screamed. The mother or the daughter, who had stopped talking about Paris.

"Let's go," said Beemer.

Pryor reached back for the last half of his hot dog and his little greasy bag of fries.

"Is that a Glock?" asked the kid behind the counter.

"It's a Glock," said Beemer.

"Cool gun," said the kid.

The cops didn't speak. Beemer didn't say anything more. He and Pryor made it to the door, backed away across the parking lot, watching the cops watching them. The cops wouldn't shoot. Too many people.

"Get in," Beemer said.

Pryor got in the car. Beemer reached back to open the driver-side door. Hard to keep his gun level and open the door. He did it, got in, started the car, and looked in the rearview. The cops were coming out, guns drawn. There was a barrier in front of him, low, a couple of inches, painted red. Beemer gunned forward over the barrier. Hell, it wasn't his car. He thought there was just enough room to get between a white minivan and an old convertible who-knows-what.

The cops were saying something. Beemer wasn't listening. He had pissed in his pants and he expected to die of a heart attack. He listened for some telltale sign. The underbody of the Nissan caught the red barrier, scraped, and roared over. Beemer glanced toward Pryor, who had the window open and was leaning out, his piece-of-crap gun in his hand. Pryor fired as Beemer made it between minivan and convertible, taking some paint off both sides of the Nissan in the process.

Pryor fired as Beemer hit the street. Beemer heard the hot dog shop's window shatter. They wouldn't be welcome here in the near future. Then came another shot as Beemer turned right. This one went through Pryor's face. He was dead, hanging out the window. Beemer floored the Nissan. He could hear Pryor's head bouncing on the door.

The cops were going for their car, making calls, and Pryor's head was bouncing like something out of the jungle on the door. Beemer made a hard right down a semidark street. He pulled to the curb, reached past Pryor, and opened the door. It swung open, Pryor draped over it. Beemer grabbed the dead man's shirt, pulled him back through the window, and pushed the body out the door. Then he reached over to close the door. Pryor was looking up at him with three eyes, one of them brand new.

Beemer drove. There were lights behind him now, a block back. Sirens. He turned left, wove around. No idea where he was. No one to talk to. *Just me and my radio.*

Who knows how many minutes later he came to a street called Oakton and headed east, for Sheridan Road, Lake Shore Drive, Lake Michigan.

People passed in cars. He passed people walking. People looked at him. The bloody door. That was it. Pryor had marked him. No time to stop and clean it up. Not on the street. He hit Sheridan

Road and looked for a place to turn, found it. Little dead end. Black on white sign: NO SWIMMING. A park.

He pulled in between a couple of cars he didn't look at, popped the trunk lock, and got out. There was nothing in the trunk but the bag of jewelry. He dumped it all into the trunk, picked up the empty canvas bag, closed the trunk, and went looking for water.

Families were having late picnics. Couples were walking. Beemer found a fountain. He soaked George Bernard Shaw and brought him dripping back to the Nissan, where he worked on the bloody car door. It streaked. He worked, turned the canvas bag. Scrubbed. He went back for more water, wrung the bloody water from the bag. Worked again. Gunga Din. Fetch water. Clean up. Three trips and it was done.

George Bernard Shaw was angry. His face was red under the parking lot lights.

Beemer opened the trunk and threw the bag in. When he turned, he saw the cop car coming down the street. Only one way in the lot. Only one way out. The same way. He grabbed six or seven watches and some little golden animals and shoved them in his pockets quickly. Then he moved into the park, off the path, toward the rocks. Last stand? Glock on the rocks? Couldn't be. It couldn't end like this. He was caught between a cop and a hard place. Funny. Couldn't laugh though. He hurried on, looking back to see the cop car enter the little lot.

Beemer found the rocks. Kids were crawling over them. Big rocks. Beyond them the night and the lake like an ocean of darkness, end of the world. Nothingness. He climbed out and down.

Three teenagers or college kids, male, watched him make his way down toward the water.

Stop looking at me, he willed. *Go back to playing with yourselves, telling lies, and being stupid. Just don't look at me.* Beemer crouched down behind a rock, the water touching his shoes.

He had no plan. Water and rocks. Pockets full of not much. Crawl along the rocks. Get out. Find a car. Drive to the motel. Get to St. Louis. Tanner might give him a few hundred, maybe more, for what he had. Start again, find a new Pryor to replace the prior Pryor, a Pryor without a gun. Beemer knew he couldn't be alone.

"You see a man out here?" He heard a voice through the sound of the waves.

"Down there," came a slightly younger voice.

Beemer couldn't swim. Give up or keep going. He kept going. A flashlight beam from above now. Another from the direction he had come.

"Stop right there. Turn around and come back the way you came," said a voice.

"He's armed," said another voice.

"Take out your gun and hold it by the barrel. Now."

Beemer considered. He took out the Glock. Great gun. Took it out slowly, looked up, and decided it was all a what-the-hell life anyway. He grabbed the gun by the handle, holding on to the rock with one hand. He aimed toward the flashlight above him.

Before he could fire he heard a shot, felt the pain, fell backward. His head hit a jutting rock. The rock hurt more than the bullet that tore at his stomach. But the water, the cold water, was worst of all.

"Can you get to him, Dave?" someone called.

"I'm trying."

Beemer was floating on his back, bobbing in the black waves. *I can float,* he thought, looking at the flashlight. *Float out to some little sailboat, climb on, get away.*

He bobbed further away. Pain gone cold.

"Can't reach him."

"Shit. He's floating out. Call it in."

Footsteps. Beemer looked up. Beyond the light aimed at his eyes, he could see people in a line looking down at him as he floated farther and farther from the shore into the blackness. He considered waving to them. He looked for the moon and stars. They weren't there.

Maybe the anniversary hit hadn't been such a good idea.

He closed his eyes and thought that he had never fired his Glock, never fired any gun. That would be a regret if they didn't save him. That would be a regret if they did. It was a damned good gun.

Beemer fell asleep. Either that or he died.

JOE R. LANSDALE

The Mule Rustlers

FROM *The Mysterious Press Anniversary Anthology*

ON A BLUSTERY San Jacinto day, when leggy black clouds appeared against the pearl-gray sky like tromped-on spiders, Elliot
and James set about rustling the mule.

A week back, James had spotted the critter while out casing the
area for a house to burglarize. The burglary idea went down the
tubes because there were too many large dogs in the yards, and too
many older people sitting in lawn chairs flexing their false teeth
among concrete lawn ornaments and sprinklers. Most likely they
owned guns.

But on the way out of the neighborhood, James observed, on a
patch of about ten acres with a small pond and lots of trees, the
mule. It was average-sized, brown in color, with a touch of white
around the nostrils, and it had ears that tracked the countryside
like radar instruments.

All of the property was fenced in barbed wire, but the gate to the
property wasn't any great problem. It was made of hog wire stapled
to posts, and there was another wire fastened to it and looped over
a creosote corner post. There was a chain and padlock, but that was
of no consequence. Wire cutters, and you were in.

The road in front of the property was reasonably traveled, and
even as he slowed to check out the hog wire, three cars passed him
going in the opposite direction.

James discovered if he drove off the gravel road and turned
right on a narrow dirt road and parked to the side, he could walk
through another piece of unfenced wooded property and climb
over the barbed-wire fence at the back of the mule's acreage. Better

yet, the fence wasn't too good there, was kinda low, two strands only, and was primarily a line that marked ownership, not a boundary. The mule was in there mostly by her own good will.

James put a foot on the low, weak fence and pushed it almost to the ground. It was easy to step over then and he wanted to take the mule immediately, for he could see it browsing through a split in the trees, chomping up grass. It was an old mule, and its ears swung forward and back, but if it was aware of his presence, only the ears seemed to know and failed to send the signal to the critter's brain, or maybe the brain got the signal and didn't care.

James studied the situation. There were plenty of little crop farmers who liked a mule to plow their garden, or wanted one just because mules were cool. So there was a market. As for the job, well, the work would be holding the fence down so the mule could step over, then leading it to the truck. Easy money.

Problem was, James didn't have a truck. He had a Volvo that needed front-end work. It had once been crushed up like an accordion, then straightened somewhat, if not enough. It rattled and occasionally threatened to head off to the right without benefit of having the steering wheel turned.

And the damn thing embarrassed him. His hat touched the roof, and if he went out to the Cattleman's Cafe at the auction barn, he felt like a dork climbing out of it amidst mud-splattered pickups, some of them the size of military assault vehicles.

He had owned a huge Dodge Ram but had lost it in a card game, and the winner, feeling generous, had swapped titles. The card shark got the Dodge, and James got the goddamn Volvo, worn out with the ceiling cloth dripping, the floor rotted away in spots, and the steering wheel slightly bent where an accident, most likely the one that accordioned the front end, must have thrown some unseat-belted fella against it. At the top of the steering wheel, in the little rubber tubing wrapped around it, were a couple of teeth marks, souvenirs of that same unfortunate episode. Worse yet, the damn Volvo had been painted yellow, and it wasn't a job to be proud of. Baby-shit-hardened-and-aged-on-a-bedpost yellow.

Bottom line was, the mule couldn't ride in the front seat with him. But his friend Elliot owned both a pickup and a horse trailer.

Elliot had once seen himself as a horseman, but the problem was he never owned but one horse, a pinto, and it died from neglect, and had been on its last legs when Elliot purchased it for too much money. It was the only horse James had seen in Elliot's possession outside of stolen ones passing through his hands, and the only one outside of the one in the movie *Cat Ballou* that could lean against a wall at a forty-five-degree angle.

One morning it kept leaning, stiff as a sixteen-year-old's woody, but without the pulse. Having been there, probably dead, for several days, part of its hide had stuck to the wall and gone liquid and gluish. It took him and Elliot both a two-by-four and a lot of energy to pry it off the stucco and push it down. They'd hooked it up to a chain by the back legs and dragged it to the center of Elliot's property.

Elliot had inherited his land from his grandfather Clemmons, who'd hated him. Old Man Clemmons had left him the land, but it was rumored he first salted the twenty-five acres and shit in the well. Sure enough, not much grew there except weeds, but as far as Elliot could tell the well water tasted fine.

According to Elliot, besides the salt and maybe the shit, he was given his grandfather's curse that wished him all life's burdens, none of its joys, and an early death. "He didn't like me much," Elliot was fond of saying when deep in his sauce.

They had coated the deceased pinto with gasoline and set it on fire. It had stunk something awful, and since they were involved with a bottle of Wild Turkey while it burned, it had flamed up and caught the back of Elliot's truck on fire, burning out the rubber truck bed lining. James figured they had just managed to beat it out with their coats moments before the gas tank ignited and blew them over and through the trees, along with the burning pinto's hide and bones.

James drove over to Elliot's place after his discovery of the mule. Elliot had grown him a few garden vegetables, mostly chocked with bugs, that he had been pushing from his fruit and vegetable stand next to the road.

James found him trying to sell a half bushel of tomatoes to a tall, moderately attractive blond woman wearing shorts and showing lots of hair on her legs. Short bristly hair like a hog's. James had visions of dropping her in a vat of hot water and scraping that hair off with a knife. Course, he didn't want it hot as hog-scalding water,

or she wouldn't be worth much when he got through. He wanted
her shaved, not hurt.

Elliot had his brown sweat-stained Stetson pushed up on his
head and he was talking the lady up good as he could, considering
she was digging through a basket and coming up with some bug-bit
tomatoes.

"These are all bit up," she said.

"Bugs attack the good'ns," Elliot said. "Them's the one's you
want. These ain't like that crap you get in the store."

"They don't have bugs in them."

"Yeah, but they don't got the flavor these do. You just cut around
the spots, and those tomatoes'll taste better than any you ever had."

"That's a crock of shit," the lady said.

"Well now," Elliot said, "that's a matter of opinion."

"It's my opinion you put a few good tomatoes on top of the bug-
bit ones," she said. "That's my opinion, and you can keep your tomatoes."

She got in a new red Chevrolet and drove off.

"Good to see you ain't lost your touch," James said.

"Now, these here tomatoes have been goin' pretty fast this morning. Since it's mostly women buyin', I do all right. Fact is that's my
first loss. Charm didn't work on her. She's probably a lesbian."

James wanted to call bullshit on that, but right now he wanted
Elliot on his side.

"Unless you're doin' so good here you don't need money, I got
us a little job."

"You case some spots?" Elliot asked.

"I didn't find nothin' worth doin'. Besides, there's lots of old
folks where I was lookin'."

"I don't want no part of them. Always home. Always got dogs and
guns."

"Yeah, and lawn gnomes and sprinklers made of wooden animals."

"With the tails that spin and throw water?"

"Yep."

"Kinda like them myself. You know, you picked up some of them
things, you could sell them right smart."

"Yeah, well. I got somethin' better."

"Name it."

"Rustlin'."

Elliot worked his mouth a bit. James could see the idea appealed to him. Elliot liked to think of himself as a modern cowboy. "How many head?"

"One."

"One? Hell, that ain't much rustlin'."

"It's a mule. You can get maybe a thousand dollars for one. They're getting rarer, and they're kind of popular now. We rustle it. We could split the money."

Elliot studied on this momentarily. He also liked to think of himself as a respected and experienced thief.

"You know, I know a fella would buy a mule. Let me go up to the house and give him a call."

"It's the same fella I know, ain't it?"

"Yeah," Elliot said.

Elliot made the call and came out of the bedroom into the living room with good news.

"George wants it right away. He's offerin' us eight hundred."

"I wanted a thousand."

"He's offering eight hundred, he'll sell it for a thousand or better himself. He said he can't go a thousand. Already got a couple other buys goin' today. It's a deal and its now."

James considered that.

"I guess that'll do. We'll need your truck and trailer."

"I figured as much."

"You got any brown shoe polish?"

"Brown shoe polish?"

"That's right," James said.

The truck was a big four-seater Dodge with a bed big enough to fill, attach a diving board, and call a pool. The Dodge hummed like a sewing machine as it whizzed along on its huge tires. The trailer clattered behind and wove precariously left and right, as if it might pass the truck at any moment. James and Elliot had their windows down, and the cool April wind snapped at the brims of their hats and made the creases in their crowns deeper.

By the time they drove over to the place where the mule was, the smashed spider clouds had begun to twist their legs together and blend into one messy critter that peed sprinkles of rain all over the truck windshield.

They slowed as they passed the gate, then turned right. No cars or people were visible, so Elliot pulled over to the side of the road and got out quick, with James carrying a rope. They went through the woods, stepped over the barbed-wire fence, and found the mule grazing. They walked right up to it, and Elliot bribed it with an ear of corn from his garden. The mule sniffed at the corn and bit it. As he did, James slipped the rope over its neck, twisted it so that he put a loop over the mule's nose. Doing this, he brushed the mule's ears, and it kicked at the air, spun and kicked again. It took James several minutes to calm it down.

"It's one of them that's touchy about the ears," Elliot said. "Don't touch the ears again."

"I hear that," James said.

They led the mule to the fence. Elliot pushed it almost to the ground with his boot, and James and the mule stepped over. After that, nothing more was required than to lead the mule to the trailer and load it. It did what was expected without a moment's hesitation.

There was some consternation when it came to turning truck and trailer around, but Elliot managed it and they were soon on the road to a rendezvous with eight hundred dollars.

The place they had to go to meet their buyer, George Taylor, was almost to Tyler, and about sixty miles from where they had nabbed the mule. They often sold stolen material there, and George specialized in livestock and just about anything he could buy quick and sell quicker.

The trailer was not enclosed, and it occurred to James that the mule's owner might pass them, but he doubted the mule would be recognized. They were really hauling ass, and the trailer, with the weight of the old mule to aid it, had slowed in its wobbling but still sounded like a train wreck.

When they were about twenty-five miles away from Taylor's place, James had Elliot pull over. He took the brown shoe polish back to the trailer and, reaching between the bars while Elliot fed the mule corn on the cob, painted the white around the mule's nose brown. It was raining lightly, but he managed the touch-up without having it washed away.

He figured this way Taylor might not notice how old the critter was and not try to talk them down. He had given them a price, but they had dealt with Taylor before, and what he offered wasn't always what he wanted to give, and it was rare you talked it up. The trick was to keep him from going down. George knew once they had the mule stolen they'd want to get rid of it, and it would be his plan to start finding problems with the animal and to start lowering his price.

When the mule was painted, they got back in the truck and headed out.

Elliot said. "You are one thinker, James."

"Yes sir," James agreed, "you got to get up pretty goddamned early in the morning to get one over on me. It starts raining hard, it won't wash off. That stuff'll hold."

When they arrived at Taylor's place, James looked back through the rear truck window and saw the mule with its head lowered, looking at him through sheets of rain. James felt less smart immediately. The brown he had painted on the mule had dried and was darker than the rest of its hide and made it look as if it had dipped its muzzle in a bucket of paint, searching for a carrot on the bottom.

James decided to say nothing to Elliot about this, lest Elliot decide it really wasn't all that necessary to get up early to outsmart him.

Taylor's place was a kind of ranch and junkyard. There were all manner of cars damaged or made thin by the car smasher that Taylor rode with great enthusiasm, wearing a gimme cap with the brim pushed up and his mouth hanging open as if to receive something spoon-fed by a caretaker.

Today, however, the car smasher remained silent near the double-wide, where Taylor lived with his bulldog, Bullet, and his wife, Kay, who was about one ton of woman in a muumuu that might have been made from a circus tent and decorated by children with finger paints. If she owned more than one of these outfits, James was unaware of it. It was possible she had a chest full of them, all the same, folded and ready, with a hole in the center to pull over her head at a moment's notice.

At the back of the place a few cows that looked as if they were ready to be sold for hide and hooves stumbled about. Taylor's station wagon, used to haul a variety of stolen goods, was parked next to the trailer, and next to it was a large red Cadillac with someone at the back of it closing the trunk.

As they drove over the cattle guard and onto the property, the man at the trunk of the Cadillac looked up. He was wearing a blue baseball cap and a blue T-shirt that showed belly at the bottom. He and his belly bounced away from the Caddy, up the steps of the trailer, and inside.

Elliot said. "Who's that?"

"Can't say," James said. "Don't recognize him."

They parked beside the Cadillac, got out, went to the trailer door, and knocked. There was a long pause, then the man with the baseball cap answered the door.

"Yeah," he said.

"We come to see Taylor," Elliot said.

"He ain't here right now," said the man.

"He's expectin' us," James said.

"Say he is?"

"We got a mule to sell him," James said.

"That right?"

"Mrs. Taylor here?" James asked.

"Naw. She ain't. Ain't neither one of them here."

"Where's Bullet?" Elliot asked.

"He don't buy mules, does he?"

"Bullet?" Elliot said.

"Didn't you ask for him?"

"Well, yeah, but not to buy nothin'."

"You boys come on in," came a voice from inside the trailer. "It's all right there, Butch, stand aside. These here boys are wantin' to do some business with George. That's what we're doin'."

Butch stood aside. James and Elliot went inside.

"So is he here?" James asked.

"No. Not just now. But we're expectin' him shortly."

Butch stepped back and leaned against the trailer's kitchen counter, which was stacked with dirty dishes. The place smelled funny. The man who had asked them to come inside was seated on the couch. He was portly, wearing black pants and black shoes with the toes turned up. He had on a big black Hawaiian-style shirt with hula girls in red, blue, and yellow along the bottom. He had greasy black hair combed straight back and tied in a little ponytail. A white short-brimmed hat with a near-flat crown was on a coffee table in front of him, along with a can of beer and a white substance in four lines next to a rolled dollar bill. He had his legs crossed and he was playing with the tip of one of his shoes. He had a light growth of beard and he was smiling at them.

"What you boys sellin'?" he asked.

"A mule," James said.

"No shit?"

"That's right," Elliot said. "When's George coming back?"

"Sometime shortly after the Second Coming. But I doubt he'll go with God."

Elliot looked at James. James shrugged, and at that moment he saw past Elliot, and what he saw was Bullet lying on the floor near a doorway to the bedroom, a pool of blood under him. He tried not to let his eyes stay on Bullet long. He said, "Tell you what, boys. I think me and Elliot will come back later, when George is here."

The big man lifted up his Hawaiian shirt and showed him his hairy belly and against it a little flat black automatic pistol. He took the pistol out slowly and put it on his knee and looked at them.

"Naw. He ain't comin' back, and you boys ain't goin' nowhere."

"Aw shit," Elliot said, suddenly getting it. "He ain't no friend of ours. We just come to do business, and if he ain't here to do business, you boys got our blessing. And we'll just leave and not say a word."

Another man came out of the back room. He was naked and carrying a bowie knife. He was muscular, bug-nosed, with close-cut hair. There was blood on him from thighs to neck. From the back room they heard a moan.

The naked man looked at them, then at the man on the couch.

"Friends of Taylor's," the man on the couch said.

"We ain't," James said. "We hardly know him. We just come to sell a mule."

"A mule, huh," said the naked man. He didn't seem bashful at all. His penis was bloody and stuck to his right leg like some kind of sucker fish. The naked man nodded his head at the open doorway behind him, spoke to the man on the couch. "I've had all of that I want and can take, Viceroy. It's like cutting blubber off a whale."

"You go on and shower," Viceroy said, then smiled, added: "And be sure and wash the parts you don't normally touch."

"Ain't no parts Tim don't touch," Butch said.

"I tell you what," Tim said. "You get in there and go to work, then show me how funny you are. That old woman is hardheaded."

Tim went past Butch, driving the bowie knife into the counter, rattling the dishes.

Viceroy stared at Butch. "Your turn."

"What about you?" Butch said.

"I don't take a turn. Get with it."

Butch put his cap on the counter next to a greasy plate, took off his shirt, pants, underwear, socks, and shoes. He pulled the knife out of the counter and started for the bedroom. He said, "What about these two?"

"Oh, me and them are gonna talk. Any friend of Taylor's is a friend of mine."

"We don't really know him," James said. "We just come to sell a mule."

"Sit down on the floor there, next to the wall, away from the door," Viceroy said, and scratched the side of his cheek with the barrel of the automatic.

A moment later they heard screams from the back room and Butch yelling something, then there was silence, followed shortly by more screams.

"Butch ain't got Tim's touch," Viceroy said. "Tim can skin you and you can walk off before you notice the hide on your back, ass, and legs is missin'. Butch, he's a hacker."

Viceroy leaned forward, took up the dollar bill, and sucked up a couple lines of the white powder. "Goddamn, that'll do it," he said.

Elliot said, "What is that?"

Viceroy laughed. "Boy, you are a rube, ain't you? Would you believe bakin' soda?"

"Really?" Elliot said.

Viceroy hooted. "No. Not really."

From the bedroom you could hear Butch let out a laugh. "Crackers," he said.

"It's cocaine," James said to Elliot. "I seen it in a movie."

"Good God," Elliot said.

"My, you boys are delicate for a couple of thieves," Viceroy said.

Tim came out of the bathroom, still naked, bouncing his balls with a towel.

"Put some clothes on," Viceroy said. "We don't want to see that."

Tim looked hurt, put on his clothes, and adjusted his cap. Viceroy snorted the last two lines of coke. "Damn, that's some good stuff. You can step on that multiple."

"Let me have a snort," Tim said.

"Not right now," Viceroy said.

"How come you get to?" Tim said.

" 'Cause I'm the biggest bull in the woods, boy. And you can test that anytime you got the urge."

Tim didn't say anything. He went to the refrigerator, found a beer, popped it, and began to sip.

"I don't think she knows nothing," Tim said. "She wouldn't hold back havin' that done to her for a few thousand dollars. Not for a million."

"I reckon you're right," said Viceroy. "I just don't like quittin' halfway. You finish a thing, even if it ain't gonna turn out. Ain't that right, boys?"

James and Elliot didn't reply. Viceroy laughed and picked up the beer on the coffee table and took a jolt of it. He said to himself, "Yeah, that's right. You don't do a thing half-ass. You do it all the way. What time is it?"

Tim reached in his pocket and took out a pocket watch. James recognized it as belonging to George Taylor. "It's four."

"All right," Viceroy said, satisfied, and sipped his beer.

After a time Butch came out of the bedroom bloody and looking tired. "She ain't gonna tell nobody nothin'. She's gone. She couldn't take no more. She'd have known somethin', she'd have told it."

"Guess Taylor didn't tell her," Tim said. "Guess she didn't know nothin'."

"George had more in him than I thought, goin' like that, takin' all that pain and not talkin'," Viceroy said. "I wouldn't have expected it of him."

Tim nodded his head. "When you shot his bulldog, I think he was through. Took the heart right out of him. Wasn't a thing we could do to him then that mattered."

"Money's around here somewhere," Viceroy said.

"He might not have had nothin'," Butch said, walking to the bathroom.

"I think he did," Viceroy said. "I don't think he was brave enough to try and cross me. I think he had the money for the blow, but we double-crossed him too soon. We should have had him put the money on the table, then done what we needed to do. Would have been easier on everybody all the way around, them especially."

"They'd have still been dead," Tim said, drinking the last of his beer, crushing the can.

"But they'd have just been dead. Not hurt a lot, then dead. Old fat gal, that wasn't no easy way to go, and in the end she didn't know nothin'. And Taylor, takin' the knife, then out there in that car in the crusher and us telling him we were gonna run him through, and him still not talkin'."

"Like I said, we killed the bulldog I think he was through. Fat woman wasn't nothin' to him, but he seemed to have a hard-on for that dog. He'd just as soon be crushed. But I still think there might not have been any money. I think maybe they was gonna do what we were gonna do. Double-cross."

"Yeah, but we brought the blow," Viceroy said.

Tim grinned. "Yeah, but was you gonna give it to 'em?"

Viceroy laughed, then his gaze settled lead-heavy on the mule rustlers. "Well, boys, what do you suggest I do with you pickle heads?"

"Just let us go," James said. "Hell, this ain't our business, and we don't want it to be our business. It ain't like Taylor was a relative of ours."

"That's right," Elliot said. "He's cheated us plenty on little deals."

Viceroy was quiet. He looked at Tim. "What do you say?"

Tim pursed his lips and developed the expression of a man looking in the distance for answers. "I sympathize with these boys. I guess we could let 'em go. Give us their word, show us some ID, so they spill any beans we can find them. You know the littlest bit these days and you can find anybody."

"Damn Internet," Viceroy said.

Butch came out of the bathroom, naked, toweling his hair.

"You think we should let 'em go?" Viceroy asked.

Butch looked first at Viceroy and Tim, then at James and Elliot. "Absolutely."

"Get dressed," Viceroy said to Butch, "and we'll let 'em go."

"We won't say a word," Elliot said.

"Sure," Viceroy said. "You look like boys who can be quiet. Don't they?"

"Yeah," Tim said.

"Absolutely," Butch said, tying his shoe.

"Then we'll just go," James said, standing up from his position on the floor, Elliot following suit.

"Not real quick," Viceroy said. "You got a mule, huh?" James nodded. "What's he worth?"

"Couple thousand dollars to the right people."

"What about people ain't maybe quite as right?"

"A thousand. Twelve hundred."

"What were you supposed to get?"

"Eight hundred."

"We could do some business, you know."

James didn't say anything. He glanced toward the door where the men had been at work on Mrs. Taylor. He saw the bulldog lying there on the linoleum in its pool of hardened blood, and flowing from the bedroom was fresh blood. The fresh pool flowed around the crusty old pool and bled into the living room of the trailer and died where the patch of carpet near the couch began; the carpet began to slowly absorb it.

James knew these folks weren't going to let them go anywhere.

"I think we'll take the mule," Viceroy said. "Though I ain't sure I'm gonna give you any eight hundred dollars."

"We give it to you as a gift," Elliot said. "Just take it, and the trailer it's in, and let us go."

"That's a mighty nice offer," Viceroy said. "Nice, huh, boys?"

"Damn nice," Tim said.

"Absolutely," Butch said. "They could have held out and tried to deal. You don't get much nicer than that."

"And throwing in the trailer too," Tim said. "Now, that's white of 'em."

James took hold of the doorknob, turned it, said, "We'll show him to you."

"Wait a minute," Viceroy said.

"Come on out," James said.

Butch darted across the room, took hold of James's shoulder. "Hold up."

The door was open now. Rain was really hammering. The mule, its head hung, was visible in the trailer.

"Ain't no need to get wet," Viceroy said.

James had one foot on the steps outside. "You ought to see what you're gettin'."

"It'll do," Viceroy said. "It ain't like we're payin' for it."

Butch tightened his grip on James, and Elliot, seeing how this was going to end up and somehow feeling better about dying out in the open, not eight feet from a deceased bulldog, a room away from a skinned fat woman, pushed against Butch and stepped out behind James and into the yard.

"Damn," Viceroy said.

"Should I?" Butch said, glancing at Viceroy, touching the gun in his pants.

"Hell, let's look at the mule," Viceroy said.

Viceroy put on his odd hat and they all went out in the rain for a look. Viceroy looked as if he were some sort of escapee from a mental institution, wearing a hubcap. The rain ran off of it and made a curtain of water around his head.

They stood by the trailer staring at the mule. Tim said, "Someone's painted its nose, or it's been dippin' it in shit."

James and Elliot said nothing.

James glanced at the trailer, saw there was no underpinning. He glanced at Elliot, nodded his head slightly. Elliot looked carefully. He had an idea what James meant. They might roll under the trailer and get to the other side and start running. It wasn't worth much. Tim and Butch looked as if they could run fast, and all they had to do was run fast enough to get a clear shot.

"This is a goddamn stupid thing," Butch said, the rain hammering his head. "Us all standing out here in the rain lookin' at a goddamn mule. We could be dry and these two could be —"

A horn honked. Coming up the drive was a black Ford pickup with a camper fastened to the bed.

The truck stopped and a man the shape of a pear with the complexion of a marshmallow, dressed in khakis the color of walnut bark, got out smiling teeth all over the place. He had a rooster under his arm.

He said, "Hey, boys. Where's George?"

"He ain't feelin' so good," Viceroy said.

The man with the rooster saw the gun Viceroy was holding. He said, "You boys plinkin' cans?"

"Somethin' like that," Viceroy said.

"Would you tell George to come out?" the man said.

"He won't come out," Butch said.

The man's smile fell away. "Why not? He knows I'm comin'."

"He's under the weather," Viceroy said.

"Can't we all go inside? It's like being at the bottom of a lake out here."

"Naw. He don't want us in there. Contagious."

"What's he got?"

"You might say a kind of lead poisonin'."

"Well, he wants these here chickens. I got the camper back there full of 'em. They're fightin' chickens. Best damn bunch there is. This'n here, he's special. He's a stud rooster. He ain't fightin' no more. Won his last one. Got a bad shot that put blood in his lungs, but I put his head in my mouth and sucked it out, and he went on to win. Just come back from it and won. I decided to stud him out."

"He's gettin' all wet," Butch said.

"Yeah he is," said the chicken man.

"Let's end this shit," Tim said.

James reached over and pulled the bar on the trailer and the gate came open. He said, "Let's show him to you close up."

"Not now," Viceroy said, but James was in the trailer now. He took the rope off the trailer rail and tied it around the mule's neck and put a loop over its head, started backing him out.

"That's all right," Viceroy said. "We don't need to see no damn mule."

"He's a good'n," James said when the mule was completely out of the trailer. "A little touchy about the ears."

He turned the mule slightly then, reached up, and grabbed the mule's ears, and it kicked.

The kick was a good one. Both legs shot out and the mule seemed to stand on its front legs like a gymnast that couldn't quite flip over. The shod hooves caught Viceroy in the face, and there was a sound like a pound of wet cow shit dropping on a flat rock, and Viceroy's neck turned at a too-far angle and he flew up and fell down.

James bolted, and so did Elliot, slamming into Tim as he went, knocking him down. James hit the ground, rolled under the trailer, scuttled to the other side, Elliot went after him. Butch aimed at the back of Elliot's head and the chicken man said, "Hey, what the hell."

Butch turned and shot the chicken man through the center of the forehead. Chicken man fell and the rooster leaped and squawked, and just for the hell of it, Butch shot the rooster too.

Tim got up cussing. "I'm all muddy."

"Fuck that," Butch said. "They're gettin' away."

Even the mule had bolted, darting across the yard, weaving through the car crusher and a pile of mangled cars. Their last view of it was the tips of its ears over the top of the metallic heap.

Tim ran around the trailer and saw James and Elliot making for a patch of woods in the distance. It was just a little patch that ran along both sides of the creek down there. The land sloped just enough and the rain and wind were hard enough that the shot Tim got off didn't hit James or Elliot. It went past them and smacked a tree.

Tim came back around the trailer and looked at Butch bending over Viceroy, taking his gun, sticking it in his belt.

"He bad?" Tim asked.

"He's dead. Fuckin' neck's broke. If that's bad, he's bad."

"We gonna get them hillbillies?"

"There ain't no hills around here for a billy to live in. They're just the same ole white trash they got everywhere, you idiot."

"Well, this ain't Dallas . . . We gonna chase 'em?"

"What for? Let's get the TV set and go."

"Got a stereo too. I seen it in there. It's a good'n."

"Get that too. I don't think there is no money. I think he was gonna try and sweet-talk Viceroy out of some of that blow. A pay-later deal."

"He damn sure didn't know Viceroy, did he?"

"No, he didn't. But you know what, I ain't gonna miss him."

A moment later the TV and the stereo were loaded in the Cadillac. Then, just for fun, they put the chicken man and Viceroy in the chicken man's truck and used the car crusher on it. As the truck began to crush, chickens squawked momentarily and the tires blew with a sound like mortar fire.

With Viceroy, the chicken man, and the chickens flattened, they slid the truck onto a pile of rusted metal, got in the Cadillac, and drove out of there, Butch at the wheel.

On the way over the cattle guard, Tim said, "You know, we could have sold them chickens."

"My old man always said don't steal or deal in anything you got to feed. I've stuck by that. Fuck them chickens. Fuck that mule."

Tim considered that, decided it was sage advice, the part about not dealing in livestock. He said, "All right."

Along the creek James and Elliot crept. The creek was rising and the sound of the rain through the trees was like someone beating tin with a chain.

The land was low and it was holding water. They kept going and pretty soon they heard a rushing sound. Looking back, they saw a wall of water surging toward them. The lake a mile up had overflowed and the creek and all that rain were causing it to flood.

"Shit," said James.

The water hit them hard and knocked them down, took their hats. When they managed to stand, the water was knee-deep and powerful. It kept bowling them over. Soon they were just flowing with it and logs and limbs were clobbering them at every turn.

They finally got hold of a small tree that had been uprooted and hung on to that. The water carried them away from the trees around the creek and out into what had once been a lowland pasture.

They had gone a fair distance like this when they saw the mule swimming. Its neck and back were well out of the water and it held its head as if it were regal and merely about some sort of entertainment.

Their tree homed in on the mule, and as they passed, James grabbed the mule's neck and pulled himself onto it. Elliot got hold of the mule's tail, pulled himself up on its back where James had settled.

The mule was more frantic now, swimming violently. The flood slopped suddenly, and James realized this was in fact where the highway had been cut through what had once been a fairly large hill. The highway was covered and not visible, but this was it, and there was a drop-off as the water flowed over it.

Down they went, and the churning deluge went over them, and

they spun that way for a long time, like they were in a washing machine cycle. When they came up, the mule was upside down, feet pointing in the air. Its painted nose sometimes bobbed up and out of the water, but it didn't breathe and it didn't roll over.

James and Elliot clung to its legs and fat belly and washed along like that for about a mile. James said, "I'm through with livestock."

"I hear that," Elliot said.

Then a bolt of lightning, attracted by the mule's upturned, iron-shod hooves, struck them a sizzling, barbecuing strike, so that there was nothing left now but three piles of cooked meat, one with a still visible brown nose and smoking, wilting legs, the other two wearing clothes, hissing smoke from the water, blasting along with the charge of the flood.

MICHAEL MALONE

Maniac Loose

FROM *A Confederacy of Crime*

HOLDING A YELLOW smiley-face coffee mug, Lucy Rhoads sat
in her dead husband's bathrobe and looked at two photographs.
She had just made a discovery about her recently deceased spouse
that surprised her. Prewitt Rhoads — a booster of domestic san-
guinity, whose mind was a map of cheerful clichés out of which
his thoughts never wandered, whose monogamy she had no more
doubted than his optimism — her spouse Prewitt Rhoads (dead
three weeks ago of a sudden heart attack) had for years lived a secret life of sexual deceit with a widow two blocks away in the pretty
subdivision of Painton, Alabama, where he had insisted on their living for reasons Lucy only now understood. This was the same man
who had brought her home Mylar balloons proclaiming, "I Love
You," and white cuddly Valentine bears making the same claims,
and an endless series of these smiley-face coffee mugs — all from
the gifts, cards, and party supplies shop he owned in Annie Sullivan
Mall and called The Fun House. This was the same man who had
disparaged her slightest criticism of the human condition, who had
continually urged her, "Lucy, can't you stop turning over rocks just
to look at all the bugs crawling underneath them?"

Well, now Lucy had tripped over a boulder of a rock to see in the
exposed mud below her own Prewitt Rhoads scurrying around in
lustful circles with their widowed neighbor Amorette Strumlander,
Lucy's mediocre Gardenia Club bridge partner for more than fifteen years; Amorette Strumlander, who had dated Prewitt long ago
at Painton High School, who had never lived anywhere in her life
but Painton, Alabama, where perhaps for years she had sat pa-

tiently waiting, like the black widow she'd proved herself to be, until Prewitt came back to her. Of course, on his timid travels into the world beyond Painton, Alabama, Amorette's old boyfriend had picked up a wife in Charlotte (Lucy) and two children in Atlanta before returning to his hometown to open The Fun House. But what did Amorette Strumlander care about those encumbrances? Apparently nothing at all.

Lucy poured black coffee into the grimacing cup. Soon Amorette herself would tap her horn in her distinctive pattern, *honk honk honk* pause *honk honk,* to take Lucy to the Playhouse in nearby Tuscumbia so they could see *The Miracle Worker* together. Lucy was free to go because she had been forced to accept a leave of absence from her job as a town clerk at Painton Municipal Hall in order to recover from her loss. Amorette had insisted on the phone that *The Miracle Worker* would be just the thing to cheer up the grieving Mrs. Rhoads after the sudden loss of her husband to his unexpected heart attack. "I always thought it would be me," said Amorette, who'd boasted of a heart murmur since it had forced her to drop out of Agnes Scott College for Women when she was twenty and kept her from getting a job or doing any housework ever since. Apparently, Lucy noted, the long affair with Prewitt hadn't strained the woman's heart at all.

Lucy wasn't at all interested in seeing *The Miracle Worker;* she had already seen it a number of times, for the Playhouse put it on every summer in Tuscumbia, where the famous blind deaf mute Helen Keller had grown up. The bordering town of Painton had no famous people to boast of in its own long, hot, languid history, and no exciting events either; not even the Yankees ever came through the hamlet to burn it down, although a contingent of Confederate women (including an ancestor of Amorette's) was waiting to shoot them if they did. A typical little Deep South community, Painton had run off its Indians, brought in its slaves, made its money on cotton, and then after the War between the States had gone to sleep for a hundred years except for a few little irritable spasms of wakefulness over the decades to burn a cross, or (on the other side) to send a student to march with Martin Luther King, or to campaign against anything that might destroy the American Way of Life.

In its long history, Painton could claim only three modest celebrities: There was Amorette Strumlander's twice-great-grandmother who'd threatened to shoot the Yankees if they ever showed up; she'd been a maid of honor at Jefferson Davis's wedding and had attended his inauguration as president of the Confederacy in Montgomery. Fifty years later there was a Baptist missionary killed in the Congo either by a hippopotamus or by hepatitis; it was impossible for his relatives to make out his wife's handwriting on the note she'd sent from Africa. And thirty years ago there was a linebacker in an Alabama Rose Bowl victory who'd played an entire quarter with a broken collarbone.

But of course none of these celebrities could hold a candle to Helen Keller, as even Amorette admitted — proud as she was of her ancestral acquaintance of Jefferson Davis. Indeed no one loved the Helen Keller story as told by *The Miracle Worker* more than she. "You can never ever get too much of a good thing, Lucy, especially in your time of need," Mrs. Strumlander had wheedled when she'd called to pester Lucy into going to the play today. "*The Miracle Worker* shows how we can triumph over the dark days even if we're blind, deaf, and dumb, poor little thing."

Although at the very moment that her honey-voiced neighbor had phoned, Lucy Rhoads was squeezing in her fist the key to her husband's secret box of adulterous love letters from the deceptive Amorette, she had replied only, "All right, come on over, Amorette, because I'm having a real dark day here today."

Still Lucy wasn't getting ready. She was drinking black coffee in her dead husband's robe and looking at the photos she'd found in the box. She was listening to the radio tell her to stay off the streets of Painton today because there was a chance that the streets weren't safe. In general, the town of Painton didn't like to admit to problems; the motto on the billboard at the town limits proclaimed in red, white, and blue letters, THERE'S NO PAIN IN PAINTON, THE CHEERFULEST TOWN IN ALABAMA. There was always a patrol car hidden behind this billboard with a radar gun to catch innocent strangers going thirty-six miles an hour and slap huge fines on them. If Deputy Sheriff Hews Puddleston had heard one hapless driver joke, "I thought you said there was no pain in Painton," he'd heard a thousand of them.

The local billboard annoyed Lucy, as did the phrasing of this radio warning; she thought that a town so near the home of Helen Keller had no business suggesting life was "cheerful" or that the

streets were ever safe. The reporter on the radio went on to explain
rather melodramatically that there was a maniac loose. A young
man had gone crazy at Annie Sullivan Mall on the outskirts of
Painton and tried to kill his wife. Right now, live on the radio, this
man was shooting out the windows of a florist shop in the mall, and
the reporter was outside in the atrium hiding behind a cart selling
crystals and pewter dwarves. No one was stopping the man because
he had a nine-millimeter automatic assault weapon with him, and
he had yelled out the window that he had no problem using it. The
reporter had shouted at him, "No problem," and urged the police
to hurry up. The reporter happened to be there broadcasting live
at the mall because it was the Painton Merchants Super Savers
Summertime Sale for the benefit of the Painton Panthers High
School football team, 1992 state semifinalists, and he'd been sent
to cover it. But a maniac trying to kill his wife was naturally a bigger
story, and the reporter was naturally very excited.

Lucy turned on her police scanner as she searched around for
an old pack of the cigarettes Prewitt had always been hiding so she
wouldn't realize he'd gone back to smoking again despite his high
cholesterol. He'd never hidden them very well, not nearly as well
as his sexual escapades, and she'd constantly come across crumpled packs that he'd lost track of. Lucy had never smoked herself,
and had little patience with the Gardenia Club members' endless
conversations about when they'd quit, how they'd quit, or why
they'd quit. But today Lucy decided to start. Why not? Why play by
the rules when what did it get you? Lighting the match, she sucked
in the smoke deeply; it set her whole body into an unpleasant
spasm of coughing and tingling nerves. She liked the sensation; it
matched her mood.

On the police scanner she heard the dispatcher rushing patrol
cars to the mall. This maniac fascinated her, and she went back to
the radio, where the reporter was explaining the situation. Apparently the young man had gone to the mall to shoot his wife because
she'd left him for another man. According to the maniac's griev-
ance to the reporter, his wife was still using his credit cards and had
been in the midst of a shopping spree at the mall before he caught
up with her in the Hank Williams Concourse, where they'd fought
over her plan to run off with this other man and stick the maniac
with the bills. She'd fled down the concourse to the other man,

who owned a florist shop at the east end of the concourse. It was here that the maniac caught up with her again, this time with the gun he'd run back to his sports van to collect. He'd shot them both, but in trying to avoid other customers had managed only to hit the florist in the leg and to pulverize one of his wife's shopping bags. Plaster flying from a black swan with a dracaena plant in its back gouged a hole out of his wife's chin. He'd allowed the other customers to run out of the shop but held the lovers hostage.

Lucy could hear the sirens of the approaching patrol cars even on the radio. But by the time the police ran into the atrium with all their new equipment, the florist was hopping out of his shop on one foot, holding on to his bleeding leg and shouting that the husband had run out the back door. The police ran after him while the reporter gave a running commentary as if it were a radio play. As the florist was wheeled into the ambulance, he told the reporter that the maniac had "totally trashed" his shop, "terminator time." He sounded amazingly high-spirited about it. The reporter also interviewed the wife as she was brought out in angry hysterics with a bandage on her chin. She said that her husband had lost his mind and had nobody but himself to blame if the police killed him. She was then driven off to the hospital with the florist.

Lucy made herself eat a tuna sandwich, although she never seemed to be hungry anymore. When she finished, the maniac was still on the loose and still in possession of the nine-millimeter gun that he'd bought only a few months earlier at the same mall. News of the failure of the police to capture him was oddly satisfying. Lucy imagined herself running beside this betrayed husband through the streets of Painton, hearing the same hum in their hearts. The radio said that neighbors were taking care of the couple's four-year-old triplets, Greer, Gerry, and Griffin, who hadn't been told that their father had turned into a maniac in Annie Sullivan Mall. The couple's neighbors on Fairy Dell Drive were shocked; such a nice man, they said, a good provider and a family man. "I'dah never thought Jimmy'd do something like this in a million years, and you ask anybody else in Painton, they'll tell you the same," protested his sister, who'd driven to the mall to plead with her brother to come out of the florist shop, but who had arrived too late.

The reporter was obliged temporarily to return the station to its Mellow Music program, *Songs of Your Life,* playing Les Brown's Band

of Renown doing "Life Is Just a Bowl of Cherries." Lucy twisted the
dial to OFF. She did not believe that life was a bowl of cherries, and
she never had. In her view life was something more along the lines
of a barefoot sprint over broken glass. She felt this strongly, although she herself had lived a life so devoid of horror that she
might easily have been tricked into thinking life was the bowl of
sweet fruit that her husband Prewitt had always insisted it was. The
surprised reaction of the Mall Maniac's neighbors and family annoyed her. Why *hadn't* they suspected? But then, why hadn't she
suspected Prewitt and Amorette of betraying her? At least the maniac had noticed what was going on around him — that his wife
was stockpiling possessions on his credit cards while planning to
run off with the florist. Lucy herself had been such an idiot that
when years ago she'd wanted to leave Prewitt and start her life over,
he'd talked her out of it with all his pieties about commitment and
family values and the children's happiness, when at the exact same
time, he'd been secretly sleeping with Amorette Strumlander!

Lucy smashed the smiley mug against the lip of the kitchen
counter until it broke and her finger was left squeezed around its
yellow handle as if she'd hooked a carousel's brass ring. There, that
was the last one. She'd broken all the rest this morning, and she
still felt like screaming. It occurred to her there was no reason why
she shouldn't. She didn't have to worry about disturbing her "family" anymore.

It had been twenty-one days now since the death of the per-
fidious Prewitt. Last Sunday the Rhoads son and daughter had
finally returned to their separate lives in Atlanta, after rushing
home to bury their father and console their mother. These two
young people, whom Prewitt had named Ronny after Reagan and
Julie after Andrews, took after their father, and they thought life
was a bowl of cherries too, or at least a bowl of margaritas. They
were affable at the funeral, chatting to family friends like Amorette
Strumlander about their new jobs and new condo clusters. They
liked Amorette (and had Lucy not distinctly recalled giving birth to
them, she could have sworn Amorette was their mother, for like
her they both were slyly jejune). Ronny and Julie were happy with
their lifestyles, which they had mimicked from trendy magazines.
These magazines did not explain things like how to behave at a father's funeral, and perhaps as a result Ronny and Julie had acted

during the service and at the reception afterward with that convivial sardonic tolerance for the older generation that they had displayed at all other types of family functions. Amorette later told Lucy she thought "the kids held up wonderfully."

Lucy was not surprised by her children's lack of instinct for grief. Their father would have behaved the same way at his funeral had he not been the one in the casket. "The kids and I are day people," Prewitt had told his wife whenever she mentioned any of life's little imperfections like wars and earthquakes and pogroms and such. "You're stuck in the night, Lucy. That's your problem." It was true. Maybe she should have grown up in the North, where skies darkened sooner and the earth froze and the landscape turned black and gray, where there wasn't so much Southern sun and heat and light and daytime. For life, in Lucy's judgment, was no daytime affair. Life was stuck in the night; daytime was just the intermission, the waiting between the acts of the real show. When she listened to police calls on the radio scanner, the reports of domestic violence, highway carnage, fire, poison, electrocution, suffocation, maniacs loose in the vicinity of Annie Sullivan Mall always struck her as what life was really about. It suddenly occurred to her that there must have been a police dispatch for Prewitt after she'd phoned 911. She'd found him by the opened refrigerator on the kitchen floor lying beside a broken bowl of barbecued chicken wings. The scanner must have said: "Apparent heart attack victim, male, Caucasian, forty-eight."

Prewitt had died without having much noticed that that's what he was doing, just as her day children had driven off with whatever possessions of Prewitt's they wanted (Ronny took his golf clubs and his yellow and pink cashmere V-necks; Julie took his Toyota) without having really noticed that their father was gone for good. If Prewitt had known he'd be dead within hours, presumably he would have destroyed the evidence of his adultery with Amorette Strumlander, since marriage vows and commitment were so important to him. But apparently Prewitt Rhoads had persisted in thinking life a bowl of imperishable plastic cherries to the very last. Apparently he had never seen death coming, the specter leaping up and grinning right in his face, so he had died as surprised as he could be, eyes wide open, baffled, asking Lucy, "What's the matter with me?"

Amorette Strumlander had been equally unprepared when she'd heard about Prewitt's sudden demise from their Gardenia Club president, Gloria Peters, the next morning. She had run up the lawn shrieking at Lucy, "I heard it from Gloria Peters at the nail salon!" as if getting the bad news that way had made the news worse. Of course, Lucy hadn't known then that Prewitt and Amorette had been having their long affair; admittedly that fact must have made the news harder on Amorette. It must have been tough hearing about her lover's death from Gloria Peters, who had never once invited Amorette to her dinner parties, where apparently Martha Stewart recipes were served by a real maid in a uniform. In fact, that morning after Prewitt's death when Amorette had come running at her, Lucy had actually apologized for not calling her neighbor sooner. And Amorette had grabbed her and sobbed, "Now we're both widows!" Lucy naturally thought Amorette was referring to her own dead husband, Charlie Strumlander, but maybe she had meant her lover, Prewitt.

Honk honk honk pause *honk honk*. *Honk honk honk* pause *honk honk*.

Amazingly it was two in the afternoon, and Lucy was still standing in the middle of the kitchen with the yellow coffee mug handle still dangling from her finger. She quickly shoved the photographs she'd found in the bathrobe pocket as Amorette came tapping and whoohooing through the house without waiting to be invited in. She had never waited for Lucy to open the door.

"Lucy? Lucy, oh, why, oh, good Lord, you're not even ready. What are you doing in a robe at this time? Didn't you hear me honking?" Mrs. Strumlander was a petite woman, fluttery as a hungry bird, as she swirled around the table in a summer coat that matched her shoes and her purse. She patted her heart as she was always doing to remind people that she suffered from a murmur. "I have been scared to death with this maniac on the loose! Did you hear about that on the radio?"

Lucy said that yes she had, and that she felt sorry for the young man.

"Sorry for him! Well, you are the weirdest thing that ever lived! You come on and go get dressed before we're late to the play. I know when you see that poor little blind deaf-and-dumb girl running around the stage spelling out 'water,' it's going to put your own troubles in perspective for you, like it always does mine."

"You think?" asked Lucy flatly, and walked back through the

house into the bedroom she had shared with Prewitt. She was followed by Amorette, who even went so far as to pull dresses from Lucy's closet and make suggestions about which one she ought to wear.

"Lucy," Amorette advised her as she tossed a dress on the bed, "just because this maniac goes out of his mind at the Annie Sullivan Mall, don't you take it as proof the world's gone all wrong, because believe me most people are leading a normal life. If you keep slipping into this negative notion of yours without poor Prewitt to hold you up, you could just slide I don't know where, way deep. Now, how 'bout this nice mustard silk with the beige jacket?"

Lucy put her hand into her dead husband's bathrobe pocket. She touched the photos and squeezed the key to the secret letters into the fleshy pads of her palm. The key opened a green tin box she'd found in a little square room in the basement, a room with pine paneling and a plaid couch that Prewitt considered his special private place and called his "study." He'd gone there happily in the evenings to fix lamps and listen to vinyl big band albums he'd bought at tag sales, to do his homework for his correspondence course in Internet investing in the stock market. And, apparently, he went there to write love letters to Amorette Strumlander. Lucy had never violated the privacy of Prewitt's space. Over the years as she had sat with her black coffee in the unlit kitchen, watching the night outside, she had occasionally fantasized that Prewitt was secretly down in his study bent over a microscope in a search of the origins of life, or down there composing an opera, or plotting ingenious crimes. But she was not surprised when, the day after her children left for Atlanta, she'd unlocked the "study" door and discovered no mysterious test tubes, no ink-splotched sheets of music, no dynamite to blow up Fort Knox.

What she had found there were toy trains and love letters. Apparently Prewitt had devoted all those nights to building a perfect plastic world for a dozen electric trains to pass through. This world rested on a large board eight feet square. All the tiny houses and stores and trees were laid out on the board on plastic earth and AstroTurf. In front of a little house, a tiny dad and mom and boy and girl stood beside the track to watch the train go by. The tiny woman had blond hair and wore a pink coat, just like Amorette Strumlander.

Lucy found the love letters in a green tin box in a secret drawer built under the board beneath the train depot. There were dozens of letters written on legal pad paper, on pink flowered notepaper, on the backs of envelopes, hand-delivered letters from Amorette to Prewitt, and even a few drafts of his own letters to her. They were all about love as Prewitt and Amorette had experienced it. There was nothing to suggest to Lucy that passion had flung these adulterers beyond the limits of their ordinary personalities, nothing to suggest *Anna Karenina* or *The English Patient*. No torment, no suicidal gestures. The letters resembled the Valentines Prewitt sold in his gifts, cards, and party supplies shop in downtown Painton. Lacy hearts, fat toddlers hugging, fat doves cooing. Amorette had written, "Dearest dear one. Tell Lucy you have to be at The Fun House doing inventory all Sat. morn. Charlie leaves for golf at ten. Kisses on the neck." Prewitt had written, "Sweetheart, You looked so [great, scratched out] beautiful yesterday and you're so sweet to me, I couldn't get through life without my sunshine."

Beneath the letters, at the bottom of the box, Lucy had found the two Polaroid pictures she now touched in the bathrobe pocket. One showed Amorette in shortie pajamas on Lucy's bed, rubbing a kitten against her cheek. (Lucy recognized the kitten as Sugar, whom Prewitt had brought home for Julie and who, grown into an obese flatulent tabby, had been run over five years ago by a passing car.) The other photograph showed Amorette seated on the hope chest in her own bedroom, naked from the waist up, one hand provocatively held beneath each untanned breast. After looking at the pictures and reading the letters, Lucy had put them back in the box, then turned on Prewitt's electric trains and sped them up faster and faster until finally they'd slung themselves off their tracks and crashed through the plastic villages and farms and plummeted to the floor in a satisfying smashup.

Now, in the bathroom, listening to Amorette outside in the bedroom she clearly knew all too well, still rummaging through the closet, Lucy transferred the key and the photos from the bathrobe pocket to her purse. Returning to the bedroom, she asked Amorette, "Do you miss Prewitt much?"

Mrs. Strumlander was on her knees at the closet looking for shoes to go with the dress she'd picked out for Lucy. "Don't we all?" she replied. "But let time handle it, Lucy. Because of my murmur I have always had to live my life one day at a time as the Good Book says, and that's all any of us can do. Let's just hope this crazy man keeps on shooting people he knows and doesn't start in on strangers!" She laughed at her little joke and crawled backward out of the closet with beige pumps in her hand. "Because there are sick individuals just opening fire whenever and wherever they feel like it, and I'd hate for something like that to happen to us in the middle of *The Miracle Worker* tonight. Here, put that dress on."

Lucy put on the dress. "Have you ever been down in Prewitt's study, Amorette?"

"Ummum." The dainty woman shook her head ambiguously, patting her carefully styled blond hair.

"Would you like to see it now?" Lucy asked her.

Amorette gave her a curious look. "We don't have time to look at Prewitt's study now, honey. We are waaay late already. Not that jacket, it doesn't go at all. Sometimes, Lucy . . . This one. Oh, you look so pretty when you want to."

Lucy followed her dead husband's mistress out to her car. Amorette called to her to come along: "Hop in now, and if you see that mall shooter, duck!" She merrily laughed.

As they drove toward the interstate to Tuscumbia through Painton's flower-edged, unsafe streets, Lucy leaned back in the green velour seat of her neighbor's Toyota (had Amorette and Prewitt gotten a special deal for buying two at once?) and closed her eyes. Amorette babbled on about how someone with no handicaps at all had used the handicapped-parking space at the Winn-Dixie and how this fact as well as the Mall Maniac proved that the South might as well be the North these days. Amorette had taken to locking her doors with dead bolts and might drop dead herself one night from the shock of the strange noises she was hearing after dark and suspected might be burglars or rapists. It was then that Lucy said, "Amorette, when did you and Prewitt start sleeping together?"

The little sedan lurched forward with a jolt. Then it slowed and slowed, almost to a stop. Pink splotched Amorette's cheeks, until they matched the color of her coat, but her nose turned as white as a sheet. "Who told you that?" she finally whispered, her hand on her heart. "Was it Gloria Peters?"

Lucy shrugged. "What difference does it make?"

"It was, wasn't it! It was Gloria Peters. She hates me."

Lucy took one of Prewitt's left-behind hidden cigarettes out of her purse and lit up. "Oh, calm down, nobody told me. I found things."

"What things? Lucy, what are you talking about? You've gotten all mixed up about something —"

Blowing out smoke, Lucy reached in her purse. She thrust in front of the driver the Polaroid picture of her younger self, flash-eyed, cupping her breasts.

Now the car bumped up on the curb, hit a mailbox, and stopped.

The two widows sat in the car on a residential avenue where oleander blossoms banked the sidewalks and honeysuckle made the air as sweet as syrup. There was no one around, except a bored teenage girl in a bathing suit who Rollerbladed back and forth and looked blatantly in the car window each time she passed it.

Lucy kept smoking. "I found all your love letters down in Prewitt's study," she added. "Didn't you two worry that I might?"

With little heaves Amorerte shook herself into tears. She pushed her face against the steering wheel, crying and talking at the same time. "Oh, Lucy, this is just the worst possible thing. Prewitt was a wonderful man, now, don't start thinking he wasn't. We never meant to hurt you. He knew how much I needed a little bit of attention because Charlie was too wrapped up in the law office to know if I had two eyes or three, much less be sympathetic to my murmur when I couldn't do the things he wanted me to."

"Amorette, I don't care to hear this," said Lucy.

But Amorette went on anyhow. "Prewitt and I were both so unhappy, and we just needed a little chance to laugh. And then it all just happened without us ever meaning it to. Won't you believe me that we really didn't want you to get yourself hurt."

Lucy, dragging smoke through the cigarette, thought this over. "I just want to know how long?"

"Wuh, what, what?" sobbed her neighbor.

"How long were you screwing my husband? Five years, ten years, till the day Prewitt died?"

"Oh, Lucy, no!" Amorette had sobbed herself into gasping hiccups that made the sound *eeuck*. "No! *Eeuck. Eeuck.* We never . . . after Charlie died. I just didn't think that would be fair. *Eeuck. Eeuck.*"

"Charlie died a year ago. We've been in Painton fifteen." Lucy squashed her cigarette butt in the unused ashtray. She flashed to an image of the maniac smashing the glass storefronts that looked out on the concourse of the shopping mall. "So, Amorette, I guess I don't know what the goddamn shit 'fair' means to you." She lit another cigarette.

Amorette shrank away, shocked and breathing hard. "Don't you talk that way to me, Lucy Rhoads! I won't listen to that kind of language in my car." Back on moral ground, she flapped her hand frantically at the thick smoke. "And put out that cigarette. You don't smoke."

Lucy stared at her. "I do smoke. I am smoking. Just like you were screwing my husband. You and Prewitt were a couple of lying shits."

Amorette rolled down her window and tried to gulp in air. "All right, if you're going to judge us —"

Lucy snorted with laughter that hurt her throat. "Of course I'm going to judge you."

"Well, then, the truth is . . ." Amorette was now nodding at her like a toy dog with its head on a spring. "The truth is, Lucy, your negativity and being so down on the world the way you are just got to Prewitt sometimes. Sometimes Prewitt just needed somebody to look on the bright side with."

Lucy snorted again. "A shoulder to laugh on."

"I think you're being mean on purpose," whimpered Amorette. "My doctor says I can't afford to get upset like this."

Lucy looked hard into the round brown candy eyes of her old bridge partner. Could the woman indeed be this obtuse? Was she as banal of brain as the tiny plastic mom down on the board waving at Prewitt's electric train? So imbecilic that any action she took would have to be excused? That any action Lucy took would be unforgivable? But as Lucy kept staring at Amorette Strumlander, she saw deep down in the pupils of her neighbor's eyes the tiniest flash of self-satisfaction, a flicker that was quickly hidden behind a tearful blink. It was a smugness as bland and benighted as Painton, Alabama's, history.

Lucy suddenly felt a strong desire to do something, and as the feeling surged through her, she imagined the maniac from the mall bounding down this residential street and tossing his gun to her through the car window. It felt as if the butt of the gun hit her stomach with a terrible pain. She wanted to pick up the gun and shoot into the eye of Amorette's smugness. But she didn't have a gun. Besides, what good did the gun do the maniac, who had probably by now been caught by the police? Words popped out of Lucy's mouth before she could stop them. She said, "Amorette, did you know that Prewitt was sleeping with Gloria Peters at the same time he was sleeping with you, and he kept on with her after you two ended things?"

"What?"

"Did you know there were pictures, naked pictures, of Gloria Peters locked up in Prewitt's letter box too?"

Mrs. Strumlander turned green, actually apple green, just as Prewitt had turned blue on the ambulance stretcher after his coronary. Amorette had also stopped breathing; when she started up again, she started with a horrible-sounding gasp. "Oh, my God, don't do this; tell me the truth," she wheezed.

Lucy shook her head sadly. "I am telling the truth. You didn't know about Gloria? Well, he tricked us both. And there were some very ugly pictures I found down in the study too, things he'd bought, about pretty sick things being done to naked women. Prewitt had all sorts of magazines and videos down in that study of his. I don't think you even want to hear about what was in those videos." (There were no other pictures, of course, any more than there had been an affair with Gloria Peters. The Polaroid shot of Amorette's cupped breasts was doubtless as decadent an image as Prewitt could conceive. Every sentiment the man ever had could have been taken from one of his Mylar balloons or greeting cards.)

"Please tell me you're lying about Gloria!" begged Amorette. She was green as grass.

Instead, Lucy opened the car door and stepped out. "Prewitt said my problem was I couldn't *stop* telling the truth. And this is the truth. I saw naked pictures of Gloria posing just like you'd done and laughing because she was copying your pose. That's what she said in a letter, that he'd shown her the picture of you and she was mimicking it."

"Lucy, stop. I feel sick. Something's wrong. Hand me my purse off the back seat."

Lucy ignored the request. "Actually I read lots of letters Gloria wrote Prewitt making fun of you, Amorette. You know how witty she can be. The two of them really got a laugh out of you."

Unable to breathe, Amorette shrank back deep into the seat of her car and whispered for Lucy please to call her doctor for her because she felt like something very scary was happening.

"Well, just take it one day at a time," Lucy advised her neighbor. "And look on the bright side."

"Lucy, Lucy, don't leave me!"

But Lucy slammed the door and began to walk rapidly along beside the oleander hedge. She was pulling off fistfuls of oleander petals as she went, throwing them down on the sidewalk ahead of her. The teenage girl on Rollerblades came zipping close, eyes and mouth big as her skates carried her within inches of Lucy's red face. She shot by the car quickly and didn't notice that Amorette Strumlander had slumped over onto the front seat.

Lucy walked on, block after block, until the oleander stopped and lawns spread flat to the doorsteps of brick ranch houses with little white columns. A heel on her beige pump came loose and she kicked both shoes off. Then she threw off her jacket. She could feel the maniac on the loose right beside her as she jerked at her dress until she broke the buttons off. She flung the dress to the curb. Seeing her do it, a man ran his power mower over his marigold beds, whirring out pieces of red and orange. Lucy unsnapped her bra and tossed it on the man's close-cropped emerald green grass. She didn't look at him, but she saw him. A boy driving a pizza van swerved toward her, yelling a war whoop out his window. Lucy didn't so much as turn her head, but she took off her panty hose and threw it in his direction.

Naked in her panties, carrying her purse, she walked on until the sun had finished with its daytime tricks and night was back. She walked all the way to the outskirts of Helen Keller's hometown.

When the police car pulled up beside her, she could hear the familiar voice of the scanner dispatcher on the radio inside, then a flashlight was shining in her eyes and then Deputy Sheriff Hews Puddleston was covering her with his jacket. He knew Lucy Rhoads from the Painton Town Hall, where she clerked. "Hey, now," he said. "You can't walk around like this in public, Mrs. Rhoads." He looked at her carefully. "You all right?"

"Not really," Lucy admitted.

"You had something to drink? Some kind of pill maybe?"

"No, Mr. Puddleston, I'm sorry, I've just been so upset about Prewitt, I just, I just . . ."

"Shhh. It's okay," he promised her.

At the police station back in Painton, they were handcuffing a youngish bald man to the orange plastic seats. Lucy shook loose of her escort and went up to him. "Are you the one from the shopping mall?"

The handcuffed man said, "What?"

"Are you the one who shot his wife? Because I know how you feel."

The man tugged with his handcuffed arms at the two cops beside him. "She crazy?" he wanted to know.

"She's just upset. She lost her husband," the desk sergeant explained.

Prewitt's lawyer had Lucy released within an hour. An hour later Amorette Strumlander died in the hospital of the heart defect that Gloria Peters had always sarcastically claimed was only Amorette's trick to get out of cleaning her house.

Three months afterward, Lucy had her hearing for creating a public disturbance by walking naked through the streets of Painton, the cheerfulest town in America. It was in the courtroom across the hall from the trial of the Mall Maniac, so she did finally get to see the young man. He was younger than she'd thought he'd be, ordinary-looking, with sad, puzzled eyes. She smiled at him and he smiled back at her, just for a second, then his head turned to his wife, who by now had filed for divorce. His wife still had the scar on her chin from where the plaster piece of the swan had hit her in the florist shop. The florist sat beside her, holding her hand.

Testifying over his lawyer's protest that he'd tried to kill his wife and her lover but had "just messed it up," the maniac pleaded guilty. So did Lucy. She admitted she was creating as much of a public disturbance as she could. But unlike the maniac's, her sentence was suspended, and afterward the whole charge was erased from the record. Prewitt's lawyer made a convincing case to a judge (who also knew Lucy) that grief at her husband's death, aggravated by the shock of the car accident from which her best friend was to suffer a coronary, had sent poor Mrs. Rhoads wandering down the sidewalk in "a temporarily irrational state of mind." He suggested that she might even have struck her head on the dashboard, that she might not even have been aware of what she was doing when she "disrobed in public." After all, Lucy Rhoads was an upright citizen, a city employee, and a decent woman, and if she'd gone momentarily berserk and exposed herself in a nice neighborhood, she'd done it in a state of emotional and physical shock. Prewitt's lawyer promised she'd never do it again. She never did.

A few months later, Lucy went to visit the maniac at the state penitentiary. She brought him a huge box of presents from the going-out-of-business sale at The Fun House. They talked for a while, but conversation wasn't easy, despite the fact that Lucy felt not only that they had a great deal in common, but that she could have taught him a lot about getting away with murder.

FRED MELTON

Counting

FROM *Talking River Review*

I TOSS THE first shovelful of crumbling dirt into the grave. They say it's an honor to be the first, like throwing out the first baseball of the new season.

Snow twirls and twists its way into the dark rectangle as if sucked into the earth's gaping void. No one says a word. John Bouchard, the soul-bankrupt banker, Lucille Emerson, the widowed neighbor with fifteen hundred acres of slumbering wheat land, Orville Mansfield with his cheap toupee, and the two to three others stand with their hands clasped neatly in front, heads bowed. I'm the only family present.

I count the shovelfuls: twenty-eight, twenty-nine, thirty. I can't quit. The shovel keeps digging. I keep counting. I swore I wouldn't cry. A man should have learned not to cry by the age of twenty-four.

A couple of pats on the shoulder, several muttered "So sorry, Amp," and I set the spade aside. I've lost count now. Even in the cold, sweat stings my eyes. The folding chair creaks beneath my weight as I sit. I pull the wool collar of my coat up against my neck, shove my tingling hands between my thighs, and stare directly into the pit. The silent snow swirls like pure white confetti.

He died alone.

When he was alive, my Uncle Keven stood yardstick straight, measuring just under five and half feet short. His round, flat face barely tolerated the tangle of hair wrestling across his head. He explained it away as "cowlicks gone awry, about as combable as a pack of pigs' tails." His blue-green eyes surveyed people, as a farmer judges distances. His thick upper body sat atop stubby, bowed legs. He was strong — stronger than any man I ever knew. He moved as if he were constantly under water. Slow. Deliberate.

He lived for baseball, but World War II killed his chances when it snatched him away from an imminent semipro career with Seattle's newest team, the Rainiers. "Heck," he'd say, "I was so short I could have caught behind the plate standing up." But by the time he came back from the Philippines, he'd lost everything youth had ever loaned him. "You can lose it all," he'd mutter, "but you'll always have family."

I grew up on a five-thousand-acre, third-generation wheat farm in eastern Washington, just outside of Endicott. The town boasted a population of more than seven hundred living on hills facing north across the Palouse, as if looking for a future that would never come its way.

My well-mannered mother and back-busting father raised me and my sister Sarah with the typical wheat farmers' attitudes: trust no one but family; never depend on the weather to do anything except knock the stuffin' out of you. My father ate, drank, and choked on that Palouse dirt. Home to him was standing knee-deep in a sea of waving, thick, green wheat. Dream wheat. Uncle Keven and I shared our own dreams. The Brooklyn Dodgers.

Uncle Keven lived three miles, as the crow flies, west of us on a wheat farm handed down to him by my grandfather. Most people found Uncle Keven stingy with conversation. I never did. We had talked baseball ever since I could catch one. "It'll be your ticket out of Endicott, Amp," he told me. "Maybe so," I answered, "but the old man'll tear up the ticket before I can ever get my hands on it."

Sarah, on the other hand, flashed her ticket around with style and grace. Bouncing blond hair, batting eyelashes. Bobby socks. Soft words and sweet smiles. Endicott High's Rodeo Queen and voted "Most Marry-able, Class of '55" her senior year. She adored the title, as did mother and father. And I adored her, thinking the five years between us somehow afforded her the wisdom of kings. But even royalty suffers.

In the summer at the end of Sarah's sophomore year a grumbling Greyhound Bus gave us Jake Fiess.

Uncle Keven and I were out tending his horses the evening Jake Fiess strolled down the gravel driveway. The horses' ears twitched at the sound of the rocks crunching beneath his steps. Jake Fiess looked like a walking scarecrow. And he was missing an eye.

"Lookin' for work," he announced.

"Around here, a man introduces himself. I'm Keven Armstrong."

"Jake." He propped his foot on the fence.

"Got a last name?"

"Fiess."

Purple veins sprawled across Jake's sinewy forearms. A pack of Camels rode high on his left biceps beneath his tattered T-shirt. His Adam's apple bobbed like a cork on the front of his willowy neck when he swallowed, and a crude mustache couldn't hide the several missing teeth. Jake cocked his head to the side when he spoke, as if he'd heard something over his right shoulder.

"This is Amp. My nephew."

Jake stared at me for a moment, then turned back to Uncle Keven. "Got any work?"

"Suppose so." Uncle Keven leaned around and glanced behind Jake's shoulder. "That all you got? Just a knapsack?"

"Suppose so."

"You'll find a bunk out in the barn."

Later that evening, I sat at Uncle Keven's kitchen table with a glass of iced tea glistening in my hands. I poured in another heaping tablespoon of sugar and watched the crystals drift in the amber color.

"You're gonna rot out those new teeth, Amp."

I held the glass up to my face and mentally measured the sugary mound on the bottom. "I'll get more."

"Not at eleven years of age, you won't."

"Will too."

Uncle Keven laughed. "Hand me another hanger."

"Why do you like to iron so much, Uncle Keven? Even all your old overalls?"

"Thinkin' time."

"Thinking about what?" I sprinkled more sugar across the melting ice cubes and looked over at him.

"Thinking about people, generally." The black iron hissed, then slid the length of the ironing board like a miniature tugboat. Uncle Keven's fingertips traced the straight edges of the denim. "I mostly think about people. Their lives. How wrinkled they are. How I wish they could just be ironed out."

"I iron sometimes, Uncle Kev. But mostly I just iron right over all the wrinkles. Makes 'em worse."

"You don't say." He chuckled. "At least it shows you cared. That's what I like about ironing — you get credit for trying." He pressed the iron down so hard the ironing board's metal legs squeaked. He lifted the iron, turned toward me, smiling, and said, "But, then again, wrinkles aren't so bad, really."

I watched him for a few more minutes.

"Do you like girls, Uncle Kev?"

"Sure."

"How come you never married one?"

"Planned on it." He folded the overalls against his waist, making sure the legs were equal length, then sat down with them in his lap and fumbled with the brass buttons. "But she made other plans when I went off to war. I got the letter a month before I was shipped home." His fingertips stopped moving. "I thought goin' off to war would be" — he sighed — "the hardest thing a man could do." He stood back up, put the overalls neatly against the pile of folded wool socks, and reached for a cotton shirt. "Sometimes," he nearly whispered, "coming home is worse than anything you'll ever do."

I watched him fiddle with the buttoned-down collar for what seemed like minutes. Uncle Keven finally turned around. "But, maybe . . ." He winked. ". . . ironing's worse."

"You think this Jake's ever been married?"

"Can't say."

I stepped over to the sink and turned on the hot water. I scraped at the mound of sugar with my spoon, licked the end of it, and rinsed the glass. "He's kind of scary. That one eye and all."

Uncle Keven's iron hissed again. "Ain't a one of us that's perfect, Amp."

"Do you ever get scared, Uncle Keven?"

Uncle Keven smiled at me. "Count, Amp. Just count anything when you're scared. Remember?"

"Like you said you did in the war, right?"

Uncle Keven's smile faded. "Count the number of times you breathe if nothing else." The iron stopped moving. "At least that way you'll know you're still alive."

"S'pose he can see out of it? That one eye, I mean."

"Can't say, Amp."

"I'm goin' to bed."

"See you bright and early."

As I turned the corner, I stopped and said, "Can I sleep in your room tonight? Just tonight?"

Uncle Keven smiled. "Go ahead."

I didn't see a lot of Jake those first two weeks. I stuck to the side of Uncle Keven like a newborn foal to its mother. Nearly every morning Uncle Keven would let me make coffee while he fried up crackling bacon and the sun still slept. I'd beg for his homemade biscuits — tell him I'd do the dishes if he'd make them. "You'll do them anyways," he answered, shaking his head. "That's our agreement for you staying here this summer. Remember? But first, go out there and fire up that old truck." I bolted out the door, hearing him shout, "Hustle makes muscle."

I sat in the idling flatbed Ford and pretended I was the sole owner of Uncle Keven's farm. The sun's rays gilded the three grain silos sitting up on the hill, just above the barn. They stood like monstrous metal paladins guarding the house. Each held more than 500,000 bushels when full, and rose stories high. Horizontal augers rested across the bottoms of the silos, waiting to corkscrew the tons of wheat into empty trucks come fall. Uncle Keven told me that his neighbor to the south, Forrest T. Manly, once had a distant cousin who accidentally fell into a half-empty silo and was buried there for over two years beneath the wheat before anybody suspected what had happened to him. "If the auger hadn't spit out that flattened boot, he'd have never been found," Uncle Keven told me.

He called his three silos "The Holy Trinity." Said they were the Father, the Son, and the Holy Mother of God watching over him. Over us. Years later, he'd tell me, "Don't ever empty the Holy Mother. She keeps us out of the jailhouse."

After the last chipped coffee cup was set upside down in the drainer, we'd drive the miles of dusty roads cutting past the fields. Uncle Keven would often stop and point out the whitetail deer. They always turned their proud heads our way, their ears flickering, their tails at attention, for one last look before trotting over the horizon. We'd listen to the radio man's scratchy voice read the latest weather forecast as we bounced along in the Ford. Most days Uncle Keven would let me ride in the back as long as I promised two things: to hold on like my life depended on it and to never tell my mother. I'd close my eyes and fill my nostrils with the sweet summer air as we topped the hill coming home. This was how I wanted to live my life forever, with my Uncle Keven.

One cool evening after a light summer rain, when the damp wheat smelled of wet rope and the scent hovered like an invisible mist, Jake found me feeding the chickens out in the corrals. I sat on the top rail, perched above the busy feathered heads, and scattered the seed like rice at a wedding, then watched the pointy beaks bobbing and pecking, beady eyes darting. I had a couple of favorites I saved bread for while the scrawnier chickens scratched furiously at the soft dirt for their meal.

"What the hell kind of name is 'Amp,' anyways?"

"Huh?" I nearly dropped the bread. Jake came and stood beside me, his head near my waist. "Uh . . . they're my initials," I said.

"Hmm. Got names for any of them banties?"

"Huh?"

"Names. Chickens like names."

"Uh-uh," I said. "Not these. They're way too dumb."

"Don't kid yourself." Jake reached for the top board and climbed up beside me. "*They* know how the world works. 'Specially the banties."

"The little ones?" I tossed a balled up piece of bread at one. Several of the other chickens raced toward it but the banty charged them and they scattered like marbles dropped on a tile floor. Jake laughed.

"See that? That's what I'm talking about." Jake elbowed me. "Look at all the others. How they cower to that little banty. Know why?" Jake waited for my answer, but I didn't offer one. " 'Cause he just *thinks* he's tough. Look at him, chest all punched out like a bullfrog on a hot night."

I did have a name for the one bird Jake admired. But, I didn't say so.

"People's the same way." Jake spat between his knees, a mean spit, not the kind men squirt between puckered lips when they're just chatting an afternoon away. "My old man was a banty rooster. Cock of the walk."

I shifted my weight, slid an inch away from Jake, pretending to scratch an itch on my side. Jake kept his eye on the chickens.

"'Only room enough for one rooster in *this* barn,' that old shit told me." Jake spat again. "That was the last thing he said to me as I was packing up."

"How long ago was that?" I asked, as I flipped more seed into the corral.

"Too long to remember, boy."

Jake got quiet. His hands gripped the rail as he leaned forward and stared at the scrambling chickens. "See how fast that one is?" He jutted his pointy chin at the one Uncle Keven and I had secretly named Jake Jr. "You gotta be fast in this world, boy. Just like that banty. Walk tough. Look 'em in the eye. Keep movin'. Always keep moving." Jake spat at the chickens. "They can't hurt you as long as you're moving." He shook his head.

The chickens continued their squabbling. Jake Jr., however, stood stock still, broadside to Jake and me. His yellow beak sat half open and his black, glassy eye blinked calmly. Watching him made me think of Jake — as if the both of them had only one good eye.

"See the spurs on him?" Jake asked.

I looked at the scaly heels on the rooster. "Yeah."

"Them's equalizers. Know what an equalizer is, boy?"

"No."

"Something to even things out." He leaned back and reached into his pants pocket. Out came what looked like a polished black handle with a raised silver button near the end. I must have frowned because Jake chuckled and said, "Never seen one, have you?"

I just shook my head.

"Here. Get a closer look for yourself." His hand floated up to my face and his thumb slid down toward the button.

FLICK!

I jerked back as a flash of silver exploded out the side of the handle. It was like snapping fingers — the thumb stopping ahead of the sound — it was so fast. It took me a second to realize what I'd just seen.

"Wow!"

"Wow's right. With this," Jake said, chuckling, "I can be the banty rooster of any goddamned barn I want."

My eyes stayed fixed on the shining blade. My tingling fingers drifted toward the knife.

"Don't even think about it, boy," Jake said. "It'll cut your gizzard out 'fore you can yell 'Daddy!'." He folded the knife and slipped it back into his pants pocket. Jake spat again, this time with less meanness.

"Who's doing all the yellin' at night?"

"Huh?" I was still thinking about the switchblade, what it'd take to get my hands on one. "Oh," I said as I looked up at the house and shifted my weight. "Uncle Keven . . . he has real bad dreams some nights. Says it's the war."

"Hmm. Hates them Japs, I bet."

"He . . . he doesn't talk to me about it. Says he can't."

"Well, what the hell do you two talk about all day? I seen you out there on the front porch. Him whittling away. You smilin' like a kid on Christmas morning."

"Baseball. Uncle Keven was good." I could feel the excitement building in me. It always started when I talked baseball. "*Real* good."

"Could swing the stick, huh?"

"Boy, could he. And catch, too."

"Shit," Jake said as he hopped down from the fence. The chickens scattered, wings flapping, throats clucking at one another. Jake turned around, leaned against the fence with his arms crossed, and stared at the house. He worked up a hard spit, the kind that puffed his cheeks out and growled as it came up. He coughed it out, then kicked at it with his boot. "Baseball," he said as he walked off, "is for sissies."

June sprinted by us as if we were standing still. During the hot days, I'd walk the fields pulling rye, getting rid of it to avoid dockage come harvest. On other days, my job was to clean out the trucks, check the oil, the radiators, and get them ready for the beginning of harvest in mid-July. When Uncle Keven wasn't looking, I'd climb the red International Harvester combine, grab the huge black steering wheel, and pretend I was driving. Nearly every morning I begged him to let me start up the green John Deere just to hear it. I thought the smell of gasoline would forever be my cologne.

Jake helped Uncle Keven replace sickle blades. From there, they'd move to the discs, always thinking ahead, even though some years Uncle Keven didn't disc the fields because the soil was already turning into brown talcum powder. Harvesting Uncle Keven's four thousand acres would take the last half of July and nearly all of August. Jake did nothing but complain about how hot and dry the Palouse was. I tried to stay away from him as much as possible. I even looked forward to the hotter days of late August, when Uncle Keven would be sending me out into the fallow fields with nothing but a hoe and a canteen to pull up the thistle and the tumbleweeds. Jake always said he had some other place to be. Somewhere else more important.

My father tended to his own crew, his own five thousand acres of rolling, undulating dream wheat. Mother didn't see him from before dawn to after dusk, so she visited with Uncle Keven and me every other day around lunchtime. She'd pile out of the Pontiac with crunchy fried chicken, cold mashed potatoes with a slab of butter punched into the center, and coleslaw. She and her brother mostly talked about the weather — and me.

"As long as the boy's eating," she said as she nodded toward me.

"He is, Katie," Uncle Keven answered. "Just look at him."

"I just wish you'd get yourself a phone, Keven," she said as she started the car.

"Haven't the need for one, Katie. I got Amp."

Sarah, I saw little of that summer. She'd come by on occasion — mostly in the evenings on her way into town — with mother's car. "Two more years, Uncle Keven," she'd remind him. "Just two more and I'm out of here."

That one Friday, that one nearly all of Endicott would remember as being the hottest Friday they *could ever* remember, Sarah drove down the gravel driveway to find Uncle Keven listening to the radio on the front porch. He was bent over, whittling away at time and a crooked pine bough, shaking his head at the Yankees' latest home run. I was trotting his roan mare between the house and the corrals when Jake came out of the barn all duded up. Payday made him walk taller than he really was. A slicked up banty rooster.

Sarah pulled to a stop when Jake walked in front of the car. He moved to the driver's side, opened the door, and offered her a hand. Sarah didn't get out. I trotted over.

"Hey, Sis," I said. "Whatcha doin'?"

"Looks to be going to town," Jake answered. "Nice skirt and fancy shoes." He nodded as if in agreement with himself. I slid down off the mare.

"That I am, Jake, thank you." Sarah reached up and adjusted the bright yellow bow behind her head. "Came by to see if you needed anything."

"That I do," Jake said.

"I was meaning Uncle Keven and Amp," she said.

"Well, it *is* Friday night. And it *is* a long walk into town for a man my age."

"I think we're okay, Sis. Uncle Keven and I don't need anything." I moved behind Jake and looked into the car. Sarah was gorgeous. Hair pulled back in a ponytail. Ironed beige blouse and saddle shoes. Pleated white skirt. Even bright red lipstick. She looked like a Grace Kelly sitting in my mother's car.

"Come on, princess. Step down from your carriage." Jake made a wide sweeping motion, curtsied, and turned his good eye on my sister.

"Thank you, no, Jake." Sarah's hands gripped the steering wheel. She barely turned her head toward us. "But, I do have to go. I have someone waiting for me."

"Well, let's go then," Jake said as he raced around to the other side of the car. I glanced up at the porch. Uncle Keven was gone. The radio sports announcer's voice hooted and howled. I turned back to my sister.

"I think it's okay, Sis." I shrugged my shoulders, leaned over, looked past my sister, and saw Jake reaching for the door handle. Before Sarah could say anything, Jake had the door open. "Uncle Keven trusts him," I said.

"Sure he does," Jake said, drawing out the first word as he sat down. "He hired me, didn't he?" He slammed the door. "Besides, Sarah. It's only a ten-minute drive into town. Surely you can spare *that* much of your precious time."

Two months later, I found Jake sitting on the bumper of the Ford, trimming his fingernails with his knife — the equalizer.

"Hey," I muttered. Jake didn't raise his head. "Can you take me and my stuff over to my parents' house a little later?" The rehearsed words spilled out of my mouth.

"Why don't you have your cute little uncle drive you over in the morning?" He chewed on his left index finger, then spat at the ground.

"Well, he's gone. Uncle Keven's gone up to Spokane with my parents. Remember?"

"And you?" Jake's head swiveled toward me. I looked into that cloudy gray eye, the one that rarely blinked.

"Well, Sarah wanted me to come to the house and stay with her. She gets scared, you know. You know how girls are." I watched Jake nibble on his ring finger.

"I thought she'd gone into town for a couple of days. Heard she wasn't *feelin' so good.*" Jake drew those last words into an accusation. A smirk peeked from the corner of his mouth as he lifted his chin and glared at me.

How, I thought, *could he talk like that after what he did to my sister?* My eyes felt like they were on fire. I looked away.

I shuffled my feet and stuffed my hands in my pockets. "Well, that's why she stayed home and Uncle Keven and everybody went up to Aunt Roberta's," I lied, "to see about Sarah staying with her for a while." My mouth was as dry as sawdust.

"You know, boy, I haven't seen you talk this much in a week's time. Somethin' going on here you want to tell me about?" He folded the equalizer and stood up. " 'Sides, you can drive. Why don't you drive your little ol' ass on out there?"

I felt caught. Cornered. My stomach twisted itself into a knot.

"I said," Jake growled, "why —"

"Uh, because . . . because —"

"Oh, hells-bells. I'll do it, boy. Let's go right now."

"Right now? You sure?"

"Shut up, boy." Jake's mouth warped itself into half-smile, half-grimace. "You ain't afraid to go with me, are you?"

"No, sir, it's just that . . ." The knot twisted on itself. *Would Uncle Keven be ready?*

"What? It's just what, little boy?" Jake leaned over and put both hands on his knees.

"Nothin'."

"Damned straight, nothin'." He stood back up and puffed his chest out. " 'Sides," he added, "I like visiting with your sister." He winked at me with his good eye. "Now go on and get your stuff."

The Ford screeched up the driveway toward the three silos, The

Holy Trinity. I said a prayer to the Holy Mother of God as Jake drove past.

Jake turned onto Highway 16 and the blacktop began snaking its way past more grain silos lining the six miles of winding road toward home. I loved to count the silos every time we drove the highway between home and Uncle Keven's. There were sixteen total, the same number as the state highway's.

I counted the first five silos before Jake said a word to me.

"Why you acting so strange, boy? One minute you're babblin' like a schoolgirl. Next minute you're all clammed up." Jake had to turn his head all the way around in order to see me with his good eye. "You don't think I like little boys, do you? Is that what's bothering you?" He turned his head back toward the highway. "Shit, boy, I like girls. I'm not like that uncle of yours, *Uncle Keven*." Jake cooed my uncle's name, then tilted his head back and kissed the air in front of him. "No sirree bob, I ain't nothin' like *that* little queer."

I kept counting the silos, hoping that concentrating on them would keep my head clear, focused.

Farther down the highway, Jake leaned into the door, cocking his head ever so slightly, like a man listening to his girlfriend whispering secrets over his shoulder. His cigarette dangled from his bottom lip and he draped his right arm across the steering wheel.

"Turn here," I blurted out at the sixteenth silo. My hands shot up and cupped my mouth as if I'd just burped at the dinner table.

Jake's right hand slapped my thigh. "Don't you think I know that, boy? I know where your sister lives," he said with a laugh as the Ford's wheels left the pavement and started up the gravel road.

We topped the last hill and coasted down the driveway to the front of my parents' house. Jake cut the engine before the truck came to a stop.

Bill and Will, our two Labs, didn't sprint out to greet the truck as they usually did. I heard them barking from inside the barn off to the right of the house.

"Why are them mutts put up?" Jake asked.

I kept staring at the house, wondering if Uncle Keven had heard the truck.

Jake's hand slapped my shoulder. "Hey," he snorted. "I asked you a question."

I pulled my hands out from under my bottom — I'd been sitting on them trying to warm them up. "Uh . . . uh . . . sometimes Sarah just puts them up. I don't know why." I kept searching the windows of the house, looking for a clue of Uncle Keven's presence.

"Hold on, boy." Jake snatched at my shirtsleeve as I leaned into the door to push it open. "I got us an idea."

I froze. I could feel my chin start to jiggle.

"I got us a proposition, boy." My shirtsleeve fell free. I heard Jake's Zippo lighter click open. I pulled my stare from the floorboard and watched him suck on another cigarette, his head slightly turned to the right, that gray eye peering at nothing. His lips pinched the cigarette and the flame flickered. The Zippo clinked shut and his brown hands moved away from his face. "Why don't you hustle on over there to that barn, saddle up one of them ol' swaybacks your old man calls a horse, and take yourself and them dogs out for a evenin' ride?" He took another drag on the cigarette. "A real . . . long . . . ride. Thataway," he blew a cloud of smoke toward the roof of the truck, "I can help your sister Sarah around the house."

My legs felt like icicles. I thought they'd snap if I tried to stand on them.

"Damn, boy. You're shakin' like a dog shittin' a peach seed." He snickered, slapped me on the arm again and said, "You ain't afraid of the dark, are you? Now, go on, boy." He turned and glared at me with his one good eye. "I'm tellin' you, you don't want to be around here while I visit with your sister."

Tears welled up in my eyes. The dashboard, the windshield, the house — everything — went blurry. I blinked and blinked but I did not make a sound. I refused to make a sound.

I bolted through the open door and sprinted toward the barn.

"That's right, gingerbread boy!" Jake shouted at me. "Run, run as fast as you can."

I collapsed into a ball when I reached the side of the barn. I squeezed my fists and pressed them into my cheeks. I couldn't think. I couldn't breathe. My mind swirled and spun and coiled back in on itself. *Don't you dare cry,* I thought. *Don't you dare cry.* I crawled my way back onto my feet and slid along the barn until I made it to the corner. I leaned my head back against the wall, drew in a deep breath, and then eased my nose around to see Jake stop on the front porch. He reached for the doorknob. Will and Bill howled furiously.

Jake twisted the knob, calling, "S-a-r-a-h." He kicked the door open. The dogs fell silent. I held my breath. Just as Jake stepped through the doorway, it hit.

The baseball bat struck mid-thigh. I heard the big bone snap. Jake squealed. He hunched over, frantically groping at the bent leg. The bat fell again, this time across his back.

"He's got a knife, Uncle Keven!" I shouted, racing toward the house. "A knife!"

By the time I jumped onto the porch, Jake lay face-down on the doorstep. Uncle Keven didn't take his eyes off him. He lifted Jake's right shoulder with the toe of his boot and rolled Jake onto his back, like flipping over a rusted sheet of tin. Jake's hands rose and fluttered in front of his face. They moved back and forth as if trying to shoo invisible demons.

Uncle Keven stood above Jake's head. He watched the hands tremble, stared at the broken, bent leg, then frowned at Jake's hands.

"Hold 'em down, Amp," Uncle Keven said, still not looking at me. "You have to hold his hands down."

"He's . . . he's got a —"

"I don't want them touching my face." The icy words just fell from my uncle's mouth, like they weren't his own.

I looked down at Jake. His head was tilted back as if he were trying to see inside the house, past Uncle Keven, but his eyes were pinched shut. His mouth opened and closed like a suffocating fish on land, sucking at the air. But the mouth made no sounds. His coarse Adam's apple bobbed beneath the stretched skin.

Uncle Keven stepped to the side of Jake. He propped the baseball bat against the door, knelt alongside the trembling hands, then grabbed the left wrist and slammed it to the floor. Jake's right hand still fluttered, as if unaware of what the other was doing.

"There can't be any blood."

"Wh . . . what?"

"Here. Step right here." I placed my boot heel on Jake's left wrist. It felt rubbery. I reached and held the doorjamb tight with both hands.

"Now, this one." Uncle Keven moved my other foot into place.

I obeyed, trapping Jake's right wrist under my other boot. Jake started to moan. I kept looking forward, down the hall, into the kitchen. My eyes searched my own home as if I'd never seen it before. I stared at the fireplace. The pink plastic flowers decorating the mantel. The white candles standing like frozen fingers. I counted them, over and over, and then started again. I saw the wood-framed photos of Sarah. Of me. My mother. Of Uncle Keven in his Marine uniform.

"There can't be," Uncle Keven whispered, "any blood."

I couldn't speak. I stood in the doorway like some cocky cowboy with his legs spread wide, towering over two grown men. My feet burned. My uncle moved silently, as if under water.

I glanced down just as Uncle Keven lay the wooden baseball bat across Jake's throat. He shifted his weight on his knees and slid both hands down to the ends of the bat. He looked like a hunched-over baker with a huge, misshapen rolling pin getting ready to knead dough.

I closed my eyes, tilted my head back, and squeezed the door-jamb with all my might, trying to hold on to a world that couldn't stop spinning. I kept counting.

Jake's mouth made no noise.

The seconds twisted into years as my Uncle Keven bore down. He finally stopped. But the crackling, the crunching, never have.

The Palouse snow slants across Highway 16, tossing shadows into an already gray January afternoon. My windshield wipers cake up with ice and screech across the glass. I pull off the highway, head up the gravel driveway, and stop at the top of the hill. There they are. The Holy Trinity sitting one, two, three. Pointed heads. Wide silver bellies.

I'm cold. Colder than I can ever remember being.

Uncle Keven's house is hollow. Empty. The bantam chickens are long gone.

I sit in the car with the engine idling. The wipers rest. I count the years since I saw Jake walk down this road. Thirteen. *Still counting,* I think, *after all these years.* My hands curl up into fists.

Sarah and my parents never visited this house, the one over the rise, sitting beneath the Holy Trinity. None of them could ever forgive Uncle Keven for disappearing off the front porch that evening. Sarah would turn her head at the sight of her uncle, my uncle. She'd call him "him." "Are you going over to visit 'him,' again?" she'd ask me. "I saw 'him' in town today." But, she never heard "him" asking her teachers how she was doing in school, if her grades were good, if she needed anything. She never saw "him" sneak out at her wedding after she said "I do" to some pig farmer's fat son who muttered the same words but didn't mean them. But I saw "him."

After that summer, Uncle Keven and I rarely discussed my "ticket" out of Endicott — baseball. I lost every ounce of interest I'd ever had in baseball. I helped him seed his winter wheat each fall but never stayed the night with him again. That year, Mother moved my bedroom downstairs, complaining, "You moan too much at night."

Uncle Keven never uttered a word about what took place that evening after Jake's fingers quit twitching beneath my boot heels. "Get on back to Sarah, Amp," is all he said. His voice never sounded the same to me after that.

I got my boyhood wish. Uncle Keven willed me the farm.

And I've never emptied the Holy Mother of God — and I never will.

ANNETTE MEYERS

You Don't Know Me

FROM *Flesh and Blood*

"HEAR THEM moving around?" She presses her ear to the door.

He doesn't hear anything, and standing in the dark outside her parents' bedroom scares him. What if they come out and catch him and her listening? And they don't know him, don't even know he's in their place. He gets anxious, like he always does when he's scared. He can't help it.

"You're afraid. What are you fuckin' afraid about? They're *my* parents, not yours."

"I gotta go," he says. The sweat is dripping off him, and his glasses slide down his nose. He has to pee.

She's disgusted with him. "You gotta do better than this or you can't hang out with me." She drags him back down the hall to the other side of the apartment. It's this huge place that goes a whole floor with their own elevator stop. She has her own bathroom.

He can't pee while she stands in the doorway watching him, talking about *them*. It's all she talks about. She hates them. "They're always on my case." She makes her voice whiny. "Why do you have to dress like that, Lila? Like you're a boy. You're such a pretty girl, Lila." She changes her voice. "Do you like the way I dress, Anthony?" Raising her baggy sweatshirt, she flashes little apricot tits at him. "You think I look like a boy, Anthony? What do you say, Anthony? Do you think I'm a pretty girl?" She stands there and waits.

"Yeah," he says. He can hardly hear himself. The piss comes gushing out of him. "You're beautiful." He feels like his feet are glued to the floor. His beeper starts going.

She lowers her T-shirt. "Forget it. Call your mama."

She scares him, but everything scares him. He doesn't want her to stop talking. He's never met anyone like her before. She's so free. She does whatever she wants to do, goes wherever she wants, says what she wants. He doesn't understand why she complains all the time.

". . . can't imagine them having a conversation," Lila says. "They never talk about anything real except when they're talking about me, and even then they don't relate to me."

Hands shaking, he zips up. It's after midnight and he's skipped his last pill. Yeah, his mom'll be on his back in a minute. Why isn't he home? It's a school night. And just like that his beeper goes off again. It's going to wake her parents.

But she laughs and lies down on her bed, her arms behind her head, and stares at him. His and his mom's whole place could fit in her bedroom. Her bed has this thing called a canopy over it. Her stupid mother's stupid idea. He feels stupid.

She jumps up and goes, "Let's get some beer and hang out."

The apartment has a back door and back stairs. This is how they get out. She steers him to the lobby's side entrance, the way they came in. The doorman is this tall jerk with no chin and a skinny mustache. Benny, she calls him. When Benny opens the door for them, he gives Anthony a wink, like he knows something.

"Go on, Anthony, what're you waiting for?" She gives him a push. He stands on the sidewalk and looks back. She's passing something to the jerk doorman.

It pisses him off, like she's got something going with the asshole. Anthony wants her for himself. "You getting something on with him?" His beeper goes off. His mom gave him the beeper so she could keep track of him. No one keeps track of Lila. She wouldn't let them.

Lila laughs at him. "Why don't you call your mama, baby?"

Fuck, she makes him mad. He grabs her arm and she shakes him off, gives him a look like he's a piece of shit. "Don't you ever touch me like that," she says, swiping him with the back of her hand. Her ring nicks him on the cheek. She goes off down the street toward the all-night grocery.

It's only two weeks since he first saw her. He'd started hanging out in the park on his way home from school, where a lot of kids his age hung out with hippies and bikers, drinking beer and smoking weed. Sometimes he'd Rollerblade. He didn't talk much, and pretty soon they were making fun of him because he didn't do weed, and didn't drink.

He was on these pills, two different ones, and he was not supposed to, not even beer, but Anthony didn't tell them that. He didn't go to regular public school because he got anxious attacks. But he was doing better at Harrison, where the classes were small and they didn't keep telling him to do better.

He'd come into the park this one day and bladed up and down the trails. When he came to the bandstand, he didn't see the usual crew, except for the two homeless men who were collecting the empty beer cans. They looked at him, then pointed down in the low valley near the lake. Getting closer, he heard the whistles and shouts. The fight was between two kids he knew who hung out. They were really smacking each other around, kicking and rolling in the grass.

"Kill him, slice him!"

Anthony looked to see where the shout came from and he saw a girl in baggy pants and a T-shirt on the path going up the hill. She lifted a can to her lips, drained it, and threw it at the fighters. It bounced off the head of the one standing over the other, who was lying on the ground.

The standing kid yelled at the girl, "Fuck you, bitch," distracted just long enough to get an up-punch in the balls from the kid on the ground.

The girl laughed and bladed off.

"Who's that?" Anthony asked Robert Paredes, one of the boys watching the fight.

"That's Lila. She's crazy, man, but she can fight. I seen her hurt another bitch bad."

Anthony followed her hut not too close. After a while she began to look over her shoulder at him. She was crazy. She'd pass people and clip them hard, then go fast so by the time they began to yell at her she was gone. One time she stuck her foot into the spokes of a bike as the biker rode by and the bike jerked and threw the rider into the road in front of a cab. The cab stopped just in time.

Anthony heard her laughing, but he couldn't see her. He kept going on the path, but he'd lost her. He was tired. He sat down on a bench next to a backpack someone had left. He looked around, prodded the backpack, looked around again. He stood, reached for the backpack, and started to go.

"Where you think you're goin' with my backpack, asshole?" She was standing in front of him, holding a can of beer. She took a long drink, then snatched her backpack from him, unzipped it, and offered him a can of beer. He stared at it, then popped it, and drank. This wild, crazy feeling came over him.

After that, he was with her. They bladed along the park paths with her yelling at people, like, "Outta my way, fuckhead," and "When they let you out, crazy ass?" He liked to see the look on people's faces when she did that. She had the power.

They ended up on the steps near the lake with some other kids and some old fart hippie bums with beards and long hair, and bikers, all smoking weed and drinking beer. Everyone knew Lila and looked at him differently because he was with her.

"Pass the beer," she said. "I got weed." She took a couple of Baggies from her backpack and flashed them. Two bags full of joints.

"We're out," one of the hippies said. "But how about some grass?"

She flung one Baggie up in the air and they all jumped for it, scrambling over each other.

His beeper went off.

She stashed the other Baggie in her backpack. "What're you, a dealer or somethin'?"

He said the truth. "My mom."

"His mom wants her baby to come home," Lila yelled. "Yeah, yeah, yeah."

He felt his face get all hot.

She laughed. "How'd you get those?"

He looked down at the scars on his wrists and back at her.

"Come on, let's get some beer," she said.

He followed her out of the park to a deli, where he watched her pick up two six-packs and lay down the bills. She had a lot of twenties all wadded up in her backpack.

"You been drinking?" the clerk asked.

"You talkin' to me?" she said.

Out on the street she said to Anthony, "So I'm a drunk, so what?"

They went back to the lake and sat around smoking and drinking till he didn't know what time it was, but it was real dark and the cops kept coming and waving their flashlights and telling them to clear out.

His mom went after him when he got home. "Whatsa matter with you? You missed your medication. Where'd you go? Why didn't you answer your beeper?"

He wanted to say to her what Lila would say, something free, but he couldn't get the words straight in his head, so he didn't say anything. But he knew Lila now and he would do what he wanted like her, and there was nothing his mom could say to him anymore that would change that.

So now he watches Lila walk away from him, like he's nothing, and he doesn't know if she means it or not. He touches where her ring nicked him and it's wet. He takes off his glasses and rubs his eyes.

"What the fuck you waitin' for?" He hears her screaming from all the way down the street.

He puts on his glasses. He can barely see her in the light of the street lamp. People turn around and look at her. Like she's a celebrity. She's like no one he knows in his whole life. He catches up with her and waits while she buys two six-packs. She hands one to him and they head out to the park.

The sky is full of dark, rolling clouds, hiding the moon. The park has this wet feel though it hasn't rained, and the air lies heavy over them. It's very dark and after closing time, and the cops are making their rounds. Lila sees better than he does and she hisses when she spots them.

The real night people are settled on the steps leading to the bandstand, talking, drinking. He knows most of them by sight now. They're all different ages. Mostly guys. Some have regular jobs, but like to hang out and drink and do drugs. Anthony's seen some do hard drugs and pass out. The drunks always end up puking by the lake.

An old black man lies snoring on the steps blocking their way. He's giving off a big stink. "Move it, nigger," Lila yells. She kicks at him. He groans and clutches the air, but can't keep himself from tumbling down the rest of the steps. He lies at the bottom of the stone steps, then picks himself up and stumbles away.

Anthony and Lila sit at the top of the stairs, and she begins passing out the cans of beer. His beeper goes off. He shuts it down.

"Get the weed," she tells Anthony, who takes some joints from her backpack and gives them to her.

This big middle-aged guy stands up from a few stairs below. He lifts his beer can to Lila.

"Hey!" Lila looks at him like she knows him.

He gives her another look and comes up the stairs to them. He's wearing this shirt with the sleeves rolled up, half in and half out of his pants. He's carrying a jacket.

"Hey," he says. He sits down on the other side of Lila.

"Remember me?" she says. "I'm Lila from rehab."

"Yeah," he says. "Lila from rehab." He slurs his words and keeps nodding his head.

It's like they're in some kind of private club together that won't let Anthony in. Anthony moves in closer to her. Lila gives him a mean look, like who the fuck does Anthony think he is, and Anthony inches away.

"Danny Boy," she says.

"Yeah," the drunk says, and like he passes out.

Not long afterward a three-wheel cop car comes along with a searchlight that swirls all over. A loudspeaker goes on and the cop tells them to disperse, get out of the park, the park is closed for the night.

Danny Boy twitches and gets up. He gives Lila a drooly smile and goes off on one of the bike trails.

Anthony doesn't go right home. He circles around and follows Lila. If she knows, she doesn't let on. She's put the hood of her gray sweatshirt up over her head. He follows her right to her apartment building, to the side entrance, where the jerk with the mustache is standing at the door. They don't see Anthony.

"Jeez," the jerk says, "you got trouble again. He called nine-one-one and the cops just got here."

"Fuck," she says, and she goes inside and Anthony doesn't see her anymore.

Late the next afternoon, after he does the grocery shopping for his grandmother and carries the bags up the stairs to the fourth floor for her, Anthony blades to Lila's building. He waits for her, smoking a joint out of sight of the doorman.

A lot of people pass him, heading for the park across the street, joggers and hikers especially, and bladers. It's spring and everyone's out. Across the way the bushes all have yellow flowers.

A taxi stops and the doorman runs over to open the door. Lila jumps out and walks in Anthony's direction. The doorman helps a tall, thin lady in a fitted suit and high heels get out. Lila's mother, though Lila is small and wears baggy clothes so you can't tell she's not thin.

"Lila," the tall lady says, "where are you going?"

"None of your business." Under her breath Lila adds, "Bitch."

"What do you want for dinner?" the tall lady asks, like Lila hasn't talked back fresh to her.

"Leave me alone," Lila shouts. "Don't you see I'm talking to my friend?"

"Ask your friend if he wants to stay for dinner," her mother says.

"He says he would rather die," Lila says real loud. "Don't you, Anthony?"

Her mother ducks her head like she's embarrassed and goes into the building.

Anthony can't imagine talking like that to his mother.

Lila makes him excited, like he's on the edge, going to jump. He touches his cock, feels the swell. It feels good. He's stopped taking his pills. He heard at the clinic they keep you from getting hard. He wants to be with her all the time.

Apricot tits. Little knobs of nipple that connect his tongue to his cock.

"Come on," Lila says, grabbing his arm. "I gotta get my blades."

She takes him into her building past the doorman and another man in a uniform.

"No Rollerblades," the doorman calls to Anthony.

Anthony stops moving.

"Forget it," Lila says. She shoves Anthony forward and he takes off on the smooth marble floor, barely able to stop himself from crashing into her mother and another woman in a hat waiting for the elevator. He bumps into a bench.

The woman in the hat makes a little noise. She stares at Lila.

"See something you like?" Lila says.

"You kids are out of control," the woman says.

Lila comes up and barks like a dog right in the woman's face.

The woman backs off and doesn't get on the elevator when the doors open.

"What is your friend's name, Lila?"

"Puff Daddy," Lila says.

"I thought you said Anthony," her mother says.

"Anthony Puff Daddy." Lila laughs, pokes Anthony so he laughs, too.

In daylight, the apartment looks like a museum.

"Would you like a Coke?" her mother asks.

"Puff Daddy and I are goin' bladin'," Lila says. She takes her blades from her backpack and puts them on.

"Lila, please don't upset everyone in the building."

"Why would I do that?" Lila says.

"Come home early," her mother says. And while her mother continues with, "You know your father doesn't like you to stay out late," Lila mouths the same words, making monkey faces.

Anthony can't get over it. She's so free. If he could only be like her.

When they get to her bedroom, she pulls off her sweatshirt and grabs a fresh one just like it from a drawer. Her apricots are stiff. She stops. "You lookin' at me?"

He cringes. "No."

"What's the matter? Aren't they worth lookin' at?"

He's sweating. "Sure."

She pulls the sweatshirt over her head. "Come here."

He crosses to her, trying to conceal the lump in his pants.

"Closer." He's standing right up against her. His cock shivers. She lifts her baggy sweatshirt and pulls it over his head, her tits in his face. He grabs her ass. He's in a dark place, her sweat salty on his tongue. Her knee nuzzles his cock. "Suck them," she says.

He comes, goes limp.

"Schmuck!" She pushes him away.

They blade through the park, drinking beer, and Lila says, "They're always on my case, come home early, don't do this, don't do that." She stops and yells at no one in particular, "We're big trouble!" A middle-aged black woman pushing a white child in a stroller gives her a look, and Lila screams, "What you lookin' at, nigger?"

The woman sits down on a bench. The child begins wailing.

Lila races off, Anthony follows. "My father called the cops on me once," Lila says. "Didn't think I was respectful enough."

"So he called the cops?" Anthony's shocked. "And the cops came?"

"I punched the stupid asshole out. That's when they put me in rehab. A lotta good it did."

It's getting dark by the time they stop at the bandstand. The usual group is there. A couple of the guys are slap boxing, but like they're loaded and they're not moving too fast and not hitting hard.

"Got any grass, Lila?" one of the old hippies yells.

"Yeah," she says. "Got any beer?"

"Not much."

Anthony's beeper goes off. He ignores it.

"Pass it around." Lila gives Anthony the plastic bag from her backpack. He sees her backpack is full of money, tens and twenties.

"Hey, girl." Danny Boy sits down next to Lila and throws his arm across her shoulder, offers her what's left of his Colt .45 malt.

She tilts her head, but there's hardly anything. She shoves the empty can at Danny Boy and takes out two twenties. "Anthony, get some beer."

"I don't have I.D."

"What a nerd," she says real loud to Danny Boy.

Anthony feels hot, dizzy, like he's going to pass out.

Everyone is looking at him.

"Here." She pushes the twenties at him. "Just do it. You know where. Give him the whole thing, Tell him it's for me."

Danny Boy laughs and raises his empty can at Anthony. "We'll be right here when you get back." Anthony wants to push it in his face.

His beeper goes off when he is leaving the park, and again at the deli.

The clerk at the deli gives him the eye. "Made you her slave I see."

Anthony smacks the twenties down on the counter. The clerk hands over two six-packs. "Well, watch out for her. She's a nut job."

Lila's not there when he gets back, and it's real dark already. He thinks he's going crazy. He goes from one to another, "Where is she? Where'd she go?"

"Get outta here, asshole," one of the hippies says, giving him a push. "She's been taking turns humping everybody."

His beeper goes off, and they all start laughing.

"Try the lake," one of the bikers tells him. "Saw her go that way with Danny Boy. But leave the beer."

Anthony maneuvers his way down the stairs to the grassy slope leading to the lake. There are dim lights around the lake, but he can't see anything. It's like she disappeared. And with that old drunk. He's not watching where he's going and hits a stump and goes flying, lands on his back, wind knocked out.

"Where's the beer?" Lila stands over him swinging her jeans. She's wearing her baggy shirt, and that's all. She sways and the moonlight makes her eyes glow.

"Left it back there."

She drops her jeans on his face, puts a bare foot on his chest, and moves it around slowly. Then she straddles him. He touches her tentatively, her ass hard and soft at the same time. Just as he is, though he hasn't taken his medication at all in the past week.

"Well, that's the last we'll ever see of it."

She squeezes her thighs against him like she's riding and he's the horse. Her cunt wets through his shirt.

"I'm sorry," he says.

She gets off him. "Let's get some movies. We'll drink my father's shit." She pulls her pants from his face, sits on him like he's a bench, takes her blades out of her backpack, holds them out to him. "Do it."

She has soft feet, like a baby, and short toes. He takes her toes in his mouth and sucks.

"I knew you were a perv," she says, taking her feet from him. She puts on her blades herself, and starts off not too steady, calling back, "Well, you coming or not?"

At Blockbuster she picks out a couple of kung fu flicks and they go into her building by the side entrance, where the jerk is on the door. "Use the stairs," he says.

Anthony takes off his blades, while Lila can't make her fingers work right and tears at hers in a fury, can't undo them, and gets angrier and angrier. "You got a knife? Cut them off me." She claws at him. "You hear? Cut them off."

He takes his knife, pops open the blade. She pulls it from his hands and hacks at the leather.

"You're ruining them," he says.

"Who cares?" Tearing the wrecked blades off, she drops them into the trash can near the back stairs and hands him his knife.

They climb twelve flights and at the back door she tells him to take off his high-tops. "Otherwise," she says, "they'll come out and tell me I can't do this and I can't do that, like I'm a prisoner." She uses her key to get in. It's a kitchen. The cleanest kitchen Anthony's ever seen. Like no one eats in it.

She's jumpy, throws the videos on her bed, starts going through her drawers, searching the floor of her closet. "You got any acid?"

Anthony shakes his head. He watches her acting crazy. She leaves the room and he waits. She's making him jumpy, too. She comes back with a bottle of dark booze and takes a long swallow, then offers it to him. He takes a swallow, chokes, coughs, hands it back to her. Tastes terrible. He's never had more than a beer.

"I gotta have acid," she says. "Let's get out of here."

They're back in the park near the bandstand, and there's a big full moon giving off light and a crowd of the night people, many who work regular day jobs and have money for weed and booze and other stuff. He recognizes them now and they know him, because of Lila. He feels powerful because she's singled him out to be with. They accept him now.

Someone passes them a sweet-smelling joint and they drink Zima and do acid, and he lies back on the steps and looks up at the moon, watching it expand and shrink and turn into a leering, snot-dripping face.

"Where'd you go, Lulu?" Danny Boy sits down next to Lila and throws his arm around her, like he owns her or something. "How about a little sugar?" He makes smacking sounds with his lips. He's so drunk he can't keep his head up, and he stinks of vomit.

Anthony feels Lila stiffen up next to him. She gives Danny Boy one of her bad looks. "That's it," she says. "We're goin' to the lake." Anthony follows her, but can hardly feel his feet anymore, and she's swinging and swaying like she feels the same as him.

Danny Boy gets up like she's invited him to go along.

Nobody's at the lake yet, but they will be because the cops will start coming around with the searchlights and drive everyone away from the bandstand. The surface of the lake is like one big dark mirror. Anthony stands at the edge and looks into it and it goes red and yellow and purple and ends up making him lose his balance.

"Watch out there, son." Danny Boy grabs Anthony's shirt. He's so drunk, he leans into Anthony, slobbering, and Anthony pushes him away. There's a ripping sound.

"You tore it," Anthony says, looking at his shirt. Everything explodes in his head. His mom'll kill him. He punches at Danny Boy, but the man is already on his knees.

"Slice him," Lila yells. "Where's your knife?"

Anthony takes his knife out, pops the blade. Danny Boy looks up at him, blinking in the moonlight. He tries to get to his feet, but falls down again.

"What're you waitin' for?" Lila screams.

Anthony has his arm low. He underhands the knife. The blade catches Danny Boy as the man comes up. Catches him in the gut. Danny Boy grabs hold of the knife and struggles with Anthony, like he wants to keep it in his gut and Anthony's trying to get it out. There's blood flying, like it's raining, and Danny Boy howls like a jungle animal. Magic music, is what it is, and when Anthony gets the knife out, he plunges it back in, and out, and in, keeping time to the music. It's so good . . . so good. So good. . . .

"Yes," Lila sings. "Yes. Yes. Yes."

Anthony shudders, his body jerks like he's a spastic. The come collects in his pants.

Danny Boy goes over backward and doesn't move. Anthony holds up the knife to the moon. The blade runs soft and red.

"Don't stop, Anthony," Lila says. "If we throw him in the lake, he'll just float up and they'll find him. We have to cut him up, take his insides out, then he'll sink. I read it somewhere."

Anthony's confused. What's she saying? His beeper goes off.

"Here." She grabs the knife from him. "I'll do it." She's going through Danny Boy's pockets, pulling out wallet and papers. She empties the wallet, throws it and the papers into a trash basket, and follows it with a lit match. The trash basket bursts into flames.

Danny Boy's insides are hanging out of him, all slimy. "Come on, move it," she says. They throw everything in the lake, but the stuff is slippery and maybe they miss some. Then they each take an arm and drag Danny Boy farther into the lake.

"Everyone out of the park," comes over a loudspeaker.

"Let's get out of here," Lila says, taking off.

The footpaths are pitch black and everything gets very quiet, except for Danny Boy's howling, which rings in Anthony's ears. He catches up to Lila and they leave the park together, heading for the side door of her building, where the asshole doorman lets them in.

"Jesus H. Christ!" He's staring at them in the dim light. "You been in a fight?"

"We were attacked by a crazy bum," Lila says. "We'll wash up in the laundry room."

"I don't want nothing to do with this," the doorman says. He turns and leaves them.

Anthony and Lila go to the laundry room and begin to wash the blood and slime off them. "Give me the knife," she says. "I'll take care of it."

He gives her the knife. They put their wet clothes in one of the dryers, drop the coins in, and while everything dries, they wait around wrapped in someone's clean towels Lila pulled from another dryer. And all the time Lila doesn't stand still, but paces the room up and down. He gets tired following her and sits on the floor and starts to go to sleep.

"Wake up." She's hitting his head like she's crazy. They get dressed and go up to her apartment the back way, and she tells him, "Take a shower."

The hot water feels good. He'll just get dressed and go home. He can hardly hold his head up.

Lila pulls back the shower curtain and steps in, takes the soap and lathers her hands. She grabs his cock with her soapy hands. "You come too soon, dickhead, and I'll kill you, I swear."

"I won't," he moans.

She jumps him like a monkey, her left hand around his neck, her right hand guiding him inside her. He holds her slippery ass while she puts both arms around his neck and starts banging. He's going to pass out, for sure.

She digs her nails into his back. "Don't just stand there, asshole."

His feet go out from under him and he goes over backward, pulling her down on top of him.

Lila's screams get drowned out by the water that's coming down on them. "Think we made an idiot baby?" She laughs, turns the water on freezing cold, and jumps out of the shower.

After Anthony turns the shower off, he just lies there. He can't move. He hears her talking. Who's she talking to? He gets out of the shower and wraps one of her towels around him. She's on the telephone.

". . . none of your business," she says. "I'm just tellin' you we were attacked by some homeless and I ran and they caught my friend." She hangs up the phone, when she sees Anthony.

"Why'd you do that?" Anthony asks.

"We should've cut his hands off," she says. "I'm gonna go wash my hair."

Anthony lies down on her bed and falls asleep. The pounding on the door wakes him. Some man is yelling, "Lila! Come out of there."

He sees her standing near the bed. She is wearing pajamas. "What do you want? I'm sleepin'," she says. Her hair hangs in her face.

"Come out at once. The police want to talk to you."

"Stay here," she whispers to Anthony. She leaves the room, but the door is half open.

Anthony gets into his clothes, pulls on his Nikes. He wants to leave, but he's trapped. He looks around the room. There's no blood that he sees. He goes into the bathroom. No blood. Maybe he can leave by the back way. They wouldn't be talking in the kitchen. He pushes the door open a crack, and someone grabs his arm and pulls him out.

"Look what we have here, Pierce. Come on out and talk to us." Anthony can tell he's a cop, though he's not in uniform. The cop brings him into a big room where Lila's parents are sitting on a couch, in bathrobes, both looking at the same time angry and scared. Lila is in a chair near the fireplace and another cop, also not in uniform, is leaning against the fireplace. Lila gives Anthony a terrible look, like she wants to kill him. Anthony can't stop shivering.

They sit him on a chair next to Lila, and take out notepads and pencils.

"So where were we?" the cop named Pierce says. "Oh, yeah, you made an anonymous phone call to nine-one-one to tell us a friend of yours was attacked in the park."

Lila doesn't say anything.

"Is this the friend?" Pierce looks at Anthony.

She gives Anthony another look. "I've only known him a couple of weeks."

Anthony has to pee. He can't concentrate. What did she do with his knife?

"Your doorman said you both came in the side entrance a couple of hours ago, covered with blood."

Lila's mother gasps, her hand over her mouth. Her father, a small guy with thin hair, puts his arm around his wife. They both look sick. Lila glows with a kind of light like Anthony's seen around the Virgin Mary at St. Anne's.

"Nice ring," Pierce says.

Lila looks at her ring.

Pierce takes Lila's hand. "How'd you get blood on it?"

Anthony can't believe it, but *she* starts crying. Her parents rush to her. She's screaming and throwing herself on the floor.

"We were drinkin' and he got jealous and did it." Lila points at Anthony. "I tried to give him mouth to mouth, but it was too late."

"Stop talking, Lila," her father says. "You're incriminating yourself."

Anthony can't move. Did she say he did it?

Lila turns on her father, smacking him. "Get away from me, asshole. You think I don't know they're writin' down what I say? I don't give a fuck."

"I know my daughter couldn't —"

Lila shrieks at him, "You don't know me."

"Hold up your foot, Anthony," Hernandez says. Anthony holds up his foot. Hernandez nods at Pierce. "Blood in the grooves."

"Let's take a walk, kids," Pierce says.

"I don't think —" Lila's father stops.

"You can come along with us, sir," Pierce says. "We're just going to see where the kids got attacked and what happened to their friend."

"You got a backpack or something?" Hernandez asks Anthony. Anthony nods. "Come along, then, and we'll get it." He's putting on latex gloves.

Lila's room looks the same only the bed is rumpled where he slept and there are wet towels on the floor. His backpack is next to the bed. He picks it up and Hernandez takes it from him. "Let me help you," he says, and then he opens it. "Nice blades." And then, "Your knife?"

Anthony stares at the knife. Hernandez says, "Get up against the wall, Anthony, spread eagle." Hernandez pats him down. "Good boy." They go back to the living room, Hernandez holding the backpack. He nods at Pierce.

"Come on, kids," Pierce says.

"You can't take her away," Lila's mother cries. "It's not safe in the park at night."

"We'll be back," Hernandez says. "We're just going for a little walk. And she'll be plenty safe with us." Hernandez takes Anthony by the arm and Lila goes with Pierce.

In the elevator. Pierce tells Lila to stand still, and he frisks her. "Hate to do it in front of your parents," he said, "but it's got to be done."

"What're you searchin' me for? Search him," Lila says.

They leave the apartment building by the main entrance. It must be three or four in the morning because it's quiet on the street, and in the park the moonlight makes Anthony think he's in a movie. Lila's parents stayed in the apartment. Anthony heard her father on the telephone as they were leaving.

Lila leads the way, like she's a dog on a trail, right down to the lake. The moon is so bright it's like daylight, or maybe it's all the searchlights and the cop cars. Anthony sees yellow tape around a place on the edge of the lake, where a dark lump lies half in and half out of the water. And the shadows of the night people beyond the tape, with the cops on loudspeakers yelling for everybody to get out of the park.

Lila is shrieking and crying. "I was afraid of him. I thought he was gonna kill me, too." She looks down at Danny Boy, blubbering and choking. "I tried to help you."

Hernandez puts his hands on Anthony's shoulders. "You have the right to remain silent . . ."

JOYCE CAROL OATES

The High School Sweetheart

FROM *Playboy*

THERE WAS an intensely private man whose fate was to become, as year followed year, something of a public figure and a model for others. Nothing astonished R____ more, and more alarmed him! Relatively young, he'd achieved renown as a writer of popular yet literary novels; his field was the psychological suspense mystery, a genre in which he excelled, perhaps because he respected the tradition and took infinite care in composition. These were terse, minimally plotted but psychologically knotty novels written, as R____ said in interviews, sentence by sentence, and so they must be read sentence by sentence, with attention, as one might perform steps in a difficult dance. R____ was himself both choreographer and dancer. And sometimes, even after decades of effort, R____ lost his way, and despaired. For there was something of horror in the lifelong contemplation of *mystery;* a sick, visceral helplessness that must be transformed into control, and *mastery.* And so R____ never gave up any challenge, no matter how difficult. "To give up is to confess you're mortal and must die."

R____ was one of those admired persons who remain mysterious even to old friends. By degrees, imperceptibly as it seemed to him, he became an elder, and respected, perhaps because his appearance inspired confidence. He had fair, fine, sand-colored hair that floated about his head, a high forehead and startlingly frank blue eyes; he was well over six feet tall and lean as a knife blade, with long loose limbs and a boyish energy. He seemed never to grow older, nor even mature, but to retain a dreamy Nordic youthfulness with a glisten of something chill and soulless in his eyes, as if, inwardly, he gazed upon a tundra of terrifying, featureless white and the utterly blank, vacuous Arctic sky above. One of the prevailing mysteries about R____ was his marriage, for none of us had ever glimpsed his wife of four decades, let alone been introduced to her; it was assumed that her name began with "B," for each of R____'s eleven novels was dedicated, simply and tersely, to "B," and it was believed that R____ had married, very young, a girl who'd been his high school sweetheart in a small town in northern Michigan, that she wasn't at all literary or even interested in his career, and that they had no children.

In one of his reluctant interviews R____ once admitted, enigmatically, that, no, he and his wife had no children. "*That,* I haven't committed."

How proud we were of R____, as one of the heralded patricians in the field! When he spoke to you, smiled and shook hands, like a big animated doll, you felt privileged, if only just slightly uneasy at the remote, arctic glisten in those blue, blue eyes.

R____ was often nominated to run for office in professional organizations to which he belonged, yet always he declined out of modesty, or self-doubt: "R____ isn't the man you want, truly!" But finally, at the age of sixty, he gave in and was elected by a large majority as president of the American Mystery Writers, a fact that seemed to both deeply move him and fill him with apprehension. Repeatedly he called members of the executive board to ask if truly R____ was the man we wanted; repeatedly we assured him, yes, certainly, R____ was.

On the occasion of his induction as president, R____ meant to entertain us, he promised, with a new story written especially for that evening, not a lengthy, rambling speech interlarded with lame jokes, like certain of his predecessors. (Of course there was immediate laughter at this remark. For our outgoing president, an old friend of R____'s and of most of us in the audience, was a well-liked but garrulous gentleman not known for brevity.)

Almost shyly, however, R____ took the podium and stood before an audience of perhaps five hundred mystery writers and their guests, straight-backed and handsome in his detached, pale, Nordic way, a fine figure of a man in an elegant tuxedo, white silk shirt, and gleaming gold cuff links. R____'s hair was more silvery than we recalled but floated airily about his head; his forehead appeared higher, a prominent ridge of bone at the hairline. Well back into the audience, you could see those remarkable blue eyes. In a beautifully modulated, rather musical voice, R____ thanked us for the honor of electing him president, thanked outgoing officers of the organization, and alluded with regret to the fact that "unforeseen circumstances" had prevented his wife from attending that evening. "As you know, my friends, I did not campaign to be elected your president. It's an honor, as the saying goes, that has been thrust upon me. But I do feel that I am a kinsman of all of you, and I hope I will be worthy of your confidence. I hope you will like the story I've written for you!" Almost, R____'s voice quavered when he said these words, and he had to pause for a moment before beginning to read, in a dramatic voice, from what appeared to be a handwritten manuscript of about fifteen pages.

The High School Sweetheart: A Mystery

There was an intensely private man whose fate was to become, as year followed year, something of a public figure and a model for others. Nothing astonished R____ more, and more alarmed him! Relatively young, he'd achieved renown as a writer of popular yet literary novels; his field was the psychological suspense mystery, a genre in which he excelled, perhaps because he respected the tradition and took infinite care in composition. These were terse, minimally plotted but psychologically knotty novels written, as R____ said in interviews, sentence by sentence, and so they must be read sentence by sentence, with attention, as one might perform steps in a difficult dance. R____ was himself both choreographer and dancer. And sometimes, even after decades of effort, R____ lost his way, and despaired. For there was something of horror in the lifelong contemplation of *mystery;* a sick, visceral helplessness that must be transformed into control, and *mastery*. And so R____ never gave up any challenge, no matter how difficult. "To give up is to confess you're moral and must die."

At this apparent misstatement, R____ paused in confusion, peering at his manuscript as if it had deceived or betrayed him; but a moment later he regained his composure, and continued —

"To give up is to confess you're *mortal* and must die."

Forty-five years ago! I wasn't yet R____ but a fifteen-year-old named Roland, whom no one called Rollie, skinny, gawky, self-conscious, with a straight-A average and pimples like hot little beads of red pepper scattered across forehead and back, lost in helpless erotic dreams of a beautiful, popular blond senior named Barbara, whom everyone at Indian River High School called Babs. Now that I am no longer this boy, I can contemplate him without the self-loathing he'd felt at the time. I can feel a measure of pity for him, and sympathy, if not tenderness. Or forgiveness.

My high school sweetheart was two years older than I, and, I'm ashamed to confess, didn't realize that she was my high school sweetheart. She had a boyfriend her own age, and numerous other friends besides, and had no idea how I secretly observed her, and with what yearning. The name Babs — unremarkable, yet so American and somehow wholesome — makes me feel faint, still, with hope and longing.

In high school, I came to dread mirrors as I dreaded the frank assessing stares of my classmates, for these confronted me with a truth too painful to acknowledge. Like many intellectually gifted adolescents I was precocious academically and retarded socially. In my dreams, I was freed of my clumsy body and often glided along the ground, or soared, swift as thought; I felt myself purely a mind, a questing spirit: it was my own body I fled, my base, obsessive sexual yearning. In actual life I was both shy and haughty; I carried myself stiffly, conscious of being a doctor's son in predominantly working-class Indian River, even as I saw with painful clarity how my classmates were only polite with me when required, their mouths smiling in easy deference even as their eyes drifted past me. *Yes, you're Roland, the doctor's son, you live in one of the big brick houses on Church Street, and your father drives a new, shiny black Lincoln, but we don't care for you anyway.* Already in grade school I'd learned the crucial distinction between being envied and being liked. Where there was laughter, there, Roland, the doctor's son, was excluded. Of course, I had one or two friends, even rather close friends, boys like myself, brainy and lonely, and given to irony, though we were too young to grasp the meaning of *irony:* where heartbreak and anger conjoin. And I had my secret dreams, which attached themselves with alarming abrupt-

ness and a terrible fixedness, at the start of my sophomore year
in high school, to beautiful blond Babs, a girl whose father, a carpenter and stone mason with a good local reputation, had
worked for my father.

Why this fact filled me with shame in Babs's presence, while
Babs herself took no notice of it at all, I can't explain.

Adolescence! Happiness for some, poison for others. The
killer's heart is forged in adolescence. Sobering for R____ in his
rented tuxedo, gold cuff links gleaming, to recall that fifteen
years ago he would have eagerly exchanged his privileged life as
a small-town physician's brainy, beloved son, destined to graduate summa cum laude from the University of Michigan, for that
of Babs Hendrick's boyfriend Hal McCreagh, a good-looking
football player with a C average, destined to work in an Indian
River lumberyard for life. *If I could be you. And no more me.* Mostly
I managed not to think of Hal McCreagh at all, but solely of Babs
Hendrick, whom in fact I saw infrequently. When I did manage
to see her, in school, in passing, I was so focused on the girl that
she existed for me in a rarefied dimension, like a specimen of
some beautiful creature — butterfly, bird, tropical fish — safely
under glass. I saw her mouth move but heard no sound. Even
when Babs smiled in my direction and gaily murmured *Hi!* in the
style of popular girls at Indian River High who made it a point,
out of Christian charity perhaps, to ignore no one, I scarcely
heard her. In a buzzing panic, I could only stammer a belated reply, half-shutting my eyes in terror of staring at Babs too openly,
her small shapely dancerlike body, her radiantly glistening pink-
lipsticked lips and widened smiling eyes, for in my paranoia I was
convinced that others could sense my yearning, my raw, hopeless, contemptible desire. I imagined overhearing, and often in
my fever dreams I did actually hear, voices rising in derision,
"Roland? *Him?*" And cruel adolescent laughter of the kind that,
decades later, still reverberates through R.___'s dreams.

For this I cannot truly blame the girl. She knew nothing of her
power over me.

Did she?

Babs was a senior, and I was only a sophomore and did not
exist to her; to be in close proximity to such a girl, I had to join
the Drama Club, in which Babs was a prominent member, a high

school star, invariably cast in student productions directed by our English teacher Mr. Seales. Onstage, Babs was a lively, pretty, and energetic presence, one of those golden creatures at whom others gaze in helpless admiration, though to be truthful, and I mean to be truthful in this narrative, Babs Hendrick was probably only moderately talented. But by the standards of Indian River, Michigan, she shone. In Drama Club I was an eager volunteer for work no one else wanted to do, like set design and lighting; I helped Mr. Seales organize rehearsals. To the surprise of my friends, who had no idea of my infatuation with Babs, I spent more and more time with the Drama Club crowd, comfortable in my relatively invisible role, happy to leave the spotlight to others.

In that context, as a kind of mascot, *Roland* became *Rollie*. What a thrill.

For Babs herself would summon me, "Rollie? Would you be a sweetheart" — with what ease and unconscious cruelty murmuring such words to me! — "and run out and get me a cola? Here's some change." And Rollie would go flying out of the school and down the street a block and a half to a convenience store, to bring back a cola for Babs Hendrick, thrilled by the task. More than once I'd run to fetch something for Babs and when I returned to the rehearsal room, panting like a good-natured dog, another of the actors would send me out again, and Rollie would fly a second time, not wanting to protest for fear of arousing suspicion.

Almost, I overheard behind me Babs's musical voice: "That Rollie! I just love him."

Between Clifford Seales and certain of his girl students, particularly blond, effervescent Babs, there was a heightened electric mood during Drama Club meetings and play rehearsals; a continuous stream of bright, racy banter of the kind that left the girls pink-cheeked and breathless with giggling and Mr. Seales (though long married and his children grown) grinning and tugging at his shirt collar. Perhaps there was nothing seriously erotic about such banter, only playfulness, but unmistakably flirtatious undercurrents wafted about us, for most of the Drama Club members were not ordinary students but students singled out for *attention;* and Mr. Seales, in his fifties, thick-waisted, porcine, with a singed-looking face and wire-rimmed bifocals that shone when

he was at his wittiest and most eloquent, was no ordinary high
school teacher. He cultivated a brushlike rufous mustache and
wore his hair long, past his collar. He'd been an amateur actor
with the Milwaukee Players in his early twenties, and he'd im-
pressed generations of Indian River students by hinting that he'd
almost had, or possibly had had, a screen test with Twentieth
Century Fox in his youth. Babs daringly teased Mr. Seales about
his wild Hollywood days when he'd been Clark Gable's double.
(Mr. Seales did resemble, from certain angles of perspective and
in flattering light, a fleshier Clark Gable.)

After the tragedy, and the scandal that surrounded it, rumors
would fly through Indian River that Mr. Seales was a pervert
who'd insisted on his girl and boy actors rehearsing passionate
love scenes in his presence, to prepare them for acting together
onstage. That Mr. Seales was a pervert who rehearsed passionate
love scenes with his girl students, private sessions. That he had
"brushed against," "touched," "fondled" Babs Hendrick before
witnesses, and made the girl blush fiercely. That Mr. Seales carried, in his briefcase, a silver flask filled with gin, and out of this
flask he secretly laced coffee and soda drinks to give to unsus-
pecting students, to render them more malleable in his pervert
hands. In the seven months I belonged to the Drama Club I'd
seen no evidence of any of this, and so I would testify to the Indian River police in Mr. Seales's defense (though my father was
furious with me afterward). Yet how strange: Never had I wit-
nessed Mr. Seales pouring anything into any drinks, including
my own, but somehow I was inspired to such an action myself,
out of despair of my obsession with Babs and out of (how can I
explain, without seeming to be trying to excuse myself?) a con-
viction of my essential helplessness. *For never would Roland have believed himself capable of what he dreamt of committing: never would he,
who believed himself a victim, have imagined himself so powerful, and lethal.*

Not gin out of a silver flask, but a heavy dose of barbiturate
from my mother's crammed medicine cabinet. It was an old prescription; I took the chance that my distracted, nervous mother
would never notice.

It was not my intention to hurt my high school sweetheart. For
I so adored her, I could not imagine even touching her! In my
sickly, fevered dreams I "saw" her vividly, or a female figure that

resembled her; beneath layers of bedclothes, as if hoping to hide myself from my father's suspicious eyes that seemed to penetrate my bedroom walls, I groaned in anguish, and in shame, in thrall to her female beauty. *I was the victim, not the girl.* I wished to free myself from my morbid obsession, and I became desperate. For had not my father (reading my thoughts? identifying certain symptoms in my person, my behavior?) warned me with much embarrassment of the danger of "unclean practices," "compulsive self-abuse"? Had not my father turned aside from me in disgust, seeing in my frightened eyes and inflamed pimply skin an admission of guilt? And yet I could not beg him for mercy claiming *I am the victim!*

In high school life, Babs Hendrick existed in a rarefied dimension, inaccessible to someone like me; I might brush against her in a corridor, or descending a flight of stairs, might sit on the floor of the greenroom backstage, six inches from her feet, yet this distance was an abyss. The girl was invulnerable, immune to anything Roland or Rollie might say or do. At such times I knew myself invisible, and though lowly, in a way blessed. Unlike other, older and more attractive boys, I had not a chance to compel this girl to love me, even to notice me, thus I risked little, like a craven but faithful mongrel. Even when someone called out "Rollie!" and sent me on an errand, I felt myself invisible and blessed. During rehearsals on the open, bare stage, which was often drafty, I liked it that Babs might send me for her sweater, or her boyfriend's jacket; I loved it that, in this place devoid of glamour, Babs yet exuded her innocent golden-girl beauty, which (I came to think) no one really appreciated but me. At such times I could crouch on the floor and gaze openly at Babs Hendrick's flawless heart-shaped face, her perky, shapely little body, for she was an "actress"; in fact, and this was a delicious irony not lost on Roland, Babs and the other Indian River stars were dependent on people like Roland, an admiring audience for their self-display, or what was called "talent." And so I made myself more and more available to the Drama Club, and to the rather vain, pompous Mr. Seales, as a way of making myself liked and trusted. How quiet Roland was, and utterly dependable! No one else in the Drama Club was either, and this included Mr. Seales himself. I was always available if, for instance, Babs needed someone patient to help her with her lines, in the greenroom, or in an

empty classroom. ("Gosh, Rollie, what would I do without you!
You're so much sweeter and a darn sight smarter than *my* kid
brother.") Mr. Seales had cast, or miscast, Babs as the wan, crippled, poetic Laura in Tennessee Williams's *The Glass Menagerie;*
this was a plum of a role for an aspiring actress, but one for
which Babs's healthy, wholesome golden-girl looks and childlike
extroversion hardly suited her. Her superficial facility for rote
memory wasn't helping her much with the poetic language of
the Williams play, and she was continually baffled by its emotional subtext. Even Mr. Seales was beginning to be impatient
with her tearful outbursts and temper tantrums, and several
times spoke cuttingly to her in front of others. These others were
to be shortly designated as "witnesses," even I, who had no
choice but to tell police officers all that I'd truly heard.

One of my frequent errands was to fetch quart plastic bottles
of a certain diet cola, explosively carbonated and artificially
sweetened, from the convenience store up the street — a vile-
tasting chemical concoction that my father claimed had caused
"cancerous growths" in laboratory rats, and that, though I ex-
ulted in going against my father's wishes whenever I could, I
found repellent, undrinkable. Yet Babs was addicted to this
drink, kept bottles in her locker and was always running out. The
fact that the cola was in a quart bottle and not a can, and that I
was often the person to open it, and pour the drink into paper
cups to pass around to the actors, gave me the idea, and an innocent idea it seemed to me, like a magical fantasy interlude in a
Disney film, of mixing something in the fizzing liquid, a sleeping
potion it might romantically be called, that would cause Babs
Hendrick to become sleepy suddenly, and doze, for just a few
precious minutes, and I alone might observe her close up, watch
over and protect her: If needed, I would wake her and walk her
home.

Babs Hendrick, walked home by Roland, the doctor's son.

This was a fantasy that sprang from one of my fevered erotic
dreams. I both loathed these dreams as unhealthy and unclean,
and craved them; I both wished to rid myself of them forever,
and cherished them as one of the few authentic creations of my
lonely life. Out of this paradox grew, like poisonous toadstools
by night, my compulsion to write, and to write of certain sub-

jects the world designates as morbid. Out of the tragedy of that long-ago time grew my obsession with *mystery* as the most basic, and so most profound, of all artistic visions. Out of my obsession with my high school sweetheart, the distinguished (and lucrative) career of R____, newly elected president of the American Mystery Writers! Though R____ is far from fifteen years old, he is not so very distant from the fifteen-year-old Roland secretly planning, plotting, rehearsing his deed of great daring. He seemed in his sex-obsessed naivete to think that he could accomplish his goal without having the slightest effect on reality, and without consequences for either himself or his victim.

Of course, fifteen-year-old Roland did not think of Babs Hendrick as a *victim*. She wielded such power!

And so it happened, as in a dream, one bleak, gunmetal-gray afternoon in March, in that limbo season poised between late winter and early spring, when the temperature seems frozen at 32 degrees Fahrenheit, that rehearsals for *The Glass Menagerie* broke off around five o'clock, and Mr. Seales sent everyone home except for Babs, with whom he spoke in private, and twenty minutes later Babs appeared in the corridor outside the classroom, wiping at her beautiful downcast eyes. Seeing me lurking nearby (but Babs wouldn't have thought her friend Rollie was capable of *lurking*) eagerly, she asked would I help her with lines? Just for a half-hour?

Murmured Rollie shyly, "Sure."

Babs led us to the greenroom backstage. As usual, she stood as she recited her lines, and moved about restlessly, trying to match her gestures with Tennessee Williams's maddeningly poetic, repetitive language. She scarcely glanced at me as I read lines, or prompted her, as if she were alone; I was Laura's mother, Laura's brother, Laura's caddish gentleman caller, yet it was exclusively her own image she gazed at in the room's long horizontal mirror. Even in this fluorescent-lit, stale-smelling room with shabby furnishings and worn linoleum tile, how beautiful Babs was! Far more beautiful than poor doomed Laura. *I loved her and hated her. For the sake of the Lauras of the world, as well as the Rolands.*

The other day, in the leafy, affluent suburban town fifty minutes north of Grand Central Station where I live, as the irony of circumstance had placed me, on Basking Ridge Drive, which intersects with Church Street, I was walking into the village to pick up my newspapers, as I do every day for the exercise, and I saw her. I saw Babs Hendrick: a lovely girl with shoulder-length wavy blond hair and bangs brushed low on her forehead, walking with some high school classmates. I stopped in my tracks. My heart clanged like a bell. I nearly called out to her — "Babs? Is it you?" But of course, being R____, and no longer naive, I waited until I could ascertain that of course the girl wasn't my lost high school sweetheart, and didn't truly resemble her. I turned aside to hide my grief. I limped away, shaken. I took solace all that day in writing this story, for I no longer have lurid, delicious erotic fantasies by night, beneath heavy bedcovers: the only fantasies that visit me now are willfully calculated, impeccably plotted contrivances of my writerly life.

I repeat: It was not my intention to hurt my high school sweetheart.

In my anxiety, I must have mixed too much of the barbiturate into the cola drink. I'd taken a number of capsules from my mother's medicine cabinet, broken them, and carefully poured the white powder into a tissue; this tissue, wrapped in cellophane, I'd been carrying in my pocket for what seemed like months, but could have been only two or three weeks. I knew that my opportunity would come if I was patient. And that March afternoon, when Babs and I were alone together in the greenroom, and no one near, and no one knowing us, and she sent me to her locker to fetch her opened bottle of cola while she used the girls' backstage lavatory, I knew that this was meant to be. Almost, I had no choice. I siphoned the white powder into the virulent dark chemical drink, replaced the top, and turned it upside down, shook it gently. Babs took no notice of the barbiturate, for she drank the cola in distracted swallows while trying to memorize her lines, and was on her feet, restless and impatient, having decided that the secret to Williams's heroine was her anger, hidden beneath layers of girlish verbiage of which the playwright himself hadn't been aware. "Cripples are always angry, I bet. *I'd* sure be, in their place."

Roland, sitting on an old worn corduroy-covered sofa, waiting anxiously for the sleeping potion to take effect, murmured yes, he guessed Babs must be right.

She continued with her lines, reciting, forgetting, and needing to be prompted, remembering, reciting, moving her arms, making her face "expressive"; the more she rehearsed Laura, the more Laura eluded her, like a mocking phantom. Ten minutes passed, with excruciating slowness; I felt beads of sweat break out on my heated face and trickle down my thin sides; fifteen minutes passed, and by degrees Babs appeared to be getting drowsy, murmuring that she didn't know what was wrong with her, she was feeling *so tired,* couldn't keep her eyes open. She knocked the cola bottle over; what remained of the liquid spilled out onto the already stained carpet. Abruptly then she slumped down at the far end of the sofa, and within a matter of seconds was asleep.

I sat without moving, not even looking directly at her, at first, for some time. The magic had worked! It wasn't believable, yet it had happened; Roland could have had no real power over a girl like Babs Hendrick, yet — this had happened. Yes I was elated. Ecstatic! Yes I was terrified. For what I had done, the crudest of tricks, I could not undo.

Not scrawny brainy Roland, that shy boy, but another person, calculating and almost calm, moved at last from his position on the sofa and stood trembling with excitement over the sleeping girl. Beautiful when awake, and animated, Babs was yet more beautiful in sleep; waxy-skinned and vulnerable, she seemed much younger than seventeen. Her face was pale and slack and her lips parted, like a sleeping baby's, her arms were limp, her legs sprawled like the legs of a rag doll. She wore a pale yellow angora sweater with short puffy sleeves, and a charcoal gray pleated skirt. (This predated the era of universal blue jeans.) I whispered, "Babs? Babs?" and she gave no sign of hearing. She was breathing in deep, erratic, shuddering breaths and her eyelids were quivering. My fear was that she'd wake suddenly and see me standing over her and know what I'd done, and begin to scream, and what would happen to Roland, the doctor's son, then? I dared to touch her arm, and shook her gently. "Babs? What's wrong?" So far, what was happening wasn't suspicious exactly. (Was it?) Kids often fell asleep in school, cradling their heads on their arms in the library, or in study hall; in boring classes nearly everyone nodded off, at times. Self-dramatizing young actors, complaining of exhaustion and overwork, stole naps in the greenroom, and tales were told of couples "sleeping"

on the infamous corduroy couch when they were assured of a
few minutes' quick-snatched privacy. Babs, like her popular
friends, stayed up late, talking and laughing over the telephone,
as I'd gathered from overhearing their conversations, and she'd
been anxious about the play, and sleep-deprived, so it wasn't so
unlikely that, in the midst of going over her lines with me, she
might become exhausted suddenly and fall asleep. *None of this
was suspicious. Not yet!*

But Roland's behavior was beginning to be suspicious, wasn't
it? For stealthily he went to the door, which had no lock, and
dragged a heavy leather armchair in front of it to prevent the
door being opened suddenly. (There were likely to be a few
teachers and students remaining in the building, even past six
o'clock.) He switched off all the lights in the windowless room
except one, a flickering fluorescent tube on the verge of burning
out. He spoke gently, cautiously to the deeply breathing, sleeping
girl, "Babs? Babs? It's just me. Rollie." For long mesmerized seconds he stood above her, staring. The elusive girl of his fever
dreams! His high school sweetheart, whom his father tried to for-
bid him. Unclean. Compulsive. Self-abuse. Daringly Roland
touched the girl again, caressing her shoulder, like a film lover,
and her arm in the fuzzy angora sweater, and her limp, chill
fingers. He was breathing quickly now, and he'd become sticky
with sweat. If he leaned closer, if he kissed her? (But how did you
kiss a girl like Babs Hendrick?) Just her forehead? Would she
wake suddenly, would she begin to scream? "It's just me. Rollie. I
love you." Suddenly he wondered, with a stab of jealousy,
whether Hal McCreagh had ever seen Babs like this. So deeply
asleep! So beautiful! He wondered what Hal did to Babs, when
they were alone together in Hal's car. Kissing? (Tongue kissing?)
Touching, fondling? Petting? It excited Roland, and infuriated
him, to imagine.

But Hal wasn't here now. Hal knew nothing of this interlude,
this "rehearsal." There was no longer any Hal. There was only
Roland, the doctor's brainy, beloved son.

He was trembling badly now. Shaking. A powerful throbbing
ache in his groin, which he tried to ignore, and a rapid beating
of his heart. This could not be happening, could it? How could
this be happening? Bringing his lips against the girl's strangely

cool, clammy forehead. It was the first true kiss of his life. Babs's silky blond head had fallen back against the soiled armrest of the sofa, and her mouth had dropped open. Her eyelids were oddly bluish and fluttering as if desperately she wanted to open them but could not. "Babs? Don't be afraid." He kissed her cheek, he stooped to kiss her mouth, which hung open, slack, helpless, a string of saliva trailing down her chin. The taste of her mouth excited him terribly. With his tongue he licked her saliva. *Like tasting blood. Roland, the vampire. That first kiss!* His brain seemed to go black. He was seized by a powerful need to grab hold of the girl, hard. To show her who was master. But he restrained himself, for Roland was not such a person; Roland was a good boy and would never harm anyone. (Would he?) Babs Hendrick was, he knew, a good Christian girl, as he was a good Christian boy. What harm could come to them *really?* If he meant no harm, harm would not ensue. He would be protected. The girl would be protected. He'd begun to notice her strange, labored breathing, audible as a grown man's breathing in stress, and yet he did not somehow absorb the possible meaning of such a symptom, though he was (but right now, *was not*) Roland, the doctor's son. He was trembling with excitement. His hand, which seemed to him slightly distorted as if seen through a magnifying lens, reached out to smooth the silky blond hair and cradle it in his fingers. He stroked the nape of the girl's neck, slowly he caressed her shoulder, her left breast, delicately touching the breast with his fingertips, that fuzzy pale yellow angora wool that was so beautiful; he cupped his hand (but was this *his hand?*) beneath the small, shapely breast, gently and then with more assurance he caressed, he squeezed lightly. "Babs! I l-love you." The girl moaned in her heavy, stuporous sleep, a sexual moan it seemed to Roland, who was himself whimpering with excitement. But she didn't wake. His power over her, Roland's revenge, was that she could not wake; she was at his mercy, and he would be merciful. She was utterly helpless and vulnerable, and he would not take advantage of her as one of the crude Indian River High boys would have done in his place. (Would he?) In even the most lurid of his dreams he hadn't defiled his sweetheart (at least that he'd allowed himself to remember). In a cracked, hoarse, half-pleading voice, whispering, "Babs? Don't be afraid. I would never

hurt you, *I love you.*" And the blackness rose, swooning in him a
second time, annihilating his brain, and he would not afterward
recall all that happened in that dim-lit windowless room, on the
shabby corduroy sofa, or was caused to happen, perceived as
through a distorting lens that both magnified and reduced vision.

When again Roland was able to see clearly, and to think, he
saw to his horror that it was nearly six-thirty. And still the stricken
girl slept on the corduroy sofa, the sound of her breathing now
filling the airless room. Her head lay at a painful angle on the
soiled armrest and her arms and legs were limp, loose as those of
a rag doll. Except now her unseeing eyes were partly open, showing a crescent of white. Anxiously he whispered, "Babs? Wake
up." He felt panic: hearing voices in the corridor beyond the
backstage area, boys' voices, perhaps basketball players leaving
practice; and Hal McCreagh was among these, or might have
been, for Hal was on the team; and what would Roland do, and
what would be done to Roland, if he were discovered like this,
hiding, guilty-faced, with Babs Hendrick sprawled on the sofa,
helpless in sleep, her hair disheveled and her clothing in disar-
ray? Hurriedly, with shaking fingers, Roland readjusted the fuzzy
angora sweater, and the pleated skirt. Whimpering, pleading for
the girl to wake up, please would she wake up, yet like Sleeping
Beauty in the Disney film, she would not wake up; she was under
a curse; she would not wake up for *him.*

For the first time it occurred to the trembling boy that he
might have given his sweetheart too strong a dose of the drug.
What if she never woke up? (But what was *too strong,* he had no idea.
Half the bottle of six-milligram capsules? That odorless chalky
white powder?)

Panic swept over him. No, he wouldn't think of *that.*

On a shelf amid the tattered copies of play scripts he found
a frayed, light wool blanket to draw gently over Babs. He tucked
the blanket beneath her damp chin, and spread her blond, wavy
hair in a fan around her head. She would sleep until the drug
wore off, and then she would wake; if Roland — "Rollie" — were
very lucky, she wouldn't remember him; and if he were unlucky,
well — he wouldn't think of that. (And he did not.) Stealthily
then he fled, and was unseen. He would leave the single
fluorescent light flickering. He would slip from the greenroom

to the darkened backstage area and make his way out into a rear
corridor, not taking the most obvious, direct route (which would
have brought him into a corridor contiguous with the corridor
that led to the boys' locker room), and so, breathless, he would
flee the scene of the crime, which in his heart he could not
(could he?) acknowledge was a crime, even into his sixty-first
year, when R____ had long replaced both Roland and "Rollie."
Contemplating then through the distorting lens of time the pale,
calm-seeming doctor's son safe in the brick house on Church
Street, and safe in his room immersed in geometry homework at
8:20 that evening, the approximate time that Babs Hendrick's
heart ceased beating.

The Glass Menagerie would not be performed that spring at Indian River High.

Clifford Scales would be suspended without salary from the
school, and his contract terminated soon after, during the Indian
River police investigation into the barbiturate death of Seales's
seventeen-year-old student Babs Hendrick. Though not enough
evidence would be gathered against him to justify a formal arrest, Seales would remain the prime suspect in the case, and his
guilt taken for granted. Forty-five years later in Indian River, if
you speak of Babs Hendrick's death, you'll be told in angry disgust that the girl's English teacher, an alcoholic pervert who'd
molested other girl students over the years, drugged her with
barbiturates to perform despicable sexual acts on her, and killed
her in the process. You will be told that Seales managed to escape prosecution, though of course his life was ruined, and he
would die, divorced and disgraced, of a massive heart attack a
few years later.

Ladies and gentlemen, you will ask: Had the Indian River police no other suspects? Possibly yes. Practicably speaking, no.
Even today, small-town police departments are ill equipped to
undertake homicide investigations in which neither witnesses
nor informants come forward. Dusting for fingerprints in the
greenroom yielded a treasure trove of prints, but all of these,
even Seales's, were explainable. DNA evidence (saliva, semen)
would have convicted the guilty individual, but DNA evidence
was unknown at the time. And the boy, the shy bespectacled doctor's son, Roland, was but one of a number of high school boys,
including the dead girl's boyfriend, whom police questioned; he

was not singled out for suspicion, spoke earnestly and persua-
sively to police officers, even defending (in his naivete) the noto-
rious Seales, and was never to behave in any way that might be la-
beled suspicious. In a state of suspended animation. No emotion,
only wonder. That I, Roland, had done such a thing. I, a victim,
to have wielded such power!

If my mother had ever discovered that a bottle of prescription
sleeping pills was missing from her medicine cabinet, she never
spoke of her discovery and what it might mean.

It would be rumored (but never printed in any newspapers or
uttered on radio or TV) that "sick, disgusting things" had been
done to Babs Hendrick's helpless body before her death; only a
"pervert" could have done such acts upon a comatose victim. But
there would never be any arrest of this criminal, and therefore
no trial. And no public revelations.

(What "sick, disgusting things" were done to my sweetheart, I
don't know. Another individual must have slipped into the
greenroom between the time Roland fled and Babs died later
that evening.)

The sick horror of *mystery* that remains unsolved.

You will ask: Did the killer never confess?

The superficial answer is no, the killer never confessed. For he
did not (did he?) truly believe himself a killer; he was a good
Christian boy. And he was (and is) a coward, contemptible. The
more complex answer is yes, the killer confessed, and has confessed many times during his long and "distinguished" career.
Each work of fiction he has written has been a confession, and an
exultation. For, having committed an act of mystery in his adolescence, he understood that he'd proved himself and need never
commit another; forever afterward, he would be an elegist of
mystery, and honored for his style. Ladies and gentlemen, thank
you for this new honor.

In the sudden silence, R_____ self-consciously stacked the pages
of his manuscript together to signal that "The High School Sweetheart: A Mystery" was over, as we in the audience, his friends and
admirers, sat stunned, in a paralysis of shock and indecision.
R_____'s story had been compelling, and his delivery mesmerizing
— yet, how should we applaud?

ROBERT B. PARKER

Harlem Nocturne

FROM *Murderers' Row*

MR. RICKEY was wearing a blue polka dot bow tie and a gray tweed suit that didn't fit him very well. He took some time getting his cigar lit and then looked at me over his round black-rimmed glasses.

"I'm bringing Jackie Robinson up from Montreal," he said.

"The other shoe drops," I said. Mr. Rickey smiled.

"I want you to protect him," he said.

"Okay," I said.

"Just like that?" Rickey said.

"I assume you'll pay me," I said.

"Don't you want to know what I'm asking you to protect him from?"

"I assume I know," I said. "People who might want to kill him for being a Negro. And himself."

Rickey nodded and turned the cigar slowly without taking it from his mouth.

"Good," he said. "Himself was the part I didn't think you'd get."

I looked modest.

"Jackie is a man of strong character," Rickey said. "One might even say forceful. If this experiment is going to work he has to sit on that. He has to remain calm. Turn the other cheek."

"And I'll have to see that he does that," I said.

"Yes. And at the same time, see that no one harms him."

"Am I required to turn the other cheek?"

"You are required to do what is necessary to help Jackie and me and the Brooklyn Dodgers get through the impending storm."

"Do what I can," I said.

"My information is that you can do a lot. It's why you're here. You'll stay with him all the time. If anyone asks you, you are simply an assistant to the general manager. If he has to stay in a Negro hotel, you'll have to stay there too."

"I got through Guadalcanal," I said.

"Yes, I know. How do you feel about a Negro in the major leagues?"

"Seems like a good idea to me."

"Good. I'll introduce you to Jackie."

He pushed the switch on an intercom and spoke into it, and a moment later a secretary opened the office door and Robinson came in wearing a gray suit and a black knit tie. He was a pretty big guy and moved as if he were working off a steel spring. He was nobody's high yellow. He was black. And he didn't seem furtive about it. Rickey introduced us.

"Well, you got the build for a bodyguard," Robinson said.

"You, too," I said.

"Well, I ain't guarding your body," Jackie said.

"Mine's not worth ten grand a year," I said.

"One thing," Robinson said, and he looked at Rickey as he spoke. "I don't need no keeper. You keep people from shooting me, good. And I know I can't be fighting people. You gotta do that for me. But I go where I want to go and do what I do. And I don't ask you first."

"As long as you let me die for you," I said.

Something flashed in Robinson's eyes. "You got a smart mouth," he said.

"I'm a smart guy."

Robinson grinned suddenly.

"So how come you taking on this job?"

"Same as you," I said. "I need the dough."

Robinson looked at me with his hard stare.

"Well," Robinson said. "We'll see."

Rickey had been sitting quietly while Robinson and I sniffed around each other. Now he spoke.

"You can't ever let down," he said. He was looking at Robinson, but I knew I was included. "You're under a microscope. You can't drink. You can't be sexually indiscreet. You can't have opinions about things. You play hard and clean and stay quiet. Can you do it?"

"With a little luck," Robinson said.

"Luck is the residue of intention," Rickey said.

He talked pretty good for a guy who hit .239 lifetime.

It didn't take long to pick up the way it was going to be.

Peewee Reese was supportive. Dixie Walker was not. Everyone else was on the spectrum somewhere between.

In St. Louis, a base runner spiked Robinson at first base. In Chicago, he was tagged in the face sliding into second. In St. Louis, somebody tossed a black cat onto the field. In Cincinnati, he was knocked down three times in one at bat. In every city we heard the word *nigger* out of the opposition dugout. None of this was my problem. It was Robinson's. There was nothing I could do about it. So I sat in my corner of the dugout and did nothing.

My work was off the field.

There was hate mail. I couldn't do anything about that, either. The club passed the death threats on, but there were so many of them that it was mostly a waste of time. All Robinson and I could do about those was be ready. I began to look at everybody as if they were dangerous.

After a double header against the Giants, I drove Robinson uptown. A gray two-door Ford pulled up beside us at a stoplight, and I stared at the driver. The light changed and the Ford pulled away.

"I'm starting to look at everybody as if they were dangerous," I said.

Robinson glanced over at me and smiled the way he did. The smile said, *Pal, you have no idea.*

But all he said was, "Uh-huh."

We stopped to eat at a place on Lennox Avenue. When we came in everyone stared. At first I thought it was Robinson. Then I realized they hadn't even seen him yet. It was me. I was the only white face in the joint.

"Sit in the back," I said to Robinson.

"Have to, with you along," he said.

As we walked through the place, they recognized Robinson and somebody began to clap, then everybody clapped. Then they stood and clapped and hooted and whistled until we were seated.

"Probably wasn't for me," I said.

"Probably not."

Robinson had a Coke.

"You ever drink booze?" I said.

"Not in public," Robinson said.

"Good."

I looked around. Even for a hard case like me it was uncomfortable being in a room full of colored people. I was glad to be with Robinson.

We both ordered steak.

"No fried chicken?" I said.

"No watermelon, either," Robinson said.

The room got quiet all of a sudden. The silence was so sharp that it made me hunch a little forward so I could reach the gun on my hip. Through the front door came six white men in suits and overcoats and felt hats. There was nothing uneasy about them as they came into the colored place. They swaggered. One of them swaggered like the boss, a little fat guy with his overcoat open over a dark suit. He had on a blue silk tie with a pink flamingo hand-painted on it.

"Frank Digiacomo," Robinson said. "He owns the place."

Without taking off their hats or overcoats, the six men sat at a large round table near the front.

"I hear he owns this part of Harlem," I said.

Robinson shrugged.

"When Bumpy Johnson was around," I said, "the Italians stayed downtown."

"Good for colored people to own the businesses they run," Robinson said.

A big guy sitting next to Digiacomo stood and walked over to our table. Robinson and I were both close to two hundred, but this guy was in a different class. He was thick bodied and tall, with very little neck and a lot of chin. His face was clean shaved and sort of moist. His shirt was crisp white. His chesterfield overcoat hung open, and he reeked of strong cologne.

"Mr. Digiacomo wants to buy you a bottle of champagne," he said to Robinson.

Robinson put a bite of steak in his mouth and chewed it carefully and swallowed and said, "Tell Mr. Digiacomo, no thank you."

The big guy stared at him for a moment.

"Most people don't say no to Mr. Digiacomo, Rastus."

Robinson said nothing but his gaze on the big man was heavy.

"Maybe we can buy Mr. Digiacomo a bottle," I said.

"Mr. Digiacomo don't need nobody buying him a bottle."

"Well, I guess it's a draw," I said. "Thanks for stopping by."

The big guy looked at me for a long time. I didn't shrivel up and blow away, so after a while he swaggered back to his boss. He leaned over and spoke to Digiacomo, his left hand resting on the back of Digiacomo's chair. Then he nodded and turned and swaggered back.

"On your feet, boy," he said to Robinson.

"I'm eating my dinner," Robinson said.

The big man took hold of Robinson's arm, and Robinson came out of the chair as if he'd been ejected and hit the big guy with a good right hand. Robinson was a good-sized guy in good condition, and he knew how to punch. It should have put the big guy down. But it didn't. He took a couple of backwards steps and steadied himself and shook his head as if there were flies. At Digiacomo's table everyone had turned to look. The only sound in the room was the faint clatter of dishes from the kitchen. It was so still I could hear chairs creaking as people turned to stare. I was on my feet.

"Sit down," I yelled at Robinson.

"Not up here," Robinson said. "I'll take it downtown, but not up here."

The big man had his head cleared. He looked at the table where Digiacomo sat.

"Go ahead, Sonny," Digiacomo said. "Show the nigger something."

The big man lunged toward Robinson. I stepped between them. The big man almost ran over me, and would have run over both of us if I hadn't hit him a hell of a left. It was probably no better punch than Robinson's, but it benefited from the brass knuckles I was wearing. It stopped him but it didn't put him down. I got my knee into his groin and hit him again with the knucks. He grunted and went down slowly. First to his knees, then slowly toppling face forward onto the floor.

The place was like a tomb. Even the kitchen noise had stopped. I could hear someone's breath rasping in and out. I'd heard it before. It was mine.

The four men at Digiacomo's table were on their feet. All of them had guns, and all of them were pointing at us. Digiacomo remained seated. He looked mildly amused.

"Don't shoot them in here," he said. "Take them out."

I was wearing a Colt .45 that I had liberated from the U.S. Marine Corps. But it was still on my hip. I should have had it out when this thing started.

One of the other men, a thin tall man with high shoulders, said, "Outside" and gestured with the .38 belly gun he carried. He was the gunny. You could tell by the way he held the weapon, like it was precious.

"No," Robinson said.

"How about you, pal?" the gunny said to me.

I shook my head. The gunny looked at Digiacomo.

Digiacomo said, "Okay, shoot them here. Make sure the niggers clean up afterwards."

The gunny smiled. He was probably good at it. You could see he liked the work.

"Which one of you wants it first?" he said.

At the next table a small Negro with a thin mustache, wearing a cerulean blue suit, said, "No."

The gunny glanced at him.

"You too, boy?" he said.

At the table on the other side of us a large woman in a too-tight yellow dress said, "No." And stood up.

The gunny glanced at her. The small Negro with the mustache stood too. Then everyone at his table stood. The woman in the too-tight dress moved in front of Robinson and me. Between us and the gunny. The people from her table joined her. The people from mustache's table joined them. Then all the people in the room were on their feet, closing on us, surrounding us, making an implacable black wall between us and the gunny. I took my gun out. Robinson stood motionless, balanced on the balls of his feet. From the bar along the far side of the room came the sound of someone working the action of a pump shotgun. It is a sound, like the sound of a tank, that doesn't sound like anything else. Through the crowd I could see the round-faced bartender leaning his elbows on the bar aiming a shotgun with most of the stock cut off.

The gunny looked at Digiacomo again. They were an island of pallid faces in a sea of dark faces. Digiacomo got to his feet for the first time. His face was no longer amused. He looked at me through the crowd, and at Robinson, and seemed to study us both for a moment. Then he jerked his head toward the big man who had managed to sit up on the floor among the forest of Negro feet. Two of the other men with Digiacomo eased through the crowd and got the big man on his feet. They looked at Digiacomo. Digiacomo looked at us again, then turned without speaking and walked out. The gunny put his belly gun away, sadly, and turned and followed Digiacomo. The other men, two of them helping the big guy, went out after him.

The room was as still and motionless as Sunday in Antarctica. Then Robinson said again, "Not up here," and everyone in the room heard him and everyone in the room began to cheer.

"Lucky thing this is a baseball crowd," I said to Robinson.

He looked at me for a moment as if he were somewhere else. Then he seemed slowly to come back. He smiled.

"Yeah," he said. "Lucky thing."

F . X . T O O L E

Midnight Emissions

FROM *Murder on the Ropes*

"BUTCHERIN' was done while the deceased was still alive," Junior said.

See, we was at the gym and I'd been answering a few things. Old Junior's a cop, and his South Texas twang was wide and flat like mine. 'Course he was dipping, and he let a stream go into the Coke bottle he was carrying in the hand that wasn't his gun hand. His blue eyes was paler than a washed-out work shirt.

"Hail," he said, "one side of the mouth'd been slit all the way to the earring."

See, when the police find a corpse in Texas, their first question ain't who done it, it's what did the dead do to deserve it?

Billy Clancy'd been off the police force a long time before Kenny Coyle come along, but he had worked for the San Antonia Police Department a spell there after boxing. He made some good money for himself on the side — down in dark town, if you know what I'm saying? That's after I trained him as a heavyweight in the old *El Gallo,* or Fighting Cock gym off Blanco Road downtown. We worked together maybe six years all told, starting off when he was a amateur. Billy Clancy had all the Irish heart in the world. At six-three and two-twenty-five, he had a fine frame on him, most of his weight upstairs. He had a nice clean style, too, and was quick as a sprinter. But after he was once knocked out for the first time? He had no chin after that. He'd be kicking ass and taking names, but even in a rigged fight with a bum, if he got caught, down he'd go like a longneck at a ice house.

He was a big winner in the amateurs, Billy was, but after twelve pro fights, he had a record of eight and four, with his nose broke once — that's eight wins by KO, but he lost four times by KO, so that's when he hung 'em up. For a long time, he went his way and I went mine. But then Billy Clancy opened Clancy's Pub with his cop money. That was his big break. There was Irish night with Mick music, corned beef and cabbage, and Caffery's Ale on tap and Harp Lager from Dundalk. And he had Messkin night with *mariachis* and folks was dancin' *corridos* and the band was whooping out *rancheras* and they'd get to playing some of that *norteña* polka music that'd have you laughing and crying at the same time. For shrimp night, all you can eat, Billy trucked in fresh Gulf shrimp sweeter than plum jelly straight up from Matamoros on the border. There was kicker, and hillbilly night, and on weekends there was just about the best jazz and blues you ever did hear. B. B. King did a whole week there one time. It got to be a hell of a deal for Billy, and then he opened up a couple of more joints till he had six in three towns, and soon Billy Clancy was somebody all the way from San Antonia up to Dallas, and down to Houston. Paid all his taxes, obeyed all the laws, treated folks like they was ladies and gentlemen, no matter how dusty the boots, how faded the dress, or if a suit was orange and purple and green.

By then he had him a home in the historic old Monte Vista section of San Antonia. His wife had one of them home decorating businesses on her own, and she had that old place looking so shiny that it was like going back a hundred years. His kids was all in private school, all of them geared to go to UT up Austin, even though the dumb young one saw himself as a Aggie.

So one day Billy called me for some "Q" down near the river, knew I was a whore for baby back ribs. Halfway through, he just up and said, "Red, I want back in."

See, he got to missing the smell of leather and sweat, and the laughter of men — he missed the action, is what, and got himself back into the game the only way he could, managing fighters. He was good at it, too. By then he was better'n forty, and myself I was getting on — old's when you sit on the crapper and you have to hold your nuts up so they don't get wet. But what with my rocking chair money every month, and the money I made off Billy's fighters, it got to where I was doing pretty good. Even got me some ostrich boots and a El Patron 30X beaver Stetson, *yip!*

What Billy really wanted was a heavyweight. With most managers, it's only the money, 'cause heavies is what brings in them stacks of green fun-tickets. Billy wanted fun-tickets, too, but with Billy it was more like he wanted to get back something what he had lost. 'Course, finding the right heavyweight's like finding a cherry at the high school prom.

Figure it, with only twenty, twenty-five good wins, 'specially if he can crack, a heavy can fight for a title's worth millions. There's exceptions, but most little guys'll fight forever and never crack maybe two hundred grand. One of the reason's 'cause there's so many of them. Other reason's 'cause they's small. Fans like seeing heavyweights hit the canvas.

But most of today's big guys go into the other sports where you don't get hit the way you do in the fights. It ain't held against you in boxing if you're black nowadays, but if you're a white heavy it makes it easier to pump paydays, and I could tell that it wouldn't make Billy sad if I could get him a white boy — Irish or Italian would be desired. But working with the big guys takes training to a level that can break your back and your heart, and I wasn't all that sure a heavy was what I wanted, what with me being the one what's getting broke up.

See, training's a hard row to hoe. It ain't only the physical and mental parts for the fighter what's hard, but it's hard for the trainer, too. Fighters can drive you crazy, like maybe right in the middle of a fight they're *winning*, when they forget everything what you taught them? And all of a sudden they can't follow instructions from the corner? Pressure, pain, and being out of gas will make fighters go flat brain-dead on you. Your fighter's maybe sweated off six or eight pounds in there, his body's breaking down, and the jungle in him is yelling quick to get him some gone. Trainers come to know how that works, so you got to hang with your boy when he's all alone out there in the canvas part of the world. He takes heart again, 'cause he knows with you there he's still got a fighting chance to go for the titties of the win. 'Course, that means cutting grommets, Red Ryder.

Everyone working corners knows you'll more'n likely lose more'n you'll ever win, that boxing for most is refried beans and burnt tortillas. But winning is what makes your birdie chirp, so you got to always put in your mind that losing ain't nothing but a hitch in the git-along.

Working with the big guys snarls your task. How do you tell a heavyweight full-up on his maleness to use his mind instead of his sixty-pound dick? How do you teach someone big as a garage that it ain't the fighter with the biggest brawn what wins, but it's the one what gets there first with deadly force? How do you make him see that hitting hard ain't the problem, but that hitting *right* is? How do you get through to him that you don't have to be mad at someone to knock him out, same as you don't have to be in a frenzy to kill with a gun? Heavyweights got that upper-body strength what's scary, it's what they'd always use to win fights at school and such, so it's their way to work from the waist up. That means they throw arm punches, but arm punches ain't good enough. George Foreman does it, but he's so strong, and don't hardly miss, so he most times gets away with punching wrong. 'Course he didn't get away with it in Zaire with Mr. Ali.

So the big deal with heavies is getting them to work from the waist down as well as from the waist up. And they got to learn that the last thing that happens is when the punch lands. A thousand things got to happen before that can happen. Those things begin on the floor with balance. But how do you get across that he's got to work hard, but not so hard that he harms himself? How do you do that in a way what don't threaten what he already knows and has come to depend on? How do you do it so's it don't jar how he has come to see himself and his fighting style? And most of all, how do you do it so when the pressure's on he don't go back to his old ways?

After they win a few fights by early knockout, some heavies get to where they try to control workouts, will balk at new stuff what they'll need as they step up in class. When they pick up a few purses and start driving that new car, lots get lazy and spend their time chasing poon, of which there is a large supply when there is evidence of a quantity of hundred-dollar bills. Some's hop heads, but maybe they fool you and you don't find that out till it's too late. Now you got to squeeze as many paydays out of your doper that you can. Most times, you love your fighter like he's kin, but with a goddamn doper you get to where you couldn't give a bent nail.

Why shouldn't I run things? the heavy's eyes will glare. His nose is flared, his socks is soggy with sweat, his heart's banging at his rib cage like it's trying to bust out of jail. It's 'cause he don't understand that he can't be the horse and the jockey. *How could anyone as big and handsome and powerful and smart as me be wrong about anything?* he will press. Under his breath he's saying, *And who's big enough to tell me I'm wrong?*

When that happens, your boy's attitude is moving him to the streets, and you may have to let him go.

Not many fight fans ever see the inside of fight gyms, so they get to wondering what's the deal with these big dummies who get all sweaty and grunty and beat on each other. Well, sir, they ain't big dummies when you think big money. Most big guys in team sports figure there's more gain and less pain than in fights, even if they have to play a hundred fifty games a year or more, and even if they have to get those leg and back operations that go with them. Some starting-out heavies get to thinking they ought to get the same big payday as major-league pitchers from the day they walk into the gym. Some see themselves as first-round draft picks in the NBA before they ever been hit. What they got to learn is that you got to be a hungry fighter before you can become a championship fighter, a fighter who has learned and survived all the layers of work and hurt the fight game will put on you. Good heavyweights're about as scarce as black cotton.

There're less white heavies than black, and the whites can be even goofier than blacks about quick money. Some whites spout off that 'cause they're white, as in White Hope, that they should be getting easy fights up to and including the one for the title. If you're that kind — and there's black ones same as white — you learn right quick that he don't have the tit or the brains to be a winner under them bright lights.

Though heavies may have the same look, they're as different from each other as zebras when it comes to mental desire, chin, heart, and *huevos* — *huevos* is eggs, but in Messkin it means "balls." Getting heavies into shape is another problem, keeping them in shape is a even bigger one, 'cause they got these bottomless pits for stomachs. So you work to keep them in at least decent shape all the time — but not in punishing *top shape,* the kind that peaks just before a fight. Fighter'd go wild-pig crazy if he had to live at top shape longer than a few days, his nerves all crawly and hunger eating him alive. And then there's that blood-clotting wait to the first bell. See, the job of molding flesh and bone into a fighting machine that meets danger instead of high-tailing from it is as tricky as the needlework what goes into one of them black, lacy deals what Spanish ladies wear on their heads. Fighting's easy, cowboy, it's training what's hard.

But once a trainer takes a heavy on, there's all that thump. First of all, when the heavy moves, you got to move with him — up in the ring, on the hardwood, around the big bag. You're there to guide him like a mama bear, and to stay on his ass so's he don't dog it. All fighters'll dog it after they been in the game a while, but the heavies can be the worst. They got all that weight to transport, and being human, they'll look for a place to hide. A good piece of change'll usually goad them. But always there is more training than fighting, and the faith and the fever it takes to be a champ will drop below ninety-eight-point-six real quick unless your boy eats and sleeps fight. 'Course, no fighter can do that one hundred percent. Besides, there's the pussy factor. Which is part of where the punch mitts come in. They'll make him sharp with his punches, but they're also there to help tire him into submission come bedtime.

The big bag they can fake if you don't stay on them, but a trainer with mitts, calling for combination after combination, see that's for the fighter like he's wearing a wire jock. But for the trainer, the mitts mean you're catching punches thrown by a six-foot-five longhorn, and the punches carry force enough to drop a horse. And the trainer takes this punishment round after round, day after day, the *thump* pounding through him like batting practice and he's the ball. I can't much work the mitts like I once did, only when I'm working on moves, or getting ready for a set date. But even bantamweights can make your eyes pop.

Part of the payoff for all this is sweeter'n whipped cream on top of strawberry pie. It's when your fighter comes to see himself from the outside instead of just from the in. It's when all of a sudden he can see how to use his feet to control that other guy in the short pants. It's how a fighter'll smile like a shy little boy when he understands that all his moves're now offense *and* defense, and that he suddenly has the know-how to beat the other guy with his mind, that he no longer has to be just some bull at the watering hole looking to gore. And that's when, Lordy, that you just maybe got yourself a piece of somebody what can change sweat and hurt into gold and glory.

Getting a boy ready for a fight is the toughest time of all for trainers. After a session with the mitts, your fingers'll curl into the palms of your hands for a hour or so, and driving home in your Jimmy pickup means your hands'll be claws on the steering wheel. The muscles in the middle of your back squeeze your shoulders up around your ears. Where your chest hooks into your shoulders, you go home feeling there's something tore down in there. Elbows get sprung, and groin pulls hobble you. In my case, I've got piano wire holding my chest and ribs together, so when I leave the gym shock keeps on twanging through me. By the time I'm heading home, I'm thinking hard on a longneck bottle of Lone Star. The only other thing I'm thinking on is time in the prone position underneath Granny's quilt.

See, what we're talking about here is signing on to be a cripple, 'cause when you get down to it, trainers in their way get hit more than fighters, only we do it for nickels and dimes, compared. So what's the rest of the deal for the trainer? Well, sir, after getting through all the training and hurting, you live with the threat that you could work years with a heavy only to have him quit on you for somebody who's dangling money at him now that you've done the job that changed a lump of fear and doubt into a fighter. But like I say, a good heavy these days only has to win a few fights for a shot at the title. If he wins that, he's suddenly drinking from solid gold teacups. As the champ, he will defend his title as little as once. But the payoff can be *mucho* if he can defend a few times. So when the champ gets a ten-million-dollar payday, the trainer gets ten percent off the top — that's a one-million-dollar bill. That can make you forget crippled backs and hands.

'Course the downside can be there, too. That's when your heart goes out to your fighter as you watch helpless sometimes as he takes punches to the head that can hack into his memory forever. And your gut will turn against you when one day you see your boy's eyes wander all glassy when he tries to find a word that he don't have in his mouth no more. You feel rotten deep down, but you also love your fighter for having the heart to roll the dice of his life on a dream. And above all, you see clear that no matter how rotten you feel, that your boy never had nothing else but his life to roll, and that you was the lone one who ever cared enough to give him the only shot he would ever have.

Yet the real lure, when you love the fights with everything that's left of your patched-up old heart, is to be part of the great game — a game where the dues are so high that once paid they take you to the Mount Everest of the Squared Circle, to that highest of places, where fire and ice are one and where only the biggest and best can play, *yip!*

Trainers know going in that the odds against you are a ton to one. So why do I risk the years, why do I take shots that stun my heart? Why am I part of the spilt blood? Why do I take trips to Leipzig or Johannesburg that take me two weeks to recover from? B. B. King sings my answer for me, backs it up with that big old guitar. *"I got a bad case of love."*

Anyway, all I was able to get Billy was what was out there, mostly Messkins, little guys wringing wet at a hundred twenty-four and three quarters, what with us being in San Antonia. But there was some black fighters, too, a welter or a middleweight, now and then. Billy treated all his fighters like they was champs, no matter that they was prelim boys hanging between hope and fear, and praying hard the tornado don't touch down. If they was to show promise, he'd outright sponsor them good, give them a deuce a week minimum, no paybacks, a free room someplace decent, and eats in one of his pubs, whatever they wanted as long as they kept their weight right. If a boy wasn't so good, Billy'd give 'em work, that way if the kid didn't catch in boxing, leastways he always had a job. People loved Billy Clancy.

See, he'd start boys as a dishwasher, but then he'd move 'em up, make waiters and bartenders of them. He had Messkin managers what started as busboys. He was godfather to close to two dozen Messkin babies, and he never forgot a birthday or Christmas. His help would invite him to their weddings, sometimes deep into Mexico, and damned if he wouldn't go. Eyes down there would bug out when this big *gringo*'d come driving through a dusty *pueblo* in one of his big old silver Lincoln Town Cars what he ordered made special. Billy'd join right in, *yip!*, got to where he could talk the lingo passable-good enough to where he could tell jokes and make folks laugh in their own tongue.

Billy Clancy'd be in the middle of it, but he never crossed the line, never messed with any of the gals, though he could have had any or all of 'em. The priests would always take a shine to him, too, want to talk baseball. He never turned one down who come to him about somebody's grandma what needed a decent burial, instead of being dropped down a hole in a bag.

One time I asked Billy why he didn't try on one of them Indian-eyed honeys down there. Respect, is what he said, for the older folks, and 'specially for the young men, you don't want to take a man's pride.

"When you're invited to a party," said Billy, "act like you care to be invited back."

That was Billy Clancy; you don't shit where you eat.

My deal with Billy was working in the gym with his fighters for ten percent of the purse off the top. No fights, no money. I didn't see him for days unless it was getting up around fight time. But he'd stop by, not to check up on me, but just to let his boys know he cared about them. Most times he was smoother than gravy on a biscuit, but I could always tell when something was pestering him. 'Course he wouldn't talk about it much. Billy didn't feel the need to talk, or he saw fit not to.

I know there was this one time when the head manager of all Billy's joints in San Antonia took off with Billy's cash. Billy come into his private office one Monday expecting to see deposit slips for the money what come in over a big weekend. Well, sir, there was no money, and no keys, and no manager, but that same manager had held a gun on Billy's little Messkin office gal so's she'd open the safe. The manager had whipped on the little gal, taped her to a chair with duct tape to where she'd peed herself, and she was near hysteric.

Billy had some of his help make a few phone calls, and damned if the boy what did Billy didn't head for his hometown on the island of Isla Mujeres way down at the tip of Mexico, where he thought he'd be safe. Billy waited a week, then took a plane to Mérida in the Yucatán. He rented him a big car with a good AC and drove on over to the dried-out, palmy little town of Puerto Juárez on the coast that's just lick across the water from what's called Women's Island.

He hung out a day or so in Puerto Juárez, until he got a feel for the place, and so the local police could get a good look at him. Then he just pulled up in front of their peach-colored shack, half its palm-leaf roof hanging loose. He took his time getting out of his rental car, and walked slow inside. Stood a foot taller than most. He talked Spanish and told the captain of the local *federales* his deal, made it simple. All he wanted was his keys back, *and* he wanted both the manager's balls. The captain was to keep what was left of the money.

That night late, the captain brought forty-six keys on three key rings to Billy's blistered motel. He showed Polaroids of the manager's corpse what was dumped to cook in the hot water off the island, and he also brought in the manager's two *huevos* — his two eggs, each wrapped in a corn tortilla. Billy Clancy fed them to the wild dogs on the other side of the adobe back fence.

Billy checked out some of the Mayan ruins down around those parts, giving local folks time to call the news back to San Antonia. Billy got back, nobody said nothing. Didn't have no more problems with the help stealing now he'd made clear what was his was his.

There was only one other deal about Billy I ever knew about, this time with one of his ex-fighters, a failed middleweight, a colored boy Billy'd made a cook in one of his places. Nice boy, worked hard, short hair, all the good stuff. First off, he worked as a barback. But then the bartenders found out the kid was sneaking their tips. They cornered him in a storeroom. They had him turned upside down, was ready to break his hands for him, but then he started squealing they was only doing it 'cause he's black. Billy heard it from upstairs and called off his bartenders, piecing them off with a couple of c-notes each. He listened to the boy's story, and 'cause he couldn't prove the boy was dirty, he moved him to a different joint, and that's where he made a fry cook out of him. The kid was good at cooking, worked overtime anytime the head cook wanted. But then word come down the kid was dealing drugs outta the kitchen. Billy knew dead bang this time and he had one of his cop friends make a buy on the sly.

See, Billy always tried to take care of his own business, unless when it was something like down in Mexico. Billy said when he took care of things himself, there was nobody could tell a story different from the one he told. So he waited for the boy outside the boy's mama's house one night late, slashed two of his tires. Boy comes out and goes shitting mad when he sees his tires cut, starts waving his arms like a crawdad.

Billy comes up with a baseball bat alongside his leg, said, "Boy, I come to buy some of that shit you sell."

Boy pissed the boy off something awful, but he knew better than to challenge Billy on it. So the boy tried to run. He showed up dead, is what happened, his legs broke, his balls in his mouth. No cop ever knocked on Billy Clancy's door, but drugs didn't happen in any of Billy's places after that neither.

It was a couple years after that when Dee-Cee Swans collared me about this heavyweight he'd been working with over at the Brown Bomber Gym in Houston. I said I wasn't going to no Houston — even if it was to look at the real Brown Bomber himself. Dee-Cee said there wasn't no need.

Henrilee "Dark Chocolate" Swans was from Louisiana, his family going back to Spanish slave times, the original name was Cisneros. Family'd brought him as a boy to Houston during World War Two, where they'd come to better themself. Henrilee's fighting days started on the streets of the Fifth Ward. He said things was so tough in his part of town that when a wino died, his dog ate him. Dee-Cee was a pretty good lightweight in his time, now a'course he weighs more. Fight guys got to calling him Dee-Cee instead of Dark Chocolate, to make things short. Dee-Cee said call him anything you want, long as you called him to dinner.

He wore a cap 'cause he was bald-headed except for the white fringe around his ears and neck. He wore glasses, but one lens had a crack in it. He had a bad back and a slight limp, so he walked with a polished, homemade old mesquite walking stick. It was thick as your wrist and was more like a knobby club than a cane. But old Dee-Cee still had the moves. The time, between now and back when he was still Dark Chocolate, disappeared when Dee-Cee had need to move. Said he never had no trouble on no bus in no part of town, not with that stick between his legs. Dee-Cee had them greeny-blue eyes what some coloreds gets, and when he looked at you square, you was looked at.

Way me and him hooked up was chancy, like everything else in fights. 'Course we knew each other going way back. Both of us liked stand-up style of fighters, so we always had a lot to talk about, things like moves, slips, and counters. Like me, he knew that a fighter's feet are his brains — that they're what tell you what punches to throw and when to do it. Since there was more colored fighters in Dallas and Houston, that's where Dee-Cee operated out of most. But he had folks in San Antonia, too. He showed up again, him and a white heavyweight, big kid, a Irish boy from L.A. calling himself "KO" Kenny Coyle. What wasn't chancy was that Dee-Cee knew I was connected with Billy Clancy.

Dee-Cee got together with Coyle, trained him a while in Houston after working the boy's corner twice as a pickup cutman in a Alabama casino. The way the boy was matched, he was supposed to lose. See, he hadn't fought in a while. But he won both fights by early KOs, and his record got to be seventeen and one, with fifteen knockouts. Coyle could punch with both hands at six-foot-five, two hundred forty-five pounds, size sixteen shoe. His only loss came a few years back from a bad cut to his left eyelid up Vancouver, Canada.

The boy'd also worked as sparring partner for big-time heavyweights, going to camp sometimes for weeks at a time. That's a lot of high-level experience, but it's a lot of punishment, even when you're bone strong, and sometimes you could tell that Coyle'd lose a word. Except for the bad scar on his eyelid, and his nose being a little flat, he didn't look much busted up, so that made you think he maybe had some smarts. He was in shape, too. That made you like him right off.

Dee-Cee was slick. He always put one hand up to his mouth when he talked, said he didn't want spies to read his lips, said some had telescopes. He was known to be a bad man, Dee-Cee, but that didn't mean he didn't have a sense of right and wrong. Back before he had to use a cane, we got to drinking over Houston after a afternoon fight — it was at a fair where we both lost. Half drunk, we went to a fish shack in dark town for some catfish. Place was jam-packed. The lard-ass owner had one of them muslim-style gold teeth — the slip-on kind with a star cutout that shows white from the white enamel underneath? Wouldn't you know it, he took one look at my color and flat said they didn't serve no food. Dee-Cee was fit to be tied — talked nigga, talked common, said Allah was

going to send his black ass to the pit along with his four handker-
chief-head ho's. Old muslim slid off the tooth quick as a quail when
Dee-Cee tapped his pocket and said he was going to cut that tooth
out or break it off.

We headed for a liquor store, bought some jerky, and ended up
out at one of them baseball-pitching park deals drinking rock and
rye and falling down in the dirt from swinging and missing pitches.
People got to laughing like we was Richard Pryor. Special loud was
the hustler running a three-card monte game next to the stands, a
little round dude with fuzzy-wuzzy hair. He worked off a old lettuce
crate and cheated people for nickels and dimes. Not one of them
ever broke the code, but old Dee-Cee had broke it from the git. He
watched sly from the fence as the monte-guy took even pennies
from the raggedy kids what made a few cents chasing down balls in
the outfield.

Dee-Cee put on his Louisiana country-boy act, bet a dollar, and
pointed to one of the cards after the monte-guy moved the three
cards all around. 'Course Dee-Cee didn't choose right, *couldn't*
choose right, so he went head-on and lost another twenty, thirty
dollars. Then he bet fifty, like he was trying to get his money back.
The dealer did more slick business with his cards, and Dee-Cee
chose the one in the middle — only this time, instead of just pointing to it and waiting for the dealer to turn it face-up like before,
Dee-Cee held it down hard with two fingers and told monte-man to
flip the other two cards over first. Dee-Cee said he'd turn his card
over *last,* said he wanted to eyeball *all* the cards. See, there was no
way for nobody to win. The dealer knew he'd been caught cheat-
ing, and tried to slide. Dee-Cee cracked him in the shins a few
times with a piece of pipe he carried those days, and pretty soon —
wouldn't you know it? — the monte-man got to begging Dee-Cee
to take *all* his money. Dee-Cee took it all, too. 'Course he kept his
own money, what was natural, but he gave the rest to the raga-
muffins in the field — at which juncture the little guys all took the
rest of the night off.

Dee-Cee got me off to the side one day, his hand over his mouth,
said did I want to work with him and Coyle? He told me Coyle
maybe had a ten-round fight coming up at one of the Mississippi
casinos, and I figured Dee-Cee wanted me as cutman for the fight,

him being the trainer and chief second. I say why not?, some extra cash to go along with my rocking chair, right?

But Dee-Cee said, "Naw, Red, not just cutman, I want you wit' me full-time training Coyle."

I say to myself, *A heavyweight what can crack, a big old white Irish one!*

Dee-Cee says he needs he'p 'cause as chief second he can't hardly get up the ring steps and through the ropes quick enough no more. 'Course with me working inside the ring, that makes me chief second *and* cutman. I'd done that before, hell.

Dee-Cee says he chose me 'cause he don't trust none of what he called the niggas and the beaners in the gym. Said he don't think much of the rednecks neither. See, that's the way Dee-Cee *talked,* not the way he *acted* toward folks. Dee-Cee always had respect.

He said, "See, you'n me knows that a fighter's feet is his brains. My white boy's feet ain't right, and you good wit' feet. We split the trainer's ten percent, even."

Five percent of a heavyweight can mount.

Dee-Cee said, "Yeah, and maybe you could bring in Billy Clancy."

Like I said, Dee-Cee's slick. So I ask myself if this is something I want bad enough to kiss a spider for? See, when a fan sees the pros and the amateurs', he sees them as a sport. But the pros is a business, too. It's maybe more a business than a sport. I liked the business part like everybody else, but heavyweights can hurt you like nobody else. So I'm thinking, do I want to chance sliding down that dark hole a heavyweight can dig? Besides, do I want to risk my good name on KO Kenny Coyle with Billy Clancy? I told Dee-Cee I'd wait a spell before I'd do that.

Dee-Cee said, "No, no, you right, hail yeah!"

See, I'm slick, too.

What it was is, Coyle was quirky. He'd gone into the navy young and started fighting as a service fighter, started knocking everybody out. He won all of the fleet and other service titles, and most of the civilian amateur tournaments, and people was talking Olympics. But the Olympics was maybe three years away, and he wanted to make some money right now. Couldn't make no big money or train full-time in the navy, so one day Coyle up and walks straight into the ship's captain's face. Damned if Coyle don't claim he's queer as a three-dollar bill. See, the service folks these days ain't supposed

F. X. TOOLE

to ask, and you ain't supposed to tell, but here was Coyle telling what he really wanted was to be a woman and dance the ballet. Captain hit the overhead, was ready to toss him in the brig, but Coyle threatened to suck off all the marine guards, and to contact the president himself about sexual harassment. Didn't take more'n a lick, and the captain made Coyle a ex-navy queer. Coyle laughed his snorty laugh when he told the story, said wasn't he equal smart as he was big? Guys said he sure was, but all knew Coyle wasn't smart as Coyle thought he was — 'specially when he got to bragging about how he stung some shyster lawyers what had contacted him while he was still a amateur. See, they started funneling him money, and got him to agree to sign with them when he turned pro. He knew up front that nobody was supposed to be buzzing amateurs, and he got them for better'n twenty big ones before he pulled his sissy stunt on the navy. When they come to him with a pro contract, he told them to stick it, told them no contract with a amateur was valid, verbal or written, and that he had bigger plans. He had them shysters by the ying-yang, he said, and them shysters knew it. Coyle laughed about that one, too.

Too bad I didn't hear about the lawyer deal until we was already into the far turn with Coyle. By the time I did, I already knew Kenny was too big for his britches, and that he was a liar no different from my cousin Royal. If it was four o'clock, old Royal'd say it was four-thirty. Couldn't help himself.

Coyle's problem as a fighter was he'd not been trained right, but he was smart enough to know it. His other trainers depended on his reach and power, and that he could take a shot. The problem with that is that you end up fighting with your face. What I worked on with him was the angles of the game, distance, and how to get in and out of range with the least amount of work. The big fellows got to be careful not to waste gas. But where I started Coyle first was with the *bitch*. See, the bitch is what I call the jab, that's the one'll get a crowd up and cheering, you do it pretty. *Bing! Bing!* Man, there ain't nothing like the bitch. And Coyle took to it good, him being fed up with getting hit. With the bitch, you automatic got angles. You got the angle, you got the opening. *Bang!* Everything comes off the bitch. I got him to moving on the balls of his feet, and soon he was coming off that right toe behind the bitch like he was a great white going for a seal pup. *Whooom!*

See, when you got the bitch working for you is when you got the other guy blinking, and on his heels going backward, and you can knock a man down with the bitch, even knock him out if you can throw a one-two-one combination right. Coyle picking up the bitch like he did is what got me to think serious on him, 'specially when I saw how hard he worked day in, day out. On time every day, nary a balk. Dee-Cee and me both started counting fun-tickets in our sleep but both of us agreed to pass on the ten-round Mississippi fight until I could get Coyle's feet right.

Moving with Coyle, like with the other heavies, is easy for me even now. 'Cause of their weight, they get their feet tangled when they ain't trained right, and I know how to back them to the ropes or into a corner. I don't kid myself, they could knock me out with the bitch alone if we was fighting, but what we're up to ain't fighting. What we're up to is what makes fighting boxing.

Billy Clancy got wind of Coyle and called me in, wanted to know why I was keeping my white boy secret. I told him Coyle wasn't no secret, said it was too soon.

"Who's feedin' him?"

"Me and Dee-Cee."

Billy peeled off some hundreds. I'd later split the six hundred with Dee-Cee.

Billy said, "Tell him to start eatin' at one of my joints, as much as he wants. But no drinks and no partyin' in the place. When'll Coyle be ready?"

"Gimme six weeks. If he can stand up to what I put on him, then we'll see."

"Will he fight?"

"He better."

Once I got Coyle's feet slick, damn if he didn't come along as if he was champion already. When I told Billy, he put a eight-round fight together at one of the Indian reservations on the Mississippi. We went for eight so's not to put too much pressure on Coyle, what with me being a new trainer to him. We fought for only seventy-five hundred — took the fight just to get Coyle on the card. When I told Coyle about it, he said book it, didn't even ask who's the opponent. See, Coyle was broke and living in dark town with Dee-Cee, and hoping to impress Billy 'cause Dee-Cee'd told him about Billy Clancy having money.

Well, sir, halfway through the fifth round with Marcellus Ellis,

Coyle got himself head-butted in the same eye where he'd been cut up in Vancouver. Ellis was a six-foot-seven colored boy weighing two-seventy, but he couldn't do nothing with Coyle, 'cause of the bitch. So Ellis hoped to save his big ass with a head-butt. Referee didn't see the butt, and wouldn't take our word it was intentional, so the butt wasn't counted. Cut was so bad I skipped adrenaline and went direct to Thrombin, the ten-thousand-unit bovine coagulant deal. Thrombin stopped the blood quicker'n morphine'll stop the runs, but the cut was in the eyelid, and the fight shoulda been stopped in truth. But we was in Mississippi and the casino wanted happy gamblers, so the ref let it go on with a warning that he'd stop the fight in the next round if the cut got worse.

Dee-Cee got gray-looking, said he was ready to go over and whip on Ellis's nappy head with his cane.

I told Coyle the only thing I could tell him. "They'll stop this fight on us and we could lose, so you got to get into Ellis's ass with the bitch and then drop your right hand on him and get *respect!*"

All Coyle did was to nod. He went out there serious as a diamondback. Six hard jabs busted up Ellis so bad that he couldn't think nothing but the bitch. That's when Coyle got the angle and, *Bang!* he hit Ellis with a straight right that was like the right hand of God. Lordy, Ellis was out for five minutes. He went down stiff like a tree and bounced on his face, and then one leg went all jerk and twitchy. We went to whooping and hugging. That right hand was lightning in human form. But what it was that did it for me wasn't Coyle's big right hand, it was the way he stuck the *bitch*, and the way Coyle *listened* to me in the corner.

Billy wanted to sign him right then, but I said wait, even though I knew Coyle was antsy to get him a place of his own. Besides, we had to wait a month and more to see if the eye'd heal complete. It took longer than we thought, so Billy started paying the boy three hundred a week walking-around money. Folks at the casino was so wild about that right hand coming outta a white boy that Billy was able to get twenty-five thousand for Coyle's next fight soon's a doctor'd clear his eye. And sure enough, Coyle was right back in the gym when the doctor gave him the okay. But he had some kind of funny look to him, so I told him to go home and rest. But no, Coyle kept showing up saying he wanted to get back to that casino. How do you reach the brain of a pure-strain male hormone when he's eighteen and one, with sixteen KOs? But one morning when me and

Dee-Cee was out with him doing his road work, we got a surprise. Coyle started pressing his chest and had to stop running. Damn if he didn't look half-blue and ready to go down. Me and Dee-Cee walked him back to the car, both holding him by a arm. I thought maybe it was a heart attack. We hauled ass over to Emergency. They checked him all over, hooked him up to all the machines, checked his blood for enzymes. Said it wasn't no heart attack, said it was maybe some kind of quick virus going around that could knock folks down. Coyle wanted to know when he'd be able to fight again in Mississippi, and I told him to forget Mississippi till he was well. On our way out, the doctor got me to the side to tell me he wasn't positive Coyle was sick.

I said, "What does that mean?"

Doc said, "I'm not sure. Just thought you might want to know."

After a couple of days' rest Coyle was back in the gym, but then he had to stop his road work outta weakness again. He looked like a whipped pup, so I figured he had to have something wrong. He said, "But I can't fight if I don't run, you said it yourself."

I said, "You can't fight if you ain't got gas in your tank, that's what that means. Right now, you got a hole in your tank."

"I need dough, Red."

He was a hungry fighter; it's what you dream about. And there he'd be the next day, even if he coughed till he gagged. You never saw anybody push himself like him. But by then, the fool could hardly punch, much less run. But he still wanted to train, said he didn't want us to think he didn't have no heart.

I said, "Hail, boy, I'm worried about your brain, not heart. You got money from the last fight. Rest."

He said, "I sent all but a thousand to my brother for an operation. He's a cripple."

Well, later on I learned he'd pissed all the money away on pussy and pool, and there wasn't no cripple. But at that time I was so positive Coyle had the heart it takes that I just grabbed the bull by the horns and told Billy it was time. Billy could see the weak state Coyle was in, but on my good word it was a virus, Billy signed Coyle up to a four-year contract. On top of that, he gave Coyle a one-bedroom poolside apartment in one of his units for free. Said he'd give Coyle twenty-five hundred a month, that he'd put it in the contract, no payback, until Coyle started clearing thirty thousand a year. Said he'd give Coyle sixty thousand dollars under the table as a signing bonus soon's he was well enough to get back in the gym. Coyle wanted a hundred thousand, but settled for sixty.

Billy said, "That's cash, Kenny. So you don't have to pay no taxes on it."

"I'll get you the title, Mr. Clancy."

"Billy."

I looked at Dee-Cee, knew the head of his dick was glowing same as mine. Damned if Coyle wasn't back in the gym working hard and doing road work in only three days. Billy's word was good, and I was there when he paid Coyle off in stacks of hundreds. Money smells bad when you get a gang of it all together.

Wouldn't you know it? Old stinky-head went right out and spent the whole shiteree on one of them new BMW four-wheel-drive deals what goes for better than fifty thousand. Coyle got to bragging about the sports package, the killer sound system, how much horsepower it had. Who gives a rap when you can't afford tires and battery? Buying them boogers is easy, keeping them up what's hard.

Besides, it was about that time that Coyle's knees went to flap like butterfly wings. See, the ladies took one look at Coyle and thought they had the real deal, what with him having that big car and flashing hundreds in the clubs.

Dee-Cee said, "How many times you get you nut this week?"

Coyle said, "That's personal."

Dee-Cee said, "So you been gettin' you nut every night."

Coyle said, "No, I ain't."

Dee-Cee said, "You is, too. If it was one or none, or even two times, you'da said so."

Coyle looked at me like he'd never heard such talk.

I said, "He's sayin' when your legs get to wobblin', you been doin' it too much. He's saying that when your legs're weak that your brain gets to wonderin' why's it so hard to keep itself from fallin' down. That's when your brain is so busy keeping you on your feet that it don't pay attention to fightin'. Son, you got to have your legs right so your mind can work quicker than light, or you end up as a opponent talkin' through your nose, and the do-gooders wants to blame us trainers. No good, it's you and your dick what's doin' wrong."

Coyle said, "I'm a fighter livin' like a fighter."

Dee-Cee said, "Way you goin', you won't be for long."

I said, "Dee-Cee ain't wrong, Kenny."

Dee-Cee said, "Boy, you can fuck you white ass black, but that ain't never gonna make you champ of nothin'."

Coyle snorted, said, "I'll be champ of the bitches."

Dee-Cee said, "You go out, screw a thousand bitches, you think you somethin'? Sheeuh, you don't screw no thousand bitches, a thousand bitches screw you — and there go you title shot, fool."

Coyle said, "Fighters need release."

Dee-Cee said, "Say *what*? All you got to do is wait some. You midnight emissions'll natural take care of you goddamn release!"

I said, "Look, we're tryin' to get you around the track and across the finish line first, but you're headin' into the rail on us."

"Yeah," said Dee-Cee, "workin' wit' you be like holdin' water in one hand."

Coyle thought about that and seemed to nod, but next day when he come in his knees were flapping same as before.

Come to find out, Coyle wasn't worth the powder to blow him to hell. Billy found out Coyle had been with three gals in the stall of the men's toilet at one of his hot spots — that they'd been smoking weed hunched around the stool, *yip!* Billy didn't jump Coyle. But instead of seeing him as a long-lost White Hope in shining armor, he saw him same as me and Dee-Cee'd come to — like a peach what had gone part bad. So, do you cut out the bad part and keep the good? Or do you shit-can the whole deal? Billy decided to save what he could as long as he could.

Billy told Coyle to flat take his partying somewhere else, like he was first told. If I know Billy, there was more he wanted to say, but didn't. 'Course big old Coyle didn't take it too good, and wanted to dispute with Billy. So Billy said not to mistake kindness for weakness. Coyle got the message looked like, and was back in the gym working hard again — he wanted that twenty-five hundred a month. We figured the bullshit was over, leastways the in-public bullshit. But who could tell about weed? And who knew what else Coyle was messing with? By then, I got to feeling like I was a cat trapped in a sock drawer.

I told Coyle that what he'd pulled on Billy wasn't the right way to do business.

Coyle said, "He's makin' money off me."

I said, "Not yet he ain't."

That's when things got so squirrelly you'd think Coyle had a tail.

First thing what come up was that stink with the plain-Jane cop's daughter who said Coyle knocked her up — said Coyle'd gave her some of this GHB stuff that's floating around that'll make a gal pass out so deep she's a corpse. Cop's daughter said the last thing she remembered was that she was in Coyle's pool playing kissy face. Next thing she knew she was bare-ass on the floor and Coyle was fixing to do her. She said she jumped up and fled.

Coyle claimed that he'd already done her twice, said she was crying for more.

See, it wasn't until it come out she was pregnant that she told her daddy, who was a detective sergeant of the San Antonia P.D. She was a only child, and Daddy had them squinty blue eyes set in a face wide in the cheekbones what the Polacks brought into Texas. That good old boy got to rampaging like a rodeo bull, and right about then his neighbors got to thinking about calling Tom Bodette and checking into a Motel 6.

Once Daddy'd killed a half bottle of Jim Beam, he loaded up a old .44 six-gun, put on his boots and hat, and went on over to shoot Coyle dead.

Coyle told Daddy he loved plain-Jane more than his life itself, said that he wanted to marry her.

Cop was one of them fundamentals and figured marrying was better'n killing, so he let Coyle off.

Arrangements was made quick so the girl could wear white to the altar and not show. But then Coyle ups and says he'd have to wait till after the kid was born, that he wanted a blood test to prove he was the real daddy. The cop went to rampaging again and was fixing to hunt Coyle down, but he was took off the scent when his daughter stuck something up herself. Killed the baby, and liked to killed herself. The family was in such grief that Daddy started to drink full-time. The girl was sent off to live with a aunt up Nacogdoches. The cop had to go into one of them anger management deals or get fired from the force. 'Course Coyle slapped his thigh.

Second deal was about sparring, and was way worse for me'n Dee-Cee than the cop-daughter deal. All of a sudden Coyle started spar-

ring like he never done it before. Everybody was hitting him —
middleweights we had in with him to work speed, high school line-
men in the gym on a dare, grunts for God's sake. The eye puffed
up again, and we had to take off more time. All of a sudden Coyle's
moving on his heels instead of his toes, and now he can't jump
rope without stumbling into a wall. A amateur light heavy knocked
him down hard enough to make him go pie-eyed, and Dee-Cee
called the session off. Most times like that, a fighter's pride will
make him want to keep on working, but not Coyle. He was happy to
get his ass outta there. Billy heard about it and quick got Coyle that
second Mississippi fight for seventy-five thousand. Got Coyle ten
rounds with a dead man just to see what was what.

The opponent was six foot tall, three hundred twenty-eight
pounds, a big old black country boy from Lake Charles, Louisiana,
who couldn't hardly scrawl his own name. But in the first round,
with his damn eyes closed, he hit Coyle high on the head with
an overhand right and knocked him on his ass. Me and Dee-Cee
couldn't figure how he didn't see the punch coming, it was so high
and wide. Coyle jumped up, and to his credit, he went right to
work.

Bang! Three bitches to the eyes, right hand to the chin, left hook
to the body, all the punches quick and pretty. The black boy settled
like a dead whale to the bottom, and white folks was dancing in the
aisles and waving the Stars and Bars. It was pitiful, but Coyle strutted like he just knocked out Jack Johnson. Me and Dee-Cee was
pissed, and our peters had lost their glow. Dressing room afterward
was quiet as a gray dawn.

Coyle took time off, not that he needed the rest. He came back
for a few days, then it got so he wasn't coming in at all. If he did,
he'd lie around and bullshit instead of work. You could smell weed
on him, and his hair got greasy. Now all our fighters started going
flaky. Sweat got scarcer and scarcer. There was other times Coyle'd
come in so fluffy from screwing you wished he didn't come in at all.
Gym got to be a goddamned social club what looked full of boy
whores and Social Security socialites. What with Coyle lying around
like a pet poodle, Billy's other fighters started doing the same.
Some begged off fights that were sure wins for them. You never
want a fighter to fight if he's not ready, but when they're being paid
to be in shape, they're supposed to be in shape, not Butterball goddamn turkeys.

I tried to get Coyle to get serious, but he kept saying, "I'm cool, I'm cool."

I said, "Tits on a polar bear's what's cool."

That went on for three months, but I wasn't big enough to choke sense into him. Besides, no trainer worth a damn would want to. Fighters come in on their own, or they don't come in. Billy wanted a answer, but I didn't have one. How do you figure it when a ten-round fighter hungry for money pulls out of fights 'cause of a sore knuckle, or a sprung thumb, or a bad elbow? Course old Coyle didn't volunteer for no cut in pay.

One day he was lounging in his velour sweatsuit looking at tittie magazines. He said to turn up the lights. I said they was turned up. He said to turn them up again, and I said they was up again. Coyle yelled at me the first and last time.

"Turn 'em all the goddamn fuck up!"

"Boy," I said, and then I said it again real quiet. "Boy, lights is all the goddamn fuck up."

He looked up. "Oh, uh-huh, yeah, Red, thanks."

About then I figure Kenny don't know shit from Shinola.

Vegas called Billy for a two-hundred-thousand-dollar fight with some African fighting outta France. He had big German money behind him, and he was a tough sumbitch, but he didn't have no punch like Kenny Coyle. Coyle said he'd go for the two-hundred-thousand fight in a heartbeat.

I knew there had to be some fun in all this pain. We whip the Afro-Frenchie and win the next couple of fights, and we're talking three, maybe five hundred thousand a fight. Even if he loses, Billy's got all his money back and more, and me and Dee-Cee's doing right good, too. If we win big, we'll be talking title fight, 'cause word'll be out that there's some big white boy who could be the one to win boxing back from the coloreds. The only coloreds me and Dee-Cee gave a rap about was them colored twenties, and fifties, and hundreds that'd make us proud standing in the bank line instead of meek. Like I say, the amateurs and the pros ain't alike, and Billy's figuring to get his money out of Coyle while he can. Me and Dee-Cee's for that, 'specially me, since it gets me off the hook.

But neither one of us could figure what had happened with

Coyle, so we got Billy to bring in some tough sparring partners for the Frenchie fight to test what Coyle had. Same-oh same-oh, with Coyle getting hit. But when he hit them, *damn!*, they'd go *down! A* gang of them took off when Coyle threw what that writer guy James Ellroy calls *body rockets* that tore up short ribs and squashed livers. But it was almost like Coyle was swinging blind. Usual-like, you don't care about the sparring partners, they're paid to get hit. But the problem was that Coyle was getting hit, and going *down*, too. He'd take a shot and his knees would do the old butterfly. We figured he'd been smoking weed, or worse — being up all night in toilets with hoochies.

Dee-Cee said, "Can't say I didn't tell him 'bout midnight emissions, but no, he won't listen a me."

But Coyle wasn't short on wind, and he looked strong. Me'n Dee-Cee'd never seen nothing like it, a top guy gets to be a shot fighter so quick like that, 'specially with him doing his road work every dawn? Hell, come to find out he wasn't even smoking weed, just having a beer after a workout so's he could relax and sleep.

Seeing all our work fall apart, I figured we was Cinderella at midnight. Me and Dee-Cee both knew it, but we still couldn't make out why. Then Dee-Cee come to me, his hand over his mouth.

Dee-Cee said, "Coyle's blind in that bad eye."

I said, "What? Bullshit, the commission doctors passed him."

"He's blind, Red, in that hurt eye, I'm tellin' you. I been wavin' a white towel next to it two days now, and he don't blink on the bad-eye side. Watch."

Between rounds sparring next day, with me greasing and watering Coyle, Dee-Cee kind of waved the tip of the towel next to Coyle's good eye and Coyle blinked automatic. Between the next round, Dee-Cee was on the other side. He did the same waving deal with the towel. But Coyle's bad eye didn't blink 'cause he never saw the towel. That's when I understood why he was taking all them shots, that's when I knew he was moving on his heels 'cause he couldn't see the floor clear. And that's why he was getting rocked like it was the first time he was ever hit, 'cause shots was surprising him that he couldn't tell was coming. And it's when I come to know why he was pulling out of fights — he knew he'd lose 'cause he couldn't see. He went for the two-hundred-thousand fight knowing he'd lose, but he took it for the big money. I wanted to shoot the bastard, what with him taking Billy's money and not saying the eye'd gone bad and making a chump outta me.

The rule is if you can't see, then you can't fight. I told Dee-Cee we got to tell Billy. See, Billy's close to being my own kin, and it's like I stuck a knife in his back if I don't come clean.

Dee-Cee said to wait, that it was the commission doctor's fault, not ours, let them take the heat. He said maybe Vegas won't find out, and maybe the fight will fuck Coyle up so bad he'll have to retire anyhow. Billy'll still get most of his money back, Dee-Cee said, so Billy won't have cause to be mad with us. That made sense.

But what happened to mess up our deal permanent was that the Vegas Boxing Commission faxed in its forms for the AIDS blood test, said they wanted a current neuro exam, and they sent forms for a eye exam that had to be done by a ophthalmologist, not some regular doctor with a eye chart. Damned if Coyle wasn't sudden all happy. He couldn't wait once he heard about the eye test. Me and Dee-Cee was wondering how can he want a eye test, what with what we know about that eye?

Sure enough, when the eye test comes in, it says that Coyle's close to stone blind in the bad eye, the one what got cut in Canada. The nuero showed Coyle's balance was off from being hit too much in training camps, which is why he couldn't jump rope, and why he'd shudder when he got popped. The eye exam proved what me and Dee-Cee already knew, which is why Coyle was taking shots what never shoulda landed. What it come down to was the two-hundred-thousand-dollar fight was off, and Coyle's fighting days for big money was over. It also come down to Billy taking it in the ass for sixty grand in signing money that was all my fault. And that ain't saying nothing about all the big purses Coyle coulda won if he had been fit.

Turns out that the fight in Vancouver where Coyle got cut caused his eye to first go bad. The reason why word didn't get loose on him is 'cause Coyle didn't tell the Canadian doctors he was a fighter, and 'cause it was done on that Canadian free health deal they got up there. The eye doc said the operation was seventy percent successful, but told Coyle to be careful, 'cause trauma to the eye could mess it up permanent. What with him dropping out of boxing for a couple of years the way fighters'll do when they lose, people wasn't thinking on him. And the way Coyle passed the eye test in Alabama and Mississippi was to piece off with a hundred-dollar bill the crooked casino croakers what's checking his eyes. When later on he told me how he did it, he laughed the same snorty way as when he told how he played his game on the navy.

That's when I worked out what was Coyle's plan. See, he knew right after the Marcellus Ellis fight that the eye had gone bad on him again, but he kept that to himself instead of telling anyone about it, thinking his eye operation in Canada won't come out. That way, he could steal Billy's signing money, and pick up the twenty-five hundred a month chasing-pussy money, too. I wondered how long he'd be laughing.

Only now what am I supposed to say to Billy? After all, it was my name on Coyle what clinched the deal. It got to be where my shiny, big old white boy was tarnished as a copper washtub. I talked with Dee-Cee about it.

Dee-Cee said, "You right. That why the schemin' muhfuh come down South from the front!"

See, we surprised Coyle. He didn't know the tests had come back, so me and Dee-Cee just sat him down on the ring apron. Starting out, he was all fluffy.

Dee-Cee said, "Why didn't you tell us about the eye?"

Coyle lied, said, "What eye?"

Dee-Cee said, "Kenny, the first rule's don't shit a shitter. The eye what's fucked up."

Coyle said, "Ain't no eye fucked up."

"You got a fucked-up eye, don't bullshit," said Dee-Cee.

"It ain't bad, it's just blurry."

"Just *blurry* means you ain't fightin' Vegas, that's what's muthuh-fuckin' blurry," Dee-Cee said, muscles jumping along his jaw. "I'm quittin' you right now, hyuh? Don't want no truck with no punk playin' me."

Coyle's eyes started to bulge and his neck got all swole up and red. "You're the punk, old man!"

Coyle shoved Dee-Cee hard in the chest. Dee-Cee went down, but he took the fall rolling on his shoulder, and was up like a bounced ball.

Dee-Cee said, "Boy, second rule's don't hit a hitter."

Coyle moved as if to kick Dee-Cee. I reached for my Buck, but before it cleared my back pocket, Dee-Cee quick as a dart used his cane *bap! bap! bap!* to crack Coyle across one knee and both shins. Coyle hit the floor like a sack full of cats.

"I'll kill you, old man. I'll beat your brains out with that stick."

Dee-Cee said, "Muhfuh, you best don't be talking no *kill* shit wit' Dark Chocolate."

Coyle yelled, "Watch your back, old man!"

Dee-Cee said, "Boy, you diggin' you a hole."

Dee-Cee hobbled off, leaning heavy on his cane. Coyle made to go after Dee-Cee again, but by then I'd long had my one-ten out and open.

I said, "Y'all ever see someone skin a live dog?"

I had to get Coyle outta there, thought to quick get him to the Texas Ice House over on Blanco, where we could have some longnecks like good buds and maybe calm down. Texas Ice House's open three hundred sixty-five days a year, sign out front says GO COWBOYS.

Coyle said, "Got my own Texas shit beer at home."

Texas and *shit* in the same breath ain't something us Texans cotton to, but I went on over to Coyle's place later on 'cause I had to. I knocked, and through the door I heard a shotgun shell being jacked into the chamber.

I said, "It's me, Red."

Coyle opened up, then limped out on the porch looking for Dee-Cee.

Coyle said, "I'm gonna kill him, you tell him."

Inside, there was beer cans all over the floor, and the smell of weed and screwing. Coyle and a half-sleepy tittie-club blond gal was lying around half bare-ass. She never said a word throughout. I got names backing me like Geraghty and O'Kelly, but when I got to know what a sidewinder Coyle was, it made me ashamed of belonging to the same race.

I said, "When did the eye go bad?"

Coyle was still babying his legs. "It was perfect before that Marcellus Ellis butted me at the casino. But with you training me, hey baby, I can still fight down around here."

"You go back to chump change you fight down around here."

"My eye is okay, it's just blurry, that's all, don't you start on me, fuck!"

"It's you's what's startin'."

"This happened time before last in Mississippi, okay? And it was gettin' better all by itself, okay?"

I stayed quiet, so did he. Then I said, "Don't you get it? You fail the eye test, no fights in Vegas, or no place where there's money. Only trainer you'll get now's a blood sucker."

Coyle shrugged, even laughed a little. That's when I asked him the one question he didn't never want to hear, the one that would mean he'd have to give back Billy's money if he told the truth.

I said, "Why didn't you tell us about the eye before you signed Billy's contract?"

Coyle got old. He looked off in a thousand-yard stare for close to a minute. He stuttered twice, and then said, "Everybody knew about my eye."

I said, "Not many in Vancouver, and for sure none in San Antonia."

Coyle said, "Vegas coulda checked."

I said, "We ain't Vegas."

Coyle stood up. He thought he wanted to hit me, but he really wanted to hide. Instead, he moved the shotgun so's it was pointing at my gut.

He said, "I don't want you to train me no more."

I said, "Next time you want to fuck somebody, fuck your mama in her casket. She can't fuck you back."

That stood him straight up, and I knew it was time to git. As the door closed behind me, I could hear Coyle and the tittie-club blonde start to laugh.

I said to myself, "Keep laughin', punk cocksucker — point a gun at me and don't shoot."

I drove my pickup over to Billy's office next day, told him the whole thing. It wasn't far from my place but it was the longest ride I ever took. I was expecting to be told to get my redneck ass out of Texas. He just listened, then lit up a Montecristo contraband Havana robusto with a gold Dunhill. He took his time, poured us both some Hennessy XO.

He could see I felt lowdown and thought I'd killed his friendship.

I said, "I'm sorry, Billy, you know I'd never wrong you on purpose."

Billy said, "You couldn't see the future, Red. Only women can, and that's 'cause they know when they're gonna get fucked."

Billy put the joke in there to save me from myself, damned if he didn't. I was ready to track Coyle and gut him right then. But Billy said to calm down, said he'd go over to Coyle's place later on. I wanted to go, said I'd bring along Mr. Smith and Mr. Wesson.

"Naw," said Billy, "there won't be no shootin'."

When Billy got to Coyle's, Kenny was smoking weed again, had hold of a big-assed, stainless steel .357 MAG Ruger with a six-inch barrel. Billy didn't blink, said could he have some iced tea like Coyle was drinking. Coyle said it was Snapple Peach, not diet, but Billy said go on'n hook one up. Things got friendly, but Coyle kept ahold of the Ruger.

Billy said, "Way I see it, you didn't set out to do it."

Coyle said, "That's right. Ellis did it."

Billy said, "But you still got me for sixty large."

Coyle said, "Depends on how you look at it." He laughed at his joke. "Besides, nobody asked about my eye, so I told no lie. Hey, I can rhyme like Ali, that's me, hoo-ee."

Billy said, "Coyle, there's sins of commission and there's sins of omission. This one's a sixty-thousand-dollar omission."

Coyle said, "You got no proof. It was all cash like you wanted, no taxes."

Billy said, "I want my sixty back. You can forget the free rent and the twenty-five hundred you got off me every month, but I want the bonus money."

Coyle said, "Ain't got it to give back."

Billy said, "You got the BMW free and clear. Sign it over and we're square."

Coyle said, "You ain't gettin' my Beamer. Bought that with my signing money."

Billy said, "You takin' it knowin' your eye was shot, that was humbug."

Coyle said, "I'm stickin' with the contract and my lawyer says you still owe me twenty-five hundred for this month, and maybe for three years to come. He says you're the one that caused it all when you put me in with the wrong opponent."

Billy'd put weight on around the belly, and Coyle was saying he wasn't dick afraid of him.

Billy didn't press for the pink, and didn't argue about the twenty-five hundred a month, didn't say nothing about the lost projected income.

"Then tell me this," Billy said, "when do you plan on gettin' out of my building and givin' back my keys?"

Coyle laughed his laugh. "When you evict me, that's when, and you can't do that for a while 'cause my eye means I'm disabled, I checked."

Billy laughed with Coyle, and Billy shook Coyle's left hand with his right before taking off, 'cause Coyle kept the Ruger in his right hand.

Billy said, "Well, let me know if you change your mind."

"Not hardly," said Coyle. "I'm thinkin' on marrying that cop's daughter. This here's our love nest."

Me and Dee-Cee was cussing Coyle twenty-four hours a day, but Billy never let on he cared. About a week later, he said his wife and kids was heading down to Orlando Disney World for a few days. On Thursday he gave me and Dee-Cee the invite to come on down to Nuevo Laredo with him Friday night for the weekend.

Billy said, "We'll have a few thousand drinks at the Cadillac Bar to wash the taste of Coyle out of our mouths."

He sweetened the pot, said how about spending some quality time in the cat houses of Boys Town, all on him? I said my old root'll still do the job with the right inspiration, so did Dee-Cee. But he said his back was paining him bad since the deal with Coyle, and that he had to go on over Houston where he had this Cuban *Santería* woman. She had some kind of mystic rubjuice made with rooster blood he said was the only thing what'd cure him.

Dee-Cee said, "I hate to miss the trip with y'all, but I got to see my Cuban."

I told Billy he might as well ride with me in my Jimmy down to Nuevo Laredo. See, it's on the border some three hours south of San Antonia. I had a transmission I been wanting to deliver to my cousin Royal in Dilley, which is some seventy-eighty miles down from San Antonia on Highway 35 right on our way. Billy said he had stuff to do in the morning, but that he'd meet me at the Cadillac Bar at six o'clock next day. That left just me heading south alone and feeling busted up inside for doing the right thing by a skunk.

I left early so's I could listen to Royal lie, and level out with some of his Jack Daniel's. When I pulled up in front of the Cadillac Bar at ten of six, I saw Billy's bugged-up Town Car parked out front. He was inside, a big smile on him. With my new hat and boots, I felt fifty again, and screw Kenny Coyle and the BMW he rode in on. We was laughing like Coyle didn't matter to us, but underneath, we knew he did.

Billy got us nice rooms in a brand-new motel once we had quail and Dos Equis for dinner, and finished off with fried ice cream in the Messkin style. Best I can recollect, we left our wheels at the motel and took a cab to Boys Town. We hit places like the Honeymoon Hotel, the Dallas Cowboys, and the New York Yankey. Hell, I buried myself in brown titties, even ended up with a little Chink gal I wanted to smuggle home in my hat. Spent two nights with her and didn't never want to go home.

I ain't sure, but seems to me I went back to the motel once on Saturday just to check on Billy. His car was gone, and there was a message for me blinking on the phone in my room, and five one-hundred-dollar bills on my pillow. Billy's message said he had to go on over to Matamoros 'cause the truck for his shrimps had busted down, and he had to rent another one for shrimp night. So I had me a mess of Messkin scrambled eggs and rice and beans and a few thousand bottles of Negra Modelo. I headed on back for my China doll still shaky, but I hadn't lost my boots or my *El Patrón* so I'm thinking I was a tall dog in short grass.

There seems like there were times when I must a blanked out there. But somewhere along the line, I remember wandering the streets over around Boys Town when I come up on a little park that made me stop and watch. It happens in parks all over Mexico. The street lights ain't nothing but hanging bare bulbs with swarms of bugs and darting bats. Boys and girls of fourteen to eighteen'n more'd make the nightly *paseo* — that's like a stroll on the main drag, 'cause there ain't no TV or nothing, and the *paseo*'s what they do to get out from the house to flirt. In some parts, the young folks form circles in the park. The boys' circle'd form outside the girls' circle and each circle moves slow in opposite directions so's the boys and the girls can be facing each other as they pass. The girls try to squirt cheap perfume on a boy they fancy. The boys try to pitch a pinch of confetti into a special girl's month. Everybody gets to laughing and spitting and holding their noses but inside their knickers they're fixing to explode. It's how folks get married down there.

'Course, getting married wasn't on my mind. Something else was, and I did my best to satisfy my mind with some more of that authentic Chinee sweet and sour.

Billy was asleep the next day, Sunday, when I come stumbling back, so I crapped out, too. I remember right, we headed home separate on Sunday night late. Both of us crippled and green but back in Laredo Billy's car was washed and spanky clean except for a cracked rear window. Billy said some Matamoros drunk had made a failed try to break in. He showed me his raw knuckles to prove it.

Billy said, "I can still punch like you taught me, Reddy."

Driving myself home alone, I was all bowlegged, and my heart was leaping sideways. But when it's my time to go to sleep for the last time, I want to die in Boys Town teasing the girls and learning Chinee.

I was still hung over on Monday, and had to lay around all pale and shaky until I could load up on biscuits and gravy, fresh salsa, fried grits, a near pound of bacon, three or four tomatoes, and a few thousand longnecks. I guess I slept most of the time 'cause I don't remember no TV.

It wasn't until when I got to the gym on Tuesday that I found out about Kenny Coyle. Hunters found him dead in the dirt. He was beside his torched BMW in the mesquite on the outside of town. They found him Sunday noon, and word was he'd been dead some twelve hours, which meant he'd been killed near midnight Saturday night. Someone at the gym said the cops had been by to see me. Hell, me'n Billy was in Mexico, and Dee-Cee was in Houston.

The inside skinny was that Coyle'd been hog-tied with them plastic cable-tie deals that cops'll sometimes use instead of handcuffs. One leg'd been knee-capped with his own Ruger someplace else, and later his head was busted in by blunt force with a unknown object. His brains was said to hang free, and looked like a bunch of grapes. His balls was in his mouth, and his mouth had been slit to the ear so's both balls'd fit. The story I got was that the cops who found him got to laughing, said it was funny seeing a man eating his own mountain oysters. See, police right away knew it was business.

When the cops stopped by the gym Tuesday morning, I was still having coffee and looking out the storefront window. I didn't have nothing to hide, so I stayed sipping my joe right where I was. I told them the same story I been telling you, starting off with stopping by to see old Royal in Dilley. See, the head cop was old Junior, and old Junior was daddy to that plain-Jane gal.

I told him me and Billy had been down Nuevo Laredo when the tragedy occurred. Told him about the Cadillac Bar, and about drinking tequila and teasing the girls in Boys Town. 'Course, I left out a few thousand details I didn't think was any of his business. Old Junior's eyes got paler still, and his jaw was clenched up to where his lips didn't hardly move when he talked. He didn't ask but two or three questions, and looked satisfied with what I answered.

Fixing to leave, Junior said, "Seems like some's got to learn good sense the hard way."

Once Junior'd gone, talk started up in the gym again and ropes got jumped. Fight gyms from northern Mexico all up through Texas knew what happened to Coyle. Far as I know, the cops never knocked on Billy Clancy's door, but I can tell you that none of Billy's fighters never had trouble working up a sweat no more, or getting up for a fight neither.

I was into my third cup of coffee when I saw old Dee-Cee get off the bus. He was same as always, except this time he had him a knobby new walking stick. It was made of mesquite like the last one. But as he come closer, I could see that the wood on this new one was still green from the tree.

I said, "You hear about Coyle?"

"I jus' got back," said Dee-Cee, "what about him?" One of the colored boys working out started to snicker. Dee-Cee gave that boy a look with those greeny-blue eyes. And that was the end of that.

DANIEL WATERMAN

A Lepidopterist's Tale

FROM *Bomb*

WHEN MY SISTER Janie and I were coming up in Smoketown, not long after Skeet came from across the street to stay and be our brother, an alley cat took to lingering around our house. Like all stray cats it lingered indecisively, torn between its two basic natures — it rubbed against your leg, but wouldn't let you pet it. It followed you everywhere, but hissed viciously if you tried to pick it up.

Skeet loved that cat. For a while. It was scrofulous and rib-thin, but with lively gray eyes it still had its pride. Skeet put up with its nasty attitude, fed it food and milk, watched it stalk and prowl. I guess he just wanted something to take care of even then. But since no one really wants a cat that can't be picked up and petted, an unfriendly cat, he stopped feeding it and petting it and letting it in. After a while the cat didn't come around anymore. I guess it was picked up or wandered off or died — I don't know which. And I guess Skeet was a lot like that cat. That cat had its own doom in it like a tumor.

It's a slight episode from my childhood, and I wouldn't have remembered it at all if Janie hadn't phoned me in tears at the office last week and asked me to meet her at Skeet's apartment. Skeet lived in a lot of places around town after we all left home eight years ago. I never saw most of the places Skeet lived, and I probably wouldn't have cared to. But two months ago, out of the blue, he turned up in the neighborhood that Janie and I always took pains to avoid, the one where we all grew up together.

This was Smoketown, where the shotgun houses run undistinguished for blocks and blocks, like brick after brick in a masonry wall. Where the tedium of the street, dull and scrubbed and empty and clean, is punctuated at odd intersections by a few corner storefronts — a convenience store or a laundromat or a bar. Where the enormous chimney of the city incinerator looms over everything, and the smoke that erupts from it all day long gives the neighborhood its name.

Skeet's few belongings were still at his place, and his landlord had asked us to clear them out. Apparently Skeet had put down Janie's name as the person to notify in case of an emergency. It wasn't an emergency anymore, but Janie had finally found the nerve to go over and see what was there. On her day off, calling me from a pay phone on the corner because Skeet didn't have a phone, had never had a phone, she wanted me to come over too. Quick.

"What is it?" I asked her.

"Just come over."

"It's a bad time, Janie," I told her. "I'm new here. I can't be running out on little errands in the middle of the day."

"Just come over. All right?"

"Listen," I said, guessing she'd just had a bad attack of the sorrows. "Leave it alone now. Tomorrow's Saturday. I've got the day off. I'll help tomorrow."

"That's not it."

"Well, what is it?"

In the pause that followed I could hear her inhale, that signature breadth of time. She was smoking again. "Just come over," she said.

"I can't. Can't you call Hal?" I asked, hoping she might consider calling her husband. A vicious silence ensued, and I remembered that Hal, who is not a bad person, had fallen from grace with my sister, his wife. I had no doubt he'd done nothing wrong, but that wasn't going to help Hal any. Janie's judgments have lives of their own, never dependent on things like good and bad behavior, one's deservings.

"Never mind," I said.

"He never knew Skeet," she said, almost a growl.

"Janie," I sighed.

"Sorry," she said, softening a little but still defensive, still the disappointed little girl. "Look," she went on. "I found something."

Just then Mr. Logan, the senior law partner for whom I work, came into the library. Seeing me on the phone, he marched over to my table. I smiled and held up a hand in greeting. He leaned forward, his fingers splayed over the tabletop, and waited.

"What?" I asked Janie.

"I said I found something."

"I know what you said. What did you find?"

"Just please come over." She'd hung up.

"Mr. Logan," I said, looking up. He raised his eyebrows at me over the top of his half-glasses, his face already dead with preordained disappointment. "I'm afraid I've got to run out for a while."

Skeet's apartment was no apartment at all, but one of those same storefronts in our old neighborhood, at the corner of Grand and Clay. I sat in the car for a moment and reread the address Janie had given me, convinced it was wrong. The store was too familiar to me, just two blocks from the house we grew up in. When Janie and I were kids it had been Murphy's Candy Store, then Bunny's Corner Market, and long after that a package store and bar — as though the building itself had seen fit to fulfill our every evolving need.

It was vacant now, though the front window was still intact, which surprised me. But the plate glass was painted pitch black, and plastered thickly with nightclub posters and concert flyers. I turned off the air conditioning in the car, rolled down the window, and waited.

The air outside was hot and still. The hollow summer sunlight, the shadows and the silence, the spare barren sidewalks all stole my momentum and I just sat there, feeling something of summers past. Further down the street two children were beating at each other with sticks. A screen door slammed somewhere behind me, and a little girl sped by on her bike, a doll tied cruelly to the rear fender. Suddenly and loudly a big yellow Cadillac ran the stop sign in front of me, its windows down and its stereo thumping, then was gone.

When I looked back at the storefront, Janie was leaning out of the store's dark doorway. She was watching me expectantly, staving off the heavy steel door with one of her strong, sinewy hands and motioning me inside with the other. I locked up the car and stepped up to meet her.

Janie retreated in front of me like a tour guide, walking back-ward deeper and deeper into the room. "Look at these," she said. But I couldn't see anything. The room, though cool and damp, was too dark to see. Janie had propped open the front door, and the weak light from it lit up the shallows. A dirty skylight in back illumi-nated the rear. Stopping, I let her go ahead, waiting for my eyes to adjust. And when they did the room seemed simple and empty. Old tongue-and-groove wood flooring, smoothed like stone by the treading of years, ran the whole length of the room. A broad dou-ble desk sat off to one side. A heavy oak swivel chair was pulled up to it. At the end of the room a mattress and box spring were stacked on the floor.

I stepped forward to follow, but something — a piece of string — fell against my face, startling me with its softness. A light cord. I reached up and pulled it.

"Busted," Janie said. "Come look at these."

At the desk Janie stepped around to the other side and faced me. She looked down at the surface, and I followed her eyes. Some boxes sat there. We looked up at each other, then back at the boxes.

"What are they?" I asked.

"You tell me," she said.

I stepped around and leaned in closer. They were display cases — plain rectangular wooden boxes with hinged lids and glass tops — two of them, lying face up. They were recognizable immedi-ately, the kind of boxes over which you might linger at a flea mar-ket, inspecting the pocket watches, pen knifes, old fountain pens, and election buttons they contain — all the ephemera and mantel-piece trinkets that people hoard and collect and imbue with some secret significance. I peered into one of them and then looked back at Janie.

"Moths?" I asked, for I was no lepidopterist.

"Butterflies," Janie crooned. "They're all butterflies."

She lifted the other box toward the weak light from the front door. Suddenly their colors — caramel, black, yellow, and blue — began to glow as though lit up from within, translucent and alive. In that box as in the other, butterflies of all kinds sat in neat spa-cious rows, orderly and at attention. Their wings were spread open in perfect equipoise, as though they'd just finished a long flight, or a ballet movement, by gently landing and taking a bow. But small black pins pierced the narrow abdomens of each one, holding them to the corkboard surface, making them seem less graceful, more dead, engaged in no dance at all.

A paper nametag was glued below each butterfly, its proper name spelled out in Skeet's erratic, struggling scrawl: *Papilio Glaucus, Lycaena Phlaeas, Spicebush Swallowtail, Silver-spotted Skipper, Stage Monarch, Red Admiral, Peking Cabbage, Blue Ipso-Columbus, Northern Cloudywing.* After reading them, I couldn't imagine which was more unlikely — Skeet attempting to pronounce the names, or actually taking the time to pen them.

"Look at the others," Janie said. She wagged a finger and guided me away. We walked down the length of the room until we came to three more identical boxes, standing upright in a row along the rear wall, like museum displays about to be hung. They too were filled with butterflies.

"Where did they come from?" I asked.

Janie moved a few paces away and turned, folding her arms. "I don't know," she said. "I honestly don't."

I bent down and inspected a few of them. "Maybe he picked them up somewhere."

"Picked them up? Picked them up where?" she asked.

"I don't know. Maybe he bought them."

"Come on," she said. I looked up at her. Her arms were folded. She was rocking on the balls of her feet. Her forehead was furrowed and she was picking at her fingers mercilessly.

"Or found them," I stabbed on, "in an alley. Or outside a lab. Or the museum. Or a garage sale. Who knows."

"Picked those up in an alley?"

"Maybe he bought them, Janie. I really don't know."

"Look in the drawer," she said.

"Why? What's in there?" I asked.

"Just look."

"There's something dead in there. Isn't there?"

"Look in the drawer."

I looked in the drawer. Scattered around inside were all of the implements Skeet had used to make his displays — tiny plastic boxes filled with colored pins, glue, tape, corkboard, rulers, X-acto knives.

"Look in the other," Janie said.

In the next drawer down, a deep drawer, were pieces of muslin and cheesecloth, two of them fashioned around coathangers to form crude butterfly nets. There was an old coffee can too. I lifted it out and the pungent odor that wafted from it — ethyl acetate, I know now — made me return it quickly. It was a killing jar, primitive and also of Skeet's own fashioning. Strewn along the bottom of the drawer was butterfly carnage, their bodies dry and dusty and disintegrating, brittle like fall leaves.

After I'd closed the drawers I turned the desk chair around and sat down. "I don't understand," I said.

"Neither do I." Janie, still standing, pulled out a cigarette and lit up. I started to cough conspicuously.

"Not a word," she warned. "I'm the nurse around here."

"You couldn't tell by looking at you," I said.

She inhaled and looked down at herself.

"I've got to get back to work," I finally said.

"What am I supposed to do with them?"

"I don't know. We'll talk about it later."

"I can't just leave them."

"You can for now," I said. "I've got to get back to work."

She started throwing her weight from leg to leg. She let her cigarette fall to the floor and crushed it with a pivot of her foot. "It doesn't make any sense."

"I know it doesn't," I said. I stood up to go.

"What was he doing?"

I stood looking at her, watching her wonder and wondering myself if she would hit upon it, remember it, allow herself to understand how the most vicious person we had ever known had come to take an obsessive interest in butterflies.

"I don't know, Janie. I've really got to go."

But I did know. The lies we tell when we're children might be called innocent lies, not because we're innocent, but because as children we know we're lying, and to what purpose or end. The lies we tell when we're older, though, are the frightening lies, because now we lie mostly to ourselves, and it's ourselves alone that we wish to delude.

Skeet once made medical history, though his name is in none of the textbooks. Why that is, I don't know. All I know is that the measures the doctors took to save Skeet's life, now so commonplace, were unheard of at the time.

He first got sick not long after he moved in with us. He began having difficulty with walking, and talking, and moving his arms, sluggish like a windup toy in the final throes of its gyrations. Mom was a nurse, attentive to those things, and saw it before any of us, including Skeet himself, I think, suspected a problem. She got Skeet the right appointments and checkups, and after many weeks of tests the doctors determined that Skeet's muscles were dying. They were dying generally, and all over. No name for his malady existed, but the doctors said it typically began in a patient's extremities. Limbs and appendages would begin to get more sluggish and numb. The arms and legs first, then the fingers and toes and the tongue. Skeet wouldn't be able to walk or eat or keep his eyes open. And then the numbness would spread inward — to the stomach muscles and the abdominal muscles and the bladder muscles and, in the end, the heart muscle would go. Skeet was nine.

Although the doctors had seen this before, and knew what to expect, they still had no way to successfully treat it. One of them had some ideas, though, and wanted to try them on Skeet. And because the treatment was experimental, and the risks somewhat uncertain, and because we had no money to speak of, the entire procedure — tests, injections, physical therapy, and hospital stays — would be free.

Mom took a couple weeks to think about it, and to try and find Skeet's mother.

Before he came to live with us, Skeet was no one special. He wasn't even Skeet. His name was Ted, and he was just the sickly looking kid who lived across the street from us, in a shotgun house like our own. Ted and his mother had moved from somewhere, Cincinnati I believe, and because Ted's mom and our mom were the only single mothers on our block, and close in age, they became friends. Skeet's mother would haul him over to play with us when she wanted to sit on the porch and talk aimless talk to Mom. She would find a sitter for all three of us when she wanted to take Mom out drinking with her, which Mom liked to do now and again.

I wasn't home when Skeet's mom brought him over to spend a few days with us — forever as it turned out. Janie was home, and she remembered that Skeet's mom seemed rushed. Apparently Skeet's father had turned up in Ohio somewhere, and she was off to find him and bring him back. Could we look after Ted for a while? Of course.

That night, with Skeet asleep upstairs and Janie on her way up to join him in the bedroom we would all come to share, I lingered in the kitchen a while with Mom, and prophetically asked her what would happen if Skeet's mom didn't come back. She laughed. "She'll be back for Ted, sweetie," she said, unable to imagine a mother abandoning a child. "That woman's had a hard way," she said, never once stopping to think of herself in those very terms. In the months that followed, Janie and I were worried and Mom was privately terrified, waiting for Skeet's mother to show up, then waiting for some city agency to discover her missing, or to question our possession of this child who did not belong to us. But nobody came, mother or father or officer of the law, and in time we all stopped worrying. It seems amazing now that a child could simply be left forever with a strange family, but I suppose you could get away with itinerant moves like that back then. You can get away with anything, really, when people stop paying attention.

Skeet never seemed to note his mother's absence. He never once mentioned her, and in time none of us mentioned her. After Skeet's illness we never spoke of her again.

If it was an awkward household before Skeet got sick our unease grew as Skeet's strength began to waste away drastically. When Mom wasn't at work she was at home, holed up in her bedroom when she wasn't making us meals, while Janie and I took Skeet around the neighborhood in the wagon, and sat him up on the porch with us. In the afternoons the three of us would watch TV, and when Mom would come out to fix dinner, Skeet, who could not move his head very well, followed her everywhere with his eyes as she moved about the room, and Mom, sensing it, would risk one glance at Skeet and start crying. She didn't know what to do for him. Neither did we. And after a month of not being able to find Skeet's mother, and with the doctor's reports evolving from "concerned" to "grave," Mom signed the releases. Skeet's treatment began immediately.

The experiment they tried, untested then, as I said, but so common now, was to administer huge doses of synthetic hormones to his system. They did this in the hospital three times a week, for four hours each time — with a few hours afterward for rest and rehabilitation. On those days Skeet went to work with Mom in the mornings, and Janie and I went directly to the hospital after school and waited with Skeet while he rested, in the aftermath of the treatment. It was not unlike the way in which my mother would take chemotherapy just a few years ago before we had lost her, and it was not unlike chemotherapy in the havoc it wrecked on Skeet's little body. He was exhausted, then exhilarated, then wracked with muscular cramps that made him scream. They had him on a rigorous program of physical therapy on his "off" days. When, after three months of treatment, his muscular control not only returned but started to flourish, Skeet continued with the workouts on his own and only went into the hospital for tests and an overnight checkup once a month.

"He's Charles Atlas gone crazy," Janie said one night at the dinner table, a year later. Mom and Janie and I were alone. Skeet had already left for the YMCA to work out. He worked out every night, always leaving the three of us at the table. Skeet had no patience for table talk, and he left us that way almost every evening. Not rudely, not unhappily, but in a distracted and determined way that seemed completely uncalculated.

"I think I'll call him Charles," Janie said, "instead of Skeet."

"Oh, I hate that name," Mom said. "Skeet is a name for hoodlums. Or hillbillies. I don't know why you can't just call him by his real name."

Janie and I looked at each other, and Janie rolled her eyes.

"Ted," we both said aloud, and started laughing. Mom smiled reluctantly and soon was laughing along with us. We were ashamed of our smiles, but we all smiled nonetheless. Skeet had been such a constant preoccupation for all of us that we could afford to take refuge in the shoddy respite of a little smile.

Skeet's name came from the sputtering sounds he made early on in his illness, when the muscle spasms were just beginning to act up and were proceeding toward his tongue. His speech devolved into a drooling hiss as he struggled to control the delicate sounds — the S's and T's on the end of his tongue — and his tongue went flying off the handle. He sounded, said the neighborhood kids, like a mosquito. Skeet still went to school then, and the kids we had known all our lives, with whom we grew up and were familiar, became unfamiliar in the way they took to teasing Skeet, cruelly. They asked him questions. They were always asking him questions, any question they could think of, and many of them. They loved to hear him speak, and when he finally wouldn't answer, humiliated, they asked him more and more questions, again and again, until he lost all restraint and sputtered out, screamed out, and the words fell apart and they called him Skeeter.

But by the end of the year, when he was almost well again, he adopted the name all our classmates had called him and would only answer to Skeet. His speech restored, he relished the slow, methodical, precise pronunciation of his name. "My name is Skeet," he would say, and the way he said it seemed sinister.

One autumn evening after school, the air metallic and cool, we all went to play in the dead fall light that filled the outdoor lot of Jemson's Brick & Tile down the street. On a cement island in the middle of the shipping yard was the neighborhood's only really tall tree. We all liked to hang and swing from the tree, and that early evening our swinging brought down from the tree's highest branches a bird's nest. It went wheeling to the pavement. There were two eggs in it, and two chicks just recently hatched, one of which seemed to have been hurt in the fall. It was shiny and newborn, its nascent feathers wet and spiky like hair, and it was struggling, its beak opening and closing, one free wing flapping about.

"Look, look, it's hurt," somebody said.

"It's not hurt. It's just starting to come out of the shell."

"No, not that one! Look! The wounded one!"

Everyone peered at the broken little bird, and after a while I looked around for Janie and Skeet. Janie was at my side, but Skeet was walking away. He was walking straight to the brick piles. I stood up from the huddle and watched him go. He came walking back into the group with a single red brick held high over his head. It was a remarkable thing to see, given that months before he could barely raise his own arms. I realized what he intended to do, and I stepped back swiftly. In the pause that followed the other kids looked up and, understanding, all scattered backwards. We waited. Skeet said something and let the brick fall from on high. We all approached slowly and looked down at the devastation. Flecks of blood and a yellow ooze spread out from under the brick. The wounded bird's lone wing was still flapping feebly. A few of the children ran off crying. Another, bewildered, just said "cool." In time they all wandered home, slowly and silently, but Janie and I stood with Skeet for a long time, until the one bird finally stopped moving. On our way back, I asked Skeet what he had said before dropping the brick. He repeated it, but so softly we still couldn't hear him. "What?" Janie asked again. He said it once more, loudly and sternly and distinctly now — "I'm not the wounded one."

The last time I ever saw Skeet we had an awkward encounter. My graduation from law school was kind of a miracle in my mind, not because I didn't do well — I was an average student — but because I just never imagined it was possible. Janie knew how much it meant to me. It meant just as much to her, I think, and she knew how much it would have meant to our mother. So Janie arranged a celebration picnic, on that first Sunday in June after the graduation ceremony, in Seneca Park. We were going to have friends of mine, mostly new friends from the college and from law school, Janie would bring Hal, and when my new girlfriend asked if we wouldn't have any family, Janie looked at me and we both said "Skeet" out loud.

Skeet was sort of beyond the pale around all us pasty types. His sheer bulk, his thick arms and neck, and his new buzz cut set him apart almost as soon as he pulled onto the grass in his hatchback, his car stereo blaring, and stepped out to join us. We'd been sitting in the sun, on the grass, drinking wine and eating cheese, and Skeet's arrival put a stop to our drunken chatter. I didn't know how I would introduce him, but I was suddenly glad he was there. There, where my future was supposed to start, I had a taste of my indiscriminate and reprobate past, setting me apart like a brash tattoo from my new friends and classmates. But as the afternoon proceeded and I watched Skeet work so hard at simply existing among us, I was ashamed. My past was Skeet's present, and I was wrong to claim any share in it, especially now that I was poised to walk away.

Barbara and Stan invited him to sit, and they tried to get him to talk about his work, but when you've just been fired as bouncer at a bar for brutally beating a patron, and now you're collecting loans for Jimmie Lavender the loan shark, the talk does not go far and everyone sits empty-handed. Later Skeet dropped under the tree and began flirting with Barbara and Margaret, who were fixing the food. He sat with his hands behind his head and gnawed at a blade of grass, Marlon Brando–like. And when he gave me a wink, though Barbara saw it and got up to walk away in silent disgust, I winked back.

He was at ease in a way I almost couldn't believe, far less removed and far more present than I could ever remember. Later Skeet and I walked off together. If I had been glad to see him, he seemed more happy for me, and happy to have been invited at all. He made me feel as though Janie and I hadn't forgotten him — which we had — but that he had forgotten us, so busy and moving and new had his life become. He was overdoing it. There was something hollow and vulnerable in his enthusiasm. Still, he insisted — he had big deals going. Responsibilities. Work to do. That's what it was all about now. Never better, never happier. Moving up. "Making my own way now," he said, as though there were any other way.

"A lawyer," he said, shaking his head, after we'd come to a stop. We were standing at the edge of the public golf course. Skeet turned and beamed at me, seemingly more proud of me than I was of myself. He held his head back and looked at me steadily. Then his admiration transformed into a leer. "Whooda thunk it," he said, and in the space of those three words I felt no pride at all.

He poked me in the side and laughed. "You wouldn't bust me, would you?"

"I can't arrest people, Skeet," I said, brushing away his arm. "I'm a lawyer, not a cop."

"Yeah. But that's not what I asked. That's technical," he said. "I asked, would you if you could?"

"No."

"No?"

"No, Skeet."

"You'd stand by me, right? Keep me out of the can."

"Right."

His expression veered sharply from suspicion to anger to wild-eyed amusement. He looked at me hard one last time, then smiled. "The fuck you would," he said.

When I took the bar last month I was asked to take a pledge. A pledge to uphold the law. I know a little about the law. Now it's even fair to say I "practice" it. But that phrase — "a practitioner of the law" — has always had an odd ring to my ear. Like a practicioner of magic, an instructor in illusions, a dabbler in the dark arts. Thinking of it that way, though, maybe it's not so odd after all. Maybe it's perfectly appropriate. Maybe all I do is dabble in illusions — the illusion of the law. I'd never voice that suspicion to a single one of my peers (a key to success in this line of work, one learns early on, is playing dumb and holding your tongue at the right time). Skeet knew nothing of the law itself. But in his limited way, maybe Skeet knew the only laws worth knowing.

Last week, on Saturday morning, Janie and I met again at Skeet's apartment to clear out all that was left over. The few clothes, the dishes, the hot plate and filthy bedding, the archival implements and the butterfly boxes. The mattress and box spring we dumped in the alley. The huge desk and swivel chair, though Janie pegged them as potential "antiques," demanded more energy than we could summon. We left them for the owner to keep, along with an envelope containing a check for the balance of Skeet's rent. After sweeping the floors, we locked up and left. It was ten in the morning. We were finished.

On the sidewalk, I waited and talked to Janie while she finished another cigarette.

"How's Hal?" I asked. I don't claim to know or understand Hal very well, even though we went to high school together. But asking after him is one way I have of asking after Janie. Things were still rocky between the two of them, so I thought I'd ask.

"He's pathetic," Janie said casually. She exhaled and glanced at me to register my reaction. I gave none. "He says hello."

"Say hello back," I told her. Janie, I guess, has always held her husband up to the masculine standard that Skeet came to represent for her. Or for both of us, really. Skeet was vicious. He often frightened me. Everywhere he walked, he walked with a steely stone scowl. The arteries in his neck twitched, alive like vital organs, and the blood rushed into his cheeks when he was coolly furious, which was often. But he made us both feel safe.

Janie stopped going out with us eventually. She was dating some, and when she wasn't dating she had girlfriends to run with. Skeet and I went everywhere together, though. High school for us was probably no different than it is for anybody else. And in the parks and parking lots where we all gravitated at night, somebody was going to get fucked up. I had Skeet to make sure it wasn't me.

One late Friday night, in the bathroom of the White Castle downtown, where everyone went on late Friday nights, two guys from St. Xavier, primping at the mirror, mumbled something not nice about Skeet and me. I don't know what they said, but they said something — "faggots" maybe. I wasn't paying attention. But Skeet was. He was waiting for it. He was always waiting for it — the off-hand insult, the snotty look, the middle finger, the rich-boy snort, the bigoted slur. He'd learned to expect those signs and was attuned to them in a way that I never was. In me they provoked a shrug if I noticed them at all. To Skeet they really mattered; they were everything.

I looked over at Skeet, standing at the urinal next to me. His eyes were narrowed and directed, burning holes in the tiles ahead. Then he just stopped peeing and zipped up in mid-stride, left me at the urinal, walked up to them in two decisive steps and smashed both of them full in the face so hard — one, two, that quick — that neither of them — both big boys in varsity letter jackets of some sort — had a chance to start. The sound of one of their noses breaking nauseated me.

Skeet didn't stop. He pulled one back by the hair and threw his head into the Formica countertop, let him fall to the ground, and then kicked him. He picked up the other one, who was cowering in the corner holding his bloody face, and kneed him in the stomach. That one fell to the floor and vomited. Skeet waited for him to finish, held his head up by the hair, and threw a sidewise punch into his jaw that made it seem as if the lower half of his face had a life of its own. When we walked out of the bathroom, every head in the restaurant was turned toward the bathroom door and Skeet cut an easy swath through them. I followed.

He did it to pretty boys at country club parties we crashed out in the county, without provocation and for fun. He did it to jocks at basketball pep rallies, in the dark, behind field houses. He got into it with the black guys who strutted by our car in Central Park. He did it at dances to guys who were too drunk to dance and too drunk to know better.

The one that Skeet killed, Gordon Lang, had dated Janie twice. Only twice, but I guess that was enough for Gordon to feel he had an investment in her. Drunk and bitter, he called her a whore to my face, slurring the words grotesquely, and I suddenly hated him. We were standing in Brad Bowman's kitchen, in a lull during one of

Brad's backyard parties. I looked around for Skeet. He brought out the best behavior in everyone who came near him, and his arrival at my side usually brought a quick apology or a retreat. The only thing that could stop him was a word from me, and often that did no good. No one else was in the kitchen, though. No one had seen or heard a thing.

After a minute of threats and posturing, Gordon walked away laughing. When Skeet returned a moment later I told him. "Who? Which one?" Skeet asked. I pointed out Gordon as he walked toward the street, and thought nothing of it, though in fact I'd just killed him. I walked away myself, to get another beer and brood on my own. The next morning Gordon Lang was found, two blocks down, in the backyard of a neighboring house, his head bruised and submerged in a two-foot-deep goldfish pond. He had "drowned." Janie cried all the next day as though she had lost one of us, and maybe for that reason alone I never told her what Skeet had told me — that he'd done it, beat Gordon's head against the creekstone and held him under. Janie never knew. She never knew and I never told her. I could never protect Janie the way Skeet could. But still, I have ways of my own — not telling her things being principal among them.

"You're still coming for dinner?" she asked me, stepping off the curb and into her car. Bachelor that I am, I eat dinner at least twice a week with my sister and brother-in-law.

"What are we having?"

"What do we always have?"

"Something grilled?" In the summertime, with Hal cooking, we always have grilled something. Janie started the car, the door still hanging open.

"That's what we're having, then. Grilled something."

"Bring beer?" I asked.

"Please," she said. "And dope."

Just after Janie left, I drove a few blocks out of the way to see the old house we had all three grown up in. It's never been very far from the places I've lived — nothing's very far apart in this city. But it was the only time since leaving it that I've ever been seized by a sense of nostalgia for my home, so I drove over and sat and looked at it. You could not pick it out from a picture; it still looks like every other house on that street, and it stands apart only because of its number: 332 Clay.

I have three of Skeet's butterfly boxes in my possession now, Janie has the others, and I've since taken the time to look up their names in Peterson's *Field Guide to Insects*. What were at first extraordinary to my eye seem so no longer. The guidebook told me that. Most of the books I read these days do that — take the extraordinary out of everything. They were the most ordinary of butterflies, despite their exotic names, easy to catch in any suburban yard or public park. Easy to catch even along a city street. They were garden variety butterflies. Not an exceptional one among them.

"I think I know," Janie says. She is sitting on the couch across from me, cross-legged, her third scotch cupped in her hands like something delicate, alive. Hal is asleep on the couch next to her, wheezing gently as he has been for almost an hour. A big meal and marijuana always make Hal sleepy. But it makes Janie alive, fills her with chatter. We've been talking for some time.

"You think you know what?" I ask.

Janie, laying a fresh cigarette in the ashtray, throws her head against the couch and stares up at the ceiling. "The butterflies," she says. "Why Skeet had the butterflies." She says it in an almost mystical way, and I guess it's just stoned talk. But as she finishes speaking her whole demeanor slides rapidly into a quiet oblivion. She looks down into her glass, then up at me, and then back into her glass, and I suppose she has understood something.

"Why?" I ask, settling back into my chair.

"Well," she says, "it's just a guess." She looks up at me sheepishly. "It may seem kind of kooky."

"I'm sure it will," I tell her. "What is it?"

"Well, do you remember the picnic, your graduation picnic?"

"Yes," I said.

Janie looks back at her feet, and lifts up her drink for a swallow. "Never mind."

"No," I tell her. "Go on."

"It's ridiculous."

"Is it?" I say.

Janie looks at me suspiciously, a little frightened. She shakes her head, but says nothing more.

Many hours later we are sitting there still. Janie, asleep, is trundled hard against Hal's shoulder and I have turned off all the lights.

They are breathing softly, the two of them, and if they wake up I will pretend to be asleep myself, for Janie will think me crazy to not have gone home. I sit here watching them sleep because it's good to sit here, good to be among family, to rest in the same room among loved ones and listen to them breathe in the dark. It has been so long since we shared a room together. So I will stay here and sip my drink, and think about what Janie doesn't care to remember, about that day in the park, when Skeet killed a butterfly in the company of my friends.

The day was dwindling. Everyone was drunk. Skeet had some music he wanted to play for us, convinced it would pick everyone up. Nobody protested, though nobody wanted it. We were pretending to enjoy the quiet. And as he opened his hatchback to take out his tapes, an insect — I couldn't see what, a bee or a wasp or a moth — began wheeling around him furiously. Skeet leapt back, clearly alarmed. That's when I looked up and saw him. He stepped back, then forward, and reached deftly into the trunk. He pulled out a beach towel. Holding it high, he aimed at the insect, still whirling around him, and swung at it frantically, thrashing like a swordsman in a duel with the air. He pulled back for one more swing, then, appeased, let his arm drop limply to his side.

"Did you get it?" I asked, not really caring, but wanting to show some interest for Skeet's sake.

He looked at me absently, with that familiar trance born of violence, and then leaned over into the trunk. Between his thick thumb and forefinger he withdrew a wide-brimmed orange butterfly. It was a monarch — I know that now. He held it up for our inspection. Then he began to study it a little himself. He held its wings up to the light, examined its underbelly, turned it back and forth. Or maybe I'm giving him too much credit. Maybe he didn't study it at all. Whatever attention he gave it, though, suddenly ceased when Janie, who had been watching too, stood up and dusted the seat of her pants. "Is it dead?" she asked.

Skeet lifted it once more and looked at it. He shrugged, then let his hand, still pinching the butterfly, fall to his side.

"Did you kill it?" Margaret asked, looking up from the cutting board. She shook her head. "Oh no," she mourned halfheartedly. "You killed it."

Janie, a hint of humor in her voice, said, "Hey, Skeet murdered the butterfly."

"Oh yuck," said Barbara. "He murdered the butterfly."

"Murderer," Stan teased.

"Murderer," laughed Barbara, who went back to weaving her wildflowers.

"Murderer," they all canted in chorus and I joined in, thinking it funny too until Skeet's confused eyes hardened into discs at the sight of me and I remembered too late.

SCOTT WOLVEN

The Copper Kings

FROM *HandHeldCrime & Plots with Guns*

AFTER MY WIFE divorced me last August, I left upstate New York
and drove west. My plan was to live in Seattle, but money ran thin
in Moscow, Idaho. I got stuck there. I devoted a lot of time and attention to heavy drinking and found I was really good at being
drunk.

Functional alcoholism requires a delicate balance of solitude,
booze, and money, and I worked on making a science of it.
Keeping the money part of the equation flowing is always tough, so
I was relieved when Greg showed up on my doorstep early one Saturday morning, talking about getting paid cash for a day's work.

Greg was a big ex-football player of a man who lived with his girlfriend and her son in one of the trailers that surrounded my little
cinder block, one-bedroom shed. Greg sold insurance, he painted
houses, but his main sideline was bounty hunting and skip tracing.
He was licensed by the State of Idaho, so most of the things he did
were somewhere in the neighborhood of legal. My first week in
Moscow, Greg roped me into helping him catch a fugitive, then we
transported the bad guy to the U.S. Marshal's office in Spokane.
He had given me some of the reward money, which I promptly
drank. Every time I saw Greg outside near his girlfriend's trailer, I
waved to him and he waved back. We were partners, in an unofficial sort of way. I saw him walking up the gravel road that wound
through the trailers, and I opened the door before he knocked.

"Hi," I said. Greg wore a denim shirt, jeans, a tan hunting vest,
and black cowboy boots.

"Early to be stinko, isn't it?" he asked, pointing his chin at the
beer in my right hand.

"That's a myth," I answered. "Alcohol doesn't even begin to affect your brain before noon."

"Sure," Greg said. He nodded. "Feel like taking a ride? I've got a potential client and we could get paid cash for working today."

"How much?" I asked.

Greg shifted his weight and looked out over the trailers. "I think that depends," he said.

"Ballpark it for me," I said. I leaned against the door jamb and sipped my warm beer.

"It's a missing person job," he said. He turned to look straight at me. "Could be a couple hundred bucks in it, and probably no guns." He paused. "Well, maybe guns, but definitely no cops."

I nodded. "I'm in," I said. I tilted my head and drained my beer, tossing the empty can back into my apartment. "Can I use your pistol?" Greg owned a Beretta that I coveted.

Greg smiled. "Sure. Let's drive over."

We walked back down the gravel road together and got into Greg's ugly truck. It was an old Toyota four-door that he had rigged with a Plexiglas barrier, separating the front seats from the back, just like the cops. He started it up and we drove across town and out into farm country. Mile after mile of lentils and corn stretched toward the horizon.

"Nice country," I said. I was wearing my work clothes — a pair of jeans, work boots, blue T-shirt, and tan work jacket. There was a bottle of whiskey in my jacket pocket. I took it out and had a swallow. I looked at the fields passing by.

Greg leaned over, reached into the glove compartment, and handed me the Beretta. I stuck it in the right hand pocket of my work jacket. "Farms always scare me," Greg said. "Too much work." He watched the road straight ahead, oceans of grain fields passing by on both sides. "I like town," he said. "No matter how small a town."

We passed a long-abandoned church and made a right turn onto a dirt driveway. A hand-lettered sign at the side of the driveway read Ryan's Farm. I sucked back some whiskey. We drove down the dirt driveway and stopped in front of a white house surrounded by farm buildings. A sagging picnic table sat on the front lawn. An old man walked off the porch toward us. An older, white-haired woman stood on the porch steps, in front of the house. We both got out of the truck and I left the whiskey under the passenger's seat.

"Hi," said the old man. His voice was a ton of gravel coming off a truck. "I'm Harry Ryan." He wore farmer's denim coveralls and a green ball cap.

Greg nodded. "I'm Greg Newell and this is my partner, John Thorn," he said. I nodded and lifted my right hand in a half-wave.

"Sam Haag said you were a good man for this job. Sam said you were tough." Harry Ryan looked at Greg, then at me. "I need somebody tough," he said.

"We're tough," Greg said.

Harry Ryan came closer. "I smell booze," he said.

"I spilled some on my boots last night, out playing pool," I lied.

Harry Ryan came a step closer. "Smells like you spilled it in your mouth first thing this morning," he said.

"It helps me be tough," I said.

Harry Ryan nodded.

"His wife divorced him," Greg said.

Harry Ryan put his hands in his pockets. "I understand," he said. He walked over to the picnic table and sat down. Greg and I followed and stood on the other side of the table. Harry Ryan looked up at us.

"Well," he said, "I want you to find my son." He held out an envelope. "He went up into the Panhandle to get a job and sent us some letters, like this one. But the letters stopped three weeks ago and I haven't heard from him." He handed the envelope to Greg and Greg opened it, taking the letter out. He held it over near me, so I could read it, too. It was written in a bad scrawl.

"Dad — here's nine hundred dollars and more is coming. Everything is fine. I'm working up north, mining, working for the copper kings and the pay is good. I'm working hard and will see you and mom soon. Love Mike."

"I want you to find him," Harry Ryan said. "If you find him, I'll give you five hundred dollars." The older, white-haired woman slowly turned and walked up the porch steps, back into the farmhouse. The screen door closed with a smack against its wood casing. Harry Ryan went on, at a low volume. "Mike was in some kind of small trouble in Boise that I didn't even know about. Some probation officer and a state cop stopped by here yesterday, but they wouldn't tell me anything. Just said they were looking for Mike." Harry Ryan put a photograph on the picnic table. "That's Mike," he said. The picture showed a smiling young man next to a brand-new pickup truck. In the back of the pickup truck was a Doberman. Greg picked up the picture.

"Is that his dog?" Greg asked.

"That's Max," Harry said. "Mike trained him and never went anywhere without him."

"Was Max a vicious dog?" Greg asked.

Harry smiled. "He'd take your leg off. Max was better than a gun, as far as I was concerned." He looked up into the giant blue sky and then out over the fields. He stood up and handed Greg some money. "That's two hundred fifty. You get the rest when the job is done." Harry Ryan started to walk slowly back toward his house.

"Fine," Greg said. He nodded and I nodded, too. "That's fine." He handed me the picture and we both got back into the truck. Harry Ryan never turned around, just walked up the porch steps and into the farmhouse. I took a slug of whiskey and watched the same fields roll by as Greg drove back to town.

We drove through town and Greg pulled over at a phone booth outside a gas station. I watched him making call after call, laughing and shaking his head in the little booth. Then he came back to the truck.

"Who'd you call?" I asked.

Greg looked at me and narrowed his eyes. "It pays to cultivate reliable underworld contacts," he said.

"Who'd you call?" I asked.

"Smitty and my ex-girlfriend," he said. Smitty was an old biker friend of Greg's who owned a bar just outside Bonner's Ferry, way up north in the Panhandle. I didn't know the ex-girlfriend. "Smitty says he knows a reopened copper mine in the hills, might be just what we want. He's going to ask around and get us directions. But we need cover."

"What?" I said.

"Cover," Greg said. "A disguise, so we can get in the place." Greg turned around in the gas station parking lot and doubled back into town. He pulled off onto a side street and stopped in front of a red house. "Just a minute," he said. A woman came out onto the front porch and from the excited way she looked at Greg, she appeared ready to move off the ex-girlfriend list, back into the active rotation. She and Greg went inside and I had a couple shots of booze. I wished for a cup of coffee to kind of even me out, but all I had was the whiskey. So I took two more swallows, just to stay steady and tough.

The minute turned out to be three quarters of an hour and finally, Greg came back down the front steps. Walking next to him was the biggest dog I've ever seen on a leash. The dog was black and tan, about the size of a small pony. He let the dog in the back seat and the whole truck rocked. Greg got in and started to drive.

"What the hell's that?" I asked.

"Mister Lucky," Greg said. "He's our cover. He'll get us in." Mister Lucky's head slammed into the Plexiglas barrier as we hit a pothole. He didn't even seem to notice it. His head was bigger than a basketball.

"What breed is he?" I asked.

"Neapolitan mastiff," Greg said. "Real killers." Mister Lucky lay down across the back seat. He looked cramped and slightly mad.

"How much does he weigh?" I asked.

"I don't know," said Greg. "Maybe two thirty, two forty. A real killer."

We drove north toward Bonner's Ferry. I looked out the window the whole way, but I didn't see anyone who looked like Mike Ryan. The Rockies were on our right and they seemed to grow as we headed north into them. I think the whiskey made me fall asleep for part of the ride.

We stopped at Smitty's. There were two motorcycles and a pickup truck outside in the dirt parking lot. Greg and I both got out and I followed him inside. It was a dark bar, with a jukebox, a pool table, and not much else. Mounted over the bar was a full-sized log, split down the middle. Somebody had used a wood-burning set to carve the words IN GOD WE TRUST AND YOU AIN'T GOD. There were three or four regulars inside. They must have been regulars, because even the most simple-minded folk wouldn't wander into Smitty's. For all the country up the Idaho Panhandle, nobody wandered. It was all very deliberate. There were places you weren't supposed to go, sort of a widely held secret. We were headed for one of those places. Smitty talked in low tones with Greg, gave me a half-wave, and we walked back out to the truck. It was mid-afternoon at this point. We got back in the truck. Mister Lucky didn't move.

"Did Smitty help out?" I asked.

"Sure," Greg said. "Here's where you earn the money." He took another pistol, a .45 Colt Combat Commander, out of the glove compartment and slid it under his left leg. "Just in case," he said. I reached into my jacket pocket and clicked the safety off the Beretta. I took my last slug of booze and put the bottle on the floor. We were ready.

Greg drove up into the mountains for forty minutes, following winding roads and occasionally cutting off one onto another. My ears popped as we went up. Eventually, we drove up about a mile of dirt road.

"I think this is it," Greg said.

Ahead of us, there was an iron gate and a small shack. A man was sitting on the gate. A rifle was propped up against the shack. We pulled up to the gate. There was a small sign that read COP-PER KINGS MINING on the shack. The man got off the gate and walked over to the shack. He called to us as he picked up the rifle.

"Mine's closed for the day, boys," he said. He walked toward us, cradling the rifle in his arms. "Mine's closed and we aren't hiring." He looked into the truck at Mister Lucky, who stood up and looked back. "Nice pup," he said.

Greg leaned out his truck window and held up two twenties. "Look at that," he said. "These are some of those new twenties." He looked closely at the bills. "Much bigger picture of Jackson," he said.

The man who was pretending to be a legitimate guard came over. He took the two twenties out of Greg's hand.

Greg nodded. "Aren't those new bills?" Greg asked.

"It's hard to tell in this light," the man who was a guard said.

"Well, you keep them for me and find out," Greg said. "I understand you might have to spend them to do it, but you be sure to find out." He gave the man who was a guard but didn't want us to think he was a guard a friendly fake smile. The man gave the same smile back to him. The man walked over to the shack and the gate went up. Greg pulled up.

"Go on in and tell Charlie you've got a dog on for tonight," the man who was guarding something that wasn't a copper mine said.

"How will I know it's Charlie?" Greg asked.

"He's the biggest biker you've ever seen," the man said. "And he's got the biggest gun you've ever seen too." Then he waved us through.

Greg drove in. There were some abandoned mining buildings, some industrial equipment and covered conveyors. A couple of pickup trucks were parked next to the buildings. There was no mining going on here.

"Smell that?" Greg asked. I nodded. It was a strange mixture of gasoline and ether. "Copper mine my ass," Greg said. "This is the biggest crystal meth plant in the world." I reached down, got the whiskey bottle, and took a sip. Ahead of us was a crowd of men, mostly lounging around on the backs of pickup trucks, talking and drinking beer. Most of them had some type of dog, ranging from German shepherds to Huskies. Once in a while, a dog barked. A huge biker, Charlie I assumed, sat behind a table in front of an entrance to a mine shaft. We heard the small roar of a crowd coming from inside the shaft, along with the sounds of dogs. Greg parked the truck and got out with Mister Lucky on the leash. "You take the gun," he said quietly. We walked up to the table. Mister Lucky dwarfed all the other dogs we saw. We stepped up to Charlie.

"You want to fight that dog tonight?" Charlie asked. He was huge, even sitting down. He must have weighed more than three hundred and fifty pounds. On the table in front of him sat the wickedest-looking gun I'd ever seen. It was a nickel-plated shotgun, short-barreled, but with a cylindrical magazine attached at the butt end. Charlie noticed my gaze. "That's a Streetsweeper. Nineteen shots as fast as I can pull the trigger, one in the chamber, eighteen in the clip." He looked at me. "Evens things up pretty fast, know what I mean?"

"I know what you mean," I answered.

He turned back to Greg and Mister Lucky. "So how about it?" he said.

Greg shook his head. "No," Greg said. "We just used him to get through the gate."

Charlie's face did something that it probably considered a smile. "Got to get better help around here." He spit into the dust and looked up at Greg. "If you're a cop, this is your grave."

"Do I look like a cop?" Greg said.

Charlie shrugged. "They look different nowadays," he said.

"Used to be easy — anyone with shiny shoes and a short haircut. But now —" He paused. "Well, it's not so easy."

"Sure," Greg allowed. "I'm just looking for somebody." He took the picture of Mike Ryan out and put it on the table in front of Charlie. The terrible sounds of dogs fighting came from inside the mineshaft, echoing out over the buildings. "Ever seen him?" Greg asked.

Charlie was quiet and then he coughed. "That kid's gone," he said. "Forever."

"How did it happen?" Greg asked.

"He stopped breathing, that's how it happened. Like it always happens." He looked at Greg. "Pure accident," he said. "Lots of accidents in this life."

"Right," Greg said. Lightning moved slower than Greg in that next instant, and I was the thunder only a second behind. He had Charlie down on the ground, his right foot on Charlie's throat and Mister Lucky's mouth less than an inch from Charlie's right eye. I had the Streetsweeper, safety off, and was keeping an eye on the men behind us. "Whisper it to me," Greg said to Charlie. "Tell me about the accident. And don't do anything to disturb the dog. He's edgy." A low growl, like a distant airplane engine, was coming from Mister Lucky. Charlie whispered.

"The kid was on probation in Boise. He worked up here for three weeks, transporting meth and winning with his dog. Then we caught him wearing a wire." Charlie's breathing was shallow. Greg increased the pressure of his foot. Charlie croaked it out. "We put him in with the dogs."

Greg took his foot off. Mister Lucky stayed ready until Greg tugged on the leash. The crowd of men behind us was quiet. Charlie got up slowly.

"No hard feelings," Greg said. "I had to know."

Charlie rubbed his Adam's apple. "Your nights are going to be very dark and scary," he said. He gave Greg a hard stare. I turned around with the Streetsweeper and my tough kicked in.

"You drugged-out freak!" I shouted. "I've got about ten of my buddies from 'Nam within an hour of here. You want me to call in a hail storm from hell?" I was shaking, the Streetsweeper less than an inch from Charlie's nose. "They'll feed you your own ass," I said. "You want some?" I stared at him. "Do you want some!" The trigger pressed against my finger and the whiskey tough wanted to squeeze it.

Charlie shook his head. He watched us as we walked back to the truck and pulled away. We waved to the man at the gate as we passed through. He'd probably be dead by morning for letting us in. He waved back.

The sun started to set as we drove back to Moscow. Greg cleared his throat as we reached the outskirts of town.

"Do you have buddies that were in Vietnam?" he asked.

"No," I said.

"You even fooled me," Greg said.

We pulled into Harry Ryan's driveway and Harry Ryan came out of the farmhouse. We got out of the truck. The older white-haired woman was sitting on the porch steps. Harry, Greg, and I walked over by the lentil field. It seemed to stretch out forever. Harry had his back to us, looking at the field.

"How's my boy?" he said. "Did you find him?"

Greg looked at the ground and then at Harry Ryan's back. He looked up at the sunset blue sky. "He's working," Greg said. As soon as Greg spoke, Harry Ryan started to gently cry. "He's working up north for the copper kings, just like he wrote you," Greg said.

Harry Ryan nodded. I could hear him crying as he spoke. "Lie to me again," he said. "Lie to me, tell me the best one you've got." He was sobbing. "The money's on the picnic table," he said, turning around. Harry Ryan started to walk toward his farmhouse. When I turned to look, the old woman on the porch was gone. I picked up the money as we walked back to Greg's ugly truck and drove away.

Contributors' Notes

Other Distinguished Stories of 2001

Contributors' Notes

John Biguenet has published fiction in such journals as *Book, Esquire, Granta, Playboy, Story,* and *Zoetrope,* where "It Is Raining in Bejucal" appeared. *Oyster,* his first novel, was published earlier this year, and his first collection of stories, *The Torturer's Apprentice,* was widely praised. He has published three books on translation and served two terms as president of the American Literary Translators Association. The winner of an O. Henry Award for short fiction, he currently holds the Robert Hunter Distinguished Professorship at Loyola University in New Orleans.

• *Zoetrope* commissioned me to write a 10,000-word story based on an idea by Francis Ford Coppola: A man named José Antonio witnesses, at age five, the murder of his mother by his father; fifty years later, he wins a lottery and uses the prize to track down his father. Mr. Coppola was particularly interested in whether the money would lead to justice.

Though I chafed a bit at first under the restraints of the commission, the sensitive and perceptive responses to my work by Adrienne Brodeur and the other talented editors at *Zoetrope* encouraged me through five drafts. I worked with them on "It Is Raining in Bejucal" for nearly a year and learned yet again that a published piece of fiction is a collaborative work of art.

Michael Connelly is the author of eleven published novels and one short story. His novels included the Harry Bosch series as well as *The Poet, Blood Work,* and *Void Moon.* A former journalist who specialized in crime, he was the recipient of numerous journalism awards before he realized they meant nothing and he devoted himself full-time to writing fiction. He spends most of his time in California and Florida.

• I'm not a practitioner of the short story. For years I fended off inquiries, requests, and demands for a short story. I simply liked the long form better and arrogantly felt small stories were made from small ideas. I figured I was a big-idea man. Of course, I was wrong. But I did not realize this until Otto Penzler cornered me and made me an offer I couldn't refuse. A short story about baseball. I nodded. Yeah, I could try that. Nothing is as big and as small at the same time as baseball. I had never played the game on any organized level, but once I moved to Los Angeles I fell in love with watching the Dodgers. I worked out many a plot point between innings at Dodger Stadium. For me it is a place of Zen in a sea of chaos. The seminal moment in modern Dodger history was Kirk Gibson's home run in the '88 series. A moment of wonderful joy before the dark times that followed. I wasn't there. I couldn't afford it. I actually saw it while standing on a sidewalk on Melrose Avenue and watching with a crowd through a doorway into a sushi bar. After the ball sailed over the wall and the game belonged to the Dodgers, the sidewalk crowd exploded, people running every which way and into the street to tell perfect strangers the news. I was one of them. It seemed like nothing could be wrong in the city that night.

Thomas H. Cook is the author of sixteen novels and two works of nonfiction. He has been nominated for the Edgar Allan Poe Award three times in three different categories; his novel *The Chatham School Affair* won for Best Novel in 1996. He has also been nominated for the Hammett Prize, as well as the Macavity Award. His short story "Fatherhood" won the Herodotus Prize and was selected for *The Best American Mystery Stories 1999*, edited by Ed McBain.

▪ I wrote my first short story while working as a contributing editor and book critic for *Atlantic Monthly*. I'd never attempted such a thing before but was pleasantly surprised to discover that writing a short story gave me the same feeling of satisfaction as reading one. As a writer, I particularly liked that the payoff, that final moment toward which you have been moving all along, came much sooner in a short story than in a novel, and, with it, the sense of creative completion.

As a reader, I find that a short story is like a brief encounter, intense and highly charged, yet capable of lingering in the heart for a long, long time. In "The Fix" I strove for that intensity and resonance by using boxing, and particularly the battered nobility of a long-maligned fighter, to suggest the daily "fixes" that beckon us, the erosion of character that inevitably accompanies our acceptance of them, and finally the dreadful, dawning truth that corruption may know every pleasure save that of self-respect.

Sean Doolittle's debut novel, *Dirt,* a crime thriller set in and around a crooked Los Angeles funeral home, was selected as one of the 100 Best

Books of 2001 by the editors of Amazon.com. Doolittle lives in Omaha, Nebraska, with his wife, Jessica, and daughter, Kate. He is working on his next novel and any short stories that tug on his sleeve.

▪ I imagine that most people, at one time or another, have probably experienced some version of the same gut-level fear: the fear of losing ability. I've heard writers say that they'll never live long enough to write all the ideas they have floating around in their heads. Personally, I've never suffered from this affliction. I tend to be the type who wonders, after putting each idea to paper, if I'll ever have another one. It wasn't until after I finished "Summa Mathematica" that I began to suspect that this particular anxiety doesn't really have all that much to do with writing.

As for this story: I was remodeling our basement (another story), trying to figure board feet or something, when I realized it had been so long since I'd done any math beyond using a high-powered PC to balance the checkbook that I had actually forgotten most of the multiplication tables I'd memorized in grade school. This bugged me a little in principle, but not that much overall. I never knew 'em all that well anyway, and I always hated math. But I remember thinking something like, "If you held a gun to my head, I couldn't times these fractions." Stephen Fielder wasn't far behind that thought.

A former reporter and restaurant critic, **Michael Downs** learned to write fiction at the University of Arkansas's graduate programs in creative writing, where he was a Truman Capote Fellow. He has published short stories in half a dozen literary reviews, including the *Georgia Review,* the *Michigan Quarterly Review,* and *Willow Springs.* This is the second of his stories to appear in *The Best American Mystery Stories* series; "Prison Food" appeared in the 2001 edition. Downs lives and writes in Montana, where he is at work on two books, both set in his hometown of Hartford, Connecticut. One is a collection of short stories; the other is a book of nonfiction, supported by a grant from The Freedom Forum.

▪ One snowy Easter morning when I was a boy of eleven or twelve, my family awoke to find police cars clogging our dead-end street. It was not long before we learned that our neighbor had killed his wife and their two dogs. I had liked the neighbors, and I had especially liked their dogs. This was when we lived in a small town in Vermont. Later in the afternoon that Easter Sunday, a reporter from the *Rutland Herald* rang our doorbell, but my father declined to say anything about our neighbors out of what I took to be a sense of propriety. Years later I became a reporter, and whenever I got frustrated that people wouldn't talk to me, I tried to remember my father's perspective. That dual vision — and, in general, the complicated needs of any reporter and any witness (in specific, my reporter and

Dudek) — infuses "Man Kills Wife, Two Dogs." I first tried to set the story in Vermont, mimicking my childhood experience, but as is often the case, fact could not accommodate fiction. Once I moved the story to Hartford and made Dudek my character (instead of a man like my father), imagination and story rocked loose. In truth, I know no more of what happened on that morning of my boyhood than Dudek knows about the murders in his landlord's apartment.

Brendan DuBois is a lifelong resident of New Hampshire, where he received his B.A. in English from the University of New Hampshire. A former newspaper reporter, he has been writing fiction for nearly twenty years and still lives in his native state with his wife, Mona. He is the author of the Lewis Cole mystery series — *Dead Sand, Black Tide, Shattered Shell,* and *Killer Waves* — and his fourth novel, *Resurrection Day,* a look at what might have happened had the Cuban Missile Crisis erupted into World War III, received the Sidewise Award in 2000 for Best Alternative History Novel. He is currently working on two new novels and has had more than sixty short stories published in *Playboy, Mary Higgins Clark Magazine, Ellery Queen's Mystery Magazine,* and *Alfred Hitchcock's Mystery Magazine.*

His short stories have been extensively anthologized in the United States and abroad. He has twice received the Shamus Award from the Private Eye Writers of America for Best Mystery Short Story of the year, and he has been nominated for an Edgar Award by the Mystery Writers of America for his short fiction three times. Visit his Web site at www.Brendan-DuBois.com.

▪ My short story "A Family Game" was written for an original collection of short fiction revolving around the game of baseball called *Murderers' Row.* Knowing that many of the other authors for this anthology would be submitting stories concerning major league play, I decided to take a look at how all baseball players get their start: by playing in youth leagues in their hometowns.

But although the play on the field in these leagues is that of children being introduced into what really is a family game, the tensions, pressures, and yes, even violence, off the field can sometimes mirror the worst aspects of the major leagues. During these times when there are often news stories about "rink rage" or "stadium rage," where angry parents get into fights with each other or referees or umpires, I was curious how someone with a criminal past — desperate to keep this past secret — might react when confronted by an angry parent intent on doing harm.

All too often the real cases of parental violence at sporting events end up in court or in the hospital. In "A Family Game," I'd like to think I came up with an original and satisfying story, where not only a bully gets his due, but a special family is protected and kept safe by a loving parent.

David Edgerley Gates grew up in Cambridge, Massachusetts. His short fiction has appeared in *Alfred Hitchcock's Mystery Magazine, A Matter of Crime,* and *Story.* He was a 1998 Shamus nominee for "Sidewinder," and another of his stories, "Compass Rose," was selected for *The Best American Mystery Stories 2000.*

He lives in Santa Fe.

- A lot of my stories are drawn from historical incident, or some contemporary oddity that floats around in my head until I can make use of it, but "The Blue Mirror" is based more nearly on my own experience. Stanley Kosciusko is modeled on a real guy I worked in a garage with, years ago, who did in fact survive fifty missions as a tail gunner in Liberators, flying against the Germans, only to later die of cancer. Much of the other detail in the story, like the biker bar and the locale of the showdown, is real enough, too, but the methamphetamine turf war is generic, not specific.

The other thing about "The Blue Mirror" is that I didn't spend a lot of time connecting the dots. I figured the private dick in the story ought to be at least as sharp as the reader, and if the reader could put it together, why wouldn't Jack?

The late Cathleen Jordan bought this story for *Alfred Hitchcock.* Cathleen was a terrific person, and a canny and sympathetic editor. She had an eye for the exact detail and an ear for clunkers. Her taste was elastic, not arbitrary, and she did me many kindnesses. I'm far from being the only one who'll miss her. To use Norman Mailer's apposite phrase, Cathleen added a room to the house.

Joe Gores lived for a year in Tahiti and three years in Kenya, spent two years at the Pentagon writing biographies of army generals, and for twelve years was a P.I. in San Francisco. He is a past president of Mystery Writers of America and has won three Edgars. His novel *Hammett,* filmed by Francis Ford Coppola, won Japan's first "Maltese Falcon" award in 1986. Other work includes scores of short stories and articles, three collections of his short fiction, and a massive fact book, *Marine Salvage.* He has also written ten screenplays, two TV longforms, and teleplays for most of the episodic TV mystery shows of the 1970s and 1980s, including *Columbo; Kojak; Magnum, P.I.; Mike Hammer;* and *Remington Steele.*

He and his wife, Dori, live near San Francisco and travel whenever they can get away.

- "Inscrutable" started with a parrot. My wife, Dori, has a friend named Carol Colucci who has three pet parrots. One of them is named Knuckles. The first time I heard this, I exclaimed, "Knuckles Colucci? He just has to be a Mafia hitman out of Detroit!" But at the time I was working on *Cases,* a novel fictionalizing my early years as a detective in San Francisco in the 1950s, and Knuckles sort of slid from my mind.

Fast-forward to 2000. My editor at Mysterious Press, Bill Malloy, asked me to contribute an original story to a projected twenty-fifth anniversary Mysterious Press anthology. Then Bill added the kicker. He wanted the DKA crew to appear in the story. By then I was working on the most recent DKA File Novel, *Cons, Scams & Grifts,* and all my DKA energies were focused on that. But I said I would try to come up with something.

A January night, pouring rain. Waiting in my 4-Runner for Dori with nothing to read. Suddenly, bada-bing, bada-bang, bada-boom, as they like to say on *The Sopranos,* three short stories leaped into my mind. One was "Summer Fog," which appeared in another 2001 anthology, *Flesh and Blood.* The second was a golf story I'm working on right now. The third was "Inscrutable." Ballard, Heslip, Giselle, and O.B. get involved in saving a Chinese grocer being threatened by . . . who else? A Mafia hitman out of Detroit named Knuckles Colucci!

I hope you have as much fun pecking all of the bird references out of "Inscrutable" as I had writing them in.

James Grady's first novel, *Six Days of the Condor,* became a Robert Redford movie picked by the *Washington Post* as one of the ten most defining films of the twentieth century. Grady has published a dozen other novels across genre lines, and three of his previous short stories have received national awards, including an Edgar nomination from the Mystery Writers of America. In 2001, the Cognac (France) International Film Noir Festival gave Grady's collective prose work its highest "master of noir fiction" award. Grady has also been an investigative reporter, as well as a script writer for both TV and feature films. He and his family live in Silver Spring, Maryland.

• Growing up in Shelby, Montana, I always felt embarrassed by my hometown's bizarre claim to fame: its nearly suicidal self-promotional sponsoring of a heavyweight championship boxing match, a world event crash-landed in the middle of the great American nowhere. I always wanted to be a writer, but swore I would never — *never!* — touch that Dempsey-Gibbons debacle.

Then inspiration ran smack into absolutism, and the resulting big bang blasted characters and a twist of history out of the most savage and sentimental sections of my soul. While the mechanics of the resulting story are fiction, its heart is as true a piece of work as I've ever done.

Clark Howard grew up on the lower west side of Chicago, a ward of the county and habitual runaway who eventually was sent to a state reformatory for being, he recalls, "recalcitrant." He later served in combat in the Korean War as a member of the Marine Corps and began writing shortly thereafter. Having written 120-plus short stories, 16 novels, 5 true-crime books, and 2 short story collections, he is an eight-time Mystery Writers of America Edgar nominee in the short story and true-crime categories, and winner of an Edgar for best short story. He is also a five-time winner of the Ellery Queen Magazine Readers Award and has been nominated for the Shamus Award, for the Derringer Award, and twice for the Western Writers of America's Spur Award.

▪ "The Cobalt Blues," like much of my work, is drawn from my early memories of the streets of Chicago and the scores of colorful people who passed through my young life there. The character of Lewis is based on an old guy I knew when I was an after-school runner picking up next-day bets for an illegal bookie (in the days before off-track betting). This old guy's whole life was lived by the starter's bell at racetracks all over the country. Potts was based on a man I served with in the Marine Corps. He was a real hard-luck guy. After he was killed, another Marine said, "What's the difference? With his luck, if he'd made it back, he probably would've got cancer or something anyways."

I like to write stories about life's losers who sometimes become winners just once before the end. Like the men do in "The Cobalt Blues."

Stuart M. Kaminsky was born, raised, and grew damned cold in the winters of Chicago. He has, for the past dozen years, lived in the warmth of Sarasota, Florida, where he writes novels, short stories, movies, teleplays, comic books, and poetry, and plays softball three days a week when he isn't on the road. Winner of the MWA Edgar for Best Novel in 1989, he has been nominated for six Edgars in three categories. His series characters include 1940s private eye Toby Peters, Russian policeman Porfiry Rostnikov, Chicago policeman Abe Lieberman, and Sarasota process server Lew Fonesca. He has also written two original Rockford Files novels. His screen credits include *Once upon a Time in America, Enemy Territory,* and *Hidden Fears.* His teleplay *Immune to Murder* was shown on A&E's Nero Wolfe Mysteries.

▪ "Sometimes Something Goes Wrong" was a first for me, an experiment. I wanted to see how quickly I could make a story move, a story in which I had no idea of what was going to happen, a story in which I started with two men in a parking lot and wrote in furious fascination to find out what they were doing there and what would happen to them. I always know who my characters are and what will happen in my novels and short stories. In this case, I had no idea and I had a great time. I plan to do it again and soon."

Joe R. Lansdale was born in Gladewater, Texas, on October 28, 1951. He left college when he decided his main interest was writing, and he worked a variety of jobs, including farming and janitorial work, while writing in his spare time. He became a full-time writer in 1981, producing more than two hundred short stories, articles, and essays, as well as more than twenty novels and several short story collections.

He is well known for his series of crime/suspense adventures featuring Hap Collins and Leonard Fine. *Mucho Mojo,* a New York Times Notable Book, has been scripted for film by Oscar winner Ted Tally.

A member of the Texas Institute of Letters, he has won numerous awards, including an Edgar for *The Bottoms,* six Bram Stokers, and the Critic's Choice Award.

▪ In my early twenties my wife and I owned a mule. I used the mule for plowing. We bought some land with a nice pond and plenty of grass, but we didn't move there. We planned to, but never made it. We ended up selling the land and moving somewhere else.

But when we thought we were going to move there, we moved our mule to our land while we made plans. I went over every day to feed it, pet it, trim its hooves, make sure it was okay.

One day it was gone.

Mule rustlers.

Really.

Many years later, I got to thinking about that, the fate of my old stolen mule. About the same time I was feeling nostalgic, I came across an article about criminals who cruised neighborhoods looking for things to steal.

That's when I came up with my boys here. And their plan to steal a mule. I decided to make them like some old boys I'd known while growing up. Not exactly nuclear scientists. Not exactly sanitation engineers, either. More like crash test dummies.

Guys who wanted quick money, and though not exactly evil, not exactly a boon to the universe either. This welded to other things I had read, experienced, heard about. This story resulted.

Keep your mules locked up.

Edgar and Emmy-winning novelist **Michael Malone,** critically acclaimed as one of the country's finest novelists, has also written books of fiction and nonfiction, essays, reviews, short stories, and television screenplays. Often compared to Dickens for his comic vision and the breadth of his fictional landscape, over the past quarter-century he has introduced readers to a gallery of memorable Southern characters in such novels as *Handling Sin, Dingley Falls,* and *Foolscap,* as well as in the internationally praised mystery trilogy *Uncivil Seasons, Times Witness,* and *First Lady,* narrated by wisecracking Southern police chief Cuddy R. Mangum and his aristocratic homicide detective Justin Savile V.

Educated at the University of North Carolina and at Harvard, Malone has taught at Yale, at the University of Pennsylvania, and at Swarthmore.

Among his prizes are the Edgar, the O. Henry, the Writers Guild Award, and the Emmy.

After a long (perhaps too long) exile in television, he has returned to the novel and to his native South. He now lives in Hillsborough, North Carolina, with his wife, chair of the English department at Duke University.

- "Maniac Loose" first appeared in the anthology *Confederacy of Crime*. Its sardonic heroine, Lucy, who could give even the most ruthless a lesson in how to get away with murder, is one of the twelve Southern women of my new short story collection, *Red Clay, Blue Cadillac*.

Fred Melton lives in Wenatchee, Washington, with his wife, Elizabeth, and their two sons, Matthew and Andrew. He is a full-time dentist whose writing has been published in *Talking River Review, California Quarterly, Black Canyon Quarterly*, as well as other publications, and is to appear in the forthcoming anthology *Scent of Cedar*. His story "Counting" has also earned a 2001 Pushcart Prize nomination. Melton's poetry and prose have been honored in the following contests: Pacific Northwest Writers Association (short stories 1996, 1997, and 1998), Seattle Writers Association Writers in Performance (1998–2001), and Washington Poets Association (2000).

Melton has lived in Spain, taken a fling at American bull riding, is fluent in Spanish, and holds a second-degree black belt in karate. He also holds a fly rod in his hand as much as possible.

- One October day, I took our younger son, Andrew, deer hunting in eastern Washington. While walking the windswept bluffs overlooking the Palouse River, we met a middle-aged wheat farmer with a stocky build and dust-caked hair. Although initially irritated by our presence, he eventually granted us permission to hunt on his property — provided we stayed clear of his grain silos. When I later learned of this farmer's lifelong bachelorhood, he became the seed for "Counting."

As I wrote about Uncle Keven, I began to see a man for whom justice and revenge were convictions connected at a gut level. I also discovered a man to whom fate refused to deal a fair hand; yet, he remained fiercely loyal to the thing that mattered most to him — family.

Born in New York, raised on a chicken farm in New Jersey, **Annette Meyers** came running back to Manhattan as soon as she could. Using her long history on both Broadway and Wall Street, she wrote *The Big Killing*, the first of seven mysteries featuring Wall Street headhunters Xenia Smith and former dancer Leslie Wetzon. The eighth is near completion. Her novel *Free Love*, set in Greenwich Village in 1920, introduced poet Olivia Brown and her bohemian friends. *Murder Me Now* followed in 2001.

With her husband, Martin Meyers, using the pseudonym Maan Meyers, she has written six historical mysteries in the Dutchman series, set in seventeenth-, eighteenth-, and nineteenth-century New York. In February 2001, Meyers and her husband were the subjects of a feature on their life and work for CBS-TV's *Sunday Morning*.

She is a past president of Sisters in Crime and current secretary of the International Association of Crime Writers, North America.

• Although I keep a file of short story ideas, I often plunder from my life experience. The character of Olivia Brown first appeared in a short story, "The House on Bedford Street," and came from my youthful determination to be a writer and my admiration for Edna St. Vincent Millay.

I wrote "You Don't Know Me" in response to an invitation to submit an erotic noir story for the anthology *Flesh and Blood*. Fuhgeddaboudit. Erotic noir is not my style. But wait, wasn't I a writer, and shouldn't the writer continue to surprise the writer?

"You Don't Know Me" came from my file of ideas. It had been on the edge of my consciousness for years and came surging out as if it were waiting to be told. This was the first time I'd written from a male point of view. It had to be that way, because it was his story.

Joyce Carol Oates is the author of a number of works of suspense and psychological horror, including most recently the novella *Beasts* and, under the pseudonym Rosamond Smith, the novels *The Barrens, Starr Bright Will Be with You Soon,* and *Double Delight.* Her suspense and crime fiction has appeared in *Ellery Queen's Mystery Magazine* and in a number of anthologies, including *The Best American Mystery Stories of the Century.* She lives in New Jersey and is professor of humanities at Princeton.

• "The High School Sweetheart" was inspired by my uneasy sense that those of us who write, and perhaps even those of us who read, crime fiction are in some ambiguous way moral accomplices to evil. To celebrate the master crime writer is to celebrate the artful appropriation of violence that, in "reality," would appall and terrify us. Yet, such actions are redeemed through "art." (Or are they?)

Robert B. Parker lives in Cambridge with his wife, Joan. They have two sons, David, a choreographer, and Daniel, an actor. Parker is the author of more than forty novels and two short stories, the second of which is "Harlem Nocturne." A novel based on "Harlem Nocturne" should appear in perhaps 2004.

• When I was a small boy living in western Massachusetts, Sunday baseball was not broadcast from Boston, so my father listened to the Dodger games on WHN, which came to us straight up the Connecticut Valley. That is why I was a near terminal Dodger fan when Jackie Robinson came to the Dodgers in April 1947. I never saw it, but I remember it as if I did. The dark skin and the white uniform. The bright green grass, and Red Barber's marvelous Southern voice remarking carefully that Jackie was "very definitely brunette." I thought then that Jackie Robinson was one of the great men of the twentieth century. I have not changed my mind.

"Harlem Nocturne" is based on no actual event that I know of. It came about because Otto Penzler asked me for a short story for his baseball anthology, and I couldn't think of one, so I asked Joan and she said, "You know so much about old-time baseball. Why don't you write about that?" So I did.

Southern Californian **F. X. Toole** wrote for forty years before being published at age sixty-nine in *ZYZZYVA,* the San Francisco literary magazine. Having that first short story accepted, Toole considered himself a success, the Adam of the Sistine Chapel.

Since then, his book of short stories, *Rope Burns: Stories from the Corner* was published — first in England, then in the United States. Translated into German, French, Italian, Dutch, and Japanese, *Rope Burns* received the Anisfield-Wolf Book Award for fiction in 2000 and was also chosen by the *New York Times* as one of its Twenty Memorable Books of that year. "Midnight Emissions" is Toole's first venture into the world of whodunits.

▪ Though I wrote "Midnight Emissions" in the first person, I considered it a dry run for a third-person novel I wanted to set in the boxing world of Los Angeles and San Antonio, *Pound for Pound.* I say "dry run" because I felt that if I could get my Texans right in "Midnight Emissions," then I might also have a good shot at getting them right in the novel. *Pound for Pound* is at 120 K at this point, only now I'm stuck with Texans and prune-pickers who won't shut the fuck up.

A native of Louisville, Kentucky, **Daniel Waterman** is a writer and editor who now resides in Tuscaloosa, Alabama. This is his first published story.

▪ Skeet's tale, his condition, recuperation, and evolution into the brute he becomes erupted from me over the span of a few weeks I spent alone in a four-bedroom ranch house, barren of furniture, in Alabama, knowing not a soul, waiting for a new chapter in my life to begin. Skeet's history and path seemed clear to me but meant nothing in themselves until I painted him with some redemptive features and paired him with a family, or at least a few individuals capable of loving him. And then it became their story ever so much as Skeet's.

I've found it interesting that although many friends, family, and colleagues have read the story, only one has ever asked, "What, exactly, happens to Skeet?" It's a fair question — I'm the first to admit that what actually happens to Skeet in the end is ambiguous — but one with an annoying and unsatisfactory answer. All I can really say is that I leave Skeet's fate to the reader's imagination. Though I have a fairly clear idea myself, I'm not sure the answer is all that important. Skeet is a golem of sorts — not without heart or thought — yet stands for a part of us that becomes leaden. And though a multitude of mysteries surround Skeet — how he becomes the man he does, what accounts for his obsessive need to collect such an improbable fauna, what it signifies that he must destroy life to hold onto it — the principal mystery seems to me to be the fate of the narrator: In molting from one life to another, what has he lost or gained, how will he resolve any feelings of guilt or betrayal, and how will he contend with an unanchored sense of self that might abide for a lifetime unresolved?

Scott Wolven is a graduate student at Columbia University, where he's finishing an MFA in creative writing. He is currently at work on a novel and a collection of short stories and lives in New York City with his wife. His stories have appeared in *HandHeldCrime, Plots with Guns, Crossconnect,* the *Mississippi Review* on-line, *Permafrost,* and *Thrilling Detective.*

▪ "The Copper Kings" is one of several stories I've written about these characters, and I'm sure I'll keep them together for a few more. I lived in Idaho for a while, and it's a beautiful and hard-boiled setting for all types of things. I like big dogs and sometimes put them in my stories. The phrase "copper kings" originated as a reference to the 1880s businessmen who owned the huge copper mines in Anaconda and Butte, Montana. More recently, Butte had a minor league baseball team named the Copper Kings. I really liked it as a title.

It also allowed me to run a loose, obscure thread through the story. One of my favorite Sherlock Holmes stories is "The Copper Beeches," where Holmes and Watson take a short trip through the English countryside by train. When Watson says he likes the country, Holmes replies that it terrifies him, much as Greg admits that farms scare him on the drive toward Ryan's. Holmes describes potential crimes in the country as "deeds of hellish cruelty," and I thought about that as I wrote the story.

Very special thanks to Alan Ziegler, Leslie Woodard, Colin Harrison, Sloan Harris, Victoria Esposito-Shea, Neil Smith (go Crimedogs!), Elise Lyons, and best brother Will.

Other Distinguished Mystery Stories of 2001

GORDON, ALAN
   www.Heistgame.com. *Alfred Hitchcock's Mystery Magazine*, December

HOPKINS, BRIAN A.
   The Tumbleweed Rustlers Snack and Save. *Crime Spree*, ed. Sandy DeLuca and
     Trey R. Barker (December Girl Press)
HOWARD, CLARK
   The Trial Horse. *Murder on the Ropes*, ed. Otto Penzler (New Millennium)

LAWTON, R. T.
   Once, Twice, Dead. *Alfred Hitchcock's Mystery Magazine*, September
LEONARD, ELMORE
   Chicasaw Charlie Hoke. *Murderers' Row*, ed. Otto Penzler (New Millennium)
LEWIN, MICHAEL Z.
   If the Glove Fits. *Ellery Queen's Mystery Magazine*, September/October
LOCHTE, DICK
   In the City of Angels. *Flesh and Blood*, ed. Max Allan Collins and Jeff Gelb
     (Mysterious Press)

MAFFINI, MARY JANE
   Blind Alley. *Ellery Queen's Mystery Magazine*, November
MARON, MARGARET
   Virgo in Sapphires. *Ellery Queen's Mystery Magazine*, December

NAYLER, RAY
   Man in the Dark. *HandHeldCrime*, January

OATES, JOYCE CAROL
   The Man Who Fought Roland LaStarza. *Murder on the Ropes*, ed. Otto Penzler
     (New Millennium)

REEVE, PAUL G.
   Chinese Puzzle. *Alfred Hitchcock's Mystery Magazine*, March
ROZAN, S. J.
   Double-Crossing Delancey. *Mystery Street*, ed. Robert J. Randisi (Signet)

SHANNON, JOHN
   The Problem of Leon. *Murder on the Ropes*, ed. Otto Penzler (New
     Millennium)
SIGEL, EFRAM
   A Cozy Spot in the Berkshires. *Pangolin Papers*, Spring
SMITH, ANTHONY NEIL
   Kills Bugs Dead. *HandHeldCrime*, November
SOOS, TROY
   Pick-Off Play. *Murderers' Row*, ed. Otto Penzler (New Millennium)

TAYLOR, ANDREW S.
   The Assassin's List. *Ellery Queen's Mystery Magazine,* March
TERREOIRE, DAVID
   Just Like Jesus. *Blue Murder,* December–January
TROY, MARK
   Teed Off. *Fedora,* ed. Michael Bracken (Wildside)